BIG FAT DISASTER

Beth Fehlbaum

MeritPress
F+W Media, Inc.

Published by Merit Press
an imprint of F+W Media, Inc.
10151 Carver Road, Suite 200
Blue Ash, OH 45242. U.S.A.
www.meritpressbooks.com

ISBN 10: 1-4405-7048-5
ISBN 13: 978-1-4405-7048-3
eISBN 10: 1-4405-7049-3
eISBN 13: 978-1-4405-7049-0

Printed in the United States of America.

10 9 8 7 6 5 4 3 2 1

Cover design by Frank Rivera.
Cover photo by Elizabeth Lariviere.

For all of us,

who wish to be loved just as we are.

I desire the things which will destroy me in the end.

SYLVIA PLATH

Chapter One

Who in their right mind thought it would be a good idea to put our family portrait on my dad's Senate campaign postcard? Why is my face covered by the address label? Shouldn't it be on the other side of the postcard?

I grimace as I peel away the label, imagining what it would be like to find these five people grinning like idiots in my mailbox. I mean, if I wasn't *me*, and I didn't know the truth about these people.

Us, that is.

Do people actually see us as Dad's "package deal"? He says that when people vote for him, they're getting the "whole package."

What does that even mean, anyway?

I hold up the postcard to the light, as if being able to see through it would change the way I see us. But the colors are too dark, and, anyway, a photo can't tell the whole story. No one who gets one of these stupid postcards has any idea who we really are.

I toss the postcard onto my father's desk and stare at the address label stuck to the end of my finger. *Package deal, my fat butt.*

My dad, Reese, played college ball for the UT Longhorns. He was a linebacker then, but he's an investment banker now, and he's running for the U.S. Senate. My mom, Sonya, used to teach fourth grade, and she was Miss Texas twenty-two years ago.

My oh-so-perfect-in-every-way older sister, Rachel, is about to leave for college (pause here to praise Jesus), and my little sister, Drew, like Rachel, looks like a carbon copy of Mom. They're all overly concerned with what they look like, I guess because they like what they see when they look in the mirror.

Sadly, I did *not* escape Dad's Incredible Hulk–like genes or his weight problem. My mom, sisters, and the mirror do a fantastic job of reminding me that I am *The Fat Girl.*

As if I could ever forget.

Last week, Drew took a break from admiring herself in the full-length mirror at the end of the hall when she noticed that I was eating ice cream in front of the TV. She flipped her hair back over her shoulder like Mom does, and sounded like *Mini-Mom*, too: "Do you know how many calories are in that? Where, *exactly*, do you think it will look best on you?"

As Drew turned back to the mirror, she dropped her hair brush. Lucky for her, she bent to pick it up at the exact moment that I rocketed the bowl through the air—*Slam!*—a direct hit to my arch nemesis, the mirror! That sucker broke into about a hundred pieces, and about the time that Drew recovered enough to start bawling, the frame fell off the wall.

Totally worth losing my iPhone. *Totally.*

Sometimes I hear the old lady campaign volunteers whisper about how good-looking my dad is—like, he's in his late forties, but anybody can still see the UT Austin football star he once was. He's unmistakably my father, but the qualities that make Dad attractive even though he's a big guy are the same ones that make me consider myself genetically doomed.

When a women's magazine profiled the Senate candidates' wives, the reporter and photographer came to our house to take some photos. They were about to leave when the reporter said, "Sonya, would you mind just one more photo? We'd like to have one of you and the children."

Drew called me out of my room. I stepped into the living room, and the photographer took me by the elbow and guided me right back out. "Sorry, this one's of immediate family only."

Drew giggled and said, "Colby's my sister, too, silly!"

We took the pic and as the reporter was wrapping up the interview, Mom leaned in and said, "Um, your people can Photoshop Colby, right? Make her look a little more like she belongs with us…?"

Sure enough, when the article ran, I still didn't look like I could be the spawn of a former Miss Texas, but I also didn't look like the person I see in the mirror.

Too bad that the person in charge of Dad's campaign postcards stuck with reality instead of Photoshop.

Rachel appears in Dad's campaign office doorway. "Colby, what're you doing? Let me sit at Dad's desk. The Young Conservatives choir just arrived. You need to go get ready." She doesn't look up from texting on her phone as she moves toward me.

I don't budge from the chair. "I don't feel like singing today. I'm not going."

Rachel sighs. "Yes, you *are*. You know Mrs. Hamlet will pop a blood vessel if you're not in place for the national anthem. Move it."

"I still think it sucks that you don't have to sing anymore. You're not leaving for college until Saturday." I align the address label vertically over Rachel's image, leaving only her spindly legs visible on the postcard. I rub it, trying to smooth the edges.

"Don't you think Mrs. Pendergrass and her crew of Dad's groupies put those stickers where they did for a *reason*?" Rachel whips the postcard away from me and tosses it atop the others in the box on the floor. "They're trying to *attract* voters, not *repel* them. Now heave yourself out of that chair and go put on your tent."

I imagine the suffocating heaviness of the American flag–sequined choir robe in the midsummer heat, and I nearly scream.

I jerk Rachel's phone out of her hands as she settles into Dad's chair before I've even cleared it completely.

"People think you're sooo sweet. If they knew the *real* you..." I tap Photos on the phone screen. Rachel lunges for my hand. I jerk it away and knock over Dad's tall mug of coffee. It pours onto his desk pad calendar and spills over the edge of the desk onto Rachel's skirt.

"You idiot! Look what you've done!" She bolts from the chair and yanks the phone away. "I'll be so *glad* to get away from you. You're an embarrassment to *all* of us."

"Run to the bathroom and grab some paper towels, will you?" I'm frantically moving stacks of papers, books, and Dad's knickknacks from the growing coffee puddle, and a framed photo of us on our spring break hiking trip sails off the side of the desk onto the floor. "Shit!" I look up at Rachel. "Please? Help me? I mean, this is partly your fault, you're the one who..."

She shakes her head and smiles smugly. "Nope. I was never here. I don't know a thing. You're on your own." She squares her shoulders and wrings the coffee from the hem of her skirt, then rotates the skirt on her waist so that the stain is in the back. Unflappable, just like always. "I'm going to the rally now. Hear that, Colby? The music's started. You're late."

I grab a box of tissues from the bookcase and sop up most of the coffee. I sing the first few words of "The Star-Spangled Banner," as if I'm where I'm supposed to be: sandwiched behind super weird Candy Geary, who never seems to shut up, and in front of super stinky Ronald Maynard, who smells like canned cat food. He wears a Friskies-scented cloud the way some guys wear Axe body spray. But I can't do so much as make a face, because I have to be nice to everybody. It's part of being *Reese Denton's* daughter.

I shove the coffee-soaked wads into the empty tissue box, toss it in the trash, and look around for another box, but my eye catches on the campaign postcard and my big fat face staring back at me from the center of my otherwise perfect family. Was it true? Did

Mrs. Pendergrass purposely place the address labels on the wrong side just so that she could cover my face? I thought that she and all the other geezers liked me. I lean down to the box on the floor, pull out a handful of postcards off the top of the pile, and quickly thumb through them.

Rachel wasn't kidding. Every one of the postcards is identical. I swallow hard and dump the remaining postcards onto the floor, then spread them out with my toe. I plop back into Dad's chair and nearly fall backward. I throw myself forward; my stomach clenches, and I remember Dad's snack stash in his lower left desk drawer.

Seconds later, I'm ripping the foil off one Ding Dong after another. I *think* I'll only eat one more; I don't even taste the chocolate-covered cupcakes as they go down. I plunge my hand to the bottom of the wastebasket and bury the wrappers beneath the trash. I'm kind of surprised when the box is empty; I stomp it flat with my foot and shove it to the bottom of the trash, too...Maybe Dad'll think he already ate them all.

I can't leave the evidence here. Dad eats too much, too, but he has no problem with lecturing me about the importance of appearance to voters. "It's not just *me* who's running for Senate, Colby. It's *all* of us. If you were a boy, people would assume you play football, like I did. What do you think they assume when they see *you*?"

If Mom finds out about the cupcake raid, she'll give me her disappointed look and say, "What you eat in private, you wear in public."

As soon as I feel less queasy, I'll take the bag to the dumpster. Seeing what I've done makes me feel even fatter. I just won't eat anything else today. It won't be that hard.

I sigh heavily at the coffee-saturated calendar. The month of July is ruined; at least it's almost over. I tear off the page and see Dad's handwriting on the first Saturday in August: *Move Rachel to school.* The page is too wet to add *Praise Jesus!* under his words. I lift the pages one by one to see how far into autumn the coffee soaked. By

Election Day in November, the pages are perfect again. I lift the desk pad and flutter the calendar pages to make them dry faster, and I notice initials and codes, like LW 400.5. Strange. There are names of banks and long numbers, too.

I toss the calendar atop the postcards and my eye catches on the damaged picture frame on the floor. I gingerly lift the frame and slide the broken glass into the wastebasket, then sit back in Dad's chair and carefully remove the spring break hiking trip pic that we took just before Dad broke his collarbone and we had to cut short our vacation. When I see another photo beneath it, taped to the frame's cardboard backing, it's as if all the blood rushes from my body and pools in my feet.

It's a picture of my dad.

And he's kissing a lady. I mean, he's *really* kissing her, and it looks like he was holding the camera to take the picture.

But it's not my mom. This lady has brown hair, and, anyway, I've never seen him kiss Mom that way. It's as if the photo burns my fingers; I throw it down and stumble back, knocking over my dad's chair. My heart's pounding in my ears and it feels like my chest is going to explode. I realize I'm holding my breath and I let it go, but it comes out really loud like a sob and I clap my hand over my mouth, then run to the doorway and look down the hall to make sure no one is there. I tiptoe back to the desk, retrieve the photo, and stare at it. Do I know her? Dad's wearing the sling from when he broke his collarbone. So...this was taken a few months ago.

I hear voices in the hallway. A door opens...footsteps...my dad's campaign manager, Patrick, is calling the staff together. I look around for somewhere to put the photo. I peel it off the cardboard backing and slide it down the front of my dress, into my bra.

I'm frozen, and the bookcases that line the office are closing in. I feel like a stranger looking for the first time at the framed photos lining Dad's office in chronological order. My parents' wedding photo...the two of them with Rachel...and me...then Drew came along. Every election season, we've had a family photo taken: a visual representation of Dad's "family values" platform.

I've been standing on stages and waving at crowds ever since I can remember, starting with Dad's campaign for the local school board. Then came the race for city councilman, and a year after that, state representative. My father has been trying to get everybody to love him ever since he was in middle school: A framed photo of him as eighth grade student council president hangs on the wall in his study, just above his Eagle Scout badge.

I go to the door, close and lock it, then pull the photo from my bra. Who *is* this woman? I plop into the desk chair, carefully lift the coffee-drenched calendar onto my lap, and go through the pages one by one, looking for the woman's name, but except for Rachel's on moving day, there's just the mysterious initials, names of banks, and numbers.

I turn on Dad's computer, but it's password protected. I frantically go through his desk drawers, study the books on his shelf, and even look behind the paintings and framed photos on the wall. I don't know why her name would be behind Dad's framed photo of him and George W. Bush when they met at a hardware store in Dallas, but I'm not exactly in my right mind.

I hear people cheering outside. Dad's campaign theme song—it's called "I Can't Hold Back," by this '80s band called Survivor—is blasting, so the rally must be wrapping up. I slide the photo back into my bra, then run my hands around the rim of my mouth just in case there's any crumbs there. My tongue is greasy, my teeth taste terrible, and I wish I had some gum.

I place the broken picture frame in the center of the calendar, awkwardly bend and fold it over as if I'm wrapping a gift, crease it, and shove it on top of the trash.

I scoop the postcards back into their box and straighten Dad's desk so that it looks normal. He'll notice if the spring break photo is out of the frame, so I pull the snack stash drawer all the way out, place the pic under the metal sliding mechanism, and close the drawer.

Then I upright Dad's chair, move to the doorway, and try to see his office as anyone else would: anyone who hadn't, of course, just seen my father—"the family man"—with his tongue down some stranger's throat.

I tie off the trash bag and head to the dumpster with it. I keep my head down and hope that no one recognizes me—but without a big white address label over my face, what are the odds?

I sneak away from the dumpster like a rat, tiptoe in through the back door of the building, and move to a window near the stage outside. I part the blinds ever-so-slightly to spy on my parents. My father stands at the top of the platform steps, shaking hands with people and smiling. Mom's at his side, just like always.

"I Can't Hold Back" starts up again. Dad grabs Mom by the wrist, pulls her into an embrace, then whirls her away. It's supposed to look spontaneous, but they do this to end every rally. Dad says it's a positive picture for voters to leave with, and, besides, it's an easy "out" from having to keep talking to people. They end the dance with a kiss, then he and Mom wave at the crowd and descend the steps. Just like always.

Rachel and her two best friends from The Young Conservatives catch me being a peeping Tom. I jump when she speaks. "The coast is clear, Colby. I told Mrs. Hamlet that you have a raging case of mono, and *that's* why you didn't show up to sing."

I noisily release the blinds and spin back to her, my mouth gaping open. "You did *what*?"

She strikes a thoughtful pose: eyes to the ceiling and an index finger to her chin. "Wait a minute; no, I didn't say that, after all. See, mononucleosis is the *kissing* disease, so no one would ever believe that *you* could catch it." Her friends laugh, and they high-five each other.

I roll my eyes. "For your information, that is a myth. *Anyone* can catch mono."

She mocks, "*Anyone can catch mono*," then strides to the desk my mom always uses when she's in the office. "Where's Mom's purse?... Oh, never mind. I found it." She pulls the Coach handbag out of a drawer, dumps the contents on the desk, and pulls some cash from Mom's billfold.

I fold my arms over my chest. The photo's sticky against my skin; I'm sweating so much that I wonder if the image will stay on later, like a rub-on tattoo. I'm tempted to lift it off my skin so that it won't, but I'm afraid Rachel will notice. "Does Mom know you're going through her stuff?"

Rachel glances at the other girls, and they smirk in unison. "Just tell her I needed twenty bucks. Chris has his mom's Suburban. We're going to a late lunch and a movie. I'll be home by ten."

"I want to go, too." I stand. Maybe I can get Rachel alone and show her the picture. Maybe she'll explain it away and tell me how stupid I am to ever think that Dad would cheat on Mom. I sure hope so.

"*I want to go, too*," Rachel mocks. She gives me the *You're an embarrassment to all of us* look. I get it. I know I don't fit; she doesn't have to remind me all the time. "No freshmen."

"But school's about to start. I'm a sophomore now—"

"It's only for graduates. It's our last Young Conservatives outing before we all leave for college." She shoves the billfold back in Mom's purse, gives me a withering glance, and gestures to her friends. "Let's go this way." She leads them to the side exit.

The building's empty except for Dad, Mom, and Patrick. My little sister, Drew, and Mrs. Pendergrass's grandson, Bobby, are on the plywood stage outside, putting on an imaginary concert for the volunteers who are folding up the chairs in the parking lot.

The sugar and fat I consumed in record time have me woozy enough, but stir in the discovery that Dad's cheating on Mom, and I'm positive I'm going to puke. I grab my iPod and stretch out on the sofa in the media center (it's just the room with a sofa and TV). Maybe if I lie really still, I won't throw up.

I'm between songs when I hear what sounds like arguing; I press Off and tiptoe just inside the doorway to try to hear what's going on. I lean forward and when I do, the photo of Dad and that lady pokes out the top of my bra. I push it back into place and peek around the corner into Patrick's office. Mom's nodding and smiling—but it's the smile of hers that looks like a dog baring its teeth.

Mom does that: She nods and smiles even when she thinks the person speaking is full of shit, and I can tell by the way she's arching her eyebrows that Patrick falls into that category.

Patrick Osmer has sweat pouring down his face. He grabs Dad by the biceps and pleads, "Reese, it's *me*, okay? If there's something you need to tell me—even if it's bad news—you need to let me know so that I can do as much damage control as possible. While you and Sonya were doing the meet-and-greet, some F.B.I. guys cornered me and told me that the campaign finance auditor contacted them. There's discrepancies, Reese. *Big* ones. I'm telling you, those agents aren't fooling around."

"Patrick, you're getting all worked up for nothing. Those guys aren't *real* agents; it's something my illustrious opponent is pulling to try to psych us out. They probably had a video camera and recorded the whole thing."

Patrick shakes his head violently, and his voice sounds tight when he speaks. "They knew details about our campaign that the other side couldn't."

Dad bites off each word: "Then. The. Auditor. Must. Have. Made. A. Mistake. Period." He turns to Mom and says loudly, "Are you about ready to blow this Popsicle stand, honey? I'll bet the girls are ready to go—"

"Listen!" Patrick's no longer pleading. "I saw their badges! They said they'll have a warrant within an hour, and they're going to search here, your business office, *and* your home. Do you hear me, Reese? A warrant!" He addresses Mom. "Sonya, if you know anything, *please*, tell me. I need to—I mean, *we* need to do what we can to protect ourselves before it's too late!"

Mom fires back, "No, *you* listen, Patrick! Reese is a rarity in politics: an honest, honorable man. If he says that the auditor made a mistake, then that's what happened. Maybe you're not the right person to run this campaign. In fact, if you can't look those investigators in the eye—if they're *really* F.B.I. agents—and tell them that you know without the slightest doubt that Reese Thomas Denton is the person he says he is, then you are *definitely* not the right man for this job!"

Patrick laughs, but it's not a funny-ha-ha laugh. "Lady, I've got to hand it to you. I've *never* met a person who trusts as completely as you do." He takes a step back and leans against his desk, looks from Mom to Dad, and shakes his head. "Reese, they said that this info they've got on you—it's bigger than the campaign. *Way* bigger. And the dollar figures they're throwing around are out of this world."

Patrick lowers his voice and leans into Dad. "I'm *not* going down with you, Reese. Tell me the truth: Have you misappropriated campaign funds? Has your investment firm been scamming your clients?"

Drew runs full-speed into Patrick's office and yells, "Hey, Mama! Those people out there said that I'm going to be a star!" She turns to Bobby. "And he's going to be my—what did they say you are?"

"I'm your backup dancer." Bobby grins.

Drew notices me in the media center doorway. "Colby! You should have come out there! We were famous!"

All eyes turn to me, and I'm high-tailing it for the sofa, but the telltale click of Mom's high heels on the tile tell me that I'm busted.

"How long were you standing there?"

I fumble with my ear buds and try to slide them in, but my hands are shaking. "Huh? Where?"

She shoots an arched eyebrow at me, takes a dramatic deep breath, and exhales, "The doorway."

I shake my head and give my best look of confusion. "Just…I heard Drew come in…and with all her yelling…I didn't know if… she was, you…you know…safe." I lie back against the armrest and push Play on my iPod, close my eyes, and hope that my "Wish I Was Anywhere But Here" playlist will help me stop freaking out. I wait until the second song ends to open my eyes and see if Mom's still there.

She's gone, and when I breathe a sigh of relief, the photo of Dad and the woman seems to exhale, too. I slide my finger down the front of my dress and touch the photo. I still can't believe the guy kissing that lady is my dad. Who *is* my father, anyway?

A couple of hours later, I pretend to be asleep when Mom raps her knuckles on the end table next to my head until I open my eyes. I *haven't* been snoozing; I've been trying to figure out what to do with what I know. Maybe there's a reasonable explanation for the photo. But I can't think of anything that makes sense.

Mom's shrill: "Wake up, Colby! We're leaving. Have you seen

Rachel?"

I sit up, swing my legs forward, and put my feet on the floor. I don't feel the photo's sharp corners against my skin and for a microsecond, I think it fell out of my bra. I frantically scan the sofa cushions for it but don't see it anywhere.

Mom's voice is flat. "If you're looking for your iPod, it's right here."

I take it from her and look down as if I'm winding up the cord, but I'm sneaking a peek inside my dress, too. Whew! The pic's still there. Maybe it's becoming part of me, like a growth or something. I don't even feel it anymore. Wish it was that easy to forget the image of my dad kissing that lady.

I mumble, "Rachel went out with the seniors. She said thanks for the twenty bucks. She'll be home by ten."

Mom straightens and puts her hands on her hips. "*That girl.* Well, I guess I can't begrudge her; it can't be easy to say goodbye to her friends until Thanksgiving."

Dad slips in behind Mom and wraps his arms around her waist. He places his chin on her shoulder and presses his face against hers. "Can't believe we'll be moving the big scholarship winner to school next week! Then it'll be just a matter of time before we have an empty nest!"

I watch Dad's face carefully—but he doesn't seem any different. He *looks* like he loves my mom. But if he loves her, then why...?

Mom croons, "That's right, honey. Someday, it'll be just the two of us again, like the honeymoon days." She pulls out of his embrace, faces him, and they gaze into each other's eyes. "Want to grab an early dinner out, sweetheart?" She brushes a hand across his shoulder and straightens his tie.

He sighs and shakes his head. "Actually, I need to speak to Patrick about these"—he throws up air quotes—"'concerns' of his, and try to find out what kind of mischief the opposition is up to. I'll grab something to eat from my snack stash."

My face feels hot; my stomach clenches, and I run my hand over my lips. I fill a paper cup at the water cooler and drain one cupful after another until I'm sure my red cheeks have faded.

"Where were you during the rally, Colby?" Mom asks from behind the steering wheel.

"I stayed inside. I...wasn't feeling well," I mumble. I stare out the window as we pull out of the campaign headquarters parking lot.

"Could it be all those chips you ate at El Fenix last night?" Mom's voice is tight, like it always is when she brings up what she calls my "food issues." She waits like she expects an answer. All I can think about is my dad and that lady. "Colby? Could you look at me, please?"

I drag my eyes to meet hers in the rearview mirror. I shift in my seat, and the photo pokes me. I want to reach in and adjust it, but I don't dare. I guess I could pull it out and show it to Mom so that she can tell me it's nothing.

Maybe it's Photoshopped! Hey, that could be it: If Photoshop can make *me* look so different, I'm sure that *anything* can be faked. I feel myself relax for the first time since I found it. *It's Photoshopped.* It's just something else the other candidate cooked up to gain a few points in the polls. But...why was it taped to the frame's backing? And why does it look like *he* was holding the camera to take the photo?

Mom's eyebrows make an inverted V. "Well? What do you think? Possible that all that fat and corn are doing a job on your insides?"

Drew pipes up. "*I* only ate twenty chips. That's a serving, right, Mama?" Drew gives me the same sort of judgy look that Mom does. She's only going into second grade, but she can name the Weight Watchers "Point" value of any food. Mom was teaching her to read nutrition labels while other kids were learning to read Dr. Seuss.

Drew is Mom's Diet Buddy. Rachel's her Fashion Buddy. I'm just Colby, *The Fat Girl*. I live in the school library, shop in the XXL section when I'm forced to buy clothes, and stay in my bedroom with the door closed. And I have my own snack stash that nobody knows about.

"Rachel ate lots of chips, too." I know as I say it that it won't do any good. Once Mom gets started on dissecting what I ate, she won't shut up until I promise to try harder to lose weight.

"Rachel has my metabolism, and you have your dad's. You know that; we've talked about it ever since you were little. You can look in the mirror and see that you take after your dad's side of the family. You don't want to end up like your Aunt Leah: a hundred pounds overweight and all alone."

I snap, "Aunt Leah's alone because she divorced Uncle Mark, Mom! He beat her black-and-blue, remember?"

"Colby! We are *not* going to discuss that situation in front of your little sister!" Mom glares at me in the rearview mirror so long that she nearly slams into the car in front of us.

"How could she not know about it already? It's all you talked about at the Fourth of July picnic after Leah and Cousin Ryan left!" I turn to my sister, knowing full well that I'm going to catch it for doing this. But I do it anyway. "Drew, what did Grandma say about Aunt Leah's divorce?"

My seven-year-old sister says sweetly, "The biggest mistake Leah ever made was leaving that man. He's *going* places!"

I mutter, "Yeah, he *should* have gone to jail for the broken nose he gave her." I'm watching my mom's face in the rearview mirror, and I can see her temperature rising.

"Colby! Enough!"

"It's not like *you* guys censor yourselves when you talk about the"—I throw up air quotes—"'*situation*'. What I don't get is why you don't believe that Uncle Mark did that, and why Grandma thinks she messed up her life because she didn't want to be hit anymore!"

Mom's definitely not nodding and smiling now: "You don't know what you're talking about, young lady. Mark Ellis is a powerful man, and he's on your dad's campaign committee. He has a lot of connections who have been very generous supporters. Besides, it's Leah's word against his, and the whole family knows that she's always been infuriating."

I shrug and look out the window. "Just seems to me that seeing as how Leah's actually Dad's flesh and blood, he'd feel some loyalty to her. At least some protectiveness, I mean, damn, she showed us those pictures of what Mark did, and—"

Mom's eyes bug out at my use of a swear word. She swerves hard into the Jack in the Box parking lot and throws the car into Park. She throws off her seat belt and whips around to me. "Look at me!" She waits until I obey. "Now you listen to me, Colby Diane Denton: Your father is an honorable man. His ethics are without question, and I will not have you disrespecting him by questioning his judgment in any way, shape, or form. Leah is a misguided, unhappy woman. Your dad says that ever since they were children, she was always the one to stir up trouble. If he said the sky was blue, she'd say it was green just to be disagreeable. Sometimes, I swear you must be her child instead of mine! You *definitely* take after her, size-wise! If she'd take a little pride in her appearance, she'd probably still be married."

"Gee, thanks, Mom." I either have a lump in my throat or a Ding Dong. Can't be too sure at this point.

Mom rolls her eyes but plunges forward. "Look, even if Mark did lose his temper once or twice, there's nothing to be gained by the whole world finding out. Besides, who knows what she did to drive him to it? I don't want to hear you bring it up again. It's unfortunate that Leah took constructive criticism personally, but the way she handled it, with all that screaming and yelling, was wrong. After all: we *are* family."

"Some of the stuff y'all said to Leah and Ryan was really mean,

Mom. Like, yelling at Ryan for telling on what those guys did to that girl? *Really*?"

Mom cuts her eyes toward Drew, grimaces, and gives a micro-shake of her head, but I pretend not to notice. "He was the *only* guy on that football team who picked up the phone and called the cops, but instead of—"

Mom shrieks, "*Enough*!" She spins back to the steering wheel, yanks her seat belt into place, and tries to start the car again, even though it's already running. The engine makes a scratchy-screeching sound, and Mom's growl echoes it. She grips the steering wheel with white knuckles and glares at me in the rearview mirror.

I look away. Even though I promised myself that I wouldn't eat any more today, the Oreo milkshake poster in the Jack in the Box window makes me want one. I breathe in deeply and let it out... glance down to see if the outline of the photo can be seen through my dress. "Hey, Mom? Seeing as how *I* didn't steal twenty bucks from your purse and Drew entertained the troops while they folded up chairs, could we get Jack in the Box for dinner?"

Mom scrunches her face angrily, then suddenly relaxes it and studies her own reflection in the rearview mirror. She runs the tip of her pinky over the flecks of mascara under her eyes, then rubs gently at a smudge of lipstick at the corner of her mouth. "We're not *dogs*, Colby. We don't reward ourselves with food."

Chapter Two

We arrive home to see three black SUVs and a couple of police cars overflowing from our driveway and lining the street in front of our house. A News Ten van nearly sideswipes us when Mom parallel parks in front of our neighbor's house.

"Who *are* those people, Mommy?" Drew asks in a worried voice.

Mom doesn't answer; she's already got her iPhone up to her ear. "Hello, Reese? Anyone still there? Pick up! Pick up the phone, Reese!...The—the—I don't know, *maybe* it's the F.B.I.? And—the police are here, too. Honey, pick up the phone if you're still in the office. *Please*! We need you here!"

She presses End but immediately dials another number. "Patrick? It's Sonya. Listen, the police are...What do you mean, your attorney told you not to talk to me? You work for Reese, and you *will* talk to me, do you underst—Hello? Hello?"

There's a *tap tap tap* on the driver's side window. A lady I recognize from the local news is standing on the sidewalk next to our car. She's holding a microphone, pointed right at Mom.

Mom freaks out, throws the car into Drive, and nearly takes out a passing police car when she pulls away from the curb. We speed back to campaign headquarters.

We find Dad in his office. It looks like a tornado blew through there. Books are knocked off the shelves, boxes are dumped out, there are papers everywhere, and the paper shredder is going full-tilt.

He's oblivious to us as he pulls handfuls of papers from a file cabinet and feeds them into the shredder.

Mom hisses, "You girls stay out here." She enters Dad's office and closes the door.

Their voices can be heard over the roar of the shredder, and Drew and I exchange worried looks. I stride to the water cooler and fill a cup, then straighten, keeping my back to Drew. I slip my hand down the front of my dress into my bra. I touch the photo, just to be sure that it's there, and exhale shakily.

Several minutes later, the shredder stops, and Mom opens the door. She says tersely, "Come in here."

Dad's drenched with sweat. He gestures to the two armchairs facing his desk and orders, "Take a seat, girls." He comes around to the front of his desk and leans against it.

No one makes a sound until my stomach bumps around a dozen Ding Dongs and I stifle a chocolaty burp.

Finally, Dad speaks in a panicked voice. "You *know* that in our family, honesty is everything. And…I *need* you to be honest with me, girls. This is very important." He looks from Drew to me and back again, ending with me. "My desk calendar is missing. I've looked everywhere for it." He gestures shakily to contents of boxes dumped out on the floor. "As you can see."

I concentrate on keeping my face neutral. I can't meet his eyes so I focus instead on his hands, which are knotted into fists.

"There was private information about people who have made… donations, on that calendar. Now, if something happened, I need to know about it so that I can"—he seems to lose his train of thought for a second—"protect the confidentiality of my, um, supporters."

Drew speaks in baby talk: "*I* didn't take your calendar, Daddy." *Why does she always use a three-year-old's voice?* I clench my fists and imagine punching her heart-shaped little face.

Dad's eyes are like lasers on me. "Colby, do you have anything you'd like to tell me? Your mom tells me that you stayed inside today instead of coming to the rally."

Mom moves to stand beside me. She places her perfectly manicured hand on my shoulder and squeezes it. I feel like I'm the size of Shrek. "You said you weren't feeling well, Colby. Did you spend any time in here?"

I swallow hard and run my hand over my lips. Finally, I nod.

Dad barks, "Drew, you're excused! Go to the media center and watch TV."

"Yes, Daddy!" Drew practically skips from his office.

He springs to his feet and stands over me, puts his face in mine. I can't tell if he's angry or frightened, but I've never seen him so freaked out, and I freeze. "Where's my calendar, Colby Diane? What did you do with it? It's very important that you didn't look at it! You're not allowed to see my private information!"

He grips the arms of the chair and jerks back and forth, as if the chair is holding a secret from him. "Where's my calendar, Colby Diane?"

I open my mouth, but no sound comes out. I've never been so scared in my life.

Mom steps forward, puts her hand on Dad's shoulder, and says firmly, "*Reese. Enough!*" She places her other hand on his cheek and presses his face up until he is forced to look at her. "E-nough." They have a bit of a staring contest, and she wins.

He growls, gives my chair one more good shake, then straightens and moves to stand in front of his own.

She slides into the small space between me and Dad's desk. It's as if she thinks she's protecting me, but she's so tiny that it's like a fence post trying to block out the sun. In the flat voice she uses with unreasonable people, she says, "It's just a calendar. It's not worth getting so upset over."

Dad sits down hard in his chair, and his lips curl into a sneer. "You don't know what you're talking about, Mar—" His eyes widen. "—I mean, Sonya." He sighs heavily, lowers his head into his hands, and it sounds like he's starting to cry. "Oh, my God. Oh. My. God."

Mom's still wearing her *You're Being Unreasonable* voice. "Think about it, Reese. Why would Colby take your calendar? You're just being silly."

It feels like the photo's burning into my skin. I swallow hard, glance at the floor, and my eye catches on a Ding Dong wrapper under Dad's desk. Guess I missed one when I was cleaning up.

Dad jerks upright and exclaims, "I know where it is!" He rolls back his chair, pulls his center desk drawer all the way out, and paws through it, in the process throwing out pens, paper clips, and scraps of paper until there's nothing else to remove. He runs his hands over the inside, then slams the drawer closed—open—closed, again and again.

Mom tries her soothing voice. "Let's go home, honey. We'll call a meeting of the campaign committee for tomorrow afternoon. I'm sure Al Nantz will get this all straightened out." She waits a beat, but he doesn't answer. She crosses around the desk to Dad and places her hand on his arm, but he jerks away like it's on fire.

His shoulders slump. "Everything's ruined," he whispers. "Everything's ruined now." He shakes his head sadly. "So much…information on it…if I can't find that calendar…" He shakes his head sadly.

Seeing him like this is killing me. I take a deep breath and exhale, "Dad. It—it was me. I took your calendar. I spilled coffee on it, and—See, well, Rachel and I were fighting, and—"

It doesn't seem possible, but his eyes get even bigger. "You? *You took it*? You have it?" He nearly knocks Mom over when he bolts out of his chair and starts toward me, his face bright red with rage. "How could you do that to me?"

I shrink back in the chair. I'm afraid that he's going to stand over me and scare the bejeezus out of me again, and I talk fast. "I—just let me explain, okay? I threw it away because—"

He freezes and gasps, "Did you see anything? Did you?"

I hold up my hands and shake my head slowly.

My father throws a temper tantrum. He pounds the bookshelf to his left and sends its contents tumbling to the floor, sweeps his arm across the top shelf, and starts to pull the entire bookcase down, but Mom shrieks, "Reese! Don't!"

His shoulders rise and fall with his hard breathing. At last he lowers his head and says softly, "What did you see, Colby?" When I don't answer, he whirls on me, his face contorted. "Tell me!"

Mom's voice is quiet but steady. "Colby Diane, answer your father."

"I—I didn't see anybody's name but Rachel's on your calendar—you know—about moving her to school next Saturday. The whole month of July was ruined and I tore it off—I mean, the month's almost over anyway—then I tried to get the rest of the year dry, and...and..." My voice cracks, and my voice is squeaky-high. "Don't you even care that the picture of us is gone?"

Dad frowns, looks confused. "What picture?"

I inhale shakily and exhale, "The one on the corner of your desk. From our spring break trip."

He sneers, "Why the hell would I worry about a fucking picture right now, Colby? I need to know where my calend—"

"Wh—Who's that lady you're kissing in the photo under ours, Dad?" It sounds like someone else said it, even though I know it was me.

My words seem to have the effect of slowing time and space, because my father's feet form roots to the floor halfway between my mother and me. Her eyebrows melt into a soft V, and her mouth droops open.

The spell is broken when Mom demands, "What picture?... What's she talking about, Reese?"

Chocolaty acid springs into my mouth and I nearly throw up. I'm not sure if it's because I just blabbed about the lady or that I can barely breathe because I'm so full of cream-filled cupcakes. "May I be excused?" I ask from behind my hand.

"No!" my mother snaps. "What picture did you see?"

I can't tell her. I *can't*.

She narrows her eyes at me, then at my dad. He finally uproots his feet, stumbles back to his chair, and pretty much falls into it.

Mom sways slightly and grabs the edge of Dad's desk to steady herself. Her voice high, she asks, "Reese? What's Colby talking about?"

He bends forward and starts rocking himself, his face contorted.

She moves unsteadily to him, gets on her knees, and tries to make him look at her, but he keeps turning away. She grips his biceps, tries to still his rocking.

He finally chokes out, "I...I didn't want you to find out like this. I'm so sorry, Sonya...so sorry."

It feels like I'm watching all of us from the ceiling, as if this is happening to someone else. This can't be *my parents. It can't.* Honesty is *everything* to us...right?

Mom's face forms an ugly grimace. She shakes her head, runs her hand up and down Dad's arm. Her voice choked, she pleads, "Reese, *tell* me that Colby is wrong about what she thinks she saw." Mom narrows her eyes, tilts her head, and whisper-sobs, "You would never do that to me. It's not who you are...Tell me that, Reese."

I *want* to be anywhere else. I *can't* be here. I shouldn't be seeing this moment between my parents. I rise from the chair and bolt for the door, but I'm not fast enough, because I hear my father say the words that change our lives forever:

"Sonya, I'm sorry. But...I don't love you anymore. I'm in love with someone else."

Chapter Three

Ever since I found that photo, my insides have felt like I'm on a roller coaster that's about to take its first heart-stopping plunge. I'm stretched out on my bed with my ear buds in, and my music's blasting way louder than Mom ever lets me listen to it. She's locked in her bedroom. I keep hoping that if I hold my pillow over my mouth and nose just right, I'll suffocate myself. If that doesn't work, I'll find some other way to die. I have destroyed my family. I can't go on living.

Can I?

In the hot blackness of my pillow, I replay the afternoon in my head.

As we left Dad's campaign office, the three black SUVs and two police cars were turning into the parking lot. They parked beside the stage that my parents were dancing on a few hours ago.

When we arrived home, our house was a wreck. All of my dresser drawers were dumped out on my bed, including my personal snack stash, which occupies the bottom right drawer. Ding Dongs, Pop Tarts, and candy bars covered my bedspread; it looked like a vending machine had exploded. All that was left of my laptop was my iPod cord. In fact, the agents took all of our laptops and the hard drive of the desktop computer in the family room.

Mom kept herself together long enough to use her bright, happy voice when she phoned her best friend, Brenda, who she used to teach with before being a Senate candidate's wife was her full-time job. She asked if Drew could spend the night at Brenda's house with her daughter, Charlotte.

Mom can do that with Brenda—tell her that she's got stuff to do and Drew's driving her crazy being bored—because Mom says Brenda lets her be a regular person instead of a politician's wife, which is like being on display 24/7. Mom complains sometimes, but I know she secretly enjoys being in the spotlight.

Drew was super upset about her room being invaded. She thought we'd been robbed, and she only calmed down when she realized that the "robbers" didn't steal her boy band CDs. I *really* hope she has no idea that Dad doesn't love Mom anymore. I wish *I* didn't know.

I don't know how Mom faked everything being normal, but she did for Drew's sake. She told her that Dad had a headache and was taking a nap, and she convinced Drew that the people who came into our house and turned it upside down had lost something and accidentally looked in the wrong place for it.

Drew put her hands on her hips and announced, "Well, they should have cleaned up their mess and left an 'I'm sorry' note!"

My little sister is *so* naive.

If Drew asked once, she asked a hundred times: "Is this about Colby and the calendar?"

Mom ignored her and rushed around gathering up Drew's clothes and toothbrush, shoving them into her backpack.

"No, honey, Daddy and I just have some meetings at the office, and I thought you'd have more fun at Charlotte's house."

Not that she tried to anyway, but Mom couldn't ship *me* off to a friend's house; I don't exactly have anyone I'm close to. I have friends, of course, but there's no one special. Mom says Rachel and

Drew are "social butterflies," but she uses words like "quirky" and "bookworm" to describe me. She says I take after Dad in that way, too.

Speaking of *The Man of the Hour*, he disappeared into their bedroom shortly after we arrived home. It's amazing that he even came home with us, because he sure didn't want to. Mom had to badger him into leaving the campaign headquarters.

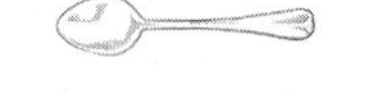

My mom is a lot of things, but more than anything else, she's one tough bitch when she's hurt, and it's easy for her to cut off anyone she feels wronged by. Dad told me that it's because she grew up in a girls' home and always had to look out for herself. Mom's public image is like she's this warm, friendly, *You'd Love to Have Me as Your Best Friend* person. But she doesn't trust people further than she can throw them, and once that trust is violated, the violator might as well be dead.

When they finally came out of Dad's office after he told Mom that he doesn't love her anymore, he headed for the media center sofa and curled up on it. She stomped right in there after him and didn't even bother with the *You're Being Unreasonable* voice or the soothing one, either. Nope; Mom went straight to *Bitch*: "Oh, no. *No, you don't.* I am *not* going to face what's at home by myself, so you get your ass off that couch and get in the car. *Now.*"

When he didn't move, she threatened to take pictures of him with her phone and text them to the news stations. That got him up.

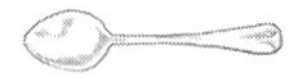

The moment Brenda pulled up and honked, Mom rushed Drew outside, then stood in the front yard and waved until the car was out of sight.

I went to my room, changed clothes, and lay face-down on the floor between my bed and the wall. I wanted to hide under my bed like I did when I was younger, but my bed's not on stilts. I sensed Mom in my doorway before she spoke. "Do you have the photograph, Colby?"

I nodded into my carpet.

She sounded choked. "Why…did you take it from your dad's office?"

I sat up and tried to look at her, but I couldn't. "I…didn't want anyone else to know about it."

Her voice was sharp. "You were going to *keep it* from me?"

I tried to swallow but my throat was so tight that I choked on my spit. "Uh—no, Mom. I had to think. I mean, it just happened a little while ago. I didn't know what to—"

She cut me off. "I'd like to see it, please."

I reached into my shirt and withdrew the photo from my bra. I glanced at it, hoping that, by some miracle, I was wrong about what I'd seen before.

I wasn't.

Mom met me where I was and took the photo from my hand. The look on her face nearly killed me. I babbled, "I'm sorry. I… didn't know what to do with it. I—"

She held up her hand to silence me. I followed her to the family room and watched as she sat on the sofa beneath the framed news clipping of Dad receiving the *Father of the Year* award from the City of Northside. She stared at the photo of him making out with that woman, then closed her eyes, lowered her head, and her tough bitch self melted away as she slid onto the floor, curled into herself, and sobbed.

I knelt beside her with my hand on her arm. She pulled into

herself even tighter and turned her face into the carpet. Every once in a while I whispered, "It'll be okay, Mom," even though I didn't believe myself.

I sat up when I heard my parents' bedroom door open. Dad carried two suitcases and a duffle bag into the family room, stepping carefully around a messy pile of board games that the F.B.I. agents pulled out of the hall closet and left on the floor.

"You okay, Colby?" he whispered. Did he think Mom couldn't hear him?

I didn't whisper. "Dad…why? How could you tell Mom that you don't love her anymore? What about my sisters and me? Do you still love us?"

His voice was flat, and he was no longer the freaked-out person he was in his campaign office. Instead, he was hyper-controlled and seemed to be wearing his *Debate Self*: the one he uses when he's facing off with an opponent and doesn't want to give anything away. He seemed to be looking at me, but it felt as if he was looking *through* me. "Of course I still love you girls, and I *do* still love your mother, Colby; just not in the same way. We will always have a very special connection, *because* of you and your sisters."

Mom wailed into the carpet and her shoulders shook with a new round of sobs.

Dad bit his lower lip and stared at his feet until Mom quieted down. When he spoke again, his voice was a little tighter. "Your mom and I have had our problems, but they have nothing to do with you. This…situation…is about me and my need for something more."

I rose up on my knees and tried to stand, but I was shaking too hard. I choked out, "Please, Dad, don't go. *Don't leave us.* Wh-who is that lady? How can you love her?"

Dad squared his shoulders and stood up straighter. "Colby, you're a child, and you can't understand what it's like for me to have feelings for another person that I never thought I would have again. Your mother is a wonderful person, and you and your sisters are everything to me. But none of you know what I have been through in the last year. You have no idea what it's like to be in my position. There's just so much pressure to be all things to all people."

I started to cry. "I'm *not* a child! You're just making excuses! *Why* did you hide that photo behind ours? Is everything a big lie?"

He fished his keys out of the bowl by the front door. "Sweetheart, I never planned on you finding out this way, but my relationship with Marcy is the real thing. My only regret is the way I've hurt you all, and for that, I am truly sorry." He shook his head and shrugged. "This is about me, not you."

He said it in the same tone of voice he'd use to tell a telemarketer that he's not interested in what she's selling.

"Well, how *were* we supposed to find out?"

He stared at his keys. "I hadn't figured that out yet."

"B-but what about—all that stuff you say in your speeches about how much you love Mom and how when you met her, you won the 'Wife Lottery'?"

He looked up as if the answer was written on the ceiling. "This feeling is not about our family. What I have found with Marcy has nothing to do with any of you. She understands that people expect me to be a certain way, and I…have to *be* that person. But not with her. I don't have to pretend to be anyone else when I'm with her." He set the luggage down but immediately retrieved it, then started to leave but looked back at me.

I wanted to ask him if we're still "a package deal," but I knew what the answer would be. "Where are you going, Dad?"

"I've got some thinking to do, and I need to be somewhere else to do it."

I went to the bathroom after Dad left and when I came out, Mom had gone to their bedroom and locked the door.

Rachel ripped the ear buds from my ears and yanked the pillow from my face.

"What the hell happened; did somebody break in? Why is Mom and Dad's bedroom door locked? Where's Drew? I got this weird voicemail from Mom, so I made Chris leave the movie early to bring me home." Rachel is completely freaked out.

Where do I even begin?

I sit cross-legged on my bed and tell my sister everything that's happened from the time she walked out of Dad's office—except for me eating a whole box of Ding Dongs—until Dad left to do his thinking about an hour ago. She doesn't believe me, and when she turns to leave my room, I jump up and grab her arm. I repeat it all, and she shoves me to the floor.

"This is *all your fault*! If you hadn't spilled that coffee, none of this would be happening! I hate you!" She slams my door on her way out.

I crawl onto my bed, place the pillow over my face, and try again to suffocate myself.

Chapter Four

Later that evening, Rachel and I are watching a reality show about wives who kill their husbands but always get caught. Mom's phone is on the kitchen counter, and it keeps ringing and buzzing with text messages. The landline rings constantly, too, as one reporter after another asks to speak to her.

Rachel and I tell them that Mom's unavailable, so they start grilling *us* about what the F.B.I. guys took out of our house. We break our parents' rule of never conversing with the press and ask them questions right back. We find out that Dad called an emergency meeting of his campaign committee and told them that he's left our mother for a woman he met at the big conference in April. He resigned from the campaign, effective immediately, and walked out of the meeting. Nobody knows where he is, and the rumor is that he's a danger to himself. Rachel turns off the TV, and we sit side by side on the sofa.

When Rachel and I can't stop crying, we turn off Mom's phone and unplug the landline. Rachel's friends keep texting her to ask what happened, and she finally turns off *her* phone. I've never seen her do that.

It gets worse. A News Ten van shows up in front of our house just as it's getting dark outside. The crew sets up lights and I try to watch as a lady reporter stands on the lawn and interviews the guy Dad was running against, but Rachel pulls me away from the window.

We ignore it when the reporter rings the doorbell and calls, "Mrs. Denton? Mrs. Denton, would you like to comment on your husband's probable arrest?"

I ask Rachel, "Is it against the law to cheat on your wife?"

She shrugs.

"You think the F.B.I. found something here?"

She sighs and rolls her eyes. "Just shut up."

The reporter goes around the house tapping on the windows, so we hide in the hallway.

Mom emerges from her room around ten o'clock. The three of us sit in the dark in silence that is broken only by our sniffling. Finally, Mom asks, "Are you girls hungry? I can heat up a pizza."

Rachel and I shake our heads. It hasn't been hard to avoid eating today. I can't stand the idea of food. My stomach's still kicking back the Ding Dongs, and that makes me think about spilling the coffee. Then this whole shitty day replays in my head.

We watch the news. The plastic-faced anchorman looks very serious next to a photo of my father from a rally he held about a month ago. Dad looks like a crazy person. I think they chose the worst picture they could.

"Good evening. Thank you for joining us. I'm Gerald Higgins. News Ten is the *only* station to bring you the breaking story of a candidate for the United States Senate who ran on a family values platform—but we've learned that his *own* marriage may be in trouble." He turns to his equally fake-looking cohost. "Deborah?"

"Thanks, Gerald, and good evening, everyone. I'm Deborah

Walters. News Ten became aware of this story after a member of Reese Denton's campaign staff called our tip line to report that the successful investment banker and senatorial candidate—who is incidentally an *outspoken* advocate for the preservation of the family unit—confessed today that he left his wife for another woman. And that's not the *only* disturbing aspect of this story. The source went on to tell News Ten that Mr. Denton is also being investigated by the F.B.I. and local law enforcement because of allegations that he has stolen from both his campaign *and* his investment firm's clients."

Mom gasps and makes a strangled cry. She claps her hand over her mouth and bends at the waist. Rachel and I put our hands on her back and rub at the same time. Our hands touch, and we lock eyes.

Deborah continues, "Even though he was leading in the polls, Mr. Denton quit the campaign, leaving his supporters stunned and seeking answers."

Gerald turns to another camera. "That's right, Deborah. As soon as the story broke, our own Susie Harlan contacted Tim Deaver, Reese Denton's opponent, to see what he has to say about the suddenly unopposed political race that he finds himself in. They met in front of the Denton home, which the F.B.I. and local law enforcement searched this afternoon."

The story opens with a close-up of our house, and Mom practically runs from the room. "I...I can't do this. This can't be happening."

Rachel and I watch Tim Deaver smile so big, it looks like his face is cracking. Susie asks, "Mr. Deaver, how do you feel about this development in the life of a man who has worked so *fervently* to defeat you in this race?"

Tim Deaver switches his face to *Serious/Sympathetic*. "It is, of course, early in the investigation, but I would hope that the voters come to the correct conclusion that the vicious rumors spread about me by the Denton campaign were just that: rumors. Who can trust a man who claimed to be the poster boy for family values but has been living a secret life?"

Susie Harlan frowns. "As you said, Mr. Deaver, it *is* early in the investigation—"

He cuts her off, breaking into a wide grin. "Traditional marriage, Susie! Right? That was Reese Denton's platform, and yet last time I checked, that means one"—he holds up a finger—"and I mean *one* man—and *one* woman—*at a time*." He wiggles his fingers and looks into the camera. "Hey, Reese, how's that working for you now, hmm?" He works his eyebrows up and down, and his smile reveals teeth so white that they look like Chiclets.

I turn to Rachel. "Our lives are over. You realize that, don't you?"

"Shut up," she whispers. She tosses her shoes to the floor, tucks her feet under a sofa cushion, and hugs a pillow tightly against her chest.

Gerald's back. "News Ten's own Mario Morales brings you this exclusive interview with Mr. Denton's campaign manager, Patrick Osmer."

Rachel picks up a shoe and throws it at the TV. "Traitor! I never did like you!"

I ask quietly, "But what if it's all true?"

She punches me hard in the arm. "Shut up, Colby!"

Mario Morales looks supernatural in the glare of the spotlight. He's standing next to a huge yard sign bearing my dad's *You Can Trust Me* face and the words *Family. Truth. Commitment. Denton.*

Mario apparently doesn't realize he's on the air. He laughs at someone off camera: "Yeah, you serious? Hey, I'd hit that, too..." He blinks a few times. "We're—we're on? We are?"

Deborah says flatly, "*Yes*, Mario, you're *on*. Loud and clear."

Mario switches to his somber face. "Thanks, Deborah. It may have started with allegations of using the campaign credit card to subsidize an affair, but that led to uncovering massive theft of his investment clients' accounts. Reese Denton is now facing felony charges of embezzlement and theft with intent to defraud. I spoke with Patrick Osmer, Mr. Denton's campaign manager, earlier this evening. We met in the office vacated just minutes before by his candidate, whose problems are just beginning."

Mario stares awkwardly at the camera a moment or two, like he's waiting for a signal. Finally, he says, "Uh, roll tape. Play the interview."

My parents' wedding portrait is on the bookcase behind Mario, who is seated in the chair near the door in my dad's office. When I was there earlier, the picture was on the top shelf behind Dad's desk. Guess they moved the photo.

"Mr. Osmer, according to my anonymous F.B.I. sources, an independent campaign finance auditor contacted the F.B.I. to report"—he consults his notes—"Mr. Denton's inappropriate usage of the campaign's credit card for personal use, substantial sums of money that are missing from the campaign coffers, and I'm told that Mr. Denton's investment banking firm is *also* likely to be indicted for fraud because of a financial scheme that he was instrumental in perpetrating. First things first: didn't he have permission to use the card?"

Patrick sighs heavily and nods his head. "Well, yes, he did, but certainly not for what *he* was spending money on. Shortly before resigning from the campaign, Reese admitted to using the campaign's credit card to take his girlfriend to the Four Seasons spa; he did that three times. He bought her tens of thousands of dollars' worth of jewelry, sent her flowers every week, and they went on weekend trips and to restaurants outside the Dallas area." He swallows hard. "Expensive...restaurants."

Mario prompts, "And, as far as you can tell, this began...?"

He sighs and chews his lip, then looks down at his folded hands, which are, incidentally, in the same spot that Dad's calendar used to be. "It started in April, when Mr. Denton was in Austin for the *Family Is the Foundation* conference. The spending binge has continued since then. We'd questioned him about it, and up until now, he'd *insisted* that this had to be a mistake on the part of the credit card company. Our committee chose to keep this quiet, because we believed him. He'd never given us a reason *not* to trust him." His eyes seem to darken, and his face turns red. He clenches his jaw and mutters, "I really don't have anything else to say about this."

The camera shifts to Mario. "My source tells me that it's possible that Reese Denton will be charged with the highest-grade felony because of the amount of money he stole to lavish on his mistress. Those spa trips add up to heartache for those who love and trusted him…and to *much* more than mere credit card abuse. Law enforcement agents have been in contact with Mr. Denton, and he is expected to turn himself in tomorrow morning. Back to you, Deborah."

"Thanks, Mario. News Ten's own Susie Harlan reached out to Mrs. Denton for a comment on this story, but she was unresponsive." They show footage of Susie knocking on our door, tapping on our windows, and tromping through Mom's flowerbeds. Deborah continues, "Late this evening, Susie tracked Reese Denton to the Northside Motor Lodge downtown, but he also declined to speak with her."

Rachel and I lean forward and watch as our father shields his face with a newspaper. He springs from his car and runs awkwardly across the parking lot. A motel room door flies open and he disappears inside. A woman's face appears in the window just before the curtains slide closed.

Rachel switches off the TV and buries her head in the pillow.

The next morning, I wake to Mom and Rachel arguing. I step to my door and press my ear against it.

Rachel yells, "No, I'm not! I'm not going now!"

"Yes, you are! You're not giving up everything you've worked for, and that is my final word on the matter!"

Rachel wails, "I don't want to go to Oregon now; don't you understand? I'm not going to leave you! I've already made up my mind that I'll call the scholarship office. Maybe they'll give me a leave of absence or something; I—"

"Rachel, you're not doing that. I *want* you to go to school. You have a place waiting for you, and that's the one thing I can count on right now. At least I know you'll have a roof over your head. I may not be able to afford a big enough place for the four of us."

There's silence; then Rachel chokes, "...What do you mean?... Aren't you going to stay here?"

Mom snaps, "The F.B.I. has frozen our assets, Rachel. That means that we can't get to any of our money, because your dad stole—I mean—they *think* that your dad stole from his investors and campaign backers."

"But this isn't your fault! You're not the one who—who—" I can't make out what Rachel is saying through her sobs, or what Mom is murmuring.

I flop back onto my bed and stare at the plastic stars above me. They've been stuck to the ceiling ever since I can remember, and now they're so old that they don't glow in the dark anymore. When I was younger, Dad would read me a story before bed; then we'd turn off the lights and play "Ask Me Anything." I could ask him any question, and he'd give me an answer. I can't think of even one time that he said, "I don't know," and I never questioned whether his answers were correct—*or true*. I believed everything he said.

I hear a car door slam. I spring off my bed and peek through the blinds. Brenda's car is in the driveway, and the News Ten van just pulled in behind it.

I throw open my bedroom door and sprint to the entryway in time to see my mom with her hand on the doorknob.

"Mom! The reporter's ba—"

She steps out onto the front porch, leaving the door wide open. Drew nearly knocks her over, wrapping herself around Mom's body like a spider monkey. Drew's face is all splotchy like she's been crying, but she isn't now.

Brenda squishes Drew when she hugs Mom. "I'm so sorry, Sonya. The girls were watching DVDs last night, so I hadn't heard about this. If I'd had any idea, I wouldn't have turned on the news this morning."

Susie Harlan and her cameraman are jogging across the yard toward us, and I'm frozen in place on the porch in my Winnie-the-Pooh pajamas. Mom, Brenda, and Drew rush past me into the house.

Rachel digs her claws into my upper arm and pulls me backward. "Don't just stand there, Colby!"

"We want your side of the story!" Susie calls. "What do you want to say about your father's imminent arrest?"

Her cameraman trips on the edge of the sidewalk and knocks over the flowerpot that I painted for my Mom's birthday when I was in fifth grade. It shatters. I yank my arm free of Rachel's grasp and stomp toward Susie.

"Go away! Leave! We don't *have* a side! We don't *know* anything!" I fall to my knees and begin gathering up the flowerpot shards, trying to put them back together. I wail and scoop up the plants. I'm crying so hard, I don't even notice my mom step around me.

Her voice is cold. "Stop filming my daughter. She is a minor child, and you do *not* have my permission to do it." I fall back on my bottom and cover my face with my dirty hands. Snot's running down my lips and off my chin, and I don't even care. I'm sitting on the sidewalk in my Pooh-Bear pajamas, boohooing like a two-year-old.

"Stop tape, Bob," Susie tells the cameraman. She speaks gently to Mom. "Mrs. Denton, the comments on News Ten's Facebook page indicate absolute support for you—and *outrage* that your husband would commit adultery and steal from those who trusted him. This is your chance to be a voice for wronged women everywhere. Won't you speak out on their behalf?"

Mom bends down and grasps my arm. I'm much too heavy to be lifted. Her voice is quiet and cold. "You're making a spectacle of yourself. Get up and go in the house. *Now.*"

I want to—I really do—but I just shake my head and bawl harder. Mom tries in vain to pull me up; she even grips me under my arms, but I'm not budging. She sighs loudly, lets go of me, and steps away. Susie and the cameraman follow her toward their van.

Rachel's narrow feet appear in front of mine, which are as wide as beaver tails. Her voice is flat. "Do you have any idea how stupid you look right now? It's not bad enough that Dad did this; now you have to make us look like a freak show. If you don't get your fat ass off this sidewalk right now, I'm going to turn the water hose on you."

I wail, "Shut up, Rachel!"

Brenda's soothing voice behind me: "Come on, sweetie. I'll help you." She steps around me and extends her hands.

I sob, "I'm...too big...you c-can't lift me." I roll onto my knees and accept Brenda's help to find my balance. She puts her arm around me, and we start toward the house. "Wait!" I run back to the broken flowerpot and retrieve the pieces that would still form a heart with the word *LOVE* on it, if I hadn't spilled that coffee on Dad's calendar.

Chapter Five

An F.B.I. agent shows up at our house first thing Tuesday morning. He tells us that their investigation has revealed that our house was paid off with money that Dad stole from his investors, and we have two weeks to find somewhere else to live because they're seizing our home.

Mom doesn't flinch. In the past two days, she's gone from being a curled-up, sobbing mess on the living room floor to having ramrod straight posture and tightly controlled emotions. And she's completely put together—dramatic makeup and beauty pageant hair—from the time she comes out of her room in the morning until bedtime. Usually she doesn't wear her poufy hairstyles when it's just us. But who *are* we anymore, anyway?

That night, Dad's on the news again. He's been booked on charges of embezzlement and theft with intent to defraud, but they don't keep him locked up. He walks out of jail holding hands with the brown-haired lady—Marcy—from the kissing photo. I guess that stealing from other people is okay with her, since she lets Dad "be who he is."

Drew bursts into tears and runs from the room. Rachel starts texting. I think about the tub of chocolate chip cookie dough in the freezer and how I can get to it without anyone seeing me.

Mom unplugs the antenna cable so that the only thing the TV's good for is watching DVDs. "I don't want you watching the news. Period." Then she goes to their bedroom and throws Dad's stuff in trash bags. She doesn't ask Rachel and me, but we get up and help her carry them to the garage. She tops the awkward pyramid of sacks with a mounted mallard duck that Dad shot a few years ago, and tucks his tube of athlete's foot cream under one of its wings.

Wednesday morning, we go to the U-Haul store, buy a shitload of cardboard boxes and strapping tape, and all of us start packing our things. It feels good to be busy, even though we don't know where we're going. I select my "Fuck You" songs playlist and listen to my iPod while I clean out my closet.

Drew squeals with delight when she opens the door Thursday afternoon to find our grandmother—my dad's mom—standing on our porch in what I've come to think of as her "uniform": long, dangly cross earrings; short, spiky red hair; perfectly applied make-up; chunky rhinestone cross necklace; oversized satiny blouse; black polyester slacks; and smelling of White Diamonds perfume. My sisters and I give her White Diamonds body powder every year for Christmas. I'll bet that when she dies, she'll be buried in that outfit, and they'll embalm her in White Diamonds.

Mom looks stunned. "Carol? What are you doing here?"

Grandma holds her arms open, and Mom walks into them. For the first time since Sunday, she breaks down and weeps.

"Aw, honey, I wouldn't be anywhere else." Grandma's deep Southern drawl, the way she stretches out each word, sounds like warm honey to my ears. She pulls back and picks a piece of lint off Mom's shirt. "Sam wanted to come, too, but he's just been elected president of the Chattahoochee chapter of *Take Back Our Country!*—and he's knee-deep in planning a community prayer breakfast. Dale will be here tomorrow to help move Rachel to school."

Rachel's jaw drops. "Uncle Dale's coming all the way here? You mean Dad's not even going to move me out?" Her voice cracks. "Seriously?" She pulls her phone from her pocket. "That's got to be wrong. I'm texting him."

Mom pulls out of Grandma's embrace. "Let me know if he answers you, Rachel, because he sure won't respond to me."

"Now, Sonya, you don't want to criticize the children's father," Grandma chides. "…Rachel, a condition of your father's release was that he not leave the state."

"You've been in touch with Reese, Carol?" Mom crosses her arms over her chest.

"Well, of course we have, sweetheart. He called us when this whole misunderstanding occurred, and we bonded him out. As soon as it's settled, we'll get our money back."

Rachel, Mom, and I exchange looks. Drew's still so excited that my grandmother's here from Georgia that she doesn't seem to realize they're talking about Dad's arrest.

Grandma flutters her hand in front of her face. "Whew! It's hot! Could I get a glass of water, please?" Rivulets of sweat look like little rivers through her thick makeup.

"Sure you can. I haven't packed the glasses yet." Mom gestures to the stacks of boxes and rolls of strapping tape. "As you can see, the house is in a state of chaos…"

Grandma furrows her brow. "Why *on earth* are you packing?"

Mom gives her a sideways look. "I guess you don't know that our bank accounts are frozen and the government is seizing the house as evidence of Reese's"—Mom swallows hard—"business practices. We're supposed to be out within two weeks. He hasn't been here since Sunday."

Grandma plops down on a kitchen chair and drops her purse to the floor. She shakes her head slowly. "I think you're acting hastily, Sonya. Reese assured Sam and me that the campaign auditor made a mistake, as did the credit card company. They'll have it all settled within a week."

Mom pulls a glass out of the cabinet and turns on the faucet.

I blurt, “He *left* us, Grandma. He cheated on Mom!”

“Don’t say it like that!” Drew wails.

Rachel heads for the back door. “I’m going to Stephanie’s house. Her family pretends they don’t know about any of this.”

Grandma looks shocked. “Sonya, I cannot believe that you would involve the children in your marital difficulties.”

Mom’s eyes get huge and she nearly drops Grandma’s glass of water. Her hand shakes when she holds it out to her. “Would you excuse us, girls?”

As usual, Drew follows orders like a little robot. She goes to her room, closes the door, and blasts her boy band CD.

I, on the other hand, stand just out of sight in the hallway and listen as my grandmother lectures my mother on what a lousy wife she is.

“Sonya, history shows us that powerful men often stray. That doesn’t mean they’re bad people; in fact, when Reese and I prayed together last night, he expressed regret at the pain he’s—”

“How long have you been in town?” Mom sounds incredulous.

“Just a day or two, I—”

“Then you *know* he’s having an affair.” Mom’s voice is rising. “You know that he resigned after admitting he’s been using the campaign’s credit card to—”

“That’s just a misunderstanding. Reese said—”

“Reese *said*?” Mom laughs bitterly. “Reese *said*? What, exactly, did Reese *say*?”

“Sonya, you need to calm down. The children are going to hear you, and—”

“Colby’s the one who discovered the affair! She found a picture of Reese kissing that goddamn slut!”

I gasp and clap my hand over my mouth. I’ve never even heard my mom say, “*Dang*.” I slide my face to the edge of the wall so that I can see them.

"Sonya! I am *shocked* to hear you use such language!" Grandma heaves herself out of the chair, tiptoes to the window, and peeks out. "Are you forgetting that reporters are sneaky and vile and will hang you out to dry if you give them the chance? Didn't what Leah did to Mark's reputation make any impression on you? Those snakes are probably slithering around on the ground outside, writing down every word you say!"

Hands on her hips, Grandma leans forward and tries to see if anyone's skulking about beneath the window ledge. She takes a long look through the window, then, apparently satisfied, tiptoes back to her chair and sighs heavily as she lowers herself onto the seat. She glances my way and I jerk back, thinking I've been discovered. But she turns back to Mom and insists, "You need to stand by Reese throughout this! Let them see you by his side, presenting a united front."

Mom shrieks, and something shatters.

Grandma freaks out. "You're scaring me! Is that what you did to Reese to drive him away? Did you throw dishes at him, too?"

Mom takes a deep breath in and blows it out. "I didn't throw that plate *at* you, and, *no*, I never lifted a finger in anger at Reese. But let me tell you what I have done. For the last twenty years, I have been the perfect politician's wife. I supported Reese without question. I raised his children to respect him as the head of our household. I didn't speak up when I disagreed with him—or with anybody else, either. I've smiled and kept up my looks and done my best to never attract negative attention.

"And this is the thanks I get: In the last four days, I've had to deal with the local news parking itself in my front yard. I've—I've watched my husband on TV, holding hands with another woman! Besides that, he could be sent to prison! Oh, and let's not forget that we have to move out, and I have no idea where the children and I will go."

Grandma sighs loudly. "Well…I can certainly see what Reese

was talking about when he told me that everything always has to be about you." Her voice cracks. "My poor son. I can't even imagine what he's had to put up with all these years. Just from what he told me last night, I—"

Mom laughs, and she sounds a little crazy. "Oh, *yes*. Reese has had it *so rough*, with a wife and children who adored him and had no idea he was stealing from his campaign to take his mistress to the Four Seasons spa three times since April!"

Grandma's voice is so low that I practically have to come out of my hiding place to hear her. "Let me ask you something, Sonya. Now, don't get more upset; just listen to what I'm saying. Please know that this question comes from a place of caring, because I love you as if you were my flesh-and-blood daughter."

Mom murmurs a strangled, "Okay."

"What are you doing to get him back?"

Dead silence…Then, it's like a bomb of emotions explodes in our kitchen: "Are you kidding me? He hasn't even bothered to call to check on the girls since he left! I've been trying to find out how I'm supposed to get Rachel moved two thousand miles to college. I've never driven a truck with a trailer. *I've* never been on a long trip like that by myself. Reese won't call me back! Then *you* show up today and announce that Dale's taking his place. It's like I'm at the mercy of the choices he makes, and I've about had enough!"

Grandma matches Mom's loudness. "There you go *again*! I'm telling you, you *cannot* keep saying things like that!" She lowers her voice and hisses, "Especially not so that others can hear you! Answer my question, please: I asked what *you* are doing to make him *want* to come home."

I don't even feel my feet move from the hallway to the kitchen: My rage has me rocket-powered. "Stop it, Grandma! Leave Mom alone! It's not her fault that Dad left!"

Mom holds up a hand. "Colby, you don't need to defend me. I'm a big girl."

"Speaking of 'big girl'..." Grandma looks me up and down. "How much do you weigh now?"

I clench my fists and lean forward. "That's none of your fucking business! Have *you* looked in the mirror lately?"

Grandma springs out of her chair really fast for an old lady and slaps me hard. I spin on my heel and stomp toward my room, with Mom hot on my trail. I try to slam my door, but she lurches forward and snatches hold of my upper arm with a death grip. Her eyes are blazing.

"*How dare* you speak to your grandmother that way? Where did you even learn that word?"

"Are you on crack, Mom? I live in the real world. I hear that word every day at school. It's in the music I listen to, it's—"

Mom sputters, "*Crack*? Are you—is that...What music? Well, you're certainly not going to listen to it anymore!" She steps into my room and snatches my iPod off my dresser.

"Mom! Didn't you hear what Grandma said? How can you be mad at *me* after everything *she* said to you?" I'm furious at myself for starting to cry.

"You were *eavesdropping*?" Her face turns bright red, and she swallows hard. "What is the matter with you, Colby Diane? You used to be such an obedient girl!" She moves to the hallway, my iPod cord dangling from her hand.

"No, I wasn't!" I yell. "I was *never* the obedient one. That's Drew! And I was never the perfect one. That's Rachel! You'd swear that I'm Aunt Leah's child, remember? I'm the one who doesn't fit!"

I slam my door and lock it, then throw myself face-down on my bed and scream into my pillow until my head feels like it's going to explode. I sob so hard that I'm sure I'm going to throw up.

Later, somebody—I think it's Drew—knocks on my door, but I can't hear what she's saying over the racket I'm making. Finally, I fall asleep.

I wake and think it's morning, but my clock radio reads 6:18 P.M. I ease open my door and peer down the hall. Silence. I pop into the bathroom and study the bright red handprint Grandma left on my cheek.

I tiptoe toward the kitchen and stick my head around the corner. There's a note taped to the cabinet.

Colby-

We've gone to grab something to eat with Grandma. Guess you were asleep. Will bring you something back.

Mom

I pull the tub of chocolate chip cookie dough out of the freezer and pop it in the microwave for a few minutes to soften it up. Then I grab a spoon, snatch the dough from the oven, and go back to my room. I lock my door just in case everyone comes back, and settle on the floor among the cardboard boxes and garbage bags that hold pieces of my life.

I shovel in heaping spoonfuls of lukewarm dough and I don't feel a thing—not the horror of finding the photo, not the deep-seated shame of being the one who told, not the indescribable ache of my dad leaving us. I don't even think about the way my mom lets me know in a hundred tiny ways that she doesn't like me, much less love me. I'm a numb mound of cells until I can't eat another bite because it feels like my insides will explode. I'm surprised that the tub's nearly empty; I bury it under some old magazines in a trash sack and crawl to my bed. My head is spinning, and raw cookie dough is backing up into my throat.

Good times.

Mom calls my name and knocks on my door, but I ignore it. She picks my lock. I close my eyes and pretend to be asleep when she sits on the edge of my bed and touches my shoulder.

"Colby?"

"Hmm?" I flutter my eyes as if I'm waking and try to sit up, but I'm still too woozy from eating nearly a pound of lightly heated cookie dough. I stifle a burning burp that I hope looks like a yawn.

"I brought you take-out from Panera Bread. Smoked ham and Swiss." She sniffs the air and makes a face. "It smells like cookies in here."

I mumble, "I don't know why it would."

She tugs at my arm. "Well, sit up. You haven't been eating enough lately, and I'm worried about you."

"According to Grandma, I'm as big as a house." I glare at Mom because I know she thinks the same thing.

Mom sighs. "She means well, she's just…" Her eyes are as dull as her voice. "I hope you'll feel up to joining us, and that you'll apologize to your grandmother."

Even though I'm painfully full, I still have room for rage. "Has she taken back what she said to you?"

Mom snaps, "You weren't supposed to hear that. I asked you to excuse yourself." She tosses the take-out bag at me and massages her temples. "I may not like what she said, but there could be a grain of truth to it. Maybe your dad just made a mistake. He is a powerful man, after all, and it's natural for women to—"

I blast her, shouting, "Seriously, Mom? You're blaming *yourself* for what he did? He lied to you! He lied to *everyone*! My whole life, I believed it when Dad said that honesty is everything to our family!"

I don't know how long Grandma has been listening in the doorway. "That has nothing to do with it, Colby! We don't air our dirty laundry to the world! Your Aunt Leah could not grasp that concept, and that's why she's barely getting by. Do you want your mother to be broke and miserable, too? Do you want your whole world to be turned upside down?"

I touch her handprint on my cheek and murmur, "I think it already is."

Around noon on Friday, Uncle Dale arrives in a pickup truck pulling a horse trailer. We all go out on the porch to look, and Rachel's eyes are huge. "I'm supposed to put my stuff in *that*?"

He claps her on the back as he comes inside. "Well, sure, sweetheart, I hosed it out before I left Shreveport this morning. That trailer's the Cadillac of equine travel. It's got AC and everything! And—no worries—I left the windows open all the way here to air out the smell."

Rachel slumps, and her voice is flat. "FML."

"Ef-em-el? What on earth does that mean?" Mom asks.

Rachel rolls her eyes. "It's French." She gives me a warning look, like *I'm* going to tell Mom that *FML* means *Fuck My Life*. She sighs. "Stephanie's going to die when I tell her this." She slips her phone from her pocket and texts as she walks to her room.

Uncle Dale watches her go and turns to Mom. "I stopped by Leah's place to see if she's still mad at us and to ask Ryan if he wanted to go on a road trip to Oregon. I thought he might be inspired to apply to the same school in a couple of years, and I was also hoping that spending some man-to-man time with him on the way back home might help. I thought that I could explain to him about how the world works, so he won't go through the rest of his life bringing a rain of fire down on himself. It's not like Leah's going to teach him about the importance of keeping his mouth shut."

Mom arches an eyebrow. "And?"

Dale shakes his head. "No dice. Leah tried to make excuses for him; said she needs him to help out in her bakery…but Ryan told me that he already *has* one asshole, and he *sure* doesn't need to be stuck in a truck with two other ones. I *suppose* he means me and Rachel."

"Such language!" Grandma spits from the armchair. "Ryan brought all his problems on himself by getting involved where he had no business. It was that girl's word against the boy's. Ryan doesn't get to be the judge of others. The Bible says—"

I blurt, "Yeah, wouldn't the Bible call Dad an adulterer and thief?"

Mom lunges at me. "Colby!"

"Last time I checked, adultery and stealing were right up there in the Top Ten." I figure she's going to latch onto my upper arm again, but she doesn't.

Uncle Dale talks to me like I'm a little kid, even calling me the pet name he gave me when I was born and looked to him like a chubby teddy bear. "You don't understand, Colby-Bear. Ryan admitted that all the guests at the party—the entire football team *and* the cheerleaders—were drinking. That girl put herself in the position of being taken advantage of, *if* that's what really happened. Ryan was wrong to turn his back on his teammate." He drops into Dad's recliner and puts his feet up.

I fold my arms and pace in front of the TV. "I'm just trying to figure out who the rules apply to, because my whole life, Dad's been lecturing me about doing the right thing, even when it's hard. So, Ryan tells the truth about what he saw and three guys beat him up for it, but instead of being proud of him, you criticize him. I think you're nothing but a bunch of hypocrites."

"Colby!" Mom steps in front of me.

I look around, and my entire family is staring at me like I've got horns and a pointy tail. I hug myself tight and glare at my feet.

"There's just one thing to do with a child like Colby at a time like this," Grandma announces. She works her way out of the chair, stands, and holds out her hands for a prayer circle. "Let us ask the Lord to remove the darkness from her soul."

I head for my room. "You do what you want. I'm going to pack." I throw back over my shoulder, "You know, since we have to leave this house, seeing as how Dad *forgot* how to do the right thing."

After Uncle Dale and Grandma leave to meet up with Dad, Mom tries to get Rachel to invite some friends over for a going-away party. Rachel doesn't want to see anyone, but Mom insists that we do *something* to try to make our last night together special. We order pizza. Mom asks Rachel to finish packing the stuff she's not taking to school, since we'll be moving it wherever we're going.

Drew and I are tired of packing and want to watch TV, but Mom still won't let us hook up the antenna cable, and the DVD player is freezing up. Since I haven't apologized to Grandma, Mom won't let me have my iPod.

Instead, she listens to it and surfs the Internet for our new life.

I wake around 2:00 A.M. to someone crying. I tiptoe outside Rachel's room. Mom's with her.

Rachel whines, "I don't *want* to go to Oregon with Uncle Dale. This isn't how it's supposed to be. We planned on going together!"

Mom's voice is low, soothing. "Aw, honey, I know. It was going to be a family vacation. I wish I could go, too, but I have about a week to find us a place to live. I'm sorry."

"Don't apologize, Mom. You're not the one who's pretending we don't exist. I don't understand what's happening. Is there something, like, mentally *wrong* with Dad?"

Mom doesn't answer for a long time. Finally, she says, "You're going to get to school and be so busy getting unpacked and finding your way around Portland, you won't have time to think about what's happened here. It'll be good for you, Rachel." Mom's trying to use her sunshiny voice, but it keeps breaking.

Rachel wails, "How am I going to make it until Thanksgiving without seeing you every day?"

Mom sounds like she's trying to convince herself along with Rachel. "You…you just *will.* You're my child, and that means you keep going no matter what. You hear me? I need you to be strong. Colby's a big fat disaster, eating everything in sight, and Drew's sliding into sadness. I've never even opened a checking account on my own, much less decided where we should live."

I sit on the floor outside my sister's room. My shoulders shake with silent sobs. I'm a disaster: a big fat disaster.

Early Saturday morning, Uncle Dale and Grandma return with the truck and horse trailer. They also bring a new hard drive for the computer in our family room.

"We picked this up at the electronics store last night. Reese was concerned about you and the girls doing without, since those investigators took all your computers." Grandma turns to Mom and asks pointedly, "Does *that* sound like someone who doesn't care about his family?"

"What about my laptop?" Rachel asks.

I jump in, too. "And mine?"

Grandma's eyes flash. "I'm not made of money! You'll make do with this, or you'll have nothing at all!"

Mom accepts the hard drive from Uncle Dale. "Of course, Carol. Thank you."

Grandma's worried about Uncle Dale driving back from Oregon by himself, so she's decided to go along for the ride. Mom and Rachel fake acting happy about "the big day finally being here," and Drew clings to Rachel in her usual spider monkey way. Uncle Dale makes a run to the local doughnut shop and returns with two dozen. I grab two frosted chocolate and two with pink icing and sprinkles, then rush toward my room to eat them.

Grandma intercepts me as she comes out of the bathroom. She snatches my paper plate from me. "You don't *need* that many doughnuts, Colby."

It's none of your fucking business! is on the tip of my tongue, but I stop myself before I say it. "I'm hungry," I lie. I mean, I think it's a lie. I can't really tell when I'm hungry. My face burns with embarrassment, and it feels like my double chin is multiplying.

"Pick *two* doughnuts," she insists. "Just two."

I lower my head. "Never mind. I'm not hungry." I step around her and rush to my room. I close my door, lock it, and slide against it to the floor. After a few minutes, I crawl to my dresser and pull my snack stash out of the bottom drawer.

The horse trailer is filled to the top with Rachel's stuff. She slams the door on Uncle Dale's pickup truck and trudges across the yard for a final goodbye. The four of us—Mom, Rachel, Drew, and I—all have spasming faces because we're trying not to cry as we huddle in a group hug. As bitchy as Rachel can be, I still don't want her to go. Not right now, when everything's upside down.

"I'll call you every day," Rachel tells Mom.

Mom nods and sounds like she has peanut butter in her throat when she talks. "I'll let you know as soon as I figure out what's next."

This time, Grandma's the one eavesdropping. "If I have anything to say about it, your mom's going to unpack and stay put. She's rushing into this instead of waiting for the misunderstanding to be sorted out. Mark my words: You're going to be sorry that you acted in haste."

Mom closes her eyes and shakes her head inside our group hug. Grandma's still talking, but we ignore her.

Uncle Dale interrupts. "If we're going to make it to southeast Colorado by dark, we need to get going."

"Thanks for helping out with Rachel," Mom tells him. "If it has to be this way, I'm glad that you're the one delivering her to college."

"Hey, that reminds me," he says. He pulls an envelope from his shirt pocket. "When I saw Leah yesterday, she asked me to give you this."

Mom takes it from him carefully, like it's contaminated. "Wonder what it could be..."

Uncle Dale laughs. "Knowing Leah, there's no telling."

Chapter Six

By Tuesday, Mom decides that we'll move to Norman, Oklahoma. One of her friends from her pageant days is now an elementary school principal and she promised Mom a teaching job. We drive three hours to get there and spend the day looking for a place to live.

After visiting several places with the leasing agent—a guy who looks and sounds so much like President George W. Bush that I'd swear it's him—Mom decides on a small house that has a fenced yard with a doghouse in it. This sets Drew to begging Mom for a puppy. Mom says she'll think about it, which sounds like "Yes" to Drew. We return to the leasing office and Mom fills out the paperwork.

While the agent runs Mom's credit, we eat an early supper at the barbecue place next door, then return to the office to sign the lease.

"There's a problem with your credit check," George W. Bush's look-alike says. He frowns at Drew and me. "Mrs. Denton, could you come with me, please?"

Mom's gone a long time. When she finally returns, her eyes are puffy and red. She snatches up her purse and snaps, "Let's go."

"What's wrong, Mama?" Drew asks. "Can I still get a puppy?"

Mom doesn't answer. Drew starts her skipping CD act, asking the same questions again and again, but I squeeze her shoulder and shake my head at her.

We get in the car. Mom pulls away from the leasing office without even putting on her seat belt, and she never gets in a car without buckling up. She screeches her tires out of the parking lot and shoots into the intersection, causing us to nearly get creamed by oncoming traffic.

I'm freaking out. "Mom! Are you okay?"

She cuts the wheel into the Walmart parking lot across the street, speeds to the rear of the building, and parks next to a dumpster.

I grab her arm. "Mom! *What happened?* What's wrong?"

She laughs crazily, shakes her head rapidly, withdraws her cell phone from her purse, and dials. Mom sounds like a machine gun, *rat-a-tat-tatting* her words: "Reese Thomas Denton, I *know* you won't call me back, but I found out that you opened credit card accounts in both of our names. I'm sure *you* know this, but we owe over a hundred thousand dollars! A. Hundred. Thousand. Dollars. You haven't been making any payments and maybe *you* don't care, but you've ruined my credit right along with yours." She hits the steering wheel: "I [*Slam*!] didn't [*Slam*!] even [*Slam*!] know about this! [*Slam Slam Slam Slam*!]" She screams, and Drew and I put our hands over our ears.

I guess Dad's phone cuts her off, because she redials his number and babbles, "*How* am I supposed to find a place for our children to live when I can't pass a credit check, Reese? We have nowhere to go! Nowhere! What have you *done* to us? We're going to be homeless!"

Mom throws her phone to the floorboard and pounds the steering wheel some more, then presses her forehead against it and weeps.

Drew throws herself face-down in the back seat and wails, "I don't *want* to be homeless!...You said I could get a puppy!"

We drive back to Northside in silence. Drew sleeps and Mom stares straight ahead. I'm spring-loaded with anxiety and watching her every second because I'm afraid she's going to zone out and drive us into oncoming traffic.

We arrive home around nine that night to find business cards and sticky notes tacked to our front door. Reporters want just five minutes and they promise to be fair, divorce lawyers want to represent Mom, and our neighbors want us out—*now*.

Late the next morning, I'm snoozing when the phone starts ringing. I groan loudly, "Somebody get the phone!" Nobody does. I roll over and just get back to sleep when it rings again. "Arrrrgh!"

I throw open my door and stomp to the kitchen. I rip the note off the cabinet: "*Running errands. Back soon.*" I snatch the phone off the charger and growl, "Hello!"

The voice is tentative. "...Sonya?"

"She's not here. May I take a message?"

"Um, is this Rachel?"

I know I sound pissy, but I don't care. "No, she lives in Oregon now. Who's this?"

"This is Leah. Who is *this*?"

My stomach clenches when she says her name. "It's Colby." I move to the dining room table and sit on the edge of a chair.

"Oh, hey, Colby, I'm returning your mom's phone call. She left a message for me late last night, but I didn't get it until this morning." Leah waits like she's expecting me to say something else, but I don't. "...Anyway, tell your mom that the answer is not just yes, but *absolutely* yes. You guys are more than welcome to it."

"Uh, we're welcome to what?"

"The trailer behind my house. You didn't know? When Dale stopped by last week and told me about your dad and mom having...problems, I sent a letter with him for your mom, offering use of the trailer behind my house for as long as you need it. Your mom left a message last night saying she'd take it, if the offer still stands."

"You mean, like, a trailer to move our stuff?"

Leah laughs. "No! To live in, silly! It's a single-wide mobile home."

"Where do you live?"

"That's right; you've never visited me. I live in Piney Creek, in East Texas. It's small and real country. But that's a good thing, because I can have a trailer behind my house and nobody cares."

"Oh…Okay. Well, thanks. I've…got to go."

"Please have your mom call me when she gets back. We'll figure out the next step."

Ever since she and my Uncle Mark split up seven years ago, Aunt Leah's been pretty standoffish as far as family gatherings. Before the divorce, she, Uncle Mark, and Ryan came over to our house a lot, although she and Dad always got into arguments easily. So, we were surprised when Leah and Ryan agreed to come to the Fourth of July picnic at a state park near Uncle Dale's house in Louisiana. Even after she stopped coming around, Aunt Leah still sent us birthday cards, usually with a ten-dollar bill tucked inside. Mom and Dad cautioned us to watch out for her because she's "unstable" and prone to blowing things out of proportion just to get attention.

"Whatever you do," Mom told Rachel and me before the Fourth of July picnic, "don't bring up Uncle Mark, politics, or religion, because that'll start a fight."

I thought that those were weird things to warn us about. Did she think I was going to say, "Hi, Aunt Leah! Tell me: What was it like to have Uncle Mark arrested for beating the shit out of you?…Election Day's coming up! You're registered to vote, right?…So, been to church lately?"…I mean, *really*.

On the Fourth of July, Dad was grilling burgers when Aunt Leah parked her yellow VW bug next to my grandparents' motor coach. Ryan got out first. He wore a neon orange cast on his wrist, and his face showed fading bruises and fresh scars that looked like he'd had stitches.

Grandma immediately raised a fuss about it: "Oh, my *goodness*, darling! Were you in a car crash?"

He looked down and shook his head.

"What on earth happened to you, boy?" Uncle Dale asked a little gruffly. "Did you take second place in an ass-kicking contest?"

Ryan kind of snorted, then moved to the trunk and popped it open. He pulled out their small ice chest, then slammed the lid closed.

Leah emerged from her car and everybody looked her up and down, too. I remembered her as not being very tall, but she was a lot heavier since the last time I saw her. She was wearing a snug tank top that showed off a tattooed wreath of flowers stretching from her back, across her shoulders, and down into the gap between her breasts. Elaborate vines wrapped her upper arms and wound all the way down to her fingers.

Dad glanced at Leah, and his mouth stretched into a smirk. He shook his head disapprovingly and spat, "Nice ink, Hoss."

I guess Aunt Leah didn't hear him, but she couldn't help but hear Grandpa when he unfolded his mountain-sized self from the camping chair by the picnic table and bellowed, "My God Almighty, Leah Jane, what have you *done* to yourself?"

Leah narrowed her eyes. "Nice to see you, too, Daddy. Well, I guess what I've done is driven nearly three hours to see my family for the first time in several years, and this is how you greet me."

Her eyes ran over my sisters and me, standing with our arms crossed just like the rest of the jury. She gave us the tiniest of smiles.

"Drew, I haven't seen you since you were barely walking. You girls sure have gotten big."

Rachel and Drew cut their eyes to me and I mumbled, "She means we're *older*, okay?"

Rachel hissed, "Yeah, right."

Uncle Dale's wife, Aunt Judy, insisted on carrying the ice chest for Ryan. "Oh, honey, let me help."

She took it from him. He stepped back and mumbled what might have been, "Thanks."

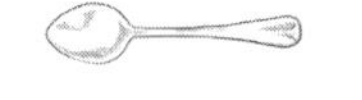

Later, as we took turns cranking the homemade ice cream maker, Leah cleared her throat and said, "This seems as good a time as any to bring this up." She ran a finger over the vines on one hand, tracing them over and over. She and Ryan exchanged a look, and she began, "Ryan's injuries are from three boys attacking him on the last day of school. He spent a week in the hospital."

Grandma blurted, "Why didn't you call us? We would have been there in a heartbeat!"

Leah swallowed hard, and her lips quivered. "Well, after the reaction you had to me leaving Mark, I didn't think you…you know"—she shrugged—"were…interested…in being there for us. I mean, over the last seven years, you haven't *done* anything to change that impression."

Grandpa's voice was flat. "It may have been seven years, but my rule is the same as it's been your whole life. If *you* create the problem for *yourself*, *you* clean it up *yourself*. You *chose* to leave that marriage. It's not my job to rescue you—especially given the way you did it: involving the press in your personal business! You nearly killed Mark's career! And, from the looks of you, I'd say I made a good call. You—a grown woman—covering yourself in that—that—trash! What do people think when they see you?"

Leah stood so abruptly that her chair fell backward. "Look, Dad, I know you don't believe that Mark was abusive to Ryan and me, but he was; he—"

Dad jumped in. "The Mark Ellis I know would *never* do the things you claim he did, Leah. Admit it: You got bored, and you wanted out."

Leah's eyes shot sparks. "The Mark Ellis *you know* is a phony, Reese." She reached into her purse and pulled out an envelope of photos. "I—I didn't show you these before, but I want to prove to you that he did what I said. These don't even show half of...just look, okay?"

At first no one would accept the envelope from her, but Aunt Judy started it off, and I peeked over my mom's shoulder when it was her turn. Of course, Leah was younger, but her face was nearly unrecognizable. Her nose was obviously broken, and a close-up photo of her neck clearly showed handprints.

She accepted the envelope back from my dad, who muttered, "I still have a hard time believing that Mark did these things. He's on my campaign committee, you know..."

Leah said softly, "He—he choked me until I passed out. If it hadn't been for Ryan—my God, he was only nine years old at the time—jumping on his back and clawing his eyes—I'd be dead."

When Ryan spoke clearly for the first time that day, it was a growl. "My dad's an asshole, Uncle Reese. I hate him. Wish I could run him over with a truck."

All of the adults except Leah started yelling at Ryan for his language and for wishing such an awful fate on anyone; then they jumped on Leah for poisoning his mind against his dad.

It was like watching a movie that doesn't make sense: Leah *proved* that what she was saying was true, but her own parents and brothers—her *family*—still didn't believe her.

Leah shrieked, "Stop it! *Stop it*! Please!" She held up both hands in surrender, closed her eyes, and her voice was barely above a whisper when she spoke. "Believe me: I would *not* be asking this if I weren't desperate. Ryan's hospital bills are swallowing me, and I can't catch up. You—you have no idea how hard it is for me to come to you, but I need help. Please...I'll pay you back; I don't know how long it'll take, but—"

Aunt Judy tiptoed over and uprighted Leah's chair, put her hands on Leah's shoulders, and gently pushed her down into the seat, then gave her three soft *pat-pat-pats*. Leah looked up at her and nodded gratefully.

Grandpa crossed his arms. "Same rule about rescuing applies here as anywhere else, Leah Jane. *Why* did those boys attack Ryan?" He narrowed his eyes and tucked his chin, giving Ryan a beady-eyed stare. "What did *you* do to them?"

"I'll bet you gave them as good as you got, right, Ryan? You *are* from Denton stock, you know!" Uncle Dale winked at him and mimed giving a one-two punch.

Ryan clenched his jaw and glared at the ground. His eyes filled with angry tears, and he impatiently brushed at his cheek with the back of his hand.

Leah calmly explained, "Last May, Ryan attended a party at one of his football teammate's homes. The parents were out of town, and there was underage drinking going on. Some girls from Cedar Points were there, too, and one of them, a girl named Kimmie, drank too much and passed out. While she was unconscious, the team's quarterback, Jared, raped her."

I gasped. "Oh, my God, is the girl all right?" It was as if my words were carried away by the light breeze blowing through our campsite.

At the mention of the word "rape," my mother ordered, "Go into the motor coach, *now*, Drew Ann."

Of course, my little sister immediately obeyed, because that's what *she does*. Mom watched her go, then snapped, "Leah, I will thank you to not use words like that around my seven-year-old daughter!"

Leah gave Mom a dull look and continued the story without acknowledging her.

"Afterward, Jared not only bragged about what he'd done; he texted a video and nude pictures of Kimmie to his teammates. He even posed in some of the photos, showing himself in the act of... violating her in a variety of ways."

My dad bolted out of his chair and stood threateningly over Ryan. "What do you have to do with this? If the press finds out that *my nephew*—"

Aunt Leah jumped up and put herself between Dad and Ryan. "Jesus Christ, Reese! Is that all you ever think about? Your fucking campaign?"

She's a lot shorter than Dad, but she kept walking forward until he nearly bumped into the flaming grill. She poked him in the chest with every word she said. "My! Son! Is! The! Only! Person! Who! Had! The! Courage! To! Report! Jared! For! Rape!" She stepped back and put her hands on her hips. "When the local police department refused to investigate, he called the county sheriff! Ryan did the right thing!"

The air became heavy, and the only sound was the birds in the forest.

Dad said nothing; just met Leah's ice-cold stare right on.

Finally, Grandma murmured, "So, why...?" She reached over and laid a hand gently on Ryan's bright orange cast. He looked to the right and down, but didn't pull away from her.

Leah dragged her feet through the powdery forest floor as she walked back to her chair. She sat heavily and put her head in her hands. After a minute or so, she spoke. "The boy—Jared—is very well-liked; very well-connected. He was bound for Baylor on a full-ride football scholarship. When the news first broke, his teammates—and much of the community—took Jared's side. They blamed *the girl* for getting drunk! All they talked about was what a shame it was that such a nice boy with a promising future would lose it all because of"—she shook her head disgustedly—"one bad decision."

Leah straightened and reached for Ryan's shoulder, resting her hand on it. "The last day of school, three of the football players severely beat Ryan. They even videoed the attack and posted it on YouTube, but it was quickly removed."

Aunt Judy was clearly horrified and asked Ryan, "Well, what happened to those boys? The ones who hurt you?"

Ryan shook his head, his angry tears flowing hard.

Leah answered for him. "Nothing, really."

Grandpa's voice was soft. "And Jared? What about him?"

"Luckily, the district attorney was able to use the texts that Ryan received from Jared as evidence. Jared is eighteen, so he'll be tried as an adult."

"You're saying he lost everything he worked so hard for, based on what *could have been* a consensual act?" Grandpa sounded like the attorney he was before he retired.

Leah looked like she'd tasted something bitter. "Were you listening to what I said, Daddy?" Her eyes grew huge, and it was like a cartoon when a light bulb shows that somebody just realized a big truth. "Jared *texted photos* that proved his guilt, just like I *showed you* photos that prove that what I'm saying about Mark is true...and yet *you choose* not to believe it."

Dad slammed the lid on the grill and strode over to Ryan. "... Well, how do *you* know that it was rape, unless you heard the girl tell him to stop? You weren't there, right?"

Ryan set his jaw and stared at the cast on his wrist.

Dad clapped Ryan on the back, then gripped his shoulder tightly. "*Right*, Ryan? *You weren't there* when this alleged rape occurred?"

At last, Ryan shook his head.

Grandpa said brusquely, "As far as I'm concerned, *everyone* at that party was in the wrong. Underage drinking! You're not going to sit here and pretend that you weren't drinking, too, are you, Ryan?"

Ryan leaned forward at the waist and dragged his toe through pine needles in a triangular pattern. Grandpa cleared his throat, and Ryan finally shook his head.

My grandfather railed, "I agree with your community, Leah Jane. That girl brought it on herself by drinking until she passed out! She may not remember giving consent, but...whatever happened, it was a perfect storm of bad choices." He looked at me. "Colby, you'd *never* go to a party where underage drinking was occurring, would you?"

I started to answer, but Rachel snorted, "Ha! As if anyone would invite *her*!"

Grandpa raised his eyebrows, and Rachel muttered, "Not that...I would go, you know, *if*...I was invited to one."

"*Of course* you wouldn't," my mother said sharply.

"*Of course* not," Grandma agreed.

Grandpa set his sights on Ryan again. "Look at me, boy."

Ryan raised his eyes at last.

"*You* need to get a job and help your mama pay the medical bills that *you* brought on her by going to a party where illegal activity occurred. You're not going to learn a lesson from this if you don't pay the price."

Ryan mumbled, "I *do* have a job. I work at Sugar's. With Mom."

Grandpa sat back hard in his chair. "Then you'd better get another one. I'm assuming you're no longer welcome on the football team?"

"I quit," Ryan said softly.

Grandpa accepted the ice cream churn from Uncle Dale and began turning the handle. "Well then, you'll have plenty of time this summer and autumn to work."

Then he set his gaze on Aunt Leah. "And, *you*: the first time I see you in seven years, and it's to ask for money. You can't expect us to open our arms and welcome you back just because you're flesh and blood. Pull yourself together, Leah Jane. Lose some weight. Pay off your debts through hard work and determination. Stop blaming Mark for your problems and, *by God*, don't teach Ryan to blame those other kids for his lapse in judgment, and maybe—just maybe—you'll come out of this stronger than when you started."

My mom sat up straight in her chair and flipped her hair back over her shoulder. "Just look at Rachel, Ryan. She's got a fully paid academic scholarship to Lewis & Clark College in Portland. She's going to be a lawyer, just like your grandpa. Get yourself on the right track again, and maybe you can do the same. Bring *pride* to our family, not *shame*."

"*That's it!*" Leah bolted out of her chair and gestured to Ryan to follow her. "I *knew* it was a mistake to come here! Just when I start to forget why I avoid this fucked-up family, you people remind me!"

She stomped over to the picnic table, tossed their potato salad into her ice chest, and told Ryan to take it to their car. As they sped away, Ryan rolled down his window and gave us all a one-fingered salute.

About the time they rounded the corner, Uncle Dale's wife, Judy, clucked her tongue. "You'd *think* a woman her size wouldn't wear tank tops in public."

"The way you acted like her best friend, I'm a little surprised to hear you say that," Mom said snidely.

"Oh, *please*. I wouldn't be seen talking to her in public. What would people think if they associated me with her? She looks like a...a...biker chick!" Aunt Judy collapsed into giggles, and Mom and Rachel joined in.

"Can I come out now?" Drew called from the doorway of the motor coach.

"Yes, it's safe," Dad grinned. "The biker chick has left the building," he said, sounding like a World Wrestling Federation announcer.

Drew cocked her head. "Huh?" The adults laughed, and she gave an adorable smile, flipped her hair from side to side like Mom does, and practically skipped down the motor coach steps.

Grandma opened her arms; Drew ran into them, and she was enveloped in a White Diamonds–scented cloud.

I brush my teeth, then sit at Mom's desk and eat a couple sleeves of Pop Tarts while I search the Internet for Piney Creek, Texas.

Mom and Drew come through the back door carrying a few Walmart bags.

"Good morning, sunshine!" Mom smiles—like, she really *smiles*—for the first time since I saw her standing next to Dad when he was shaking hands with supporters at his rally about ten days ago. Feels like it's been a lifetime.

I wonder if she's about to go crazy again. "*You're* in a good mood."

Mom pops the top on a diet soda and takes a sip. "I spent time in prayer last night. I've handed our future over to the Lord."

"Hmm." I look up from reading the *Piney Creek Chamber of Commerce* website. "Aunt Leah called. She said it's cool if we live in the trailer behind her house." I watch Mom's face to see if this statement strikes her as odd.

It doesn't seem to; Mom looks relieved as she empties the plastic sacks. "See there? Prayer works! I'll call her back in a sec."

I log off the computer and lean back in the chair with my feet on the desk. "So…you *want* to move to Piney Creek?" I gesture to the monitor. "Have you *seen* Piney Creek?"

Her eyebrows bump up and she shrugs. "Well, the offer of a place for us means I don't have to ask your grandma or Uncle Dale to let us live with them. It's not like I'm overflowing with family to rely on."

Drew kicks off her flip-flops and sits cross-legged on the sofa. "I thought we didn't like Aunt Leah and Ryan. You and Aunt Judy made fun of her for looking like a biker chick, and everybody said it's Ryan's fault that he got beat up, 'cause he has a big mouth just like Aunt Leah."

Mom crosses to the coffee table, picks up the TV remote, and clicks it On. She doesn't look at us but mumbles, "I didn't say that."

Drew insists, "Yes, you did! Remember? Remember, Mama? You, Aunt Judy, and Grandma were trying to figure out why she got all those tattoos, and Uncle Dale, Grandpa, and Daddy kept talking about how she already ruined Ryan."

Mom stares, trancelike, flipping the channels, but going so fast that there's no way she could be seeing each TV show.

"…Mama?" Drew just doesn't know when to give up. "…Mama? Didn't you say that?"

I whisper, "Drew! Knock it off!" I catch her eye and shake my head.

Drew throws her hands up and mouths, "*What?*"

I mouth, "Shut up!"

Mom blasts, "*Yes*!" She whips around, and her eyes look wild. Just as suddenly, it's like she hits a switch in her mind and stares at the remote in her hand. She sputters, "Yes…I said some…things… that day. And…just because I accepted Leah's offer doesn't mean that I've changed my mind about…everything. We're still the same people we were."

Her words echo off the walls of our packed-up home, and I wonder if they sound as empty to her as they do to me. I heave myself out of the chair and place myself between Mom and Drew. "So, when are we moving?"

Friday morning, just before the crew Mom hired shows up with a moving truck, I drag a stepladder to my room, peel a glow-in-the-dark star from my ceiling, and slide it into my pocket.

Within a couple of hours, the house is just a shell. Mom and

Drew give it one last walk-through while I start the car and roll down the windows to release the August heat. Mom's locking the front door when the News Ten van pulls up at the end of our driveway, blocking us in.

Susie Harlan hurries up our driveway. Her cameraman follows a few feet behind. She glances at me in the car and continues toward Mom, then abruptly stops and comes back to me. My stomach clenches.

She smiles. "So, you're moving, huh?"

I nod.

"That's exciting. Where are you going?" Her notepad seems to appear out of thin air. I narrow my eyes at her. Drew opens the rear passenger door and gets in without a word.

"That's none of your business," Mom says from behind the cameraman.

Susie turns to her. "Good morning, Mrs. Denton. I see that you've vacated the house within the two-week window that the government gave you."

Mom's doing her *nodding and smiling* thing, but her eyes are shooting lasers.

"As we speak, the grand jury is meeting to decide whether to indict your husband on charges of embezzlement and theft with intent to defraud. Do you have any comment?"

Mom gives me a split-second glance that I read as *"Not a word,"* and turns her icy stare back to Susie. She shakes her head, says nothing.

Susie presses, "Are you leaving town, or will you be remaining in the community?"

Mom moves to the driver's side and opens the door. She tosses her purse onto the seat, gets in, and cranks up the air conditioner.

Susie leans into the car. She's so close to me that I can see the line where her makeup ends on the underside of her jaw. "Do you still believe that your husband is the 'family values' candidate?"

Mom starts rolling up the window on Susie, who freaks out a little. "Hey!" She jerks backward.

Mom leaves the window open about a fourth of the way from the top. She speaks loudly above the blasting air conditioner. "I do have one comment for you, if you'd like it."

Susie lunges toward the window, her eyes just above the glass. "Yes?"

"You have thirty seconds to move that van before I call the competing news station and give an *exclusive* interview." Mom glances at her watch. "Your time starts...now."

When Susie doesn't budge, Mom pulls her phone out of her purse, appears to press some numbers, and says, "Yes, I need the number for KVUE in Dallas, Texas...thank you." She glances at Susie. "It's ringing."

Susie's obviously irritated. "Mrs. Denton, I'm just doing my job, reporting the news. Your husband is a public figure, and, to be honest, most people believe that you *had* to know something was going on. Would you care to dispute that?"

Mom ignores her and speaks into her phone. "Hello, my name is Sonya Denton. I was Miss Texas twenty-two years ago. My husband is Reese Denton, the now former candidate for United States Senate. I'd like to speak to your producer. I have a story for you." She shoots a look at Susie and adds, "An *exclusive* story."

Susie squeaks, "You're really going to give *them* an interview?"

Mom holds up a finger for Susie to wait. "Hi, Stu. You're the producer, correct?" Mom introduces herself again, then: "Could you hold a moment, please?" She rolls the window more than halfway down and gives Susie an evil grin. "Guess you'll find out when you see the news tonight, won't you? Last chance: stop blocking my driveway."

Susie folds her arms and juts out a hip. "Well, I'm *not* going to move that van. It's on the street, which is public domain, so—"

Mom shrugs, throws our car into Reverse, zooms back until she clears the front walk, then slams it into Drive and does a one-eighty in the front yard. We fly over the curb and hook a sharp right onto the street, narrowly missing the News Ten van. She brakes long enough to throw her arm out the window and signal to the guys in the moving van to follow us.

"Whew!" Mom tosses her phone into her purse and swipes her hand across her brow.

Drew asks, "What about Stu, Mom?"

"Who's Stu?"

"Um, the guy you were talking to on the phone? The producer?"

"Oh, I wasn't talking to anyone," she states matter-of-factly.

"You mean…you lied?" Drew's mind is clearly blown. "I thought we weren't *supposed* to lie."

I blurt, "Know what, Drew? I'll bet Aunt Leah won't mind if you have a puppy."

"Yay! I want a girl puppy and I'm going to name her Angel. Can I get her today? Please?"

Chapter Seven

Piney Creek is only about two and a half hours southeast of Dallas, but it may as well be on another planet. The East Texas roads are like roller coasters, rising and falling narrowly between gargantuan pine trees. Reddish-brown sand fills the space between the forests and the road, and huge hawks and black vultures circle overhead.

Pretty soon, I notice a pattern: The highway narrows to two lanes as it approaches a town, everybody hits their brakes when they see the local cop shooting radar, and then they punch the accelerator at the city limit sign. Unlike Northside, there's no strip shopping centers or gated neighborhoods with names like "Wildwood" with only tiny saplings for trees. Instead, there are real forests as far as I can see, and the tiny towns each seem to have a Dairy Queen and a gas station, but not much else.

A faded billboard lets us know that we're getting close:

Welcome to Piney Creek!
Home of the Fightin' Possums!

There's a cartoon possum dressed in a football uniform. He's baring his pointy teeth, but a speech bubble next to his mouth reads, "Visit for a day! You'll want to stay!"

I murmur, "Don't possums play dead?" but Mom doesn't answer. She's trying to drive and read the directions she wrote on a paper lunch bag. I take it from her. "You want me to read this to you so we don't crash into the possum on steroids?"

Mom glances in the rearview mirror at the moving van. "Just

watch for the post office. Leah said that if I pass the post office, I've gone too far."

The only buildings I see are the Piney Creek Family Pharmacy, an Exxon, and a David's grocery. We keep looking for our turnoff, but before we know it, we pass the city limit sign.

Mom sighs. "I didn't see a post office; did you?"

"It wasn't one of the three places I counted." I reread the directions. "We were supposed to turn by the sign that said *Goats for Sale*, right? Maybe there's more than one place that sells goats around here." I spy stadium lights in the distance. "I think that might be the football stadium, where the Fightin' Possums play dead on Friday nights."

"Ooo-kay…" Mom hooks a U-turn and gives the moving truck time to do the same. We're nearly to the "Welcome to Piney Creek" sign when Mom exclaims, "Hey! *Goats for Sale*!" She makes an abrupt left onto a narrow asphalt road.

We pass a burned-out double-wide mobile home and a shack with plywood siding that has the back seat of a car on the front porch. It doesn't look like anyone lives there. Mom hits a pothole. She gasps loudly and slams on her brakes. Two dogs run out from under the porch and bark at us.

The next house has a fenced front yard with no less than thirty dogs in it, many with bald patches and scaly, melty-looking skin. "What's wrong with those dogs, Mama?" Drew asks worriedly. "This street doesn't look very nice."

"Let's not judge the neighborhood just yet, girls…Leah said she lives at the base of a hill and that if we cross the bridge, we've gone too far."

Mom's phone rings. "Get that for me, would you?"

I try to answer it, but there's no signal. "Missed call. Rachel."

She sighs. "Poor baby. She's having such a hard time adjusting right now…Oh. My. Goodness." We slow to a near stop at the sight of a dented white mobile home. There's aluminum foil in the windows and a big *No Trespassing* sign tacked to a piece of wood over a window on the end of the trailer. The front yard holds old tires, a washing machine, two trucks with their hoods raised, and a speedboat with a tree growing up through the middle of it. But the thing that *really* stands out is the cage—like, a cage-fighting cage—surrounded on all sides by rotting wooden bleachers.

Drew makes more worried sounds. "Please don't let that be it; *please* don't let that be it." I glance back at her; she's closed her eyes and clasped her hands in prayer.

Mom laughs. "Our trailer is *behind* Aunt Leah's house, sweetie. She didn't mention a fighting cage, either." We take a roller coaster dip down a steep hill and see twin gates with bright orange flowers all over them. "I'm pretty sure this is her driveway. She told me to look for entry gates with trumpet creeper vine on it." We pull in, and the moving truck follows us down the winding driveway to a small, white, Victorian house with a wraparound porch and a dull gray aluminum roof. A big black-and-white mutt with a spot on its head and a smaller brown and white terrier come trotting out to us. They're barking but wagging their tails at the same time.

Drew shouts gleefully, "She's got dogggggs!"

Leah's seated on the top porch step. She leaps up and skitters down the stairs, waving and smiling.

"Aunt Leah's wearing a tank top again," Drew says in her know-it-all voice. "Remember when Aunt Judy said—"

Mom cuts her off. "*Don't* talk about that!" She pulls in next to Leah's yellow VW bug and turns to Drew. "It's very generous of Aunt Leah and Ryan to allow us to live here while I figure things out. It would be unkind to repeat what you heard at the Fourth of July picnic. Do you understand what I'm saying, sweetheart?"

Leah yanks open Mom's door before Drew can answer. "I'm so glad you decided to come!" Mom gets out of the car. Leah wraps her beefy arms around her and squeezes tight.

"She's covering Mom in her tattoos!" Drew hisses from the back seat.

I sigh. "Shut up, Drew." We step out of the car. The late summer heat feels thick and damp—the way it feels in Northside when a storm's about to hit—but there's not a cloud in the sky. The dogs lick Drew from head to toe, like they've been waiting their whole lives for her to arrive.

Leah smiles. "Looks like Charley and Zeeke made a new friend."

The moving truck driver approaches us. "You want us to start unloading? I can put the truck right up against the front porch."

"Not this house—there's a trailer behind it." Mom looks to Leah. "Right?"

Leah nods. "Yeah, see the dirt path to the right of the house? You should be able to pull the truck in just fine...If that truck's full, though..."

Mom's eyebrows shoot up. "What?"

Leah shrugs. "The trailer's not that big. Don't know if all your stuff will fit in there."

The driver frowns. "I doubt there's enough room to turn the truck around back there. We may have to unload it all in front of the house, then charge you extra to carry it to the trailer." He takes off around the corner without waiting for a response.

Mom sounds tired. "Let's go have a look, shall we?"

We follow the dirt path—it's just tire tracks worn into the grass—to the mobile home, which looks kind of like a peanut butter sandwich, with its tan-colored siding between pale trim on the top and bottom. There's one large square aluminum window to the left of the off-white plastic front door, and three narrow horizontal windows spread out evenly along the length of the trailer.

"Once you said you wanted to live here, I opened the windows to air it out." Leah leads us up rotting wooden steps to the front door of the trailer. "I can get my friend Buzz to build some new steps. I just didn't have time before you—"

Mom cuts her off. "It's fine. We're grateful to have a place to stay."

Leah holds the door open for us to walk in ahead of her. Black wasps swoop at our heads; Drew shrieks and swats at them madly. Leah says calmly, "They're just mud daubers, hon. They don't sting. There's a can of bug spray under the kitchen sink. I sure thought I'd killed them all."

A mud dauber lands on the doorjamb by Leah's head, and she smacks it with her hand. She wipes her palm on her shorts and leads us into the living area. "The trailer's twenty-two years old. I know it doesn't look like much, but it's in pretty good shape to be that age. Mark and I bought it used when we got married. The Victorian that I live in is part of a mansion built in 1895 in Gladewater. It belonged to a doctor, and when he died, his family couldn't agree who'd get the house, so they broke it into four pieces and sold it off at auction. We bought one part and had it moved to the spot it is now, and we lived in the trailer while we remodeled the house. My tenant moved out last month, and I was about to advertise it for rent when Dale told me about Reese being a selfish prick."

Mom freezes. At first I think she's going to go off on Aunt Leah for her language, but she doesn't even seem to hear that part. "I didn't realize that it's rental property, Leah. The movers are taking just about all the money I've got left. I've got to find a job, and..." She shakes her head and fixes her gaze on the kitchen counter.

"Aw, hon, don't you worry about that. Let's get you on your feet first; then we'll figure it out. I mean, it would be good if you can at least cover your own utilities, but I'm not worrying about a thing." She puts a hand on Mom's shoulder. "I *know* what it's like to have your life blown apart. Makes it hard to get out of bed in the morning when you're trying to figure out why the sun's bothering to rise."

I remember how the Fourth of July picnic ended, and I'm amazed that Leah can be so nice to us. I guess she's forgotten about it.

Mom's eyes fill with tears and she nods, but says nothing.

Drew calls from the far end of the trailer, "I want this room!"

We move single file down the hall and stand in the doorway of a bedroom that takes up the entire end of the trailer. Leah laughs, "Well, honey, this is the master bedroom, but that's between you and your mama."

There are two other bedrooms—a tiny one next to the master, and a nearly-as-tiny one at the opposite end of the trailer. I get that one.

Sure enough, the movers can't fit all our furniture into the trailer. My new room is so much smaller than the one in Northside that I have to walk sideways between my dresser and bed. The window blinds are bent and broken off in places, but Leah assures me that the only creatures who might see in are the deer and wildlife that live in the woods surrounding us.

We push the dining room table against a wall in the kitchen so that we have room to turn around. The den—which is really just an open space on the other side of the long bar in the kitchen—will only hold the TV, sofa, and one armchair. We leave our end tables, coffee table, two of the kitchen chairs, Dad's recliner, and the other armchair in Leah's front yard.

Mom pays the driver and he slowly zigzags the truck up the driveway. The rest of us practically collapse on our furniture under the pounding rays of the midday sun. Mom trudges over and hands us each a cold water bottle, then perches on an armrest.

Leah throws an arm over her eyes. "Whew! Sure would have been nice if Ryan had been here to help, too—but I needed him to hold down the fort at Sugar's."

"What's Sugar's?" I ask.

"That's my bakery. It's grown into a café now, too. Started out making birthday and wedding cakes, but now we've added breakfast and lunch service, too. I'm looking for part-time help, Colby, if you're interested."

Drew leans forward with her elbows on her knees. "I'm hungry... and hot! Could we go to Sugar's and get some food?"

Mom sounds tired. "Drew...Aunt Leah's already done so much for us." She takes a long drink of water. "We'll fend for ourselves. Thanks, though."

Leah rolls the icy bottle over her neck, unscrews the lid, and dribbles water on her forehead. "No, Drew has a great idea. You've got to get the grand tour of Piney Creek sometime. It'll take maybe five minutes to see our booming metropolis; then we'll head to Sugar's and you can eat. Let's go!"

Aunt Leah's not joking. Piney Creek is so tiny that kindergarten through twelfth grades are in the same building. Besides the school, there's a post office, pharmacy, gas station, grocery store, and four churches that are all on the same street. One of the churches, First Baptist Piney Creek, has a giant steeple that casts a shadow over the other buildings.

Leah barely slows down for us to read the signs. "That's Church Street, for obvious reasons. I don't attend; I've had enough holier-than-thou bullshit crammed down my throat to last a lifetime, but feel free to partake in what they're selling, if that's what you want to do."

She gestures to the right as she turns left. "When people talk about going to town, they mean Cedar Points, which is on the other side of the lake. You just follow this road to get there." She waves at a lady who passes us, then gestures at a metal building. "Piney Creek's police and fire department are there, and that red truck under the carport is supposed to be the fire chief's, but he quit last month. He got a job pumping out septic tanks. Pays better."

She slows as she comes up on a little yellow house with blue and white checked curtains in a large window and a bench by the front door. The gravel parking lot is nearly full, and there's a steady stream of people in and out.

"This is Sugar's. The house was built in the 1920s. I converted it to a bakery with a dining area."

We park and go in. Ryan's laughing and talking to a customer, but when he looks up and sees us, a curtain falls. He turns away.

Leah pulls a couple of cardboard menus off the wall and presses them at us. "I'm going to help Ryan with the end of the lunch rush; when you're ready to order, just come on up. It's on the house."

Mom starts to protest, but Leah's not listening. She's already pulling an apron over her head and joining Ryan at the front counter.

There's a three-tier wedding cake on a rolling cart near the kitchen entrance. I notice Mom staring at the bride and groom figurines. Her chin is quivering. Drew thumbs through a photo album of birthday cakes. The whole place smells like cake icing; I think about my dad and our tradition of baking and decorating our family birthday cakes together. He never asked Rachel or Drew for help. Just me.

The air is heavy, and even though an oscillating fan in the corner is set on high, it's no match for the heat from the kitchen. The electric breeze coats our sweaty bodies in sweetness.

A glass display case next to us holds fudge slabs and cake ball lollipops. I run my hand over my mouth, surprised the drool isn't running off my chin. If nobody else was here, I know I could eat it all without thinking twice.

I tap the photo album in Drew's hands. "I thought you were starving."

She's preoccupied. "Oh, yeah…I forgot."

I snap, "How on earth do you *forget* being hungry?" I don't know why, but her lack of interest in eating makes me furious.

The crowd clears out, and we approach the counter in front of the kitchen.

"What can I get you?" Ryan's voice is flat. He doesn't acknowledge that he knows us.

"Hi, Ryan, how are you?" Mom's got her smile in place, but Ryan's not buying it.

"We're out of chicken salad. If that's what you want…we're out." He drags his pen down the center of his notepad repeatedly until it tears the paper.

"Oh…okay…" Mom turns the cardboard menu over and over, as if the items have changed since she studied it when we were seated at the table by the front door.

"Your face doesn't look as weird anymore." Drew's on her tiptoes, trying to get a better look at Ryan over the display case.

"Don't lean on the glass," he snaps. He abruptly turns, nearly bumping into the pregnant woman behind him. "I'm taking my break."

She steps up to take his place, eases herself onto a stool, and exclaims, "Whew! It's a scorcher!"

Mom fans herself with a menu. "You've got that right. Hi…I'm Sonya, Leah's sister-in-law."

The lady grunts as she leans over the counter and shakes Mom's hand. "Nice to meet you. I'm Dulcie. Leah told me y'all were moving into her trailer."

"Yes, we've got everything moved in that's going to fit. Just a matter of unpacking, now. When's your baby due? My first child was born in the summer. It was eighteen years ago, but I still remember how miserable I was."

"He's due any minute. I'm a little worried because Leah hasn't found anybody to take my place yet, and I'm going to be staying home after I have him." She picks up a water bottle, takes a sip, and runs her eyes over Drew and me. "Did y'all decide what you want to eat?"

Mom grabs my arm and pulls me forward. "Colby can help out. Leah already told her about the job. You'd like that, wouldn't you, Colby?"

My mind is screaming, *"No! There's no way I can be around this stuff; I'll eat every second that I'm here!"* But I can't say that because nobody knows how much I fear and crave sweets at the same time. It's like the two people inside of me are fighting to control what I eat, and the one thing they have in common is hatred for me—for what I look like and how it feels to be in my body; for my inability to stop once I start.

But how can I refuse to help out when Aunt Leah gave us a place to live when we had nowhere else to go? Mom says we owe her big time.

I nod. "Yeah, that'd be great. I've always wanted to work in a bakery."

Chapter Eight

Mom, Drew, and I spend Saturday unpacking and settling in. We move Rachel's belongings and our boxes of fancy dishes, books, photos, and winter clothes to the Victorian's screened-in back porch. We're able to move most of our extra furniture from the front yard into Leah's small barn, but there's no room for Dad's oversized recliner.

"It'll just have to stay where it is for now," Mom says. "It's not supposed to rain for a while anyway." Just then, Leah's dog, Charley—sopping wet and covered in sand—leaps onto the recliner, flips onto her back, and suns her belly.

I expect Mom to leave the shade of the screened-in porch to shoo the dog out of Dad's chair, but instead she smirks at the sight. "Hmm. Well, if your dad ever comes down here to get his chair, at least it'll be well-seasoned for him."

The screened door slams behind Drew. "Daddy's coming to see us?"

Mom grimaces, like she wouldn't have made a smart-ass comment if she'd known my little sister was around. "Aw, honey, not that I know of."

Drew frowns. "But he knows where we are, right? He'll be able to find us if he wants to come get us?"

Mom runs her hand over Drew's long blonde hair, stroking it. She sighs. "Sweetie, I don't think Daddy's going to be coming back. But we'll be okay, we—"

Drew's huge blue eyes fill with tears. "But—we're Daddy's package deal, Mama!"

I snap, "No, we were just dumb enough to believe it when he said it."

Drew shoots me a look like I'm not making sense. "Mama, does Daddy know where we are or *not*? He *needs* to be able to find us—"

Mom blasts, "He'll find out when he's served with divorce papers, Drew Ann! As soon as I get enough money, I'm—"

"You're getting divorced?" Drew's voice is squeaky-high. "You're…getting…divorced?" She bolts from the screened-in porch and races toward our trailer.

Mom sits hard onto a box of books and puts her head in her hands. Her phone rings; she pulls it out of her pocket and tries to answer it. "Missed call. It's Rachel again." She sighs. "Leah told me that if I drive up the hill and park next to the *Goats for Sale* sign at the end of the road, the phone will receive a signal. Guess that's what I'll do." She shakes her head a few times and blinks. "What has my life come to?" She rises and heads for the door.

"Mom—"

She stops. "Yes?"

I'm struck by how much older she looks, even though her hair's pulled back in a ponytail and, as always, she's wearing full makeup. I want to tell her that everything's going to be okay, but I can't. I act like I forgot what I was going to say. "Nothing."

I dig through my dirty clothes pile and pull the plastic ceiling star that used to glow in the dark from my shorts' pocket. I stand on my bed, use a piece of clear packing tape to stick the star to the ceiling, and cup my hand around it, hoping it'll glow even a little bit. I bite my lower lip and pray, *"God, if You're really there; if You're going to fix this shitstorm that is my life, make this star glow. Please."* I cup my hands around that star until my arms go numb.

It may have glowed; I wouldn't know. I couldn't see a thing through my tears.

Around 6:00 P.M., Ryan knocks on our door. He's wearing the same scowl from the day before at Sugar's. He stares so hard at a dent in the siding by the front window that I look at it, too. "Mom sent me over to tell y'all that she's making burgers to celebrate you moving in, and they'll be ready at seven." He looks skyward and sighs. "She said to say, 'Sorry for the late notice. We would have been home earlier, but we had to deliver a wedding cake.'"

I'm not hungry; I polished off the stuff in my snack stash when Mom was trying to get Drew to calm down about the divorce. But I can't tell him that. "We haven't eaten yet. So...thanks." I glance at him; he still won't look at me.

Ryan snaps, "Don't thank *me*; if it were up to me..." He purses his lips, shakes his head, and mumbles, "So...come over at seven." He reaches for the doorknob and pulls it closed.

Aunt Leah's jaw drops at the sight of Drew's swollen eyes and blotchy red face. "Oh, my goodness, honey, are you having a bad day?"

Mom says, "Leah, don't—" but it's too late, because Drew starts wailing all over again: "Mama's going to divorce Daaaaaaaddddy."

Ryan says sarcastically, "*Why* am I *not surprised*? Pass the mustard."

Leah frowns. "Ryan—"

He shrugs. "What? It was going to happen eventually."

I narrow my eyes. "Well, you don't have to be an ass about it in front of my little sister."

Aunt Leah puts her hands between us like she's breaking up a fight. "Come on, y'all. This isn't an easy time for anybody. We need to focus on supporting each—"

Ryan stands up so fast that our drinks splash onto the table.

"*Really*, Mom? The way they've helped us out when we need it? The *awesome* support they showed us at the Fourth of July clusterfuck?"

Mom gasps, and he puts his palms on the table and leans into her. "I *don't* feel sorry for you. Get that? I *love* that your perfect little world is blowing up in your face!" He looks at us like he wants to spit on us. "I'm not hungry." He starts out of the room.

I blurt, "*I* didn't say anything to you! On the Fourth of July—I didn't say *anything* to you!"

Ryan freezes in the doorway and says, "Typical." He goes to his room and slams the door.

Drew's sniffling is the only sound anyone makes after Ryan leaves. I lock my eyes on the tray of cupcakes in the center of the table and imagine the wrappers flying off as I inhale them.

Finally, Leah speaks up. "So, Colby, do you think you can start at Sugar's on Monday? Dulcie's water broke at work today, so she's having the baby. I'm going to be short-handed, and I'd like to teach you to decorate cakes."

I start to tell her that Dad already taught me how, but I see one last chance to keep from having to work at Sugar's. "I've been meaning to ask you about that. Doesn't school start in a few weeks? Are you sure you want to go through training me when I'll only be working for a short time?"

Leah looks surprised. "Well, I was hoping you'd come in after school and on Saturdays."

I picture myself eating spoonful after spoonful of cake icing. I'm simultaneously excited and horrified. "Oh, good! I was hoping you'd say that!"

Sunday morning, I wake to Drew pounding on my door. The door sticks when she opens it, and she nearly falls onto my bed. I manage to open one eye, sit up on my elbows, and glare at her.

"Something's wrong with Mommy," she wails.

I spring out of bed and nearly run over my sister. I thud down the long skinny hallway to Mom's door and try the doorknob. It's locked. I freak out. "Mom! Mom! Open the door!" I ram my shoulder against the door like I've seen people do it in the movies, but the door just makes a splintering sound.

I hear footsteps, fumbling with the lock, then the door swings open. Mom's rubbing her face—she's still wearing her clothes and makeup from the day before, and her mascara's so smeared that she looks like a raccoon.

Her voice is raspy. "Wh-what's wrong?"

"Are you okay? Drew said there's something wrong with you!"

Mom blinks, trying to focus on Drew. "Why did you think that?"

I notice for the first time that Drew's dressed in her church clothes, holding her Bible, and trying not to cry. "It's Sunday! You *always* get up and make pancakes on Sunday before we go to church!"

Mom shuffles back to her bed and sits on the edge. She bends at the waist with her elbows on her knees and stares at the worn carpet. Drew moves to the bed, leans against her, and softly asks, "Aren't you going to make pancakes...before church? Aren't we going to church? We didn't go last week because you said that everybody at our old church is mad at Daddy. But we could go to that church with the big steeple. It looks nice."

Mom sighs and shakes her head.

Drew jumps up and stamps her feet. "Why does everything have to change? Is this because you're getting a divorce?"

Mom takes Drew's wrist and pulls her back. She yawns. "I'm not ready for meeting new people. I need some time."

Drew yanks her hand free and stomps to Mom's bedroom door. "I want to live with Daddy! I don't want to stay with you! I miss Daddy!"

Mom looks at her dully but says nothing when Drew vanishes into her room and slams the door. A few seconds later, we hear glass shatter.

I get to Drew's room before Mom does and find her staring slack-jawed at the Bible-sized jagged hole in her bedroom window.

Drew falls to her knees, sobbing. "I want Daddy to come back! Why is he mad at us?"

Mom joins her on the floor and wraps her arms around her. She speaks soothingly, "Oh, honey, Daddy's not mad at you."

Drew wraps herself around Mom. "Why did everything have to change?" She throws her head back and wails. "I want my old house! I hate this ugly house with the big black mud bobbers inside it!"

Mom pats her back, rocking her. "I understand, honey, but we won't be here long. Don't worry."

Drew hiccups, "Are…you…sure?"

Mom closes her eyes, nods. "Yeah. I'm sure."

I'm in the tall grass under Drew's window, watching out for snakes and carefully placing the pieces of broken glass in a cardboard box. Mom comes around the corner with Leah. Ryan trails behind them, his arms crossed and face scowling as usual.

Leah acts like the broken window is no big deal. "We'll just tape up some cardboard for now. Accidents happen. Don't worry about it. When Buzz repairs the steps, I'll have him replace the glass, too."

"That's really nice of you. I'll pay for the repairs as soon as I get some money." Mom babbles nervously, "Drew was so upset; she thought that Reese left because he's angry at her. Can you imagine such a silly thing?"

Ryan snaps, "Like the *real* reason is that much better? My mom left my dad because he was an abusive prick, but that doesn't matter to you guys, apparently. What: Mom was supposed to keep letting him do it until he killed her?"

Mom grimaces. "I'm not sure where you're going with this."

Leah murmurs, "I think it's a legitimate question, given what was said to us on the Fourth of July, Sonya."

Mom squares her shoulders and sounds more than a little defensive. "It's just...the rest of us never saw Mark behave like that, so it wasn't...real to us." She shrugs. "It made it hard to believe, since there were no witnesses. And Mark is such a good guy, he—"

Ryan steps up to Mom and looks her in the eye. "*I* was the witness, remember? And sometimes I was his punching bag, too, depending on how quickly I retrieved another beer for him. It's bad enough that you guys ditched her when she needed you the most, but even when my mom showed you proof, you *still* didn't believe it." He takes another step in, and Mom backs into a thorny vine. "Why is reality such a *problem* for you people?"

Mom looks down and crosses her arms. "Romans 3:23: *'For all have sinned and fall short of the glory of God.'*"

Ryan reaches down and yanks out a handful of tall grass. "What the hell is *that* supposed to mean?"

Mom sighs. "The only thing I know for sure at this point in my life is that *everybody's* broken." She takes the box of glass shards from me and disappears around the corner.

I watch her go, then turn to my aunt and cousin. "I get it: You don't want us here."

Leah puts her hand on my shoulder, "Yes, we do, Colby. We're glad you—"

Ryan cuts her off. "Don't lie, Mom. You told me there was *no way* they'd take you up on your offer, because they'd never *lower* themselves to living with us." He snorts. "Well, this really worked out the way you thought it would!"

Leah shrugs. "Okay, Ryan, you're right." She looks me in the eye. "I never thought your mom would actually want to live here."

I feel like I've been punched in the chest. I nod at Ryan. "I get that *he* hates us, but *you* don't like us, either? I mean…at all?"

Her face softens and she shakes her head. "It's not a matter of *liking* you. It's a matter of helping a family in need. I would have done the same thing for *anyone*. I took in my last tenant because his house burned down and he had no insurance. He stayed in the trailer and paid what he could until he got back on his feet."

She drapes an arm over Ryan's shoulders. "My whole life, my family had this public image of being so giving and kind, but when it came down to it, if helping others wasn't convenient at the time, they looked the other way. 'Do unto others as you would have them do unto you,' my dad always said…but if the 'doing unto' had any sort of inconvenient sacrifice attached to it, you could forget it."

The sun shifts in the sky. She and Ryan move out of the squint-inducing rays into the shade of the trailer, and she pulls me over to them. "Your family is welcome to stay here as long as you need. What Reese did to everyone who trusted him is awful, and I reached out to your mom because it was the compassionate thing to do. But make no mistake: I will *not* be judged on my turf the way we were at that picnic. I'm not stupid, Colby; I can imagine the things that were said about us after we left. Remember: I used to be one of them, until I broke the cardinal rule of not airing dirty laundry. I know what kinds of catty things are said behind people's backs. And as for what they said was a 'mistake' on Ryan's part: I completely support his decision to report the rape of that girl, because it was the right thing to do. Yes, there were sacrifices involved, but we actually do try to 'do unto others,' even when it's messy."

I look at my feet and nod. "I get it."

Ryan gives me a long, hard stare. "Somehow, I doubt that you do."

Chapter Nine

Monday morning, Mom drops me off at Sugar's, then heads to the school administration building to ask about open teaching positions. I haven't told her about my conversation with Leah and Ryan behind the trailer. What good would it do for her to know that Leah's not really thrilled about us moving to Piney Creek?

Leah shows me around the kitchen. "Ryan and I came in at 4:30 to stock the cases with doughnuts and muffins for the breakfast rush. Once the crowd thins, we'll clean up, then bake rolls, prep salads, and assemble sandwich fillings. Your job will be to help in all areas, but, like I told you before, I'm hoping you have an artistic side and can pitch in with cake decorating. For now, I'd like you to work the front counter. Oh—you'll need to pull your hair back in a ponytail. Pop these on, too." She hands me a hair net and an apron, then heads for the front counter. "Come on."

I stop in my tracks and laugh uneasily. "How do you keep from eating all this stuff?"

Leah spins around. "Are you asking me that because I'm fat?"

My stomach drops to my feet. "N-n-no, I just—"

She puts her hands on her hips and gives me the stink-eye.

I remember what Grandma said to me about my weight. "I didn't mean…uh, look at me, I'm a…'Big Girl,' too…"

Leah arches an eyebrow. "I don't see cookies on those trays. I see *dollar signs*. Do you have a problem controlling yourself around food like this? Your dad always did. Anytime my mother made cookies, the rest of us were lucky to score a few before Reese ate them all."

I shake my head slowly and fiddle with my hair net.

Ryan calls, "Mom, I could use some help up here."

"As long as we understand each other: this business is my livelihood. We are artists, and cakes are our canvas. Don't eat up my profits, okay?"

I nod.

Leah smiles, and she looks like the same person who welcomed Mom with a big hug when we moved to Piney Creek. "Coming, hon."

The ice machine freezes up around 10:30, and Leah leaves to buy bags of ice. Her car's barely out of the parking lot when three guys—one white, one black, and one Latino, all wearing gray *MCHS ATHLETICS* T-shirts—come in. They're drenched with sweat and talking loudly.

The African-American boy wrestles the Latino boy into a headlock. "What'd you say about my mama, José? Huh? You want to say that again?"

José tries to speak but can only choke out, "Let me go, Fredrick! Let…me—"

Fredrick shoves him into a table.

The white boy says, "Let's see how our friendly neighborhood narc is today." He marches right up to where Ryan's counting out cash for a deposit and pounds the bell by the cash register.

Ryan turns his body slightly and continues counting. He sets his jaw and lowers his eyebrows.

I self-consciously tug at my hair net and step up to the glass display case. "May I help you?" I pluck a square of waxed paper from the box as if I'm ready to fill an order.

The boy continues pounding the bell until Ryan snatches it away. The kid swipes at Ryan's head and laughs when he flinches. I notice a name written in marker on the back of his shirt: M. Taylor. He saunters over to the refrigerated case, pulls out three bottles of water, calls to his friends, "Heads up!" then throws two of the bottles like they're footballs.

The other guys aren't watching. One bottle bounces off the display case, and the other rolls under it and bumps up against my foot. I retrieve the bottle and hold it up to the boys, but they ignore me. I clear my throat and ask, "Would—would you like something to eat?"

I glance over my shoulder, hoping that Aunt Leah's miraculously appeared in the kitchen, but of course she hasn't. Ryan shoves the money back into the register, closes the drawer, and mutters, "Assholes."

José slaps his palms on the glass and yells, "What did you say?"

Ryan rolls his eyes and sighs loudly.

"Hey, homes, Ryan just called us 'assholes,'" José announces. Fredrick and M. Taylor join him in a staring contest with Ryan. "You want to say that again, *cabrón*?"

I choke out, "Um, if you want something to eat, I can—"

José snaps, "*Cállate, puta gorda!* You look like you already ate it all!" They high-five each other.

"That'll be three bucks for the waters," Ryan says flatly. "Anything else, Michael?"

M. Taylor—Michael—steps back and studies the chalkboard menu. "Yeah, I'll take a chili cheese dog with fries."

I glance at Ryan. "We—don't have that...do we?" Ryan gives me a disgusted look and shakes his head.

"*We don't have that, do we*?" Michael mocks.

I'm thrown off by the way they're talking to me, and my mouth goes dry. I choke, "I'm...new. It's my first day."

The front door swings open and Drew hurries in, followed by Mom. José elbows Michael. "Check it out!" The three thugs eyeball my mother from head to toe. Sometimes I forget how beautiful my mom still is, even though she's in her forties.

"Mommy got a job!" Drew squeals. Mom shakes her head and holds up her hand. "It's not for sure just yet—but I think I've got a good shot at it."

José works his eyebrows up and down and leers. "*Mamacita*!" My mother gives him a strange look.

"That's great, Mom. Congratulations."

Fredrick looks from my mother to me and back again. "You two *family*?" He shakes his head and snorts. "No way."

Drew pipes up, "Colby looks like my daddy, and I look like my mommy." She smiles and tosses her hair from side to side. *Ugh.*

"Lucky Daddy," Michael croons.

Mom's eyes get big. "Oookaaay..." She shifts her purse from one shoulder to the other and looks uncomfortable.

"Don't you guys need to go back to practice so you can run around and tackle each other?" Ryan asks flatly.

"Yeah, you miss it, don't you? But you don't have what it takes. Never did." Michael crumples his empty water bottle and throws it at Ryan. It misses by a long shot.

Ryan crosses his arms and leans against the wall behind the register. "I'd rather stab myself in the eye with a fork than be part of your team, now that I know what you're all about."

Michael grabs a fork from the silverware bin. "That can be arranged." He bolts toward Ryan.

The teacher side of Mom comes out and she barks, "Stop that!"

Fredrick glances at her and pulls Michael back. "Come on, man, we've got to go. Coach will make us run suicides if we're late getting back from break, and it's way too hot to run sprints up and down that field until we puke." They head for the door.

"You owe me for the water," Ryan calls as they leave. Michael flips him off.

It feels like my heart just now starts beating again. "Are those the guys who...?"

Ryan shakes his head and resumes counting out the deposit.

"Don't worry about it."

"Your mother should talk to their parents," Mom says. "If they steal from you again, you should report them to the police for theft."

Ryan snorts. "Michael's dad *is* the chief of police. When those three beat me up on the last day of school and Mom told him, Chief Taylor called up the county health inspector and said that he found rat shit in his sandwich. We got shut down for two days."

Mom's voice is high. "So…nothing at all happened to those boys for what they did?"

"Why do *you* care? You weren't there, anyway, so it may as well not have happened, right?" He slides the cash into the zippered bag, slams the cash register closed, and stares at Mom until she looks away.

Later that week, money that Mom borrowed from her friend Brenda arrives in the mail, so we go to the Walmart in Cedar Points to buy groceries. Drew keeps putting name-brand foods in the basket, and Mom tells her to choose store brands instead. I place a box of knockoff Ding Dongs atop the multipack of Great Value mac and cheese.

"We're not getting those." Mom places the cupcakes back on the shelf.

"But they're store brand. See? Choco-Treats. They're fifty cents cheaper than the Ding Dongs."

Mom gives me a look. "Don't you think you should lose some weight before school starts? Have you tried on your jeans from last year yet?"

An old lady on a motorized scooter gives me a judgy look as she putt-putts by us. I make a face at her.

Mom's waiting. She says loudly, "Well? At first I thought you weren't eating enough, but I saw you from the side yesterday, and you've packed on the pounds. I don't know when you're eating, but it's obvious that you're not missing any meals."

I cringe. "Wow, Mom, I think there's a guy at the back of the store who didn't hear you." I feel my face getting hot, and the lump in my throat is choking me. "Fine! I won't get the damned cupcakes. Can we go now, please?"

Mom gives me her moon-sized "teacher eyes" and her words feel like BBs stinging me all over. "Maybe you should try writing down everything you eat, along with the calorie count. Let's go over to the book section and see if they have a calorie counter book. We don't have extra money for such things, so that should tell you how important it is to me that you lose weight." She abruptly turns, heads to the end of the aisle, and studies the department signs on the ceiling. "Ah! There it is." She turns back to me, but looks right through me. "Come on."

As usual, Drew is *Mommy's Little Clone*: "Yay! Can I write down everything I eat, too? I want my own calorie book!"

Mom shakes her head, and her voice is gentle this time. "You don't need to do that, Drew. You're just fine the way you are." Drew looks disappointed, but she shakes it off and joins Mom as they push the basket away from me.

I watch them go until the tears in my eyes blur them into a blonde-haired blob. I take my oversized self to the front of the store and park my wide butt on a bench by the bathrooms.

We're on our way home when Mom's phone rings. "Hi, Rachel!" Mom says brightly. She always puts on her sunshiny voice when Rachel calls.

"He did? Oh, that's good. Glad your dad finally called you..."

Mom's eyebrows lower and she veers into the right lane. A guy in a pickup truck swerves onto the shoulder to avoid being hit; he yells and shakes his fist at us. She doesn't even notice. Other cars are zooming around us, and a couple more people shoot us dirty looks as Mom slows the car to fifteen miles per hour. The more she listens, the slower she drives. "Oh, honey, I'm so sorry. I hoped that your dad would come through for you. I know you hate to ask; I know… oh, sweetie, no, I don't have any money to send you. Have you called your grandparents?…I can't call them, Rachel. I just *can't*."

"Mom…" I try to get her attention, but she waves me off. "Mom, why don't you pull off the road?" She frowns but nods and slides the car into the Piney Creek Family Pharmacy parking lot.

She stops so abruptly that we jerk forward. Her voice cracks, "He does?…No, no, I don't mind that you told him." She closes her eyes, her hand on her chest. "Okay, okay, I know. I love you, too." She slides the phone into her purse and leans back against the headrest.

Drew pops up between Mom and me. "What's going on? Is Daddy coming back to us?"

Mom shakes her head slowly. "No. He's pled guilty to all charges and will be sentenced in a few months. Could be anything from probation to ten years in prison. He's agreed to pay back the money he stole from the campaign and the company's clients." She stares blankly and seems to be talking to herself. "I'm not sure how he's going to do that, seeing as how he told Rachel that he can't send her extra money to live on, but…"

Drew says, "Huh?"

Mom takes a breath and closes her eyes as she blows it out. "Daddy told the judge that he knows he made serious mistakes, and now he's waiting to find out if he has to go to jail or not."

"Did he ask about us?" I dread the answer, but I ask anyway.

"Rachel didn't say if he asked, but she told him where we are."

Drew's voice is squeaky-high. "Is he…still with that lady? The one he was holding hands with when we saw him on the news?"

Mom nods, her voice barely above a whisper. "Marcy. Her name is Marcy…and Daddy told Rachel that he's truly happy for the first time in his life."

The next week, the assistant superintendent asks Mom to come by to discuss the job opening. She stops in at Sugar's when it's over, and I can tell it's not good news.

"So? Did you get the job?" I ask hopefully.

She shakes her head. "This district's so small that there's only one teacher for each elementary grade, and the secondary teachers usually teach more than one subject. Openings are rare, but they have one for fifth grade because a teacher's husband got a job transfer. It was between me and one other person for the job, until the assistant superintendent did an Internet search for my name."

Her eyes fill with tears. "They're afraid to hire me because of my 'baggage.' He said that if people around here find out who I am, it could cause a lot of upheaval. I've already been judged as guilty of theft by association." Mom drops into a chair and stares at the floor. "Hard to believe that just three weeks ago I was in the dark about all my 'baggage,' and quite happy."

Ryan pauses in sweeping the floor. "Yeah, you were a mushroom."

Mom looks confused. "Excuse me?"

"Reese kept you in the dark and fed you shit. Like a mushroom."

Mom studies the ceiling a moment, seeming to consider the idea. Finally, she nods. "That's a pretty accurate description." She shrugs and gives him a tiny smile. "See, Ryan? We're not so different. We can agree on some things quite nicely."

For the first time since we moved to Piney Creek, Ryan looks at my mom and doesn't scowl.

Chapter Ten

Since Mom can't find a teaching job and Ryan and I will only be part-time after school starts in a week, Leah suggests that she start working at Sugar's. I wonder if this is another one of her "compassionate" offers that she'll end up regretting.

Saturday morning, I try on my school clothes from last year and, sure enough, they're way too tight. Mom screeches, "Those clothes are barely worn, Colby! It's so irresponsible of you to eat like there's no tomorrow, when you know that I don't have money to buy new clothes!"

I wonder if she knows how crazy she sounds. I'm standing in my bedroom doorway in jeans that I can't get up over my thighs, and I feel myself blush from head to toe.

I want to yell, *"I don't think about you when I pig out! I don't think about anything!"* Instead, I scream, "Well, Drew's too tall for her clothes now. You going to yell at *her* for growing? If I had gotten *taller*, would you be so pissed off?" I curse myself silently for crying.

I wait for her to answer, but all Mom does is sigh loudly and scroll through her bank statement on the computer for the millionth time. I guess she expects a money genie to have made a deposit. She lowers her head like she's praying, then snatches up her phone and checks for a text. I want to smack her upside the head. Hasn't she figured out yet that Dad doesn't care about us anymore?

I try to slam my door but of course it sticks, so I lean against it until it closes. I slide to the floor, then crawl to my dresser and pull out the bottom drawer. All that's left in my snack stash is foil Ding Dong wrappers. I pull out the drawer, hoping some wayward Ding

Dong might have fallen behind it. My frantic feelings are swallowing me whole.

A while later, Mom taps on my door as she shoves it open. She doesn't look mad anymore, and she's using her bright voice. "I have an idea! When I was growing up in the girls' home, I found a lot of my clothes at garage sales and secondhand stores. Get dressed, and we'll make an afternoon of hunting for bargains. It'll be fun!"

She waits like I'm supposed to jump up and down and squeal, *"Yay! We get to go dumpster diving for clothes!"* I stay where I am on the floor with the upturned drawer on my lap.

Mom gives me a strange look. "What are you doing?"

I look down—there's a foil Ding Dong wrapper in plain sight. I casually adjust my leg to cover it up. "I'm cleaning out my dresser to make room for the new clothes I get today…new to *me*, I mean."

Mom starts to nod, but she looks confused. "Good. I'll tell Drew to put her shoes on. Bet we find a lot of great bargains!" She starts to slump but catches herself and straightens, then shoots me a smile that looks a little like a dog baring its teeth.

We head toward Cedar Points, keeping an eye out for garage sales along the way. Mom slows but doesn't stop at the first few that we see.

"*They* had clothes for sale," Drew says as we pass each one.

"Yeah, but that one just didn't look…right. It didn't look like any girls your age live there."

"But aren't we looking for bargains for Colby, too?"

"Yes, but the people were too…" Mom pops the top on a Diet Coke and takes a sip.

It dawns on me: Mom's looking for *fat people* garage sales. We pass several more sales and I'm trying to convince myself that I can't be right, but, sure enough, Mom slows down when she sees a huge lady sitting under a canopy next to a table with a *Pay Here* sign on it. Mom says, "This looks like a nice one!" and whips the car into the driveway.

We get out of the car and Mom calls, "Hi, there! Sure is hot today, isn't it?"

The lady holds a battery-operated fan that sprays a cooling mist. She nods.

A girl about my age—but half my size—steps out onto their front porch. "Mom, do you want a Coke or sweet tea?"

"Sweet tea. Thanks, Tina."

Mom wanders over to a pile of clothes on a card table and starts sifting through them, looking at size labels. "What do you think you are now, Colby? A 20 or 22?" She pauses and looks horrified. "You *don't* think you're a 24 yet, do you?"

I shrug, grab a random book from a pile, and pretend that I'm too interested in it to answer.

Mom's voice is sharp. "Colby, I *asked* you a *question*."

I turn the page, not even seeing what's on it.

Drew comes up beside me and giggles. "Colby, why are you reading *Everyone Poops*?"

I toss the book away. "*What*?"

Mom latches onto the back of my upper arm and gives it a sharp pinch. "We do not have time for silliness, young lady, now get over there and help me find something that will fit you!"

The lady with the fan eyeballs me up and down. "I'd say she's *at least* a 20. Most of those jeans are 22s. They ought to fit her just fine."

Tina emerges from the house carrying a tall glass of iced tea. She glances at us. "Oh, good. Looks like I might make some money today after all! The jeans are four dollars each." She hands her mom the tea and gestures to some shirts hanging from a clothesline. "Shirts are two apiece." She removes a shirt from the line, pushes her sweaty hair back from her forehead, wipes her hand on the shirt, and holds it up to herself. It looks like it could wrap around her twice. "Yeah, I only wore this one a few times before I lost weight."

Mom pounces on that. "How much weight did you lose?"

"Eighty pounds."

Mom gasps, "See, Colby? Here's someone your own age who's an inspiration!" She takes the shirt from Tina and holds it up to me, and all I can think about is Tina's sweat on it. I close my eyes and will myself not to make a disgusted face.

"This shirt is *perfect*!" Mom's nearly giddy. "I prayed we'd find clothes for you, Colby, and here we are! God is good!"

Tina's mom raises her sweet tea in a toast. "Amen!"

You want to answer a prayer, God? Here's one: *Kill me now.*

The Goodwill store in Cedar Points doesn't have much in the Big Girl department, unless you count polyester floral-print tents and old lady pants with elastic waists, but I've got four big bags of Tina's *fat clothes* in the trunk of our car anyway. Drew lucks out and finds school clothes as well as a winter coat. She tries to get Mom to buy a ragged rabbit fur vest for her, but Mom refuses.

Drew slips on the vest and crosses her arms, tosses her hair, and prances up and down the aisles like she's in a beauty pageant. "Look, Mommy! I'm Miss Texas!"

I warn, "That thing's got the same skin disease as those dogs up the road from Aunt Leah's house. You're going to get bald patches and melty skin, too."

"Ohmygosh! Ohmygosh! Ohmygosh!" Drew freaks out, throws the vest off, and slams into a wispy caramel-skinned girl who's carrying an armload of clothes toward the fitting room. The girl drops the clothes and nearly falls.

I grab her arms and steady her. "Sorry, I didn't mean for that to happen!" Drew recovers enough to gather the girl's pile of plaid western shirts and worn blue jeans.

She doesn't make eye contact; just accepts the clothes from Drew and hurries into the fitting room.

Drew gives me a wounded look, and I laugh. Mom's not paying attention; she's adding up the price tags on Drew's clothes and looking worried.

Mom washes all the clothes, irons them, and proudly presents them to us. "Now you have clothes to start the year! Nobody has to know where we shopped. They won't know if you don't tell."

Drew is in heaven, combining her tops and jeans and admiring herself in the mirror as if her school wardrobe came from the most expensive store in the mall.

I try on my clothes and know right off that Tina's mom was right: I *am* "at least a 20." I'm also *way* more than a 22. I don't have the nerve to tell Mom that Tina's *fat jeans* are too tight.

I make up my mind that the jeans will fit if I starve myself the entire week, but I can't stay out of the sample box of broken cookies on the counter at Sugar's. There's a sign on the box that says *Free*, so I figure I'm not eating up Sugar's profits. Every time Leah or Ryan turns away, I'm sneaking handfuls of cookie pieces. The more I worry about what I'll wear to school, the harder it is to stop eating.

Mom starts working in the bakery, too. She's mixing up muffins and quick breads and picks up easily on cake decorating. She's so busy, she doesn't notice when I take a spoon and a measuring cup full of icing to the bathroom with me and wolf it down. It tastes just like my dad's recipe and I find myself thinking about him, but instead of the punched-in-the gut feeling I usually get since he left, I don't *feel* anything.

It's like I'm a robot and my hand is programmed for shoveling. Before I know it, the container's empty. I check my face for icing before I open the door and hide the measuring cup behind my apron as I walk to the sink and drop it into the sudsy water. No one notices. About twenty minutes later, the sugar and fat have my head spinning and my stomach churning.

I promise myself that I'll never do it again.

At night, I run my hands over the rolls on my stomach and pull my bed sheet up to the top of my neck so that my double chin doesn't touch against it. I think about the first day of school, and I wonder what I'll wear. I *can't* tell Mom that the jeans don't fit; it's not like she can return them to a garage sale.

I click on my lamp and stare at the plastic star on my ceiling. I wonder why my dad doesn't send Rachel or us any money. Don't other kids get money from their dad when their parents split up? I think about the address label across my face…I hate myself for being ugly. I *hate* myself for eating like I do. My stomach kicks back the icing and cookies, and stomach acid burns my throat. I close my eyes tight and pray that when I wake up in the morning, I'll be normal-size like Rachel and Drew.

The next day, I do it all over again.

Early on the first day of school, I pull Tina's jeans up just past my thighs, then shimmy and dance around until the material reaches my hips. The floor shakes and thunders with each stomp, and I worry that I'll plunge right through to the dirt under the trailer. Mom yells, "What are you *doing* in there?"

I grab a wire coat hanger off my dresser and fall back onto my bed. I thread the hanger hook through my zipper and pull on the hanger as the zipper strains upward. I hold my breath as I work the top button through the button hole until my fingers feel like they're bleeding, but I finally get it fastened. I can't sit up, so I roll side to side until I gain enough momentum to hurl myself toward my headboard, which I use to pull myself up. When I manage to stand, I release my breath. My lower back is screaming and my middle hangs over the top of the jeans, but, by God, they're on.

I yank a purple shirt off a hanger—this one says *Hallister* on it—and it looks like it'll be loose enough to cover the overhang of fat. But it's not. So I pull it over my arms just enough to stretch it with my elbows side to side. I twist the shirt around and stretch it front to back. When I've got it as loose as I can get it, I pull it over my head and push my arms through the sleeves. I walk stiffly to the full-length mirror on the back of my door and gasp when I realize that I forgot to put on my socks *before* I wrestled myself into the jeans. I slide my bare feet into my shoes, step back from the mirror, and try on a smile. *My* smile's not convincing, so I imitate Mom's fake smile.

It really does look like a dog baring its teeth.

Mom offers me a Slim-Fast bar for breakfast, but I'm in too much pain to think about eating. I can barely breathe.

She hugs Drew. "I filled out the paperwork for the free lunch program when I enrolled you in school. The teacher will give you a student ID number, and you'll use that instead of money to pay for food."

Drew's voice is high. "You're not going to make my lunch? You *always* used to make my lunch."

"Honey, if the school will feed you for free, we need to save money and let them do it."

Mom turns to me and pushes my hair out of my eyes. "Try to make healthy food choices, Colby. Don't choose all junk."

I pull away from her. "Speaking of choices, you kept putting me off when I asked about my classes. Am I supposed to see the counselor to fill out my course selection sheet? I don't even know which electives this school has."

Mom abruptly steps away, pulls her phone out of her purse, and checks it for messages. She does that constantly, and she never says so, but I know she's hoping she's missed a call from Dad, or that he at least texted her: *some* sign that we still matter to him. She frowns and places the phone face-down on the kitchen table. "You were busy at Sugar's, so I stopped in at the high school and filled out the papers for you."

I reach for her arm. "Do they have choir? You signed me up for choir, right?"

Mom keeps her eyes on her phone. "They *do* have choir, but you're taking life skills. It's like a health class; I figured you could apply what you learn to lose weight."

I kick a table leg, and Drew's orange juice spills.

"Hey! Clean that up right now!" Mom pulls a bunch of paper towels off the roll and shoves them at me.

I knock her hand away. "Why didn't you ask me what *I* want? I'm fifteen years old! You had no right!...You think I don't know how to eat?"

Mom snaps, "Oh, you *know* how to eat, all right!" She leans against the counter and folds her arms tightly across her chest. "I'm your mother, and I can't keep watching you destroy yourself. I don't know when you're doing it or why, but it's got to stop! Are you doing this to get back at *me*?"

I kick the table leg again, and the milk in Drew's cereal sloshes over the edge. "*You*? Why do you think that everything is about *you*?

Just say it, Mom: You're ashamed of me. I'm not tall, blonde, and thin. I take after Dad, and you hate me as much as you hate him!"

"*Hate* you? I could *never* hate you, Colby. I don't hate your *father*. I hate what he's done to us, and I hate what you're doing to *yourself*. You have such a pretty face; if you'd just lose weight, you could—"

"Stop it, Mom!"

"You could be so much more, but you…" She takes in a deep breath and blows it out. Her voice cracks. "If you'd just push away from the table!…Or…maybe you need counseling…maybe we *all* do. It's just…I don't even have health insurance anymore. I can't pay for a therapist."

I spy a knife on the counter and nearly grab it. Images scroll through my mind at lightning speed: cutting and carving the fat from my body and throwing it at my mom. As if she reads my mind, Mom moves between me and the knife, puts her hands on her hips, and stares me down. "I think you need help, Colby. Maybe the school counselor can work with you."

I pull my backpack over one shoulder and head for the door. "I don't need some counselor telling me what to eat. I get to learn all about that in my only elective!"

Drew whines, "I'm having a hard time. Can I go to counseling, too?"

I picture Drew's face covered in a bloody chunk of my fat, too. "You're perfect just the way you are, Drew. You're not a big fat *disaster*."

Mom pleads, "Colby, I'm doing the best I can."

My voice drips with sarcasm. "Yeah, and what a *great* job you're doing." I slam open the front door and stomp across the porch. My foot breaks through the second step. I yank my foot clear and scream so hard that my voice gives out.

The school bus stops at the end of Leah's driveway. Ryan, Drew, and I get on. I can barely climb the steps in my super-tight jeans. I keep my head down because I know what I look like when I've been crying: *Genetically Doomed* × *Hideous* × 1,000.

If Ryan notices, he doesn't say a word. He stares at his phone and smirks.

The bus driver says, "Morning," and we're enveloped in the universal bus smell of diesel and rubber. A girl points at Drew and me. "Who's *that*, Ryan?"

He glances at me and shrugs as he falls into a seat behind the driver.

I can tell that Drew wants to latch on to me like a spider monkey, but she's trying not to be obvious about it. We choose a seat near the front, and I'm a plank of wood sliding against it. I want to unbutton my jeans so I can breathe, but I'm afraid the zipper will open and I'll have no way to refasten it. It's not like I can stretch out in the bus aisle with a coat hanger! I snort aloud at the thought, and Drew gives me a worried look.

We lurch to a stop in front of the trailer with the fighting cage in the front yard. There are red plastic cups and beer cans scattered under the tilting bleachers. The driver honks twice, and three Latino kids tumble out the front door and race each other up the driveway. They step up into the bus and I lock eyes with the tallest of the three. It's José, the boy who said, "*Cállate, puta gorda!*" in Sugar's. I looked up the phrase online. It means "*Shut up, you fat whore!*"

He looks to his right at Ryan and calls out, "*Pendejo!*" then he leans over to me and whispers, "*Putaaaaaaaa.*" He bumps his eyebrows up and down, comes in like he's going to kiss me, then pulls back, throws his arms up in horror, and exclaims, "Agh!"

Drew buries her face against my upper arm. I want to tell her that it's okay, but I'm afraid that if I open my mouth, it'll be obvious that I'm freaking out, too.

One country road looks like another and it all blends together: barbed wire separating the road from cows and horses in pastures. Old houses with cars on blocks in the front yards. Parents with little kids waiting at the end of long dirt roads.

Several people open the bus windows and the cool air, heavy with wet grass and manure, replaces the stuffiness. A farmer on a tractor waves at us to pass him; then the countryside fades into the tiny town. We pull up to a huge white brick home with gargoyle statues on either side of wrought iron gates. The bus driver honks a few times. Finally, Michael Taylor trudges down the driveway. His nearly-white blonde hair is sticking up all over his head, and he looks like he just rolled out of bed. His eyes are so heavy-lidded, I'm surprised he's able to find his way onto the bus.

Ryan stares straight ahead as Michael fakes like he's going to topple onto him. He wobbles down the aisle and he's greeted like a rock star. His friends reach out to high-five him, and Michael laughs and pantomimes taking a drag off a joint.

Our last stop before reaching school is Tina's house. She's wearing a tight-fitting top, skinny jeans, and wedge heels. She strides onto the bus; a few people whistle. Tina smiles and makes eye contact with me as she passes my seat. If she remembers me from the garage sale, she gives no indication.

One girl stands. "Oh, my Gawd, girl! Where did the rest of you *go*?" Several people rise to gawk at her. "What did you do with the old Tina?"

Tina laughs. "I killed her."

"Y'all sit down," the bus driver snaps. She frowns in the visor mirror, and when she catches my eye, I look away.

Drew tries to be brave, but her eyes fill with tears as we walk into the building. "You're not just going to leave me the second we get inside, are you? You'll help me find my classroom, right?" She holds my hand so tightly that the sweat is making our palms slide.

I twist my hand away, wipe my palm on my jeans, and take her hand again. "Yes, I'll walk you to your room." We step just inside the building and I look side to side. "Elementary is this way." We start to the right.

"Colby, stop!" Drew plants her feet and won't move. "I need to ask you something...come here."

I bend to her and she whispers, "Are...they going to be mean to me, too?"

"What are you talking about?"

"The kids here—they're so mean to Ryan, and that boy on the bus scared me when he made those kissy sounds. He doesn't even know you. Which makes me think...do people here know about what Daddy did?" Her voice is cracking, and she's on the verge of losing control.

There's a bench by the office. I lower myself awkwardly onto it and pull Drew down next to me. I whisper, "Nobody here at school—except Ryan—knows about Dad, okay?...And...the reason they're mean to Ryan is that when he told on one of his friends for doing something bad, the friend got into big trouble."

Her eyebrows furrow. "But...if he did something bad, *shouldn't* he be in trouble?"

I glance at the clock in the hallway. "Drew, this isn't the time. We're going to be late."

Drew's shoulders are rocking as she fights to keep from sobbing.

I narrow my eyes. "Are you *seriously* worrying about this or something?"

Her chin quivers and she nods her head.

A lady in a black suit approaches us. "Is everything all right?"

Drew tightens her grip on my wrist. I tell the lady, "We're fine.

She's just a little nervous because it's her first day. We're new here."

The lady bends down and places her hand on Drew's shoulder. "Oh, are you Drew Denton? I've heard all about you."

Drew bursts into tears. "You *said* nobody knew, Colby!"

The lady gives me a quizzical look and I shrug. "She means…I told her that nobody would know how nervous she is. That's…what she's talking about." I force myself to laugh. I sound stupid.

The lady slides onto the bench next to Drew and puts her arm around her. "Aw, honey, I just meant that I figured out who you are because I met your mama when she enrolled you in school. I'm Mrs. Foster, the elementary assistant principal. You *look* just like your mother, too!" She glances at me. "And who is this with you?"

Drew sniffles, "M-my sister, C-Colby. She's in tenth grade."

Mrs. Foster looks surprised. "You're sisters? Well, I never would have guessed."

Drew automatically swings her hair side to side. "I look like my mamma and she looks like my…I m-mean—uh—never mind… him." She glances at me. I nod at her; her lower lip quivers.

"Let's let Big Sister go on to her class, and I'll take you to Mrs. Thurston's second grade classroom, okay, hon?" Mrs. Foster stands and offers her hand to Drew.

I push myself up off the bench and adjust my shirt so it's not as tight on my stomach. I'd hoped that my jeans would be loosening by now, but they're just as binding as the moment I wrenched them onto my body. "Going to be okay now, Drew?"

She looks at her feet and nods.

"I'll meet you on the bus this afternoon. Save me a seat, okay?"

She says nothing; just nods as Mrs. Foster leads her toward the elementary wing.

I head for the high school hallway and approach a tall, pretty girl with long brown hair who is laughing and talking with a shorter girl whose pointy nose and buck teeth make her appear rat-like. "Um, hi, could you tell me where I can pick up my schedule?"

The shorter girl's eyes lock on the *Hallister* logo on my chest. She nudges the taller girl and cuts her eyes back to it. "Are you new?"

"Yeah. My mom enrolled me, but I don't have my schedule. Could you—"

The tall girl cuts me off. "What's your shirt say? *Hallister*?" She giggles and they exchange knowing glances. "Never heard of *Hallister*. Where'd you get a shirt like that?"

I grimace at the white block letters embroidered across my breasts. "It's the name of a store."

The girls laugh. The shorter of the two arches an eyebrow. "So, you got it at the *Hallister* store?"

My face burns, but I hope they don't notice. I shrug.

"Um, that's *Hollister*, New Girl. I think you got ripped off." The bell rings, and they're laughing so hard that they're bumping into other people as they ooze down the hall.

"Kayley and Kara are bitches. Don't let them bother you," someone behind me says. I turn to find a girl with copper hair and heavy dark brows. I can't tell if her lipstick is blue or black, but it makes her skin appear shockingly white. She talks fast. "I like your shirt. Purple's a nice color—it's not *my* color; I like to wear black, as you can see, but anyway, what's your name?"

I try to swallow past the lump in my throat. "I'm Colby. And… thanks." I swipe at a tear as it trickles down my cheek.

"I'm Anna. Your schedule should be in the counselor's office. I'll show you where it is." She takes my upper arm. "Really: don't worry about them. They think they're better than everybody. I call them *Abercrombie and Bitch*."

We round a corner and run into a line outside the counselor's office.

Anna says, "Whoa, this is going to take a while. Think you'll be okay? I don't want to leave you, but I also can't be late to class."

"Sure." I hope I sound more confident than I feel.

"Chances are, we'll have a few classes together. If not, look for me at lunch. I'll save you a seat."

"How do you know we'll have the same lunch period?"

Anna gives me a funny look. "Are you kidding? This school is *tiny*. The entire high school eats lunch at the same time. I'm not hard to find. My buds and I eat on the stage."

"...You have a *stage* in your cafeteria?"

She snorts. "Cafe*torium*, thank you very much. It's a cafeteria and auditorium all in one. We're small-town *country*. The school's got all twelve grades in it; our school library and public library are one and the same...I'm surprised we don't come to school on farm tractors. People around here treat Walmart like it's the mall."

I wrinkle my nose. "Do you ever feel like you're missing out?"

Anna gives me a head-tilt. "If you don't know what you've never had, how can you miss it?"

Chapter Eleven

I'm way late to my first class, biology, because it takes me a while to figure out that it's in a portable building. I enter through a door in the back of the room and grimace at the first three faces I see: Fredrick, José, and Michael. Kara, the rat-faced girl who made fun of my shirt, and Tina notice me, too. Tina leans across the aisle to talk to another girl. There's no sign of a teacher. I breathe a shallow sigh of relief. The pain from my tight jeans radiates all the way up to my ribs.

I *hope* Tina's not telling that girl about my clothes. I kick myself for not realizing that I might be going to school with the person who used to own these! Rage bubbles fill my chest. I hate my life! I hate my dad for not giving us any money! I hate my mom for hating my body! I…hate.

Somebody near the front of the room has shoulder-length copper hair. I'm relieved that it's Anna, and there's an empty seat at her table. She smiles when she sees me. "Hey, are you okay?"

I'm scowling so hard that my face hurts, and I try to relax it. "Oh, yeah. Just, you know, first day, being new." I show her my schedule and we compare classes.

"Oh, cool! We have Fun Math together!"

I'm skeptical. "*Fun* Math? Every math class I've ever taken was the exact opposite of fun. I suck at math."

"Oh, they don't mean 'Fun,' like, 'Oh, boy!'—They mean 'Fun' as in, short for 'Fundamentals of Math.' I suck at math, too. Some people call that class 'Math for Dummies.'"

Kara hisses, "Hey, *Hallister*!" and explodes in giggles. I glance back and see Tina step over to Kara's table. Anna springs out of her chair and stomps back to the two of them. I don't know what she's saying, but her body language isn't friendly. She's returning to our table when Kara calls out, "Bitch!"

Without looking back, Anna shoots her the bird and slides into her chair.

"Is that ladylike behavior?" A woman who looks to be at least eighty stands directly in front of our table. Her wrinkly face is coated in powder. She's wearing a bright pink floral print blouse, turquoise scarf, and what I'm pretty sure is a curly blonde wig, since it's sitting crookedly atop her head. She blinks behind her thick glasses and frowns at Anna.

Anna jabs a thumb over her shoulder. "But, Miss, she—!"

The teacher ignores her and moves to stand in front of her desk. Her voice is crackly, and she speaks slowly. "I'm Mrs. Mary Clay. Please check your schedules. If it says 'biology,' then you're in the right place. Anybody in the wrong place?" She blinks a few times, waiting, before consulting her attendance roster.

"I recognize a lot of these names. I taught your parents, and in some cases, I taught your grandparents. You know what that tells me?"

Nobody answers, and she continues. "Tells me that you can't get away with much, because I already know which of you do the right thing and which are rotten to the core. So don't try anything. I may be old, but I'm sharp as a tack."

She moves slowly to her desk, creaks into the chair, and announces, "Michael Taylor, come up here right now."

Michael doesn't budge from his seat in the back row. "What'd I do?"

Mrs. Clay narrows her eyes behind her thick lenses and locks a gaze on him that must act like a tractor beam, because he saunters up and stands before her desk. She reaches over to a vase of roses, plucks a petal, and pops it in her mouth. She chews slowly, seeming to take pleasure in the class's reaction, which ranges from stunned silence to "Ew!"

Michael shifts his weight from one foot to the other and says impatiently, "What? What do you want?"

Mrs. Clay swallows loudly and crooks her finger, pulling Michael closer with that invisible tractor beam of hers. I swear, everybody in that room leans forward, trying to hear what she says.

"Let me tell you something, Mr. Taylor. I taught your daddy, and he was a spoiled piece of fruit: a toxic, entitled young man. Well… at that time…a real whiz-bang of a turd. For *some* reason…"—she plucks another petal and studies it—"I get the impression that you're following in his footsteps. Am I…incorrect in that assumption, Mr. Taylor?" She sticks out her tongue and places the petal on it, pulls her tongue in, and chews slowly while watching him.

Michael takes a step back and flails his arms. "You are batshit crazy, old lady, and everybody knows it. My dad told me you were nuts when *he* had you a million years ago." He starts back to his seat.

"Stop right there, Michael," Mrs. Clay's voice crackles like burning wood. "You've just confirmed my suspicions."

Michael freezes and mouths, "Fuck." He slowly turns and faces her. "So? What are *you* going to do about it?"

Mrs. Clay works her way out of her chair, shuffles to the desk directly in front of her own, and taps a frosty pink fingernail on it. "This is your assigned seat, Mr. Taylor. You shall be my research project this year: nature versus nurture. I hypothesize that, given intense intervention, you might not in fact be confirmed to be of the species *Taylorous assholious*. Despite all indications thus far to the contrary, of course."

Michael's voice is high. "Did you just call me an asshole?"

Her eyes widen behind her glasses. "Such language, Mr. Taylor! I may be a batshit crazy old lady with nothing to lose, but I *certainly* would never call a student an *asshole*. Even if he *is* one." She shuffles back to her seat, plucks another petal off the nearly bald flower, and pops it in her mouth. She's just starting on the second rose when the morning announcements begin.

I'm following Anna down the portable building steps when there's a tug on my arm. Tina hisses, "I need to talk to you!" and pulls me off the sidewalk.

I wince because my pants haven't loosened in the least. I glance down, expecting to see a ring of blood around my waist. It must be rubbed raw by now.

Tina reads the pain as fear. "Don't worry, I just need to tell you something. When Kara was—"

Anna stomps back to us. "What's up?"

"This is private," Tina snaps.

Anna squares off with her. "What, you think that just 'cause you got skinny, you're too good to hang out with the *Nobodies*?"

"What's wrong with you, Anna? We used to be friends!"

"Yeah, *used to*, until you changed and started hanging out with *Abercrombie and Bitch*!"

Tina holds up a hand. "Look. I just need to talk to—what's your name?"

"Colby." I turn to Anna. "It's okay. I'll find Fun Math on my own." I glance at my schedule. "Room 105, right?"

She frowns. "Yeah. Go in the double doors, and it's two doors down, on the right. And don't be late! My big brother told me that Coach Allison is a real dick about tardies." She gives Tina a warning look and saunters off.

Tina starts over. "Look: When Kara was making fun of your shirt, I didn't tell her that it used to be mine. I just wanted you to know that. And, to be honest, I'm sorry I sold you that shirt, because I only wore it once."

I glance down and shrug. "Looks brand-new."

She shakes her head. "You don't get it: I only wore it *once* because Kayley and Kara made fun of *me*, too. They've only started being nice to me since I lost eighty pounds." She pauses while some kids pass us, then whispers, "My mom bought the shirt at a flea market because it was cheap. She didn't know that it was a knockoff; that *Hollister* was spelled wrong. She was just, I guess, happy that I could have a name-brand shirt, since my dad's disabled and we can't afford to shop at, you know, the *real* Hollister store. I've never told anyone that, so please don't repeat it. Anyway, I'm sorry they're giving you shit about the shirt."

"It's okay; it's not like you planned for this to happen."

The tardy bell rings. Tina sputters, "I—I just wanted you to know that nobody's going to find out that you bought your clothes from me. I've got Fun Math next, too." She smiles. "Guess we'll find out together if he's a dick about tardies."

We enter the classroom just as the teacher, Coach Allison, glances up from a clipboard and says, "Second call: Denton, Colby." He's of average height with a belly that drapes far over his belt, and his face is shiny with oil. He's wearing a white collared shirt, black pleated pants, and a black-and-white ball cap with PCHS on it.

"I'm here." I cram myself into the first empty desk near the door. The pain around my waist has evolved into a burning sensation.

Coach Allison's voice heavy with an East Texas accent, he blasts, "Number one, Miss Denton, you and your friend are *late*, and it better not happen again. Number two, open your eyes and you'll notice that no one else is seated, except for..." He consults his clipboard and jabs a fat finger at the three students in desks: "Anderson, Ian; Bates, Kyle; and Cummings, Kayley. Please join your classmates along the wall. I assign seats alphabetically."

The only sound is my desk squeaking as I wriggle out of it. He waits as I gather my things to join everyone else lined up along the back wall. I feel everyone's eyes on me. My foot catches on a chair leg and I stumble. A few people laugh.

I'm almost to the wall when he calls, "Denton, Colby." I turn, and he points to a desk that's practically in the same place I was when I first entered…next to rat-faced Kara's tall friend, Kayley. She smirks at me as I sit down.

He continues, "Ellis, Ryan."

I had no idea Ryan was in this class! He emerges from behind the American flag in the corner, scowl firmly in place. He throws his binder onto his desk and slides into his seat without acknowledging that he knows me.

The seat assignments continue: "Houston, Anna…Miller, Trent… Odor—I mean, Odum, Tina…" The class explodes in laughter.

Somebody cracks, "What's that *smell*?"

Coach Allison barks, "Zip it!…Rodriguez, José…"

José strides up the side aisle, crosses the front of the room, and moves down our row. He swings his bulging backpack and thumps it squarely against Ryan's face. Ryan makes a sound like "Ooomph!" and clutches his head.

José feigns concern. "Aw, you all right, buddy? My bad." Then he leans down and hisses, "*Pendejo!*" His friends snicker. The coach says nothing; just continues seating students.

I reach for Ryan, who's bent over his desktop. "Are you okay?" He doesn't answer, and I shake him. He jerks away but keeps his head down. I ask him again but he ignores me.

Coach Allison adjusts his ball cap. "For those of you who don't know me, I'm the head football coach. I am not a math teacher per se; I am merely the person required to monitor this class. You may thank your state legislator for the budget cuts to education, because that is the only, and I repeat, *only* reason that I am in charge of a remedial math class."

He slaps his clipboard against his thigh as he paces the front of the room. "This is Fundamentals of Math. I realize that it says 'Fun Math' on your schedule, but that is a misnomer. You wouldn't *be* in this class if you deserved to have fun in math. Your lack of achievement on last year's standardized test has saddled you with me. Some of you will earn your way out by midyear and go on to Algebra I. The rest of you will remain stagnant and drown in a cesspool of your own making. There's nothing I can do about that. The district provides a workbook that you will complete independently. Do yourself a favor: If I'm working on the playbook or I'm on the computer reviewing video of a game, don't bother me."

Ryan mutters, "There's a lot that doesn't bother *you*."

Coach Allison snaps, "Problem, Ellis?...Ryan? You got something to say to me?"

I hiss, "No! You don't have a problem!"

"What's that, Miss Denton?" Coach Allison slams his clipboard down on my desk, and I jump. It feels like my stomach miraculously shoots past my waistband and slams onto the floor. I shake my head slowly.

Coach Allison crosses his arms over his chest. "Is that a response?"

I glance sideways at Ryan; he's scowling, as usual. "N-no, sir."

"What did you say to Mr. Ellis?"

I swallow and choke on my own spit. "I—was telling Ryan—that—he doesn't have a problem."

Ryan plants his elbows on his desk and leans his forehead on his palms.

Coach Allison's face is bright red. "Now *that's* where you're wrong, Miss Denton." He steps to Ryan's desk and addresses the top of his head. "Look at me, boy."

The room is so silent that when my stomach gurgles, it's like an alarm going off. I press my hand against my abdomen and try to silence it.

"I said, *'Look at me,'* boy." Coach Allison's fists are on Ryan's desk, and I see that even his *hands* are bright red. He's pissed off from head to toe.

When Ryan won't raise his eyes, Coach Allison bends down and aligns his face a few feet from Ryan's, so that he has to meet his stony stare. His voice is low but somehow loud at the same time. "I do not want you in this class, and I am going to do everything in my power to see that you are removed. What you did to Jared Moore was inexcusable. The idea of him sitting in a jail cell instead of on the fifty-yard line makes me *sick*." He leans forward until the two of them are practically nose to nose. "Chief Taylor and I are buddies."

He backs up the slightest bit; watches Ryan's face for a reaction. "I know about the false police report your mother filed on Michael for the misunderstanding you boys had in here on the last day of school. Now, I wasn't present, of course, but I don't buy that pack of lies you told. You try to make any more problems for my players this year, and you'll be sorry. Got it?"

Ryan's jaw muscles flex beneath Coach Allison's death stare, and his eyes are so dark, they look like charcoal briquettes. Through clenched teeth, he seethes, "Yes."

The man breathes the words, "Yes…what?"

Ryan's chest is rising and falling; his flat voice drips hatred from every word, just like it does any time he talks to me. "Sir…Yes…*Sir*."

The coach rises and walks hurriedly to the hallway. He looks left and right, then steps back, closes the door, and gestures to a stack of math workbooks by the wall. "Rodriguez and Miller, distribute those to your classmates." He strides to the whiteboard, writes "Unit 1, Exercises A-E. Due tomorrow," then plops into his chair and pulls up Solitaire on the computer.

The first thing I notice on the wall outside the life skills classroom is a poster: *Normal People Worry Me.* The teacher, a young woman with blue eyes and chin-length strawberry blonde hair, shakes the hand of each person as they come through the door. She's dressed in a long blue tunic and white leggings. "Good morning! Welcome! Sit anywhere."

Other than Kyle from Fun Math, I don't recognize anyone from my earlier classes. I slide my backpack onto a chair and sit at a table by myself. There's a girl sitting alone at another table. She looks familiar: She has a splatter of freckles across her nose, her skin is the color of coffee ice cream, and she has shaggy brownish-black hair. I catch her eye and give her a close-mouthed smile, but she immediately looks away.

The teacher pulls the door closed and moves to stand between our tables. "We're going to be doing a partner activity today, so I need you two to sit together, please." When the girl makes no move toward me, I gather my stuff and join her. The teacher smiles, "Thanks...and your name is?"

"Colby."

"Nice to meet you, Colby. I'm Mrs. Lowe. And you are...?" She glances at my shy table mate, who says softly, "Becca Schuler."

Becca slouches in her seat, tucks her hair behind her ears, and fingers the pearl buttons on the plaid western shirt she's wearing. It looks like a man's shirt, and it's way too big for her. Her jeans are faded with holes worn in the knees, and she's the only student I've seen so far wearing cowboy boots. Even though Piney Creek is country, the kids dress mostly like they did at my old school in a suburb of Dallas.

I realize where I've seen her before: the Goodwill store. She's the girl that Drew nearly mowed down in her rush to get away from the mangy rabbit vest.

Mrs. Lowe distributes a worksheet with a triangle on it, strides to the whiteboard, and draws a huge triangle. She labels it *Maslow's*

Hierarchy of Needs, divides it into five sections, and turns to us. "This class is called life skills, and it's about learning how to take care of yourself so that you not only survive—you *thrive*. I'm not going to waste our first day talking to you about how I *need* you to act in my class; you're young adults and you know what you need to do at school. But…how do you get *your* needs met? What are the most important things *in life*? Go ahead: call out what you think you need to survive."

One kid says, "Money!"

Mrs. Lowe writes it outside of the triangle. As each person calls out something, she adds to the list: "A car. I *need* to get off the bus."…"A smartphone!"…"A laptop."…"My little brother needs to stay out of my room. Like, forever."

She makes the time-out sign, then turns and labels the bottom section of the triangle, *Physical Needs*. "Okay, let's narrow our focus to this part only, which we could also call *Survival Needs*. Think: if you don't have these three things, you die."

The same kid yells out, "Money!" and everybody laughs. But he wasn't joking. "Well, don't you die without it? If you don't have money, you can't buy food—"

Mrs. Lowe exclaims, "Ding-ding-ding! Yes!" She jots *Food* on the board and turns to us. "Exactly how long one can survive without food depends on several things, such as how much a person weighs, their genetics, how good their health is to begin with, and, most importantly, whether or not they are sufficiently hydrated. So, another essential of life is…"

"Water!"

"That's right: Humans *need* water to live. We lose water when we sweat, go to the bathroom, and even when we breathe. Your body needs water to survive. That said, some doctors say that people can go three to five days without water. But don't try it. Don't even go a day without—" She turns to the board and adds *Water* to the *Physical Needs* section of the triangle. "And the last necessity of life is?"

Kyle from Fun Math says, "TV?"

Mrs. Lowe rolls her eyes but smiles. After a few moments of silence, she prompts, "Tell me this, Kyle: Are you going to watch your television inside a cardboard box under a bridge?"

He looks confused at first; then a slow grin spreads across his face. "Oooooh…a place to live."

"Right." Mrs. Lowe completes the *Physical Needs* section with *Shelter*. "You have to have some kind of structure that protects you from the elements, you know, like freezing weather, Texas heat, tornadoes, hail, and so on." She steps away and gestures to the triangle like she's Vanna White on *Wheel of Fortune*. "Physiological needs come first. If your body's not having its needs met in a healthy way, it's hard to focus on anything else. Let's move up to the next level: *Safety Needs*, the need to feel safe and to trust. Turn to your table partner and come up with three ways that people's safety needs are met. You have five minutes." She sets a timer. "Go."

I try a joke to break the ice with Becca. "Well, I guess *one* way to feel safe when shopping is to not be knocked over by a seven-year-old."

She furrows her brow, clearly confused.

"Two Saturdays ago? My little sister plowed into you?" I lean down and whisper, "At the Goodwill store? Remember? I caught you just before you hit the ground and went *'Splat'*?"

Becca looks at me—*really looks at me*—for the first time, and I see that she remembers. She doesn't smile. "Oh, yeah."

"Sorry about that. I told my sister that the rabbit vest she was wearing had a disease, and she freaked out."

Becca nods and looks down again.

I write my name on my paper. "So, we're supposed to come up with three ways to feel safe and to trust. Do you have one?"

"I'm finished." She slides her paper toward me. She's listed: *Mom & Dad*, *Home*, and *Best Friend*.

I grimace and remember tucking the picture of Dad and that lady—Marcy—into my bra so that no one else would see it. My chest hurts with pangs of jealousy that Becca has parents she can count on. My mom thinks of me as a big fat disaster; I haven't seen or heard from my father since the day he walked out the door—unless I count the video of him being chased by news reporters as he raced to a motel room where his girlfriend pulled the curtains closed—and now I'm living in a shitty little trailer with a plastic star taped to my ceiling. And…best friend? Of course I've had friends, but I've never had anybody I was super close to.

"You have a minute and a half," Mrs. Lowe calls.

I grit my teeth. *I can't write what Becca wrote.* "I think Mrs. Lowe means like, you know, smoke alarms or locks on the front door."

Becca sets her pen on the table and folds her arms.

I write, *smoke alarms, locks, and…*that's safety. What about trust?

I picture my dad sliding his arms around my mom and spewing some bullshit about being like honeymooners again in a few years. *Package deal, my ass.*

My stomach clenches. I close my eyes.

Mrs. Lowe warns, "Thirty seconds." Most everyone else is finished and they're talking about what they did over the summer. *I* helped destroy my family, and it only took spilling coffee and finding a photo to do it.

I slam down my pen and claw my head. The hum of conversation stops and I feel people staring. Mrs. Lowe puts her hand on my shoulder, leans down, and whispers, "Don't stress about this, Colby. It's not for a grade, and there are no wrong answers."

Tears fill my eyes, and I feel like a kid on the first day of kindergarten. I hate the lump in my throat. I tell myself that it's stupid to get this upset about an answer on a worksheet, even though I know that's not what it's about.

It takes all my self-control not to reach under the table and unfasten the top button on my jeans. I look down and see that my shirt has bunched up against the table, revealing the roll of fat around my middle. I feel myself being watched; I glance up and see that a boy at the table next to mine is staring at my bare skin. He's got his hand over his mouth, leaning over to the girl by his side. I pull the shirt down and lower my head so that he can't see me cry. I wish I was home—but the home I picture is the one in Northside: the one that Dad took from us when he forgot that *honesty is everything* to our family.

I tune out the class discussion of *Safety Needs*, and I'm relieved when Mrs. Lowe explains *Love and Friendship Needs* without requiring that I work with Becca. I'm gathering my things to leave class when Mrs. Lowe asks, "Colby? Did you hear the homework assignment?"

I shake my head and pretend to adjust my backpack strap.

"I asked you to consider what Self-Worth Needs are. Just come up with five things that you think a person can do to feel self-worth." She watches the last few kids leave. "You're new, right?"

I nod. My eyes fill up again and I lower my head.

"Do you want to talk about what's bothering you?"

I'm trying so hard not to cry that it feels like my skull is going to come apart. A sob comes out as a snort, and she mistakes it for a giggle. I'll take it.

"What's so funny?"

"J-just the idea that talking about my problems is going to make it easier to..." I try to inhale but find it's impossible. I'm in too much pain.

"To what, Colby?"

I can't think of any other answer. "Breathe."

It's lunchtime, but not for me. I'm not sure if it's my nerves or the way my jeans are slowly grinding my body in half, but I can't even think about eating. I slide into a chair near the food line exit and watch the endless stream of pizza, hamburgers, and nachos go by.

I remember the last time we went to the movies as a family. Dad and I got nachos and split an extra-large tub of buttered popcorn. I've known girls whose fathers took them camping or taught them how to work on cars. Eating is what my dad and I did together. We'd stand at the kitchen counter and dig the Oreos out of a gallon of Cookies & Cream ice cream. Mom would fuss at us, "You don't need that!" and we'd just laugh.

But my favorite time with my dad—my *favorite*—was when he baked our birthday cakes. He makes the best cake icing in the *world*. He doesn't even need a recipe. Rachel and Drew were never asked to help out, but from the time I could sit on the counter without falling off, I was in charge of handing my dad the ingredients for icing.

A bag of powdered sugar, a half stick of butter, vanilla, a little milk…the smell of the mixer getting hot…and the big moment, when he pronounced the icing just right, popped the beaters out, and handed me one to lick. He took the other one, and we always agreed that it was the best icing he'd ever made. He slathered a thick layer onto the cake, used a decorator's bag to pipe flowers and border, and there was always enough left over for us to have big, melt-in-your-mouth spoonfuls. Aunt Leah's cake icing is nearly as good as Dad's.

It dawns on me: He didn't make Rachel's birthday cake in June. Even though he still ate a lot of junk food and kept his own snack stash in his desk drawer, he'd started yelling at me for eating the way we always had. He was cranky a lot of the time, and sometimes he even called me a pig. He'd snap, "Seriously, Colby! What are my supporters going to think when they see that one of my children has no self-control?"

Self-control? Um, hello, Dad, but I think that cheating on Mom is a sign of sucky self-control. Guess you don't have to worry about what your supporters think anymore, and of course you have Marcy, the only person in the whole wide world who lets you be you. Woohoo for you, *Dad.*

Tina walks by with Kayley and Kara. There's a tiny slice of pizza and a bottle of water on her tray. I wonder if it's true: Did Kayley and Kara only decide Tina was cool enough to be a friend when she lost weight? I try to visualize Tina being as big as I am, but I can't.

Mom put me on my first diet when I was in second grade. She started pointing out women who were so big that you couldn't tell if they were pregnant or just really fat. "You don't want to be one of *those*, Colby."

She posted pictures of me on the fridge under alphabet letters spelling *Before*, and she'd post pics of tall, lean, athletic fashion models under *After*. I suppose she could have just put Rachel's pictures under *After*, but maybe she thought that would be too weird... which goes to show that my mother may have a sense of what's over the top, after all.

Here's the thing: My wrists are twice the size of Rachel's. No matter how badly Mom wishes I could be a Rachel clone, God, in all His [*cough-cough*] wisdom, made me in the image of my college linebacker father. I hope He didn't also make me a two-timing piece-of-shit thief who walks out on my family someday.

"Helloooo...are you in there?" Anna waves her hand in front of my face. "I've been calling you and doing everything but standing on the table to get your attention. Are you going to join us or what?"

I pop into awareness. "Oh, hey. Didn't see you."

She puts her hands on her hips. "Obviously. Did you already eat?"

"I'm not hungry."

Anna pulls me to my feet and drags me toward the round tables on the stage. She skitters up the steps and I follow slowly, just managing to lift one leg at a time in the jeans, which have not relaxed at all. She makes a beeline to some kids who, like Anna, dress all in black.

"Sean, this is Colby," Anna announces to a skinny guy with chin-length dirty blonde hair and a stubbly chin. He stabs a plastic spork into a chicken nugget and waves it at me. "And, Colby, this is Nikki." A girl with bluish-black hair raises one black fingernail but doesn't look up from texting.

I'm adjusting my backpack straps so it won't fall off the chair when I hear, "Ryan, this is Colby."

I look up to see my cousin placing his tray on the table. He blurts, "What're *you* doing here?"

I freeze. "Anna invited me—"

He glares at her; she throws up her hands. "What's that dirty look for?…You two know each other?"

Ryan says nothing; just curls his lip into a sneer.

Anna orders, "Sit down, Colby. Ryan: you, too."

But we don't. Anna stands and puts a hand on each of our shoulders. "Hey. I don't know what the deal is, but *everybody's* welcome at the *Nobodies*' table. Remember, Ryan? All your little football buddies treat you like shit now—but *not* the *Nobodies*! Aren't you glad you've got friends who stick by you?" She playfully punches his upper arm, winks at him, and tries to get him to smile. He remains stone-faced.

I announce, "Ryan and I are cousins." I lower myself slowly to the chair and glance up at him. "So, are you going to eat or just stand there glaring at me?"

Sean breaks out a Scottish brogue. "Aye, a spirited lass! I like a woman with fire in her belly and meat on her bones!" He addresses the texting girl. "Nikki, you could learn a thing or two from such a brave outspoken creature!" She nods but doesn't look up.

Ryan's voice drips with sarcasm. "Oh, yeah. Colby's *real* good at speaking up. *Especially* when it matters."

I slam my palm on the table. "How long are you going to stay pissed? I'm *sorry* about what happened on the Fourth of July! I never said I agreed with my dad or anyone else!"

Ryan's eyes light up; he puts his hands on the table, leans toward me, and says loudly, "Yeah, speaking of your dad—Mr. *I'm All About Families*—what's the name of the woman he left your mom for? You found a picture of them making out, right?"

A hush descends on the cafetorium, and Ryan straightens to his full height. He yells, "Come on, Colby, while you're being so outspoken, tell us all about your dad stealing money from his campaign, and how his company ripped off people who trusted him. When's the trial? How long do you think he'll go to prison?" He pauses, and his mouth stretches into a smirk. He leans across the table and yells in my face: "You think if his cellmate rapes him but the guards aren't around to hear him say 'No,' it's still rape?"

For the first time since I squeezed myself into jeans that are two sizes too small, getting out of a chair is no problem at all. I don't feel the metal button jabbing my middle, and I'm barely aware of falling down the stage steps. The room explodes in a mixture of gasps and laughter. I don't know how I pick myself up, but I do. The next thing I know, I've bolted out the front doors of the school and I'm running toward the towering steeple atop Piney Creek Baptist. I know that Sugar's is a couple streets over from Church Row. The echo of laughter in my head is almost as loud as my heartbeat in my ears.

I barely make it out of the long school driveway before I'm wheezing so badly that I slow to a stumbling walk. I keep the steeple in my sights and pray to God to pick me up and deliver me to Sugar's, because I don't think I can walk another step.

It becomes clear pretty quickly that God may answer Mom's prayers for a place to live and fat girl clothes for me, but He's not listening to mine.

Chapter Twelve

Turns out, that steeple on Church Row is so big and tall that it looks a lot closer to the high school than it is. By the time I reach Sugar's, I'm blacking out from the heat. The last thing I remember after slamming through the front door is the shocked face of a woman I've never met. I don't even feel myself hit the floor.

A man's voice: "Colby? Can you hear me?"

I think I'm still in a heap at the bottom of the stage stairs, and I try to get up, but my arms and legs are bound. I hear the sound of hissing air, and something is sticky against my face.

"Colby, it's okay." Mom's voice is shaky.

I sense wet and cold on my forehead, under my neck, and on my groin. The pain and tightness around my waist is gone. I open my eyes. There's a guy in a dark blue uniform adjusting a valve on an oxygen tank.

Mom hovers over me. She looks terrified. "You're in an ambulance, honey. What happened? Why did you leave school?"

I shake my head; pain shoots through my eyes and I can barely focus. The man says something to Mom, and she sits back.

His face appears over mine. "Just breathe in deeply and slowly, sweetie. You're dehydrated, and you may have heat exhaustion. We're working on cooling you down, and the docs at the ER will get you rehydrated."

We stay in the emergency room for several hours until the doctors are satisfied that my body temperature is in a safe range and I finish a bag of I.V. fluids. When they find out that I haven't eaten all day, they give me juice and crackers.

Mom waits until the nurse walks out; then she pulls the privacy curtain closed. She holds up what's left of my *Hallister* shirt and suffocating jeans. "The paramedics cut your clothes off, so I went to the store when you were asleep and bought new clothes." She reaches for a bag and pulls out an oversized T-shirt and comfy-looking elastic-waist shorts. "I also bought a couple more pairs of jeans for you…in a *much* larger size."

"Thanks, Mom." I shakily sit up on the edge of the bed and start to slide off the hospital gown, but I don't want Mom to see my body. I hate the face she always makes at my fat rolls and stretch marks. I pull the shorts on under the gown.

"Are you ready to tell me why you left school in the middle of the day?"

I shake my head slowly and immediately regret it; the pounding pain hasn't quite gone away.

"Okay, how about this one: Why didn't you tell me that the jeans you were wearing were so tight?"

I lower my head into my hands. Her question, combined with everything else that's happened today, is more than I can take. I burst into tears. I try to talk but I can't; all I can do is shake my head and bawl.

Mom sits next to me and drapes her arm over my shoulders. "Aw, honey, I'm sorry. You could have told me they didn't fit."

"Wh-what—c-could y-you h-have done? You t-told me that we don't have any m-money. I didn't think we could buy more clothes."

"But your jeans were *dangerously* tight, sweetie. Look at your skin…" Without waiting, Mom pulls the gown up and yanks down the shorts' elastic waistband to reveal the deep red grooves and lines that still remain on my skin. There's dried blood on some of my stretch marks.

Embarrassment and shame wash over me. I push her hand away and mumble, "I-I'm sorry that I'm such a d-disappointment to you. I wish…you didn't hate my body so much." I sob, "I mean, I think I hate it enough for *both* of us."

The nurse sticks her head in to check on us. Mom waves her away. I duck my head again.

Mom whispers, "Ssh! Ssh, Colby. Not so loud…Oh, honey, I don't hate your body." She takes my face in her hands and forces me to meet her eyes. "I just want you to be healthy, and, well, you *know* you'll never get a boyfriend, looking like this, don't you?" Her eyes fill with tears. "I wish I knew what to do to help you. I just want you to be happy." She looks away.

I touch her arm and plead, "C-could you just make me feel like you love me no matter what?…Please? Could you just…love me the way I am?"

Mom closes her eyes and her mouth crumples. She whispers, "Of course," but she's not at all convincing.

Leah, Ryan, and Drew are waiting on the Victorian's front porch when we get home. Even in the semi-darkness, I can see that Leah looks pissed beyond belief.

Ryan hangs back on the porch with his arms crossed tightly, but Drew skitters down the steps and throws her arms around me. "Oh, Colby! I'm so glad you're okay!"

I feel instantly guilty. "I'm sorry about not meeting you on the bus, Drew, I—"

"That's okay! Ryan sat next to me and I was fine." She whispers, "He really is nice, Colby!"

The dogs are covering my legs in wet kisses, and I bend over and ruffle their ears: *anything* to keep from looking at Ryan. I start to follow Mom and Drew back to our trailer when Leah calls, "Um, Sonya, could we speak to you and Colby, please?"

Mom whispers something to Drew, and she takes off around the corner with Charley and Zeeke nipping playfully at her ankles.

Leah grabs Ryan by the arm, yanks him forward to stand next to her, and bites off each word: "Ryan has something to say to you." *Ah, so she's angry with him. Thank God it's not me.*

I scrape my bottom teeth over my upper lip and stare at a knot-hole in the bottom porch step.

Mom begins, "Does this have anything to do with why Colby left school? She won't tell me—"

Leah cuts her off. "Yes, it certainly does; *doesn't it*, Ryan?" I force myself to look up. Leah's eye to eye with Ryan, and they seem to be having a staring contest. Their scowls are mirror images of each other. "Tell Sonya what you did…*now*."

Finally, Ryan gives the same speech to my mother that he gave to *everyone* in the cafetorium, including the line about Dad possibly being raped and whether it's rape if the guards don't hear him say "No." The thing is, even though Aunt Leah looks ready to pull his head off, he doesn't *sound* sorry at all.

Leah's voice is shaking. "I am so incredibly sorry, Colby." She shoots Ryan a look that could peel paint off walls. "I'm sorry that he hurt you. And, Ryan, I am *incredibly* disappointed that you would tell all those people about what Reese did."

Ryan blasts, "Wow, Mom, you sound just like Grandpa and Grandma being pissed at you for exposing Dad as the *Grand Poobah of Assholes*."

Leah looks like Ryan struck her, and I think he's going to apologize, but instead he shrugs and says sarcastically, "Fine, Mom; you want an apology?" He turns to me and says sarcastically, "Colby, I'm *sorry* that you were so upset that you decided to go for a jog in hundred-degree weather and ended up in the hospital…Then again, that's a *choice you made*, so I surely do hope that you can get two jobs to help your mom pay the medical bills." He turns to go inside, but Mom lunges forward and grabs his arm. He knocks her hand away and starts through the front door.

Mom shrieks, "Colby could have died today! Now, it *was* her choice to take off like that, but I hold you responsible for what you did. I want this to end, and I mean right now!" She stomps down the steps like she's heading for our trailer, but stops, shakes her head, and turns back. Her voice is weary. "I'm *sorry* about what happened on the Fourth of July. Maybe we were wrong to tell you that you shouldn't have reported your friend. Maybe…*maybe*, we're even wrong about your dad; maybe he *used* to be a bad person. But I don't think he is anymore. But it's not for us to judge; ultimately, only God can judge—"

Ryan blasts, "Jesus H. Christ, *seriously*?"

Mom screeches, "Listen to me! Will somebody please listen to *me* for once?" She balls her fists and it's pretty clear that she's not just talking about Ryan interrupting her.

"Ryan, please. Hear her out." Leah seats herself on the top porch step and reaches for him. He hesitates; she repeats, "*Please*." He shakes his head in disgust, but joins her.

Mom raises her eyes to the evening sky, then closes them as if in prayer. She nods like she's gotten an answer. "These last several weeks have shaken me to the foundation of my being. The life the girls and I knew is *gone*." She snorts, and her shoulders sink. "Having everything ripped away…Reese's selfishness…the way we've been tossed aside…" She locks eyes with Ryan. "If you wished suffering on us because of how you were treated, trust me: You've gotten what you wanted."

She moves to the steps, plops down on the second-to-the-last, and turns toward a rose peeking through the handrail. Head down, she cradles a blossom in both hands. Within a couple of minutes, it's apparent from her sniffling that she's crying.

Leah crab-crawls down the steps, wraps her arms around my mom, and holds her tightly. Mom turns toward her, and Leah murmurs words I can't hear.

Ryan and I lock eyes over our moms embracing, and his expression softens. He hops over the handrail and joins me on the grass. He shrugs, chews his lip, and seems to choose his words carefully. "So…you going to be okay?"

"Yeah. Just have to take it easy for a few days. No P.E. class. No midday prison breaks." I circle my toe around a dead patch of grass.

Ryan finds his own small circle of dead grass and does the same. "Well, if it makes you feel any better, my mom wants me to get counseling. She thinks I'm messed up 'cause I got the shit kicked out of me on the last day of school. The Fourth of July—all that crap everybody said—didn't exactly help, either."

I sway a little, and he grabs my arm to steady me.

"I—you may not believe me, but I *am* sorry. I don't mean to be such an asshole." His voice wavers. "Who knows, maybe I *am* fucked up, and somebody needs to fix me. Couldn't hurt to try, right?"

He's still clutching my upper arm tightly; I shrug it away. "Mom thinks I need help, too. But…not for being shit-kicked." I glance at my mother and whisper, "She wishes I was anyone but me."

The next morning on the bus, José hisses "*Pendejo*!" at Ryan, then turns to me, makes a kissy face, and croons, "*Putaaaaa*." Drew shrinks back in terror, and José laughs. Ryan glares at the back of the bus driver's head, and Drew buries her face against my side. Tina's wearing a new-to-her outfit that nobody but me knows is second-hand. Michael Taylor looks like he hasn't slept at all when he strolls down the center aisle. He mimes taking a drag off a joint and is greeted like he's Michael Phelps at the Olympics.

We get to school, and Drew takes off for her classroom. I inhale as deeply as I can around the box of Pop Tarts that I snuck this morning before Mom and Drew woke up. I stuffed myself, but I can still appreciate the smell of cut grass because my new jeans allow me to breathe, and eventually my stomach will stop feeling like it's going to explode. I've carefully chosen a shirt that I'm positive won't attract criticism, and last night, I managed to do my life skills homework in spite of a killer headache.

I had no idea what *Self-Worth Needs* are, so I did an Internet search and came up with an answer: *The need to feel important, capable, confident, respected, and recognized*...I'm about as likely to feel any of these things as I am to be crowned Miss Texas.

I'm starting to think that since nothing unusual happened on the bus, maybe I'm wrong in assuming that everybody in the cafetorium heard what Ryan said about my dad. Then I walk into the building, and my day goes to shit.

Kayley and Kara are by the water fountain in the hallway. Kara wrinkles up her pointy rat-nose. "Hey, *Hallister*, when's Reese's trial?"

The Pop Tarts gurgle in my gut and jump toward my throat. "*How*?"

"Um, hellooo, have you heard of the Internet?" Kayley pulls lip gloss out of her purse and rolls it on, watching me the whole time. "That video of him running away with a newspaper over his head was *awesome*." She narrows her eyes and tilts her head like she's staring at a painting in a museum. "You look a lot like your dad, you know...what I could see of his face, anyway. The *rest* of his body's sure not hard to miss." She hulks up her shoulders and totters from side to side, then bursts into laughter.

Kara grins. "I checked my Facebook page a second ago, and that video has forty-six shares so far. Good stuff."

She looks to Kayley, who nods in agreement. "Oh, yeah. Quality entertainment."

It feels like all the blood rushes from my head. "You don't understand: We didn't know anything about what he was doing—"

Kayley runs a brush through her hair, checks her reflection in the library window, and spins back to me. "No, Hallister, *you* don't understand. We *don't like* your kind of people here. You and your snitch cousin—you're not native Piney Creekers, and *you're not welcome*...Wouldn't surprise me one bit to find out that you're all Satan worshippers...Like her." She points at Anna, who has just come out of the restroom.

Anna doesn't even break stride as she holds up her fingers like devil horns and waggles her tongue, then flips them the bird. Inspired by her bravery, I blurt, "Yeah. Fuck off, *Abercrombie and Bitch*."

I start to walk away, but there's a hand on my shoulder. "Come with me. *Now*."

I turn, and Coach Allison's beet red face is inches from mine. The pores on his nose are *huge*. I start to speak, but he shoves his palm in my face, turns on his heel, and jerks his index finger toward the office.

My throat feels like there are giant hands squeezing it. Over my heartbeat pounding in my ears, Kara calls, "Later, *Hallister*!"

I'm practically vibrating on the chair in the hallway outside the principal's door. I hear Coach Allison repeating what I said to Kayley and Kara. But he doesn't stop there; he complains about Ryan being in his classroom, too. "I have the right not to have disruptive people in my class, Howard, and that boy is out to destroy my football team. I can't stand the sight of him!"

I don't know what the principal, Mr. McDaniel, says to Coach Allison, but the coach must not like it because when he leaves, he throws open the door so hard that it bounces off the wall and closes again. A few seconds later, a tall, thin man who looks way too young to be a principal opens the door. He's got a beard, but it doesn't go with the rest of his face.

"Colby Denton?"

I swallow past the lump in my throat. "Yes, sir."

"Come in and have a seat." He leans on the edge of his desk and crosses his arms, watching me.

I start babbling the way I do when I get nervous. "I really am sorry—I've never been in trouble before and I promise it won't happen again—I'm not the type of person who usually does things like this." I gasp for air.

He frowns. "Well, you managed to send Coach Allison's blood pressure through the roof this morning. Are you happy with yourself?"

I don't know what to say to that; what I did had nothing to do with Coach Allison or his blood pressure. "I…I was just…mad."

His eyebrows make a V over his eyes and he rubs his beard. "And the best way to deal with that was dropping the F-bomb in my hallway?"

I choke out, "No, sir."

His face softens and he rubs one eye. "Let's hear your side: I'd love to know the circumstances that led you to being in my office on the second day of school."

There's a knock on his door and his secretary sticks her head in. "The air conditioner's not working in the art room. I've put a call in to maintenance." She glances at me. "You're the one who left campus without permission yesterday, aren't you?"

Mr. McDaniel's eyebrows shoot up. "Is that so? I knew we had a runner, but I didn't know it was you."

I visualize a person in a foot race. "A…runner?"

"Yes, a student who runs away from campus. That kind of runner."

I close my eyes and nod slowly. I shoot a quick prayer up to God: *Kill me now. Please. Just…kill me now.*

He narrows his eyes like he's connecting the dots. "I heard about some disturbance at lunch. Would you like to tell me about that?" He glances at his secretary. "Bring me Colby's file, please." He circles to his chair and falls into it, then picks up a coffee mug and takes a sip. He's not careful when he places the mug on his desk calendar, and coffee sloshes over the sides. "Dang it!"

Mr. McDaniel reaches across his desk for the tissue box and bumps the framed photo of his wife in her bridal gown. It teeters off the edge of the desk, and I catch it just before it hits the floor. The next thing I know, I can't even see the photo in my hands because I'm crying so hard.

"Well, bless your heart." Mr. McDaniel leans forward in his chair and offers me the tissue box when I finish telling him everything. "That's quite a lot of change to go through in about a little over a month's time. I've seen the news stories about your father, but I didn't make the connection."

I pluck a couple of tissues and mumble, "I wish everybody else hadn't, either." *My throat is closing up. I'm sure of it. Maybe I'll drop dead soon. Hope so.*

He pages through my file. "Looks like you're a strong student in just about everything except math. That right?"

I drag my eyes up to meet his and nod silently.

He closes the file and places it atop a stack of papers. "Thanks for being honest with me about what's going on in your life. I'll speak with Kayley and Kara about their behavior, but I need you to promise me that you're not going to go off on anybody else. Can you do that?"

I thread the tissue between my fingers and nod. I feel nearly as tired as I was when I woke up in the ambulance.

"Okay, I'm just going to give your mom a quick call to let her know that I'm addressing the problems you're having with Kayley and Kara."

I sit up straight. "But she doesn't even know about them. You don't need to do that."

Mr. McDaniel shakes his head. "Nope; I'm a big believer in that old adage, an ounce of prevention is worth a pound of cure."

He dials the number to Sugar's. "Yes, may I speak to Sonya Denton, please?...Oh, hello, Mrs. Denton. I'm Howard McDaniel, principal of Piney Creek High School. Colby's here in my office; she had a verbal altercation with some other students this morning, and—" He glances at me and traces the coffee stains on his calendar with his finger. "—No, ma'am, I wouldn't say it's *Colby's* fault; actually, these other students have been harassing her in part because of her, um, clothes..." He sits up slightly in his chair and peers over his desk at me. "What she's wearing today is fine, completely within dress code...No, they're not too tight; not at all...Actually, I think the other girls' main focus today was on your husband's...issues." He leans back in his chair and looks at the ceiling.

I don't know what Mom says to him, but his face turns red and he rotates his chair away from me. He lowers his voice, which is pretty useless seeing as how I'm sitting right across from him in his small office.

"Ma'am, I simply called to let you know that it's being dealt with, in the event that you were concerned that she was being bullied." He leans back in his chair but immediately lurches forward and lowers his voice even more. "No, I don't think your daughter is telling, well, *anyone*, about finding a photo."

Mr. McDaniel turns his chair back to his desk but won't make eye contact. He retrieves my file, picks up a pen, and jots some notes on the outside of it, but I can't read them from where I am.

"I think your perception of this situation is inaccurate, Mrs. Denton. Colby is *not* causing problems; my impression of her is that she is a good student...yes, except for math. That's why she was placed in our remedial math class." He listens a while longer, nodding in response to what she's saying. "...Yes, and I appreciate you giving me all that information about Colby...No, we don't do that here; we'd have no way to monitor what she's eating at lunch. If you're concerned that Colby has an eating disorder, perhaps you can contact the counseling office. No, ma'am, you'd need to do that. Well, you have a nice day, too...Mmm-hmm."

He hangs up the phone, stares at it for what feels like a long time, then blinks a few times. "Wow. Wow-*wow*-wow." He finally looks up at me and gives a forced smile.

"Hey, Colby, I'm...going to give you just a little advice that somebody once gave me, because I think that you and I might have a lot in common in the *parent department*. What I'm going to say is directed at the issues with your dad...and, *maybe*, with your mom, too. Sometimes, you've got to succeed *in spite* of your parents, instead of *because of* them. Parents have their own problems, but those are about *them*. They're *not* a reflection of you. And that can be hard, especially when a parent does something spectacularly stupid, or, you know, maybe, they don't seem very...supportive. No offense."

I wave my hand and shake my head. My eyes are so swollen that I can barely blink.

"You're going to have to stand tall and let all the bull crap that people throw at you just bounce off. I'll do what I can on my end to see that Kayley and Kara lay off, but your cousin Ryan can tell you that I can't be everywhere. If I could, what happened on the last day of school..." He shakes his head and looks away.

"What exactly *did* happen, anyway?"

He purses his lips. "I shouldn't have brought it up." He glances at me. "It was awful. Some other boys retaliated against Ryan for reporting the sexual assault of a girl at a party he attended, and—"

"Michael, José, and Fredrick?"

"I can't divulge their names."

"But I already know—"

He shrugs. "Sorry, I can't do it. The attackers set Ryan up. The one who actually *did* the beating waited in an empty classroom, while the other two told Ryan that the teacher wanted to see him. There was a smartphone video of Mi—of the attacker—preparing himself. Actually, they caught the whole attack on video. It was uploaded to YouTube by 5:00 P.M. that afternoon."

"Why are those boys still here, then? Why aren't they in jail?"

Mr. McDaniel leans his chair back and steeples his index fingers under his chin.

"I can't discuss the investigation or administrative side of the issue, but I can tell you this: It's my second year as principal here. I'm not a native of Piney Creek, so I'm learning the political system as I go along."

I'm confused. "Isn't it the same system as the rest of the United States? They have the same president, right?"

He smiles, but it's not a genuine grin. "I don't mean *those* kind of politics. I'm talking about the system of who you *know* and who they *are*." His eyes widen. "I didn't say that, and if you repeat it, I'll deny it."

"I won't say anything."

He stands, strides to his door, and opens it. "That's a good policy to have when people say rude things, too: Don't say a thing; just walk away. We'll consider this a warning, Colby. Read your student handbook, and you'll see the flowchart of consequences for breaking the rules."

Maybe my head's so full of snot that my mouth overrides my brain. I blurt, "So, since I'm a nobody, if I cuss in the hall I'll get in trouble, but if I was a *somebody*, I could beat another person half to death and nothing happens?"

Mr. McDaniel grimaces and pulls me back into his office. He closes his door but keeps his hand on the knob. "That's *not* what I said. Administrative decisions are made on an individual basis, given the information I have. In your case, a staff member overheard profanity. In Ryan's case, there were no adult witnesses, which hampered the investigation."

I whisper, "But there was a video. It was on YouTube."

His voice is so low that I can barely hear him. "Deleted within an hour, and the phone was somehow run over by a car." He opens the door. "Again: consider this a warning. I don't want to see you in my office again for swearing at other students."

I'm late to Fun Math. Coach Allison doesn't even notice when I come in. He's talking to his computer screen, and it takes me a second to realize he's Skyping with somebody about the Friday night football game. I pull my workbook off the corner of his desk and pretend that I don't hear Kayley whisper, "Thief!"

I steal a glance at Ryan; he's got his head on his desk, sleeping. I check the board for the assignment, flip the workbook open to the assigned page, and stare blankly at it until the bell rings.

As soon as the tardy bell rings, Mrs. Lowe starts life skills class. "So? Did everybody figure out five ways to meet the need for self-worth?"

Oh, crap. I didn't search for how *to* do *it, just what self-worth* is. I slide down in my chair and try to become invisible; swallow hard and shake my head. *Why did I even bother getting out of bed today? Shit!*

Mrs. Lowe apparently notices. "Are you okay?"

"I...don't think I did the assignment the way you wanted it done."

"Just breathe, okay? It's not about being perfect." She leans against her desk and folds her arms. Today she's wearing a T-shirt dress that's embroidered with the words *Chloe's Mom* along the neckline. The stitches look like flowers. Her necklace is made of unevenly shaped clay beads on a length of yarn, and her leggings of the day are hot pink. I can't stop staring at the necklace; some of the beads look like dried dog doo.

She catches me staring. "You like it? My four-year-old"—she points to the stitched name on her dress—"Chloe, made it for me in Pre-K." She fingers a bead and smiles. "The style is primitive, and that's one of the things I love about it."

I try to imagine my mom wearing a dog-doo necklace. Her reaction to the fabric-painted T-shirt I made for her birthday two years ago was, "Where exactly do you picture me wearing this? People expect me to be well put-together at all times. Maybe if you'd taken your time in making this, it wouldn't look so homemade."

Later, I saw the T-shirt at the bottom of a box of stuff marked for Goodwill in Mom's closet. When she gave me weight loss books for my birthday, I pulled the shirt out of the box, wrapped it around the books, and put it back in the bottom of the box. A few days later, my dad took the box to Goodwill.

She asks me once in a while if I've read the books yet so that I can lose weight. I ask her when she's going to wear the shirt I made her, and she shuts up.

Mrs. Lowe says one word: "Listen." She pulls a small boom box from a counter behind her desk, places it on the center table, and pushes Play.

"What is it?" the girl next to Kyle from Fun Math asks. "I'm not allowed to listen to anything but Christian music."

"It'll be okay," Mrs. Lowe whispers.

The song is unlike anything I've ever heard. It's about a guy who is trying to be who someone else wants him to be, and he realizes that even though they love each other, he can't fix the person, and the other person can't make him a whole person, either.

The music fades out and Mrs. Lowe says, "I'm going to play it once more, and I want you to think of a time that you felt empty inside and tried to fill that feeling in ways that didn't work."

"I thought we were talking about self-worth," the girl next to Kyle says impatiently.

"*We are.* Self-worth is about believing that you *as a person* have value. If you are depending on others to provide that feeling for you," Mrs. Lowe shrugs, "you're going to be just like a broken cup. No matter what other people say or do, it'll just leak out through the cracks in your self-worth." She glances at me. "People try to seal up the cracks in all kinds of ways."

I cringe and automatically run my hand over my lips as if there are still telltale crumbs from the box of store-brand Pop Tarts that I pigged out on before school. I'd pretended that I didn't know what she was talking about when Mom asked me if I knew what happened to the brand-new box of toaster pastries.

My head is so full of thoughts about how much I hate myself for eating like I do that I barely realize the song is ending again. Mrs. Lowe makes a T-Chart on the whiteboard with the headings "*Yes*" and "*No*." Under "*Yes*," she writes "Volunteering to teach someone to read." Under "*No*," she writes "Abusing alcohol or drugs."

She whips around. "Becca, give me another '*Yes*.' What's something else someone could do to increase their self-worth?"

She thinks a moment. "Um, singing in the choir?"

Mrs. Lowe writes "Singing or playing music." "What do you guys think? How could committing oneself to a role like singing in the choir lead to a feeling of self-worth?" She waits a beat or two, but no one responds. "Colby? What do you think?"

I shrug and run my finger over and over the metal coil on my spiral notebook. "I...used to sing in the choir, but it was pretty much because my parents made me. I mean, I like to sing, but not when I'm forced to wear a sparkly choir robe and hang out with weird kids who talk too much or smell like cat food."

Mrs. Lowe takes a few steps toward me. "So...you quit? How did your parents take it when you told them that you didn't want to be in the choir anymore? Standing up for oneself is a '*Yes*' for building self-worth."

My face is burning, and I wish I'd never opened my mouth. *What to say? How* did *I get out of* The Young Conservatives *choir? Even if I* wanted *to sing with them now, they wouldn't let me.*

When I finally do speak, I sound like Kermit the Frog. "We moved here, so that pretty much solved the problem."

Chapter Thirteen

I slide my lunch tray onto the *Nobodies* table at the same time that Ryan dumps out his backpack. His history book catches the edge of my tray, and my burger and fries go airborne. He doesn't even notice.

Anna jerks her food out of the way. "What are you *doing*?"

Ryan's freaking out. "I can't find my cell phone! I had it when I came to school, and now it's gone!"

I retrieve one of my fries from Sean's chili pie and wipe off the chili with a napkin. I don't even try to hide my irritation. "You're not the only one having a rotten day, Ryan. Maybe you can try not to make it worse by throwing a shit fit."

He slams his binder onto the table and our drinks erupt simultaneously, like lava from a volcano. He leans into me and sneers, "Want me to give another speech that'll send you running away again, like your dad did from those reporters?"

So much for his apology.

"Oh, yeah…" Sean says slowly. "I saw that video of your dad on Facebook, Colby. That's some cold shit, right there."

Anna hisses, "Sean!" I glance at her; her eyes are huge. "*Ix-nay* on the *ideo-vay*!"

I dip the fry in ketchup. "I know about it already. Kayley reenacted it for me when I walked into school this morning. Forty-six shares, I think they said."

Sean taps the screen on his phone. "Now it's a hundred thirty-two."

Anna accuses, "You're friends with those bitches on Facebook, Sean?"

Sean glares at her. "If *you're* not, how do you know about it, too?"

"Everybody does! I mean—" Anna grimaces and cuts her eyes to me. "Yeah, everybody does. Sorry, Colby." She turns on Sean again. "But you didn't have to bring it up right now! Jeez!"

"How else am I supposed to keep up with what's going on? Anyway, if I keep my head down and don't make waves, they leave me alone." Sean frowns at the look Anna gives him. "I know, I know: I'm a sheep. *Baaaa-baaaa-baaaa*."

Anna's voice drips acid. "No, you're a *fucking* sheep, Sean. A *fucking* sheep. If you're going to go with the crowd, then you *probably* don't belong at our table."

Sean stands up so fast that his chair topples over. "Oh, yeah? Since when did you become as much of an asshole as Kayley? At least she and Kara don't even *try* to pretend they're anything but who they are."

The shrill blast of a whistle silences the entire cafetorium, and Coach Allison bellows at us from his post across the room. "Is there a problem you need help solving? *Sit down*!"

Sean immediately sits; he slides down in his chair so far that I expect him to end up under the table. Ryan's still standing, and Sean reaches up and yanks Ryan into a chair.

Ryan reloads his belongings into his backpack. He mutters, "I had my phone on the bus…then in art, because I took a picture of the painting we're supposed to use as an example…then I got to math, and…*Shit*! I fell asleep!" He glares at me. "Did *you* take my phone? You sit next to me, so—"

I shake my head. "I was late, remember? I missed my first class because I was in the office."

"Well, did you see my phone on my desk?"

I shake my head. "Why would you have it out in class at all? That's just asking for Coach Allison to take it up."

Ryan's shoulders sag. "Aw, man. I'll bet he did. God, I don't want to ask him for it back. He hates me."

Anna is sympathetic. "What's your mom going to say when you tell her it's gone? *My* mom would throw a wall-eyed fit."

"Yeah, that's what mine's going to do, too. She just bought that phone about a month ago, and money's tight, just like it always is. I'm pretty much screwed." Ryan zips up his backpack, drops it to the floor, and puts his head in his hands. "So, so screwed."

It takes me a while to find my English class, and I slide into an empty seat just as the tardy bell rings. The teacher, Mr. Van Horn, has his back to us as he writes board notes:

Do you think it is a <u>sin</u> to have a child out of wedlock?

Is it a *crime*? Is adultery <u>a sin, a crime, or neither</u>?

Mr. Van Horn turns from the board and folds his arms, watching us stare back at him. "Well? Let's see some smoke coming out of those ears, people. Get your brains in gear, because I want to know what you think."

Mr. McDaniel appears in the doorway. Our eyes meet and he gives me a tiny nod. His eyes scan the classroom and land on the back row. He addresses the teacher. "Hey, Max, could I see you a second?"

Mr. Van Horn says, "Sure," then reminds us, "You guys be ready to discuss those questions when I come back."

Kara hisses from the back of the room, "Hey, *Hallister*, ask him to add *stealing* to the list of sins!"

Quiet laughter ripples across the room and one kid says, "Great video, by the way."

I know I'm supposed to be thinking about Mr. Van Horn's questions, but all I can think is, *"FML."*

Mr. Van Horn returns from the hallway. His eyes zip from me to Kara and back again, making me think that Mr. McDaniel filled him in. "Most of you probably know someone who is not married but has had a baby: That's having a baby out of wedlock. How is that different from adultery?"

Formerly-fat-Tina raises her hand. "Adultery is where you're married and you're fooling around on your wife or husband."

"Right, right, but what about if you're married and you haven't seen your husband in two years; then, you have a baby…What's that called?"

"That's called being a dirty skank," Fredrick says. "My brother's wife got with another guy when he was deployed in Afghanistan. He come home and she done had some other dude's kid. She's a skank."

"That's one way of looking at it," Mr. Van Horn nods. "But unless you're directly involved in the situation, you can't know all the facts. Is it possible that you can agree to that?"

Fredrick lowers his eyelids and shakes his head slowly. "That girl's a low-down dirty skank, and there ain't no two ways about it. Right is right and wrong is wrong."

Knowing that Fredrick helped Michael and José beat the snot out of Ryan on the last day of school, it seems ironic to me that he's such an expert on right and wrong. I glance at Ryan. He's got his forehead resting on his palm, and he's staring at his desktop.

Mr. Van Horn taps the word "*Sin*" on the whiteboard. "So, is having a baby out of wedlock a *sin*?"

"Doing it—you know—*it*—with somebody you're not married to is a sin," Becca says softly.

One kid blurts, "My parents aren't married!"

Kara's friend Sarah says sarcastically, "Braggart."

Mr. Van Horn makes the time-out sign. "Let's put this discussion in the context of mid-1600s Boston, where a young woman, Hester Prynne, whose husband is presumed dead, has given birth to a baby girl named Pearl. Hester has been found guilty of adultery, and ordered to wear a symbol that identifies her as what you guys would call 'a dirty skank' upon her chest forever. When the story begins, she's standing in the center of town on a scaffold—kind of like a stage—for three hours—so that her fellow citizens can make fun of her. Do you think that she *deserves* such a punishment?"

A tidal wave of raucous laughter comes from the back row. I turn just in time to see Kara grab a black cell phone away from another girl.

Ryan nearly jumps out of his seat. "Hey, is that my phone?"

Kara sits up straight and sneers, "No. Why would *anybody* want your phone? *Backstabber.*"

"That is *enough*, Kara!" Mr. Van Horn snaps. "Now, put your phone away or I'll take it up and turn it over to the office." He waits while she complies, then: "Anna, what do you think? Does she deserve that punishment?"

Anna grins. "Yeah, I *totally* think you should take her phone."

Mr. Van Horn looks like he might pop a blood vessel, but he manages to sound sort of calm. "No, I'm talking about our hypothetical young mother: the one who's been found guilty of adultery."

"Oh, right…well, what about the guy who knocked her up? Why isn't he in trouble, too?"

"That's a very good question, and one that I hope you'll all be able to answer by the time you finish reading *The Scarlet Letter*, by Nathaniel Hawthorne."

The class groans, and Mr. Van Horn's eyebrows shoot up. "What, you guys thought I just wanted to talk about dirty skanks and sex?"

Fredrick mumbles, "I was hoping…"

Mr. Van Horn snatches a worn paperback book off the corner of his desk and holds it up high. "You'll find sex, intrigue, and much, much more within these pages." He distributes a novel to each of us. "Page one, Chapter One! We're on the hunt for sinners, sanctimonious hypocrites, and sympathetic fools."

"—And skanks," Fredrick grumbles.

"Right..." Mr. Van Horn nods. "Although you just might be surprised at what you find when you know the whole story."

In the hallway after class, Anna hands me a slip of paper. "This is my phone number. Call me if you want to hang out sometime."

"Oh, cool, thanks. I don't have a phone of my own anymore, but—"

From behind us, Kara blares, "Hey, *Hallister*!" I turn, and all of her back row buds give a thumbs-up and yell, "*Like*!"

"No, Kara, it's *Loser*, remember? *Lose—er*." Anna forms an L with her fingers and sticks it in Kara's face.

Kara's friend Sarah steps right up into Anna's face. "Better watch out, bitch, or you'll have a fan club, too."

Kara shoots the girl a look. "Shut. Up."

Anna takes me by the hand. "Come on, Colby."

Tina steps in front of us; her eyes are huge. "I just want you to know that I didn't have anythin—"

Anna moves protectively in front of me. "Step off, bitch!"

Tina's jaw drops. "Anna, stop it! I've got to talk to Colby!" She leans around my self-appointed bodyguard. "Have you seen it? *Have* you?"

Anna cuts her off. "Look, Tina, I already told you once: When you chose *Abercrombie and Bitch* over the *Nobodies*, we were done."

Anna's dragging me away; I jerk my hand free and take a few steps back to Tina. "What are you *talking* about?"

Mr. McDaniel strides down the center hallway, clapping his hands. "Come on, people! Get to class!"

Tina reaches for me. "Just—just—I swear I didn't know, Colby. I don't really '*Like*' it; I just clicked '*Like*' so that I could see what everybody else is talking about."

Mr. McDaniel pulls us apart. "Now, girls. You can visit later."

My last class of the day is P.E. I show the grumpy-looking teacher, Coach Sharp, my doctor's orders to rest up for a few days. She jerks her head toward the bleachers, and I get the idea that I'm supposed to sit there while everybody else trudges out to the grassy area and goes through warm-ups. It's co-ed, and by the looks of most of the people, the school dumped all the nerdiest people into one class. The only people I sort of know are Becca and Sean, the scraggly-chin guy from the *Nobodies* lunch table.

I pull *The Scarlet Letter* from my backpack and start reading. I read through "The Custom-House," which is like an introduction to the story and is kind of confusing, but I do get the idea that the narrator feels super ashamed about his family participating in the Salem Witch Trials, and he's digging through old family stuff when he finds the scarlet A that Hester wore. He places it on his chest, and the fabric burns him and falls to the floor. Then he finds a paper that explains what the A was for, and he decides to rewrite the story of Hester Prynne. I close the book and wonder if the narrator ever wished he didn't know the truth about his family, too. Maybe I need a scarlet D, for *Destroy*, since finding that photo blew my family apart. Or, even better: *Disaster*.

I shake my head at the thought. I'm *wearing* my D: It's there every second of every day, even when I pull my sheet up under my chin so I can't feel it against my neck. It's what I pray to God to take away, even though it's obvious that God ignores me. I mean, really: if God really answered prayers, would my dad pretend we're all dead? Would I live in Piney Creek, Texas, in a shitty little trailer behind people who only let us live there because one of them felt sorry for us?

God's not going to make me normal-size, and any time I start feeling good about myself *in spite* of being a big fat disaster, my mom just has to look at me the way she does to remind me that my weight is everything to her.

I'm craving icing so badly right now that if Leah hadn't let us know last night that she needs us to work at Sugar's today, I'd be whipping up Dad's cake icing recipe at home. I'd just have to get rid of the evidence before Mom gets home. Drew's no problem; she always disappears into her room and plays her CDs. That's just about the only thing that hasn't changed since the day Dad walked out the door.

Being at Sugar's will make it easier: I'll fill a measuring cup with cake icing—not like it'll be missed, so Leah won't bitch about me eating her profits—and disappear into the bathroom to get numb. The thoughts are like electrical currents driving me toward the inevitable pig-out about to take place.

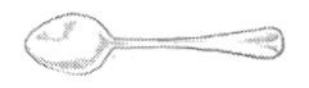

We board the bus. Ryan looks like he's been sentenced to stand before a firing squad. There's no sign of his phone, and if anyone knows who has it, they're not talking. I fall into the nearest seat and Drew shoots by me, tripping over my feet. "I get to sit by the window today!" I fight the urge to kick her. I slouch in my seat, close my eyes, and pretend to be sleepy, but Drew won't shut up. Her questions feel like a pesky mosquito interrupting my pig-out planning, and her voice is nothing but incoherent buzzing.

She taps me on the upper arm and babbles, "So, do you think so?...Do you?"

I jolt upright, knock away her hand, and snarl, "Leave me alone! I have a headache!"

She sits back abruptly, then turns her face toward the window. Within seconds, I hear her sniffling.

I know I should apologize for being such a bitch, but I don't. I close my eyes, sigh loudly, and wish we were already at Sugar's.

Chapter Fourteen

As we step off the bus, Leah meets us and sticks her hand in Ryan's face. "Give me your phone. Now."

Ryan blinks a couple times. "I was going to tell you, Mom! Wait a minute; how do you…?"

"*Now*, Ryan." Leah's chin is quivering, and her eyes are full of tears. "*Now*."

"I don't have it; it must have gotten stol—"

Leah turns abruptly and stomps into Sugar's, slamming the front door in our faces. Ryan and I exchange wide-eyed looks. "Wh-what the hell?" he stammers.

Drew puts a hand on her hip. "What did you two do *now*?" Ryan and I shrug in unison.

He twists the knob and pushes the door open slowly, like he expects somebody inside to yell, "Boo!"

I follow him in, still intending to make a beeline for the big bowl of cake icing that's always in the fridge. I'm actually kind of relieved that Ryan's in trouble; maybe nobody will notice when I'm in the bathroom a while.

The dining area is empty, and we can hear our mothers yelling at each other from Leah's office behind the kitchen.

"I'm telling you, there's *no way* that Ryan did this! He's the one who reported Jared for what he did. Do you *honestly* believe he'd do anything even *slightly* resembling it?"

"Who else could have done it? Do you think anyone else could have made that video?"

I step into Leah's tiny office; Mom immediately moves to block my view of the computer monitor. I reach for her arm. Mom and Leah exchange looks.

From the computer speakers, I hear, *Thud, Thud, Thud* and someone's soft laughter. A whisper: "What a fat ass."

Then, a woman's voice, maybe Leah's, from far away: "Ryan? Where are you?"

The whispering voice again: "Oh, shit!"

Rustling. Running.

Clearly Ryan's voice this time, a little breathless: "I'm here."

Then, Leah's: "What were you doing?"

From behind me in Leah's office doorway, Ryan gasps and stumbles back against the wall.

I pull my mother away from the desk, lean down, and stare at the banner photo across the top of a Facebook page: It's a blurry image of someone on her back—*oh my God*, it's me using a hanger to zip up my pants! The smaller profile picture is my face—but my eyes are half closed and my mouth's hanging open. When was that taken? The page is titled, *Colby Denton Fan Club*. Smaller print reads, "A page dedicated to my cousin, the *Fat Ass*, whose father is a two-faced cheating thief."

My hands are trembling, but I navigate the mouse to the first entry on the page: a video. I click Play.

The footage is shaky at first as the person filming it adjusts the camera so that it's lined up perfectly with the gaps in my bedroom blinds. There I am, jumping, stomping, and shimmying, trying to slide Tina's fat jeans onto my body. The *Thumps* are loud even from outside my room, and the camera shakes with the photographer's laughter.

"Dance, *Fat Ass*, dance!" whispers the voice on the video. It's Ryan. I know it is. I glance at him now, and all the color has drained from his face.

Drew erupts in giggles. "That's *you*, Colby!'

I shriek, "Get out of here, you little bitch!" Mom stabs her index finger at the hallway, and Drew complies.

I turn back to the monitor and watch as I fall onto my bed in my struggle. I stretch the hanger out until it's long and skinny. I don't remember making those grunting sounds. Outside my window, Ryan whispers, "Gross."

Leah reaches over, pushes the power button on the monitor, and the close-up of my face as I'm trying to roll onto my side instantly becomes a tiny white dot on a black screen.

She moves to Ryan, where he remains bent at the waist with his hands on his knees, leaning against the wall outside her office. Leah grips his upper arm and speaks through gritted teeth. "How *could* you, Ryan? *How dare* you use your phone for something like that! Hand it over, now!"

"I can't, Mom…I don't know where it is."

Leah blasts, "Don't give me that shit! *Where is your phone*?"

Ryan slides down the wall to the floor. When he finally speaks, his voice is choked. "I—fell—asleep—in class—today—and I think—Coach Allison—took it. Or…" He shakes his head and whispers, "It was stolen."

Mom is incredulous. "Are you saying that someone *else* uploaded the video of Colby to this page you started?"

He nods at the floor; then his head snaps up. "Wait—*what* page?"

Leah's voice is shaking. "Says right here that the page is dedicated to your cousin, the *Fat Ass*."

"It's not mine. I didn't do it." His eyes are pleading; he glances at me, then back to Leah. "Please believe me, Mom."

My mom says, "But you took this video of Colby, didn't you? You stood outside her window and filmed her as she dressed, didn't you?"

He takes a deep breath in and nods as he sighs it out.

"How could you do that to me?" I whisper. "Why do you hate me so much?"

Ryan shrugs. Leah tries to yank him up by the arm, but he remains on the floor. "Don't shrug! Answer her! Why would you do something so horrible? Is that the way I've raised you?"

He starts to shrug again but catches himself. "I...thought it would be funny. I wasn't going to show it to anybody...Probably."

I wobble on my feet. Mom grabs my arm and guides me onto Leah's office chair. She tries to force me to put my head between my knees, but that's worse than feeling like I'm going to pass out. I sit up and lay my head on Leah's desk instead.

"Delete it. Now. *Right now.*" Leah pulls me away from the desk and jerks her head at the computer. "Now, Ryan." He slowly stands, and she shoves him toward the keyboard.

Ryan leans down, pushes the power button on the monitor, and stares at the screen. "I can't, Mom."

Leah barks, "Why not? Just do it!"

"Well, first of all, I didn't create this page, so I don't know the password, and I can't delete the video unless I'm an administrator. Second..." He lowers his head and his voice is barely above a whisper. "The video's already been shared fifty times. Even if I could delete it, it's out there, and there's nothing anyone can do to stop it now."

Mom and Leah avoid each other while they both try to make this go away. Leah works at her computer, trying to contact Facebook to take down the *Colby Denton Fan Club* page. Mom burns up her cell phone minutes. She calls 911 to report the video, and the officer she's put in touch with tells her that it doesn't qualify as an emergency according to the Piney Creek police department protocol. So then she tries to call Dad, but he won't answer. Now she's talking to Mr. McDaniel, asking him for help to find out who did it (if Ryan really didn't). I can tell that she doesn't believe his story. Ryan swears that he didn't create the page or post the video online.

I *still* can't believe he'd film me through my window. So much for all their talk about "doing the right thing" even when it requires sacrifice.

My cousin and I are sitting at separate tables in the dining room. Drew's behind the counter, trying her hand at frosting some day-old cookies. I stare at the display case of cake pops and my mouth waters, but I'd never eat one in front of Ryan—or anyone else. I hate eating sweets in front of people; can't stand the judgy way they look at me and, anyway, seeing my rolls of fat bouncing up and down on a computer monitor has me coated in a thousand pounds of shame.

So far, no trip to the bathroom with icing like I'd planned, although I did go in there to barf just after Leah called out to Mom that the number of video shares is up to 122.

Still on the phone to Mr. McDaniel, Mom plops onto the chair across from me. She shoots Ryan a dirty look as she recounts Leah's efforts with Facebook to get the video and page removed. Ryan stands, shuffles to the big bay window, and looks out on the street.

Leah strides to the front door and flips the *Open* sign to *Closed*.

Ryan murmurs, "How did you find out about the video, Mom?"

"Well, all of this started around three o'clock, when Dulcie stopped in—I thought to show us the baby—but it was because her niece told her about the video. We were trying to find it on Facebook when Michael Taylor's mom came storming in to yell at me because *you* posted nudity online. That woman's got a mouth like a megaphone, so everybody's going to hear about it before long."

Leah pulls the broom out of the corner and sweeps the floor. "Of all the people to talk to me about parenting skills! Anyway, I wouldn't call that video 'nudity.' There's not much bare skin—at least not the kind you think of when you hear the word '*nudity*.' It's *sure* not the same kind of nudity as Jared sent out to everyone." Leah seems to realize how it sounded after she says it. "Um, I mean…it's still horrible." She glares at Ryan and yells, "*Horrible*!"

"I was in my room, with my door closed. I thought I was alone."

I say it softly, like I'm calm inside. But then I close my eyes, and liquid rage boils behind my eyeballs.

Mom wraps up her conversation with my principal. "I'll appreciate anything you can do, Mr. McDaniel. Thank you." She pushes End.

Leah joins us at the table. "Any luck, Sonya?"

Mom starts to reply, but her phone rings. "Hi, Rachel." Her voice is flat; she doesn't even try to put on her sunshiny voice. "Drew called you? When? Oh, never mind, it doesn't matter...Yes, it's terrible...Well, we're staying put for now. It's not like I have anywhere else to go..."

She glances at my aunt, who can't seem to look at her right then. "Anyway, Leah's...handling it...Yes, she really is. He knows he did wrong, I think." She sighs heavily, leans her forehead on her palm, and says through gritted teeth, "If Colby wasn't so fat, *none* of this would have happened. *Nobody* would ever think that watching her get dressed would be funny, if she'd just lose weight."

Leah gasps, "Sonya! *How* can you say that?"

News flash: the liquid rage behind my eyeballs is gasoline, and Mom just threw a match on it.

Two words: *I'm done.*

I'm. Done. I rise from my chair and casually walk toward the front door.

"Where are you going, Colby?" Leah asks in what sounds like her own version of Mom's sunshiny voice.

I sigh shakily; my throat is tight, and my voice is high and pinched. "I need some time alone. I'll be outside."

Mom's words scald me to the depths of my soul: *If Colby wasn't so fat, none of this would have happened.*

I step into the sunshine and become fixated on the heat rising off the asphalt. The sun's rays are rippling, dancing, and I see myself—stomping, shimmying, lifting one leg high and then the other, as I struggle to get those goddamned jeans on.

An awful awareness settles in and stays: Everyone knows. People are watching the video at this moment, and they are laughing at my disgusting body.

A car speeds past and catches a pothole. Thud.

Thud. Thud. Thud. What a fat ass.

My mind is buzzing with pain, electrified by my mom's words, and there, on the narrow walk in front of Sugar's, I am struck by a cyclone of everything that's happened since that day in my dad's office.

> *My father with his tongue down that woman's throat...*
> *Rachel shoves me away: "I hate you! If you hadn't found that picture..."*
> *"If Colby wasn't so fat, none of this would have happened..."*
> *"We need to pray for Colby."*
> *I'm hopeless. Hopeless. It's hopeless.*
> *"Hey, Hallister, where'd you get that shirt?"*
> *"The grand jury indicted Mr. Denton..."*
> *"Colby's a big fat disaster."*
> *Please, God, make me normal-size.*
> *"I don't want to be homeless!"*
> *What a fat ass.*
> *What a fat ass.*
> *What a fat ass.*

Honk!

I jump out of my skin, and the passing truckload of football players laughs. One of them stands and nearly falls out of the pickup bed when he imitates my shimmying jeans dance.

No more. No more. The forces that were driving me toward the cake icing just an hour before have multiplied times a million, and they're zooming toward a solution. *I'm out of here. I can't take it.* The tears I've held in since I saw myself in the video escape all at once, and a sob erupts that feels like it comes from the soles of my feet.

At that moment, I'm convinced that I am completely and utterly alone in this world. I doubt that my father loves me anymore, or if my mother ever has. I'm a fat, worthless wretch of a person who is done with this shit. *Enough.*

Even though I'm sure He's not listening, I say it anyway: "God, if You have ever loved me at all, You'll let me die."

I walk casually and stop in front of an old white house a few lots down from Sugar's. There's nobody in it; the place is for rent. It's located at the top of the first hill as people come into town. Leah's always bitching about how fast drivers clear the rise; it's like they don't realize they could run somebody over until it would be too late. I sit on the steps and notice a kitten that's been hit by a car. It's near the curb. Once in a while the warm breeze blows slightly and flutters the kitten's fur.

An idea crystallizes in my mind, and I know I'm going to do it this time. It's not the first time in my life that I've envisioned becoming roadkill; it's just the first time I've decided to give it a shot. I rise from the steps and stand on the curb, looking down at the dead kitten.

I dart out in front of the first car that clears the hill, but the driver jerks the wheel and avoids hitting me. He slams on his brakes and makes a quick U-turn, rolls down his window, and chews me out for nearly getting killed.

I pretend to apologize for being in the road and walk slowly back to the Sugar's parking lot. A few cars pass, but they're going much too slowly to really hurt me. I sit on the bench in front of Sugar's and bargain with God:

> *If You don't want me to kill myself, make a rainbow appear in the sky, like when You promised Noah that You'd*

> *never flood the world again. It's the least You can do for me: Look at the parents You saddled me with.*

There's not a cloud in the sky, and patience is not one of my strengths, so I give God one more chance to convince me not to kill myself:

> *If You don't want me to kill myself, make Mom come outside and apologize for saying that none of this would have happened if I'd just lose weight. I'll forgive You for my dad walking out on us, if You make my mother at least* pretend *to not be a heartless, horrible person.*

I scoot all the way to the end of the bench, lean to the left, and peek in the big bay window. Mom is sitting at the table, staring at her phone. Probably checking her text messages. Drew calls to her and she laughs, smiles, and stands.

She…smiles? How can she smile when a video of me is spreading like wildfire through the school? How can she smile with the same mouth she uses to say horrible things to me?

I give God—and Mom—one more chance. I peek in the window again.

Mom looks toward me.

Our eyes meet.

My heart skips a beat.

She takes a step toward the front door.

Relief floods my body: There *is* a God, and He is sending my mom outside to apologize to me.

I sit back on the bench and quickly dry my face with the neck of my shirt. I rub my eyes and take a few deep breaths. *I can forgive her, if she'll just say she's sorry for hurting me so badly. Maybe we can start over. She'll understand how much I need her to love me the way I am. And I—I can try harder to be interested in the stuff she likes.*

Maybe I'll ask her if we can start going on walks together. I might even lose weight. That'll make her happy.

Moments pass: I don't know how many, but the sun shifts in the sky. Bells chime from the Catholic church a couple of streets over. One...two...three...four...five.

We arrived at Sugar's around 3:30. How long have I been sitting out here? Maybe I'm supposed to look for the sign. I do a quick scan for a rainbow, but all I see are three black vultures circling.

Three's my lucky number; I'll give Mom a third chance. I lean over and look in the window again. She's moved behind the counter with Drew, and she's helping her decorate the day-old cookies. Drew holds up an iced cookie; Mom nods and smiles at my perfect little sister's masterpiece.

She's not coming.

A numbness—kind of the same fuzzy feeling I get from stuffing my face—spreads from my head to my toes, and I know without a doubt that I'm going to do it this time.

I walk purposefully back to the house for rent and wait for my chance. I can hear the low rumble of a semi-truck approaching the top of the hill. I step off the curb, and, just in case anyone's watching, I pretend be looking for something in the center of the road. My hair falls over my face, and I'm watching for the gleam of the truck's grill as it clears the rise. *Relief. No more. I can't take it anymore.*

I close my eyes. *Why did I have to be the one to find that photo? Why can't I stop eating like I do? Why does my mom hate me so much? And that video! Oh, my God, the video...*

The truck is getting louder; I spy an oil stain in the oncoming lane and step into the center of it. The road shakes; a hot wind gently lifts my hair from my shoulders, and I am frozen by the sight of the truck's grill coming straight for me.

The airbrakes squeal. I close my eyes tightly and hold out my arms like Jesus on the cross. Over the deafening roar, I think I hear someone call my name. I grimace, waiting for the truck to slam into me.

I'm hit, but it's not what I expected. I thought I'd be killed instantly, but instead I'm thrown sideways, and I feel no pain until I land with a *Thud* and a *Snap*. I'd swear that my lungs collapse. It seems that the screaming truck is upon me, and I expect to be hit again. I gasp and inhale a lungful of acrid, burning-rubber-tinted air.

I'm confused; I expected to see a white light and feel God's arms around me. *Am I on fire? My skin feels like it's on fire. Maybe I'm in Hell.*

Pounding footsteps, then a sound unlike anything I've ever heard before, like a waterfall of loss. A woman's voice: "Oh my God, oh my God! No-No-No-No-Noooooooo!"

Blackness.

I don't know how long I'm out, but it's as if I jolt into consciousness and see a half-full Coors beer bottle inches from my face. An orange and black beetle nearly smacks head-on into the bottle but veers around it at the last moment. I look back, up, and to the right and see the three vultures still circling against the blue sky. I face the beer bottle again and sharp stones and sand rub against my ear. I close my eyes. My left side feels as if I've been skinned alive.

Alive. *I'm alive.* My mind replays the moment I stepped into the road, raised my arms, and saw the truck bearing down.

I become vaguely aware of voices—of one voice in particular. Someone is wailing. There is an intense pulsing under my body.

From far off, I hear sirens. Then up close, footsteps and shuffling in the sand. Someone says, "Oh, my Lord, here's where the other one landed. Is this your sister, little girl?"

Drew yells, "Mama, we found Colby!" My sister's blonde hair is soft on my face. She covers my upper body with hers and whimpers, "Colby, are you dead, too?"

Dead…too?

I try to speak, but I can't. The baby-shampoo smell of Drew's hair mixes with that of burning rubber, and a jolt of terror zaps my body. I gasp and instinctively throw my right arm across her back, pull my little sister tight against me. *What is Drew doing in the road? She could get hit!*

Her voice is muffled. "Colby, I can't breathe! Let me go!"

But *I can't.*

Someone peels my arm off of Drew, and she pulls away from me. Relief floods my body when I see her face. "You're...safe," I sob.

Drew nods, her voice tiny. "Yeah, I'm okay. But..." She gazes toward the road.

But...what?

Drew bends at the waist and presses her face against my forehead. She kisses me again and again, says into my skin, "Oh, Colby, I'm so glad you're not dead, too."

I hear a woman's voice but I don't understand what she says. Drew slides back onto her heels and gets to her feet. I think I'll join her; I slowly roll onto my back and the pulsing beneath me explodes into excruciating pain. I scream, but it doesn't sound as if it's coming from me.

I look down at my left arm; it's bent all funny. I stare at it, try to wiggle my fingers, and sharp pain jolts all the way up to my shoulder. A blue print dress fills my vision and a woman says soothingly, "Now, now, baby, stay where you are. Help's on the way." She kneels beside me, slides her purse off her shoulder, and uses it to elevate my head.

That's when I see them.

Through the hazy heat rising off the road, Leah kneels by Ryan's body. She cradles his bloody head in her hands and it falls back, eyes open, staring at me. A stream of blood runs down his cheek onto her arm like he's crying blood.

I realize in horror that I'm here; *I'm alive*, because of him. *He knocked me out of the road.*

I gasp, choke on my own spit, and spew, "No, no, this can't be happening! This isn't what was supposed to—"

Drew calls out, "Mama! Here! Colby's arm is hurt!"

My mother walks slowly toward me. Her arms are wrapped tightly around herself, as if she's afraid to let go because her insides will open up and spill everywhere. She's shuffling like she's walking on ice.

I sob, "Mom? Is Ryan really...?" I choke on the word. I can't say it.

She kneels by me, but she won't look at me. Her voice is strangled. "He's...he's not good, Colby."

I slam my head side to side and kick my heels against the pavement. "Nooooo! Nooooo! This wasn't supposed to happen!"

Paramedics arrive with a stretcher and ask me to scoot onto it, but I demand, "Go help Ryan!"

The taller of the two won't look at me. He says flatly, "We're helping you right now, ma'am. Please cooperate by—"

I become enraged and not only refuse to get on their stretcher, but fight them tooth and nail when they try to apply a splint to my arm. I'm growling like a wild animal.

Mom gets in my face. Her eyes shoot sparks. "Colby Diane Denton! Stop making a scene and let these people help you!"

I roll my head and sob, "No, no, noooooo...just leave me here. Leave me."

They finally manage to get me onto the stretcher, but I won't lie still long enough for them to fasten the buckles on the straps. Finally, one of the paramedics holds me down by putting his body across my upper chest and pushing my head to the left. I watch, transfixed, as a police officer pulls Leah off Ryan's body while another cop tries to cover him with a blue sheet.

She escapes the officer's grasp and lunges for the ground, covers Ryan's body with her own, and weeps. His head flops to the side, his eyes on me. I freak out. It feels like my mind is melting, and I stop breathing just long enough to make the cop next to us wave his hand in front of my eyes like he thinks *I'm* dead.

Mom steps into my line of vision. "Don't look, Colby."

"You got her now?" the paramedic atop me asks his partner.

"Yup." He sighs. "Finally."

The paramedic carefully lifts himself off of me, and the gurney bumps toward the back of the waiting ambulance. Mom walks alongside with one hand on my shoulder and the other pulling Drew.

Chief Taylor stops the taller paramedic and asks, "Are the injuries on the boy consistent with pedestrian suicide? My officers think that the girl was trying to stop the boy from killing himself, but I want to get your take on it."

His partner answers, "That's for the coroner to decide. You know that."

Chief Taylor withdraws a notepad from his back pocket and repeatedly clicks his pen open and closed. "I need to ask your patient some questions."

The guy who had to restrain me snaps, "Can't it wait? This kid's ape-shit as it is, and she's teetering on full-blown shock."

The police chief acts like he doesn't hear him. He leans down to me. "What happened?"

Mom uses her no-nonsense teacher voice: "I insist that you wait until Colby has been treated before questioning her." She locks a stare on him and arches an eyebrow.

Chief Taylor returns Mom's glare as he flips his notepad closed and slides the pen into his front pocket. "I'll be in touch." He hands her a business card. "Give me a call when she's home from the hospital."

Mom and Drew follow the paramedic into the back of the ambulance with me.

I wail, "I'm sorry, so sorry. Please, please…oh, God, Ryan. Ryan, I'm sorry." I turn my face to the ambulance wall. I'm crying so hard that I start choking. I feel a sharp prick on my right arm.

The paramedic says loudly, "Colby, I just gave you a little something to help you calm down, all right, sweetie? You will start to feel like you're floating, mmkay?"

I shake my head, whisper, "You—you don't understand. Please, listen to me, I—"

He puts an oxygen mask over my face and gives the top of my head a little pat. My eyelids flutter, and a light buzzing fills my head. I'm very aware of the hiss of the oxygen, and my sister sounds like she's in a canyon.

"Why is Colby sorry, Mama? Is she in trouble?"

I force my eyes open, turn my face toward Mom and Drew, and I see a double image of my mother staring out the back windows of the ambulance.

Drew taps Mom's arm. "Is she, Mom? Is Colby in trouble with the police?"

My mother glances at me, shakes her head, and her face crumples. "No, why would she be? She can't help it if Ryan..." Her voice lowers to a whisper, "Killed himself." She leans forward and places her hand on my leg. "It's not your fault that this happened. You did your best."

I roll my head side to side and mumble beneath the oxygen mask, "Ryan—Ryan didn't try to kill himself...I—I was—" The restraints feel like they weigh a thousand pounds. I float out of them in my mind and whisper, "I—I've got to go. *I'm...done.*"

As I fade into darkness, I hear my mother's voice. It has an edge to it. "Are you sure you gave her enough sedative? I think she's in shock. She doesn't remember trying to save her cousin."

Chapter Fifteen

I awaken in the emergency room. I blink and try to focus on the bright lights above me. I roll my head to the side and gasp at the awkward shape of my arm, which is on a board covered with a blue cloth. I close my eyes and in an instant my mind is swirling with vultures flying overhead, the shiny steel of the semi-truck's grill, and Ryan's eyes, bloody and blue, staring at me.

A woman's voice, deep with an East Texas twang, says loudly, "Colby? Sweetie, we're almost done. Take in a deep breath for me."

I must not respond quickly enough, because she kind of shakes my right shoulder and says, "Hear me, Colby? Deep breath in."

I comply, and she says, "Good girl. We're almost finished. We're giving you just a little more medicine for the pain, okay, hon?"

I manage to open my eyes and try to raise my right hand, but it's tied down. I flex my fingers and feel tape and something stiff in the top of my hand: *an I.V. Just like yesterday, when I passed out from the heat. Maybe it still* is *yesterday, and this is a bizarre dream. I'll be glad when I wake up.*

Somebody fusses with the tubing coming out of my hand, and I watch as the nurse injects a needle into it. Whatever they put in feels cold; then I am covered in warm fuzziness.

I jolt awake and look around. There's a blue curtain pulled around the emergency room bay. I hear Mom talking on the other side of it. She sounds perturbed.

"Look, Reese, I just thought you'd want to know that your daughter nearly died today, and she has a broken arm...Well, I guess Ryan did it because he felt so guilty about posting a video of her dressing...Oh, so you *did* hear my message about it? Well, *thanks a lot* for calling me back...No, Reese, I'd never expect *you* to do anything about it. You're *only* her father.

"...Leah's in bad shape; how would you expect someone to be whose son just committed suicide?...She refuses to believe it; says he'd never do anything like that, and that there *has* to be more to the story...But he *told* us he felt like killing himself because of what he'd done to Colby.

"One minute he was sitting in Leah's office, and the next minute he left out the back door...We heard this awful noise, went outside, and saw Ryan in the road. Some woman found Colby just off the shoulder. Right now the police are saying that it looks like Colby tried to push him out of the way but slipped on some gravel and ended up...*No*, she would never do that!...Reese, you and I both know that even if Colby *was* trying to kill herself, Ryan would never be able to knock somebody her size clear off the road...*Because I know so*, Reese; she's gotten even bigger since last time you saw her..." Mom's voice fades as she walks away.

I close my eyes tightly and see Ryan's head hanging limply to the side, draped over Leah's arm. I try to turn over, but my arm is in a bulky splint. I grit my teeth and push my head back into the pillow. *So...I'm too fat to be saved.* Nice to know what she really thinks. *Well, the joke's on you, Mom, because I* was *trying to die, and he* did *save me. So there.*

Ryan's dead.

Ryan's dead.

I am alive, and Ryan is dead.

I killed him. I gasp and shake my head furiously. *No, no, it can't be.*

My throat constricts, and the tickly feeling of tears running down the sides of my head only makes me angrier at still being alive.

We arrive home late in the evening to find cars parked along the road and lining Leah's driveway. We meet Dulcie coming down Leah's front steps; she shifts her baby to one arm and hugs Mom first, then me, then Drew.

She pulls up the neck of her shirt and wipes her tears. "I'm so sorry, y'all. So, so sorry. I—I thought I couldn't cry anymore, but..." She waves her hand in front of her face. "I guess I'm not finished yet. My husband needs our car for his night shift, so I've got to go. Y'all take care of Leah. I tried to get her to call your in-laws so they can support her through this, but she absolutely refuses to have a thing to do with any of them. I'm so glad y'all are here for her; otherwise, she'd be all alone as far as family's concerned."

Her voice breaks, and it takes her a moment to continue. "I'll be back first thing in the morning."

Mom says, "Of course. Thank you, Dulcie." She watches her go and turns her gaze back to Leah's house. "I think we'd better get you home, Colby."

Drew's voice is high. "We're not going to check on Aunt Leah, Mama?"

Mom snaps, "No!" She looks back at Leah's house; someone in the front window quickly closes the curtains. "Colby's been through a lot. We need to get her into bed and elevate that broken arm."

An owl hoots and startles me, causing me to jump. I wince in pain.

"See, there? Colby needs to rest." Mom presses her hand into the small of my back, takes Drew's hand, and guides us to the trailer. In that moment, it almost feels like she sees me as more than just a big fat disaster. Maybe she *does* love me as much as she loves Drew and Rachel.

The next week is a blur. The doctor gave me pain meds, and I take them whether my arm hurts or not. Within thirty minutes of swallowing that little yellow pill, I can't feel my head. Even better than that, I don't have to remember that it's my fault that Ryan is dead. Mom keeps the pill bottle in her purse; otherwise, I'd take the pills all at once and be done with it.

I feel wired with anger, and it only subsides when I'm doped out of my mind. When the meds wear off, my thoughts are electrified by the desire to die. I'm surprised when the sun comes up each morning. Why does it bother?

Drew's second grade class makes Get Well cards for me. Her teacher, Mrs. Thurston, delivers them one day after school. "I noticed your mail came, too, so I hope you don't mind that I pulled it out of your mailbox for you."

Mom gushes, "That's so nice of you!" She's loving all the attention we've been getting, and she's even pulled her *You'd Love to Have Me for Your Best Friend* self out of storage. She thumbs through the mail. "Why, look, Colby Diane! Your sister, Rachel, sent a letter from Lewis & Clark College in Oregon!" Mom smiles at Mrs. Thurston. "Rachel earned a fully paid scholarship to Lewis & Clark. That's a private college, you know!" She takes a few steps over to me and hands me Rachel's letter.

I take the letter to my room and stretch out on my bed to read it. The first thing I notice is that it's dated the same day as what we're calling "The Accident."

August 28
C.-

Mom's been telling me what a selfish little bitch you're being lately. She didn't use those words exactly, but come on, Colby. Why would you let her buy four bags of clothes that <u>you knew wouldn't fit</u>? It's your fault that she had to buy all those new clothes in the first place! Hellooooooooo, it's called self-control, Colby. Lose some weight. If not for yourself, then think of Mom and what she's dealing with.

Speaking of that, giving yourself heat exhaustion and ending up in the hospital is just what Mom didn't need right now. If I were there, I'd sit you down and tell you to think of someone besides yourself for once.

Maybe you don't realize how bad things are for us, money-wise. I may have a full-ride scholarship, but I have <u>no spending money at all</u>. Dad doesn't send anything to help, and thanks to <u>you and your selfishness</u>, Mom has no extra money to send me, either. My friends whose parents can help them get to go out all the time, and I just have to sit in my dorm room. I've been trying to find a job, but it's hard since I'm taking fifteen hours of classes.

At least you can talk to Mom any time you want. I can't get a call through to her unless she's at work or sitting by a stupid Goats for Sale sign so that her cell phone has a signal. You've got it a lot better than I do, so grow up, Colby!

R.

I read the letter several more times. This *has* to have been sent early on the day of "The Accident." But knowing Rachel, she'd have put it in my casket if I *had* died, just to make sure that even in the Afterlife, I know what a wretched waste of flesh I am.

I slide off my bed, pull out my snack stash drawer, and withdraw a gallon-size bag of frosted cookies that I stole from Sugar's. I gorge on them until the pain medicine makes me so sleepy that I pass out on the floor.

Mom finds me later, and from the way she reacts to finding me with my face smudged with icing and cookie crumbs all over the place, there's no doubt that the *You'd Love to Have Me for Your Best Friend* version of Mom left the house at the same time Mrs. Thurston did.

When Chief Taylor calls to say that he's coming over to interview me about the day Ryan died, I immediately ask Mom for a pain pill.

She props me up on the sofa with a stack of pillows under my arm. Two seconds later, there's a knock on the door. She invites him in, then settles herself next to me.

Chief Taylor clears his throat. "Mrs. Denton, I'd prefer to speak to Colby alone."

Mom pushes back into the sofa cushions, tilts her head, and softly says, "No." She gives him her beauty queen smile, tosses her hair back, and crosses her arms. She's apparently decided to be charming instead of stiff. *Nice move, Mom.*

Chief Taylor looks a little surprised and drops into the chair across from us. "All right, then; Colby, tell me what happened the day Ryan died." He's got his pen poised above his notepad.

My pain pill hasn't actually kicked in yet, but I pretend that it's hard to keep my eyes open. I blink repeatedly and allow my head to fall forward a few times.

He leans forward with his elbows on his knees. "Is your daughter presently medicated, Mrs. Denton?"

"Yes; she's taking pain pills for the broken arm she received when she tried to stop Ryan from taking his own life. Your officer told me that it appeared that she slipped on some gravel. It's by the grace of God that she wasn't also killed. I would think you'd be honoring Colby for bravery instead of treating her like a suspect." Mom's words are blunt, but her voice is coated in honey.

He flips his notepad closed and asks gruffly, "Did you *see* it happen? Because I have a driver who said that Colby purposely stepped in front of his car. He didn't see Ryan at all."

Mom's eyebrows furrow; she turns and pokes my shoulder. This time, her voice is more sandpaper than sugar. "Hey."

I allow my eyes to close.

She does it again: "Hey! Wake up!"

I pretend it works. "Huh? What?"

Her tone is accusing: "He says that somebody saw you out in the street before Ryan was there. Is that true?" She's teetering on brand-new disappointment in me, and what's left of my soul shrivels up and dies a little more.

I make a face and speak slowly, "N-no, I was just sitting on the steps of that house for rent, thinking about the video that Ryan posted of me...Why would I be in the street?"

Chief Taylor flips open his notepad again and scrawls some notes.

"So, you did not enter the road until...when?" He narrows his eyes and watches me carefully.

I swallow hard and imagine how it might have happened. "Ryan just, like, showed up out of nowhere. He ran past me—past the steps, I mean—to the top of the hill and stood with his arms out, you know, like Jesus on the cross, and I said, 'Hey, Ryan, what are you doing?' and he said, 'Leave me alone. I want to die. I'm done.'

"I heard the truck coming and I was afraid he was going to get hit, so I ran toward him as fast as I could. I tried to reach him…and I was just about to knock him out of the way of the truck, when I slipped on some rocks…and the next thing I knew, I was on the side of the road with a broken arm."

He narrows his eyes at me. "The truck driver says it all happened lightning-fast, but he is ninety-five percent certain that you were in the road before Ryan was. The problem is, the driver had trace amounts of alcohol in his blood, so we can't take his testimony at face value."

Mom gasps. "You mean the driver was drunk?"

Chief Taylor shakes his head. "No, his blood alcohol level was too low to consider him impaired. It's just standard procedure to test commercial drivers' blood any time there's a fatality accident."

I feel the yellow pill kicking in: Woozy warmth is coating the inside of my skull and spreading through my body. I breathe in slowly and let it out. "I've told you what happened." I turn to Mom. "My arm hurts. I need to go lay down."

She stands, moves to the front door, and holds it open, signaling Chief Taylor that our interview is over. "You should be satisfied now. If you're not, then I don't know what you're looking to find here. It's not Colby's fault that Ryan was killed. She didn't force him into that road. He put himself there."

Leah has Ryan's body cremated, and Mr. McDaniel offers to hold a memorial service at the high school. The cafetorium stage is lined in funeral wreaths, and the place is so full of teenagers, it looks like lunchtime.

One kid after another comes up on the stage to speak about Ryan and what he meant to them: how he was so funny, and the way he was always there for them when they needed someone to talk to. I never knew *that* Ryan.

I wish I could quiz each speaker: *Excuse me, but did you bail on Ryan-the-Traitor after he reported Jared for raping that girl named Kimmie? Or did you keep having these deep, funny, meaningful conversations with Ryan-Your-Best-Bud?*

It's like a beauty pageant of mourning. Each speaker is just a little more broken up than the last one about the person so many people had labeled "The Friendly Neighborhood Narc" and "Snitch." But nobody calls Ryan any names at his memorial service. Nobody mentions that he got the shit kicked out of him on the last day of school, the YouTube video of the beating that immediately disappeared, or that when he walked down the hall they gave him the middle finger and mouthed, 'Fuck you!' behind his back. I keep an eye out for Mark, José, and Fredrick, but I don't see them. Doesn't mean they aren't there; I ask Mom for a pain pill about halfway through the service, so my mind gets a little fuzzy.

When it's over, I spy Kayley and Kara as we're walking to the car. They appear to be arguing, passing something back and forth. They notice us, and Kayley gives Kara a shove in our direction. Kara approaches Leah with something black in her hand.

"I found this phone in the girl's bathroom the day Ryan died. I wasn't sure whose phone it was, but somebody told me they thought it was Ryan's because his phone was, you know, stolen. Or something. So..."

Leah doesn't respond, and Kara throws her arms around her shoulders. She sounds like she's crying, but there are no tears. "I—I thought it might have, you know, pictures or videos on it that you might want to have since, you know, Ryan took lots of them. I mean, there's lots of them on his phone, I guess, I mean—I—I didn't look at all of them or anything...Anyway, I wanted you to have it."

"Thank you," Leah says woodenly.

She doesn't hug Kara back.

Anna and Sean drop in to see Leah after the memorial service, and she directs them to our trailer. I snuck an extra pain pill when Mom left her purse on the kitchen counter, and I'm resting on my bed waiting for renewed numbness to set in. When Mom taps on my bedroom door and announces that I have company, I try to wake up.

Anna gingerly hugs me and fluffs my pillows for me. "Hey, we miss you at the *Nobodies* table."

"You barely know me," I mutter. "It's like what you said about your shitty little school: How can you miss what you've never known?"

She looks like I slapped her. "Well, I knew Ryan, and I loved him. You're his cousin, so that means I care about you, too. Besides, if you'll remember, I took up for you when *Abercrombie and Bitch* were bugging you. I thought we were friends."

"Yeah, if you say so," I mumble. Anna's eyes flash, and I expect her to flip me the bird the way she does everyone else.

Sean fidgets with a rip in the knee of his jeans, making it larger. His hands are shaking and he chokes out, "It's...it's pretty awesome that you tried to save Ryan like that. Even though, you know, he still...died."

I glare at him. "That has got to be the dumbest thing anyone has ever said."

Anna leans forward. "I know you feel bad, but at least you tried. I mean—"

I cut her off and ask bitterly, "Did you '*Like*' the page, too, so that you could see the video that *Mr. Wonderful* made?"

Her eyes are huge. "Facebook took it down already."

I sit up; my head swims. "That's not what I asked. Did you *see* the video he made?"

She glances at Sean; they both look at their feet.

"Yeah, that's what I thought." I lie back onto my pillows and carefully readjust my injured arm. I stare at my lower dresser drawer and wish it still held my snack stash. It's gone now, though, thanks to Mom catching me with the cookies.

Anna blurts, "Look, we're here, okay? Yeah, we saw the video, but...we're here. It didn't change the way we feel about you. We're sorry about Ryan—about him dying...about *everything*. I can't imagine him doing something so dickish as making that video! Something must have made him do that—something crazy—because the person I knew was really sweet."

I choke out, "Like, if I wasn't so fat, he wouldn't have made it?" *Jeez, maybe I'm the only person in the world who thinks it's fucked up that my mom said that.*

Sean's voice is high. "What? No, man, that's crazy. Are you... What kind of drugs are you *taking*? Ryan made a mistake, okay? But he's not the one who uploaded the video to Facebook. He *couldn't* be." He sat on the edge of my bed. "I mean, look: when Ryan wanted to report what Jared did to that girl, *I* tried to talk him out of it. I told him that if he did it, he'd be bringing a *huge* shitstorm down on himself, and, boy, was I right...The thing is, Ryan *insisted* that he had to tell. Said he couldn't live with himself if he didn't. So...I guess what I'm saying is, even though Ryan fucked up by filming you through your window, I *know* he wasn't such a jerk that he'd upload it online. There's *just no way*."

Sean kneels next to my bed, like he's pleading. "Ryan and I were friends for years, and he'd *never* do something that cruel. I mean, yeah, Ryan could be a jerk sometimes, but he wasn't a heartless asshole or anything. Seriously, Colby." Sean's voice cracks and even though I refuse to look at him, I can tell he's starting to cry.

I sniff and say coldly, "Then I guess I don't regret trying to save him." *If everybody believes this story, why not go with it? The only person who knows the truth sure isn't talking. Hell, he's not even a whole* person *anymore. This could be my chance for a brand-new start,* if *people can forget about the Colby Denton Fan Club and my Fat Ass jeans dance. Now that I've had time to think about it, I'm not even sure I would have tried to save him if he had been trying to die.*

Moments pass with no one speaking. Sean unfolds himself and gets to his feet in the cramped space between my bed and dresser. Finally, Anna speaks up. "Look, we're going to go, okay? It's obvious that you don't feel like being around anybody, and we'll see you when you come back to school. I hope you feel better."

Sean scoots sideways until he's standing directly in front of me. I stare at the stainless steel chain draped between his belt loop and pocket, and I imagine wrapping it around my neck until I can't breathe. He says softly, "Peace out, Colby."

"Peace out," I whisper.

I took my last pain pill on Sunday around noon, and I'm dreading school without something between reality and me. While Mom's busy putting on her makeup Monday morning, I rifle through her purse, hoping that one of my pills might have fallen to the bottom of it. I find my iPod hidden in the zipper compartment. I take it out and slide it into my pocket.

There are two lint-covered Midol tablets under her billfold, but I don't bother swallowing them. Bloating and cramps are not my biggest problem.

I enter Mom's bathroom, lower the lid on the toilet, sit fully clothed, and watch Mom expertly apply eyeliner. "Can I please stay home just one more day? What if someone bumps my arm? The bone might get knocked out of place."

She frowns. "Look, Colby, I know you don't want to go to school and face all the questions. If people ask you about "The Accident," just tell them you don't want to talk about it."

I watch a wolf spider crawl stealthily out of the clothes hamper and sneak along the baseboard. "We're still calling it that? '*The Accident*'?"

She gives me a sideways look. "Out of respect for Leah, yes. The medical examiner could not conclusively rule Ryan's death a pedestrian suicide, and she still doesn't believe that he was trying to kill himself. You and I know what really happened, but we don't have to keep hammering Leah with it."

Mom fluffs her bangs with a brush, spritzes them with hairspray, and helps me to a standing position. She takes my face in her hands. "I've been thinking, Colby. So many people have expressed this to me in the last week, and…it's really made me realize that even though I dislike your food issues, and I *wish* you could find it in yourself to change, well…just knowing that you were willing to sacrifice your life for Ryan's has made me see you in a whole new light. Other people see you as a hero, and it has made me realize that you *are* a hero. *You are.*" She blinks back tears. "I don't think I've appreciated you for the selfless person you are until now. I am very proud to be your mother." She kisses me on top of the head. "I don't say it often enough: I love you." She gently wraps me in a hug.

It's all I've ever wanted.

Chapter Sixteen

Mom sends Drew and me out the door with instructions to eat at school. She's out of money, and we're out of groceries. Guess I shouldn't have eaten that entire box of Pop Tarts last week…at least not all at once. Good thing they're reopening Sugar's today, so Mom can make some money.

Leah's house is overflowing with prepared meals that her friends have dropped off in recent days, but I'd rather be hungry than go to her house for food. It'd mean I have to face her.

She's like a zombie, in a daze, mindlessly putting one foot in front of the other. The only person she really loved in the whole world is gone, and even though she hasn't said so, she must know that it's my fault. She *must*. Maybe I'm wrong about needing to wear a scarlet D for "Disaster." Maybe I need an M for "Murderer."

I try to tug Drew to our usual seat on the bus, but she insists on sitting in Ryan's old place. She scoots over to the window and uses her finger to write Ryan's name in the condensation on the glass. She draws a heart around it, then pulls her knees up to her chest and buries her face.

I stare at my feet and dread what my day will bring. Without the yellow pills to put my mind to sleep, it's whirring with images of the semi bearing down, Ryan's unseeing eyes, and Mom kissing me on the forehead and telling me that she's proud of me.

The electrified thoughts that make me pig out—or seek a face-to-face with an oncoming semi—are urging me to try again to die. I clutch my skull. Why won't the inside of my head be quiet?

Deep down, I know the thoughts are right: I don't deserve to live. I used to hate myself for not being beautiful like my sisters, but it's multiplied times a thousand now that I'm a lying sack of shit, too. Just like my father.

José doesn't do his "*Puta*"-kissy-face routine at me when he gets on the bus, and of course, Ryan's dead, so he can't call him "*Pendejo*"—"asshole" in Spanish—anymore.

Michael does his usual "I'm God's gift to the World" act as he bumps his way down the aisle, but his fans are very quiet today.

Mr. McDaniel meets me at the front doors of the school. He crooks a finger at me to follow him into his office. A lady I don't know is waiting for us.

"Have a seat, Colby," Mr. McDaniel says as he falls into his chair. "This is Mrs. Healey, one of our counselors. She's here to help make your transition back to school as smooth as possible."

I cradle my casted arm and lower myself into the chair.

Mrs. Healey places a hand on my shoulder. "I am sorry you've been through so much, Colby. Mr. McDaniel filled me in on what your family was dealing with before you moved to Piney Creek. I can't even imagine the sense of loss you must be feeling in light of Ryan's death. He was one of my favorite people in the world. A real sweetheart. You could say that I was his Number One fan."

I nearly ask, *"Are you serious?"*—But instead I mumble, "I didn't really know him that well. We…hadn't been around each other long enough to become close."

I look at my hands and sniffle, because here's the deal: People expect others to be a certain way, so they act the way they're expected to act—even if it's all bullshit. I learned *that* from my dad, and I have to agree with him: It's not easy. But if he kept it up for so long, I know I can, too.

Mrs. Healey's eyes fill with tears and she rubs my upper back, ending with a *pat-pat-pat.* "What can I do to help you deal with the loss, Colby?"

"Absolutely," Mr. McDaniel interjects. "PCHS is here for you."

This is what I *want* to say: *"You know what, Clueless People? Ryan videotaped me while I was dressing, laughed at me, and called me a Fat Ass. Because he did that, somebody—maybe not him, who knows?—posted the video on Facebook, and now everyone in this fucking school has seen my big fat ass bouncing all over the page. So, to tell you the truth, 'Ryan's Number One Fan' and Mr. 'PCHS Is Here for You'? I'm undecided as to whether he's that big a loss."*

This is what I *do* say: "Just...maybe...get some of the girls who were giving me a hard time about my dad to leave me alone? So I can get over...what happened?"

"I'm on it," Mr. McDaniel says. "I'd already spoken to Kayley and Kara about their behavior before, but I give you my word that in light of what occurred to Ryan, they have a new understanding about the need for compassion. Ryan's death has shaken the student body to its core, Colby. I think you'll see a kinder, gentler side of people now. That's the sense I get. What about you, Mrs. Healey, based on the counseling you've done since this tragedy?"

She nods. "Oh, most definitely." She turns toward me, puts her hand on mine, and says softly, "Your classmates are so *in awe* of what you did. I can't begin to tell you how many of them say that they would not have been brave enough to throw themselves in front of a speeding truck to try to save another person's life. There's no question that Ryan's death is unspeakably sad; however, perhaps because of what happened, your classmates will think about others more than themselves."

Mr. McDaniel speaks up. "Your heroism on that day is like a stone thrown into a still pond. It will have a ripple effect that no one can overestimate. Perhaps knowing that others consider you a hero will provide some small comfort to you. What you did that day will live on forever, Colby. There's no going back."

Mrs. Healey looks into my eyes until her face crumples, and she turns away to grab a tissue.

"Go on to class now," Mr. McDaniel says in a thick voice. He looks like he's about to start bawling, too. He scrawls out a pass and hands it to me. "We're here for you, so please don't hesitate to let us know if you need help."

I rise and move toward the door. My eyes are brimming with tears as it sinks in completely: If these people find out the truth, they will hate me just like my mom hates Big Fat Disaster Colby. I am fucked, and there's no going back.

I have to try again.

I have to die.

I hand Mrs. Clay the pass and move to my seat.

"Colby, come back here, please."

I awkwardly slide my backpack off my good arm, loop the strap over my chair, and approach her desk.

Mrs. Clay doesn't just eat rose petals; she reeks of them, too. Her perfume is so strong that my eyes burn a little, and I blink a few times. Her smile reveals frosty pink lipstick all over her yellowed teeth. Arms wide, she shuffles around her desk and envelops me in a suffocating hug, rocking me back and forth. At last she pushes away, but holds me by the upper arms. She cuts her eyes to the side. "Michael, come here."

From his seat front and center of her desk, he demands, "What'd I do now?"

Her voice fairly sizzles. "It's what you're going to do, Mr. Taylor: Given her injury, Colby is in need of a personal assistant. You, sir, shall be that person."

She notices that he hasn't budged and orders, "Get yourself up here now, Michael Taylor, or I will tell your father about the *marriage-y-juana* that you bought behind the field house after school yesterday."

He bolts out of his chair. "How do you?...Who told you?"

When she nods at me to return to my seat, the light reflects off her glitter-shadowed eyelids. She arches a penciled-on eyebrow in Michael's direction. "It was a lucky guess, Mr. Taylor. That's where your father bought his *marriage-y-juana* when he was my student." She moves so close to Michael that he backs up a step, and she plunges forward after him. For a moment, they appear to be dancing.

"I told you, Mr. Taylor: You are my personal project. I am determined to confirm my hypothesis: that you are *not* beyond saving. You shall prove the same to me by showing compassion to a person in need." She points a long pink fingernail in my direction. "Colby needs someone to carry her books, her lunch tray, and, perhaps, tie her shoes from time to time. You shall be Johnny-on-the-Spot."

Michael throws himself back into his desk so hard that it skids across the floor. He sneers, "What if I just pay someone to do it? Is that good enough to keep you quiet?" He punctuates the sentence with a snort and mutters, "Crazy old bag."

Mrs. Clay plucks a rose petal and holds it up to the light, studying it. She sighs. "Well, in that case, I suppose I'll have no choice but to tell your father about the headlights on the police cruisers that you shot out with your minions, Fredrick and José."

Michael jerks around in his seat and shoots an accusing glance at his teammates, whose eyes are as big around as CDs.

"Just do it, dude!" Fredrick whispers loudly.

José hisses, "Yeah, man up!"

Michael slides my backpack over his shoulder and asks, "Where to now?" He shoots lasers in Mrs. Clay's direction. She returns his bold stare and gives him a yellowed, lipstick-stained smile. He sighs heavily, rolls his eyes, and mutters, "Ugh. Fuck my life."

"I've got Coach Allison next: math class. But you really don't have to do this. I can manage just fine; I—" I reach for my backpack.

He jerks away. "Oh, no; no way! My dad finds out it was me who shot out those headlights, and I'm dead. I don't know how that old bitch found out about it, but I'm not taking a chance on her telling."

"What about Fredrick and José? What'll happen to *them* if he finds out?"

Michael shrugs. "Who cares?"

"You're not helping my case for redemption, Mr. Taylor," a crackly voice says from behind us.

Michael's eyes widen. "Let's go!"

He's halfway down the hall by the time I exit the room.

Anna is at her locker. She glances at me but immediately looks away. She's wearing a black T-shirt that's fabric-painted: "R.I.P. Ryan. We Love You!" I look around and realize that lots of people are wearing the same style shirt. I shake my head. Did Ryan realize how much his classmates loved him? Why would he kill himself? Then I remember that he did not, in fact, kill himself. Even *I'm* starting to believe the suicide story.

I doubt anyone will wear a shirt like that after I die.

Michael nearly knocks me over as he leaves Coach Allison's room. "I dumped your crap on your desk. I'll be back for it at the end of class. OkayOkayBye."

Coach Allison leans against the wall by my desk. I loop my backpack over my chair, unzip it, and withdraw a pencil and my workbook. I settle into my seat, trying to ignore the feeling of being watched.

Coach Allison clears his throat, and I follow his gaze to Ryan's empty desk next to mine. He looks at me with heavy-lidded eyes. "I just want you to know that I didn't like your cousin, but I wouldn't wish the choice he made on anybody."

He takes off his hat and holds it over his heart. "I guess that betraying people must've weighed heavily on him, and..." He sighs and frowns. "It's a damned shame." He shakes his head, puts his cap back on, trudges to the whiteboard, and writes "Unit 2, Exercises D, E, F, G. Due tomorrow." He returns to his desk and pulls up Solitaire on his computer.

I'm slogging my way through Exercise E when somebody taps me on the shoulder. I turn; a folded paper sails past my face and lands on my desktop. I glance at Coach Allison to see if he's watching, but he's asleep in his chair.

I unfold the note and read it:

> *Colby,*
> *I'm sorry about Ryan. I know who stole his phone. He's* <u>*not*</u> *the one who started that Facebook page. I know it doesn't matter now, but I thought you would want to know that he didn't do it.*
> *Tina*

I write back "*Who did it*?!" and refold the note. I pick up my pencil, slide out of my chair, and move toward the electric sharpener on the table near Tina's desk.

I glance at Coach Allison: still asleep. His head is tilted back, and his mouth hangs open. He snorts, looks wildly around, and barks, "Why are you out of your seat?"

I hold up my pencil and nod toward the sharpener. He blinks rapidly, surveys the classroom, then leans back in his chair and immediately falls asleep again. I toss the note on Tina's desk and return to my seat without sharpening my pencil.

Tina bolts for the door as soon as the bell rings. I grab my backpack and try to catch up with her; I just make it into the hallway when I'm jerked backward. "Oof!"

"Goddammit, are you *trying* to ruin this for me?" Michael yanks my backpack off my shoulder and slides it over his own. He nods toward Mrs. Clay. She's on patrol in the center of the hallway outside her room, watching us behind those thick glasses of hers. She gives Michael a little smirk and shuffles back toward her door.

I stomp my foot. "I need to talk to Tina. Follow her!"

"Well, *I* need to get to my next class, and I have to drop you and your crap off first, so where to?"

I'm still trying to watch where Tina goes.

Michael pokes me on the shoulder. "I *said*, 'Where to?'"

"Oh. Life skills."

"Jesus Christ; that's clear on the other side of the world from Ag! Hurry up!" He takes off.

I slide into my seat as the tardy bell rings.

Michael tosses my backpack onto the table, turns to Mrs. Lowe, and oozes charm. "Ryan and I had become close friends, so I'm paying tribute to him by helping Colby any way I can, but my next class is in the Ag barn on the other side of campus. Would you be willing to write a pass, please?"

Mrs. Lowe embraces Michael in a sideways hug. "That is so sweet of you to help her. I'd be happy to write an admit pass! You're Michael Taylor, right? Chief Taylor's son?"

He smiles in an "*Aw, shucks*" kind of way and nods.

She scribbles a pass and hands it to him. "Here you go."

Michael cuts his eyes to me and bumps his eyebrows up and down. I frown and shake my head.

Mrs. Lowe distributes a handout titled *The Life Change Index*. She strolls to the front of the room and says, "In the 1960s, two doctors conducted a study about the changes people had undergone over the course of a year. As a result of their research, they created a way of charting stressful events by assigning a point value to them; for example, moving to a new town or state is worth 62 points, while beginning or ending a school year is worth 10.

"As you know, we're working on meeting our needs in positive ways. It's important to understand the causes of stress so that we can choose healthy responses to it. You're going to assess the amount of stress in your life. Place an X next to any event that's happened to you in the last twelve months, and then total your score. You may begin."

Mrs. Lowe smiles at Becca, who I notice is wearing her usual plaid western shirt, jeans, and boots. I'm starting to think of it as her uniform. Our teacher slides into the chair next to me, leans over, and whispers, "How are you, Colby?"

I shrug and stare at the handout.

She nudges my hand. "I was at Ryan's memorial service. It was so nice to hear people speak well of him. He was in this class last year. During our investigation of family relationships, he shared openly about what it was like to live with an abusive person."

The photograph of Leah with a broken nose and handprints on her neck zips through my mind. I immediately feel ashamed for the way she was treated on the Fourth of July, but I try to keep my face neutral.

"I'm sure I'm not telling you anything new, I mean, since you're his cousin, you probably know about what they went through."

It seems like she's waiting for an answer, so I give her the one that seems to work: "I didn't know him that well...yet."

"Well, you hang in there, okay?" Mrs. Lowe gives me a sympathetic smile, pats my hand, and slides out of the chair to circulate among my classmates.

I stare at the *Life Change Index* handout and look for *"Asshole Cousin records video of Big Fat Disaster squeezing into impossibly small jeans,"* but apparently that's not a very common event.

I hear whispering and turn to see the boy who stared at my stomach hanging over my jeans last week. He's got his hand over his mouth, leaning over to the girl next to him. He glances at me, whispers, "Yeah, that's her."

I lower my head so that my hair acts as a curtain and spy on them. The girl sneaks her smartphone out of her purse and taps the screen. She glances at me to see if I'm watching, so I shift in my seat and tuck my hair behind my ear. I act like I'm studying the stupid-ass chart.

Mrs. Lowe's voice is firm: "Angela, no phones out in class."

She murmurs, "Sorry," slides her phone into her purse, waits for Mrs. Lowe to turn her back, and pulls it out again. Within seconds, she frowns. She hisses to the boy, "It's not there anymore. That sucks! I wanted to see it."

The boy breathes, "Yeah, too bad. It was awesome."

So, according to this *Life Change Index*, my life is more fucked than even I realized it is:

Parents are separated or divorced (90 points);

Personal illness or injury (broken arm: that's good for 80);

Death of a close friend (75…although, since we weren't friends and we weren't close, maybe I should only count 37.5 points for that one. Furthermore, maybe I don't suck at math as much as I thought I did);

Moved to a new town (62);

Change in financial status (58 points for my dad never sending us any money. *Go, Dad*);

Problems with friends (Is Anna really my friend? She won't be if she finds out the truth about Ryan. Oh, what the hell: 55 points);

Working while attending school (30 points, but working at Sugar's does provide me with cake icing, so that could balance it out…);

Began school year (10 points…although I've only been to school 2½ days so far, so does that really count?);

Drum roll, maestro? The grand total is…460, unless I knock off 37.5 points because Ryan and I weren't close friends, which leaves 422.5.

Mrs. Lowe claps her hands and says, "Time's up! Did anyone have a score higher than 250?"

I start to raise my hand until I notice that no one else is as fucked up as I am.

Mrs. Lowe gives me another of her sympathetic looks. "That's not surprising, Colby. Death of a loved one is extremely stressful."

Why does everyone assume that I loved him?

Mrs. Lowe hands out another worksheet: This one is titled *Long-Term Stress versus Short-Term Stress*. There are five blanks, one for each type of stress. "Okay, now complete this chart by describing your stressors. I'll be coming around to help you figure out if your stress is long-term or short-term."

I stare at the page. *What's the point? I'm not sticking around much longer anyway.* I raise my hand. "Um, may I please go see Mrs. Healey? She told me to check in with her if things feel too overwhelming for me."

"Of course, sweetheart." Mrs. Lowe scribbles a pass and hands it to me.

I give her a wobbly smile, then head for the hallway and make a left like I'm going to the counselors' office, but I cut down the first hallway on the right and duck into the girls' bathroom. I go into a stall, lock the door, sit on the toilet fully clothed, and put my head in my hands.

I hear footsteps and lift my feet so that I'm hidden. Someone tries to open my stall door, but they find it's locked.

The person hisses, "Shit," and goes into the other one instead. I guess whoever was in there before didn't flush, because she groans, "Grossssss," and pushes the handle. I wait for the usual bathroom sounds to happen, but instead I see knees on the floor, and soon I hear gagging, dry heaves, and spitting. It finally ends, and the toilet flushes. The stall door flies back against the wall. I leave my hiding place atop the toilet and peek out between the stall wall and door.

It's Tina. She's splashing water on her face and rinsing out her mouth. I open the door and step out. She straightens and sees me in the mirror but immediately looks away.

I ask, "Are you sick?"

She focuses on the running water. "Um. . .yeah, I think it's something I ate."

I move beside her at the sinks. "Who did it?"

She gives me a funny look. "Huh? Oh, we had, um, eggs for dinner last night, and—"

I set my jaw. "No, that's not what I mean. Who made the Facebook page? Your note said that Ryan didn't do it and that you know who stole his phone. So? Who did it?"

Tina pumps soap into her palm, runs a little water over her hands, and rubs them together. "Just—all you need to know is that *he* didn't do it, okay?" She rinses her hands, shakes them off, and moves to the air dryer.

I step forward. "No; not okay." I reach for her shoulder and kind of pull on it.

She jerks away like my hand is on fire. "Don't touch me, Colby. I'm not going to tell you. I can't."

The liquid rage boils inside me. "Tell me who made that page, Tina." My throat's getting tight and I feel myself starting to cry, which makes me even angrier. "It's not fair! Do you get that? It's—not—fair!" I shove her hard.

"What are you girls doing in here?" Coach Sharp's voice cuts through the blasting air dryer. She's standing in the doorway with her hands on her hips and a scowl on her face.

Tina glances at me. "I was…sick, and Colby was…checking on me." She tilts her head and gives me a warning look.

Coach Sharp narrows her eyes. "That's not what it sounded like from out in the hallway, ladies."

I rub my hand over my cast and stare at my feet. My heartbeat is pounding in my ears, and the air dryer's whining like it's stuck on. Something about it echoes the roar of the semi, and Ryan's bloodied face whizzes through my mind.

"You girls get to class," Coach Sharp says gruffly. She makes clear that she's waiting for us to leave, so we walk out ahead of her. I pull the hall pass out of my pocket and find that it's soaked through with my sweat.

I go back to life skills class. Mrs. Lowe is at the board, outlining the four stages of stress: alarm, resistance, adaptation, and exhaustion.

I put my head down on the table, and even though I've pretty much sworn off bothering to ask God for even the simplest things, I offer up a prayer that He'll please make Ryan's bloodied face disappear from my mind and never come back again.

Michael's a no-show after life skills. I feel stupid, standing there holding my own backpack while waiting for him to arrive to carry it for me, so I head for lunch.

I'm standing outside the exit door of the cafetorium food line, watching for Tina, when my very own personal assistant emerges, carrying a tray of food. "Oh, my God, *there* you are. When I made it to your classroom after Ag, you were gone." Michael shoves the tray of food at me. "Here…Oops, I'm supposed to carry it. Where do you want it?"

I make a face. "That's *your* lunch—"

"I know, but I can get another one." He tilts his head toward the long table at the back of the room where all the teachers eat and speaks through gritted teeth: "Crazy Miss Clay is watching us. Tell me where you want to sit. Now!"

Just then, Tina emerges with Kayley and Kara. I order, "Follow them."

"Seriously? *Those* are your peeps? I had no idea."

"Sure," I say sarcastically. "Didn't you know that we're best friends?"

He shrugs but does as I ask.

Kayley's eyes widen when I slide into the chair opposite Tina, whose lunch tray is overflowing with pizza, chips, cookies, and fries. Her head's down and her hand is set on "shovel."

Kara's right next to me, but she's so focused on Tina that she hasn't even noticed. "Jeez, girl, did you leave any for the last lunch group? I thought you didn't eat that kind of stuff anymore. Aren't you afraid you'll turn into *El Tubbo* again?"

Tina speaks through her food but doesn't look up. "I'm just hungry, that's all." I'm vibrating with anger that she knows who made the Facebook page but refuses to tell me. She may be determined to focus on her food, but I've made up my mind that I'm going to get an answer.

I have a pretty good idea and I go for it, setting my sights directly on Kara. "Sooo, you found Ryan's phone in the bathroom, huh?"

Kara's head snaps to the left. "Huh? Oh. Hey, *Hallis*—I mean, Colby. Um, yeah." She looks away, and redness starts in the center of her neck, then crawls toward her head. "Yeah, it's like I told Ryan's mom. I found it in the bathroom. On the sink."

I tilt my head. "Tina says she knows who made that Facebook page...you know, the *Colby Denton Fan Club*." My voice is shaking, along with my insides. I look down at the food on my tray and start to pick up a French fry, but my hand is trembling too much.

Kara shoots lasers at Tina, who is too busy gorging herself on cookies to notice, then turns the hateful look on me. She gets it right back. "Are you trying to say that *I* made that page?" She bares her bucked teeth and wrinkles her rat-like nose. "I wouldn't waste my time creating anything with your name *or* your fat ass on it." She leans in so close to me that I can see where she has plucked away what would be a unibrow. "Want to know what I think, Colby?"

My anger-fueled confidence vanishes, and I'm hyper-aware of my overwhelming fatness in comparison to her. I say nothing; my heartbeat is thundering in my ears.

Kayley leans forward, grips Kara's forearm, and speaks in a singsong warning tone: "Hey, K-K, don't forget what Mr. McDaniel said..." She waits for Kara to meet her gaze, but she won't. "Hey. K-K—"

Kara shakes free and turns her upper body until it mirrors mine. It feels like my mass is casting a shadow on her small shape, like an eclipse.

She whispers, "I think the biggest tragedy of all is that you weren't killed alongside your asshole cousin." She pulls her lips back over her buckteeth into a horrible smile and nods slowly, watching my reaction. "*Everybody* feels that way, *Hallister*. They're just acting like they care because Mr. McDaniel held this tear-jerker of an assembly and told us that when you came back to school, we'd better"—she throws up air quotes—"show compassion, or else." She snorts. "*As. If.*"

I finally find my voice, even though it's only a whisper: "You're a miserable bitch, Kara."

Suddenly, Tina pushes back from the table and runs for the hallway. I bolt after her, partly to escape Kara and partly to demand that Tina confirm my suspicions. She dashes into the bathroom, and I'm hot on her trail.

Tina chooses a stall with a faulty lock, and the door swings open just as she deposits her lunch into the toilet.

I step forward. "Are you o-ka—"

She violently wretches again: her shoulders rounded, her back a perfect curve. A moment later, she reaches up and flushes the toilet.

My voice echoes off the walls. "Tina? Do you need me to get the nurse?"

Still kneeling on the floor, she shakes her head furiously and says weakly, "No—no. Just—just get out. Leave me alone." She wobbles to a standing position and moves to the sink, bends down and rinses her mouth under the tap. She repeatedly runs her hand over her mouth, echoes of my own strange habit. She might be half my size now, but in that moment, I know who she is: *Tina is me.*

"It's gone," I say. "There's no evidence."

She furrows her brow. "Huh?" She turns to the mirror and closely examines her face.

"Nothing." I turn toward the door to go, but stop and pivot back. "I'm not going to ask you anymore. I know why you won't tell me that Kara made that page."

Tina's face is ghostly white, and beads of sweat on her forehead are visible in her reflection in the mirror. She closes her eyes. "I can't do this with you right now."

I take a step toward her. "It's because if you tell the truth, you'll lose Kara as a friend, and you'd rather keep things the way they are than be alone again. Right?"

She shrugs. Then nods.

I move to the wall by the sinks and lean against it. "Can I ask you something else?"

Tina places her forearms on the edge of the sink and bends until she's practically folded in half. "Why not?" Her voice is rough, like she has sandpaper in her throat.

"Is this how you did it? How you lost eighty pounds? You know...throwing up?"

She nods. "Not at first. And...I don't do it very often. Well...I try not to do it more than once a day. It's just...I...I can't gain it back. I can't go back to being like—" She catches herself, stops.

"Like me." I step forward. "You can say it. You don't want to be like me. A big fat disaster."

Tina straightens and turns to me. The sunlight through the high horizontal windows perfectly captures the shadows under her eyes. She swallows and grimaces in pain; clutches her throat. "Right," she says hoarsely. "I can't do that."

Michael paces behind my empty spot at Kayley and Kara's table. He's got my backpack over his shoulder. *Abercrombie and Bitch* are nowhere to be seen. He sees me approaching, and his eyes flash. "I *demand* a copy of your schedule. I have no idea where to dump your stuff, and I can't be waiting around all the time just because you've got some kind of bullshit girl drama going on."

I say nothing; just turn on my heel and head for Mr. Van Horn's room.

Michael easily catches up. "So? You're going to give me your schedule, right? If I have to do this, it shouldn't be an inconvenience. There's probably some kind of rule against—"

I root my feet to the floor, but Michael keeps moving. It takes him a second to notice that I'm not beside him. He stomps back to me. "Seriously? What is this, some kind of conspiracy to make me late to every class?"

"Why'd you beat the snot out of Ryan on the last day of school?" It's like somebody else is saying it, even though I know it's me.

His jaw drops, but he quickly recovers. "Wh-who told you I did that? Did Ryan tell you that? Because if he did—"

"If—what? What can you do to him now?"

Michael's mouth is moving, but no sound is coming out.

I feel my bravery waning, and I stare at the logo on his shirt. "Why'd you do it? And, besides that, why did you have to post the video of the whole thing on YouTube? I mean, wasn't it enough to just beat him up? Why'd you have to try to let everybody else in the world watch, too?"

Michael allows my backpack to slide down his arm to the floor. "Know what?" He bends down to me, and all I can see is his finger in my face. "*Get fucked, Colby.* I don't have to put up with this shit." He whirls on his heel and walks away, still babbling. "I don't have to put up with this. There are *rules* against this shit. There are *laws* against making me be a slave for a fat ass bitch. I'm *sure* there are…"

The second I walk through the door, Mr. Van Horn hands me a copy of *The Scarlet Letter* with a list of make-up assignments tucked inside it. "The class is through Chapter 6," he says. "You'll need to read and catch up. You should be able to complete today's assignment even without reading, though. If you need it, take a week to get your make-up assignments to me." He turns away and starts writing notes on the board, abruptly stops, and puts his hand on my shoulder. "I'm sorry about Ryan. If there's anything I can do, please let me know."

I nod and move to my desk. Fredrick calls from his seat a few rows over, "*Where's* your helper? *Why* isn't he carrying your stuff?"

"He quit." I unzip my backpack and pull out my binder. I'm reading over the list of assignments when I look up to find Fredrick standing next to me.

He places his palms flat on my desk and leans into me. "What you mean, 'he quit'? He can't quit!"

I frown and whisper, "You need to take that up with him, because he told me to get fucked and walked away."

Fredrick's eyes are huge. He straightens, takes a step back, and swipes the air at some imaginary target. "He don't get to quit! Ma-a-a-a-n, he *don't* get to quit. My granny finds out 'bout that stuff and, *m-a-a-a-a-a-n*!"

"Take your seat, Fredrick," Mr. Van Horn calls. "We're getting started."

Fredrick saunters back to his seat. He swipes the air again and shakes his head. "I'll—I'll talk to him." He nods, reassuring himself. "I'll talk to him about this. He don't get to quit. He don't. It ain't all about him. Nope."

Mr. Van Horn observes dryly, "Good to know you're a problem-solver, Fredrick."

He circles to the front of his desk, leans against it, and crosses his arms. "We know that at this point in *The Scarlet Letter*, Hester Prynne is an outcast. She lives among others in her community, but they have little to do with her other than to treat her like a social pariah. She is struggling to raise her daughter, Pearl, who refuses to conform to the expectations of her mother *and* what the society of that era defines as normal behavior. Meanwhile, Hester has decided that she will stay in the village where her sin took place, and try to purge her soul.

"Jonathan Edwards was a famous Puritan minister in the 1700s. When he was nineteen, he created a list of *Resolutions* to live by. Not the same type of New Year's resolutions that we tend to make today, like paying off bills or working out more. His *Resolutions* were about living a life to please God with regard to relationships, how people treated their bodies, their attitude toward life, and so on." He pulls the projector screen down, moves behind his desk, and taps a few keys on his computer. Within seconds, a list appears.

Mr. Van Horn moves to stand beside the projector screen and points to the list. "These are some of Jonathan Edwards's *Resolutions for Young People.* He considered the list a 'life code,' and it's something that a person in Hester Prynne's situation—or any young Puritan of the time—might very well have tried to live by. This is only a partial list; there are seventy *Resolutions* in total. Once a week, Jonathan reviewed all seventy to see how he was doing.

"Your mission is to study this partial list, choose one of the *Resolutions*, and pay special attention to keeping it over the next week. One week from today, you will report on your progress in keeping the *Resolution* you chose. I'll give you fifteen minutes to free-write in your journals about why you think your *Resolution* will help your life. Be ready to share which you chose and why. Ready?...Go."

I begin reading:

> *Resolved, never to DO, BE, or SUFFER any thing in soul or body, less or more, but what tends to the glory of God.*
>
> *Resolved, never to lose one moment of TIME, but to improve it in the most profitable way I possibly can.*
>
> *Resolved, to maintain the strictest temperance in eating and drinking.*
>
> *Resolved, to live with all my might while I do live.*

Resolved, never to do any thing, which I should be afraid to do if it were the last hour of my life.

Resolved, to think much on all occasions of my own dying, and of the common circumstances which attend death.

Bingo! I don't need to read any further.

Mr. Van Horn calls time and starts asking people to share their *Resolutions*, whether they raise their hands or not. I'm relieved when I'm not asked to share my choice: *To think much on all occasions of my own dying.* Stepping in front of a speeding truck didn't turn out the way I wanted it to, so I need to figure out a for-sure way to off myself.

Then again, maybe I don't *have* to do it. I mean, I'm making it through this first day back, and my teachers are being pretty nice. Maybe I can make up with Anna and have a spot at the *Nobodies* table again. Maybe all this Ryan stuff will fade away, and it won't matter so much that he was trying to save me, not the other way around.

"Colby?"

I snap back into awareness.

Mr. Van Horn taps my desk. He's standing right next to me, and I just noticed something: He smells really good. "What do you think of Becca's *Resolution*?"

"Um..."

"You weren't listening, were you?" He flips through a couple of blank pages in my journal. "And, you didn't write anything during free-write time, did you?"

I shake my head and feel my face burning.

"I know it's difficult, but try to pay attention and participate, okay? You missed out on a week of study, and we're not just talking about the *Resolutions* right now; I'm also connecting them to the novel." He taps on my desk again. "Can you try to tune in for me?"

He gives my shoulder a little squeeze and moves on.

From behind me, I hear whispers, and someone giggles. It may not have anything to do with me, but suddenly I'm uber-aware of my size, and my double chin is sticky against my neck. In my mind, I see Mom's disappointed look. I try to replace it with the way she was this morning when she kissed me and said that she sees me differently now. *As long as she doesn't find out the truth, I can do this. I can keep this secret for as long as I need to.*

I feel a little hopeful then, and I tune back in to the discussion. Maybe I'll change my *Resolution* to the one about eating right. Wonder how much weight I could lose in a week? I could eat barely anything. Then Mom will be really proud.

It could happen.

Chapter Seventeen

I'm heading to P.E. class, and I hear clop-clopping footsteps approaching quickly from behind me. Boots.

Becca appears at my side. Doesn't say anything; just clop-clops next to me. I give her a sideways glance. She's got her chin tucked into the top of her notebook, staring straight ahead.

I walk a little faster, and she does the same. We're rounding the corner to go out the double doors to the gym when she reaches out and grabs my right arm. "Colby—stop. I need to talk to you about what happened the other day."

I shake her off. "We're going to be late, and even though I can't dress out, I don't want to be—"

She moves to block the doors and rapidly shakes her head. "No. This is important. I've got to tell you something about my best friend."

I snap, "Look, I'm really happy for you that you have a best friend. *How nice* for you to feel so safe and have someone to trust. Now move out of the way, or I'm moving you."

Becca says loudly, "It's not about life skills class, Colby. It's about when you tried to kill yourself."

"What?" I look around to see if anyone else heard. I lean in close and whisper, "What are you talking about? I didn't try to kill myself. Ryan was…Look, I saved *him*. I mean, I *tried* to save him. Didn't you hear the story?"

She purses her lips and shakes her head slowly. "Stop lying, Colby. You and I both know that you tried to kill yourself. Now, about my best friend—"

The tardy bell rings and I sigh heavily. *FML.* "Seriously, Becca? You think I give a shit about your best friend? What does she have to do with me trying to kill myself? I mean, *that* didn't even happen, so…"

Her mouth falls open. "How can you *say* that? How can you lie about Ryan? If it weren't for him, I wouldn't still *have* a—"

"Stop it!" The urge to spit on her is almost more than I can stand. I take a deep breath in, blow it out, and hold up a hand in surrender. "I'm going to go park my fat ass on the bleachers and watch the rest of you run around and sweat. Nice talking to you."

She doesn't move. Instead, she locks her eyes on mine. "I saw you in the street."

My heart drops through the soles of my feet; I feel like I've been punched in the chest. I try to speak, but no sound comes out.

Becca clutches her notebook so tightly that her knuckles are nearly white. "My grandpa owns the white house on the hill. We were cleaning it that day, getting it ready for new tenants. I *saw* you through the window. You were sitting on the front steps. You ran out in front of a car, but it didn't hit you. The driver turned around and yelled at you."

My throat is tightening, and I feel like I'm going to pass out. Becca moves away from the doors to a bench on the opposite wall. "Do you want to sit?" she asks. "You're really white."

I shake my head. My feet are cemented to that place in the hallway. I try to swallow, but I can't.

Becca continues, her voice barely above a whisper. "You disappeared for a while…maybe thirty minutes; maybe longer. My mother and I were about to leave. She picked up her purse and stopped to rub a smudge off the window, when she saw you in the street. You were like this." She places her notebook on her lap and spreads her arms like Jesus on the cross.

I hear a noise—like a puppy whining—then I realize it's coming from me. I stumble backward but am stopped by the gym doors.

"I threw open the front door to yell at you just as Ryan came running around the corner for all he's worth." Becca's eyes fill with tears. "I've never seen anyone run that fast. That truck was bearing down on you, and he didn't even *hesitate.* He slammed into you, and then the truck…" She closes her eyes, and her mouth is a straight line. Her face crumples, and she bends at the waist until her upper body is resting on her notebook. Her shoulders shake like she's sobbing, but there is no sound.

I'm standing in the hallway watching Becca cry over my cousin, but a video zooms through my head: Ryan's bloodied blue eyes are staring at me. His head is stuck at a right angle to his neck.

Becca's voice draws me back. "I—I couldn't move. I've never *seen* anyone get killed. My mama ran outside. Suddenly, there were people everywhere. Your little sister was wandering around looking for you. Mama took her by the hand, and they found you knocked clear of the road, just off the top of the hill. Mama put her purse under your head."

I gasp; realize that I've been holding my breath.

Becca runs her hands over her face to wipe away the tears. She looks me so deep in the eyes, it's like she can see my soul. "Ever since that day, I've been hearing about what a hero you are. I went to Ryan's memorial service, thinking you would let people know who the hero really was."

Her words are harsh, but her voice is soft. She uses her index finger to trace the edges of a photo in her clear plastic binder cover. She holds it up for me to see a girl who looks very much like her, but with long, straight hair. She's wearing a shiny pink fringed western shirt, white cowboy hat, and a *Rodeo Princess* sash.

Becca chokes out, "This is my cousin, Kimmie Schuler. Jared Moore raped her, then sent out photos and videos of…" She loses control of herself and can't seem to catch her breath.

I step to her, put my hand on her shoulder, and say softly, "I'm sorry about your—"

She shakes her head rapidly; holds up a finger for me to wait. It seems like it takes a long time, but it's probably not even a minute later when she sobs, "*Your cousin*, Ryan, is the *only* person who had the guts to turn him in to the police!"

I struggle for an answer. "I'm really sorry that that happened to Kimmie, Becca...but me telling the truth about Ryan's death isn't going to do anything to bring him back." I turn toward the gym doors.

She blasts, "Nobody else took up for Kimmie, but Ryan did! If it weren't for him—"

I whirl on her and plead, "You made your point, okay? Now just drop it!"

She shakes her head rapidly. "I *can't* leave it alone. Ryan didn't kill himself, and it's not fair to his mama for everybody to think he did."

My voice is squeaky-high. "Are you going to tell what you saw?"

Becca covers Kimmie's photo with her palm and looks up at me. "That depends. Are *you* going to tell the truth?"

"I...You don't understand, Becca. If you...Everyone will *hate* me if they know it's my fault that Ryan died!"

Becca stands and squares her shoulders. "Kimmie is my best friend in the world. She blames *herself* for what happened to her, and that's wrong. All summer, she was in and out of the hospital—the kind for people who are in so much pain that they don't even want to live anymore. The only thing that's giving her hope is the fact that Jared Moore is locked up and he's going to be tried for what he did to her. If it weren't for Ryan, Jared would have gotten away with it."

She comes so close to me that I can see the flecks of gold in her green eyes. Her voice is flat, and she's a far cry from the girl who wouldn't meet my eyes the first day of school. "Ryan is the *only* reason that rotten piece of shit is in jail. I'm giving you until 5:00 P.M. tomorrow to set the record straight." She gives me a long, hard look. "Do the right thing, Colby, or *I will*. I owe it to Ryan."

She moves around me into the gym. I practically fall onto the bench and stare at the doors until the end-of-the-day bell rings.

The bus drops Drew and me off at Sugar's. Drew gets right to work on her homework at a table in the dining room. I grab a handful of broken cookies from the sample box on the counter and cram them in my mouth, then go to the kitchen and look around for other stuff to eat. Mom's running the mixer with her back to me, and Leah's in her office with the door closed. There's a fire truck–shaped chocolate cake cooling on the rack and a fresh bowl of bright red cake icing next to it. I fill a four-cup measure with it, fluff the remaining icing with the spatula to try to hide the fact that I stole roughly half of it, and slip into the bathroom. I lock the door, lower the lid on the toilet, and sit down—then realize that I forgot a spoon. *Shit.*

I move to the door and listen; the mixer has stopped. Leah and Mom are discussing a birthday cake order.

If I open the door, Mom's going to bombard me with questions about how the day went, and I'll have to see Leah, too. I can't deal with the empty sadness in her eyes right now. I look around, but not surprisingly, there are no spoons in the bathroom. I think about hiding the icing until I can come back to it later, but where? Plus…I want it now. Scratch that: I *need* it now.

I sit down with the measuring cup between my knees and dig in with my fingers. Once I set my hand to "shovel," I don't think about how messy and sticky the icing is. I don't feel anything, and I don't see Ryan's bloody blue eyes watching me.

The second the measuring cup is empty, I feel two things: shame at having wolfed down four cups of cake icing, and an overwhelming need for more of it. At that moment, if I had to choose between my mother being proud of me and eating more cake icing, Mom would lose big time. The rest of those broken cookies would work, too. Any cookies will do. They don't have to be broken.

I lean back against the toilet tank and try to breathe in deeply, let it out. My head is swimming, and I feel a numbness that is similar to what I felt from my little yellow pills. I jump a foot when somebody bangs on the bathroom door.

Mom calls, "Colby? Are you in there? I didn't even realize that you and Drew got off the bus."

I jump up, and the plastic measuring cup clatters on the floor. I run my hand around my mouth and look in the mirror above the sink. There's dried icing all over my cheeks, chin, and a little on my neck. I run the water, rinsing my face again and again, but I can only use one hand, so it's not very effective. I grab a paper towel and dry off, then realize with horror that the red icing has stained my skin. I turn back to try using soap this time, but Mom's pounding on the door. She sounds freaked out. "Are you okay, Colby? Did you have a bad day?"

"I'm...coming..." I look down: There's still dried red icing under my fingernails; on my forearm, shirt, and jeans. My God, I don't remember being that sloppy with it. I don't remember much of eating it at all.

I unlock the door and it pops open. Mom's face practically melts off her skull when she sees me. "Oh, my God, Colby!" She runs to me and grabs my right forearm. "Did you cut yourself?" She flips my arm over and runs her finger from my wrist to my elbow. Her eyes register confusion; then she spies the empty icing cup on the floor. Her lips curl, and I see Kara's ugly sneer.

"What are you *doing* in here?" She examines my hair. "What *is* this...?" She yanks out a wad of dried frosting, along with several strands of hair.

"Ouch!"

"What are you…?" She steps past me and snatches the icing cup off the floor. She whirls on me and shakes it accusingly, but all I can see is the revulsion on her face. "Cake icing?…What are you…Are you *eating* in the bathroom? That's disgusting!"

I've never been caught sticky-handed before; I'd perfected the art of being sneaky. At least I thought I had. I feel two inches tall and two thousand pounds heavy.

I've seen those old TV shows before where a character feels like she's falling into a spinning black-and-white hole. I always thought, *"What a cheesy special effect. No one would ever really experience that."*

I was wrong.

Mom drags me out of the bathroom. She yells, "Why are you doing this to yourself? Are you trying to have a heart attack? Can't you see how *huge* you are?"

"I…just—"

Mom throws up a hand. "No! No excuses! There is *no excuse* for eating the way you do! And"—she shakes the empty measuring cup at me—"where did you even *get* all that icing?" She throws the measuring cup into the sink full of suds, sending a geyser of bubbles into the air.

"From the looks of it, she took it from here." Leah holds the icing bowl at an angle to show that half of it is gone. She sighs. "Now I have to make more, and the order's supposed to be ready at six. Hope I can get the tint just right again." She turns away and starts pulling ingredients off the shelf.

I drag my eyes back to my mother. Her arms are wrapped tightly across her chest like they were when I was on the ground after Ryan got hit. She's radiating anger. Or maybe it's just the usual disappointment, times a thousand. She yanks off her apron, grabs her purse, and growls, "Get in the car."

On our way home, Drew does her scratched CD routine, asking a million questions. "What's wrong? What's wrong? Are you mad at Colby? What'd she do?"

Mom ignores her.

I burp loudly. I *really* want to throw up. I think about doing it and wonder how Tina got to the point of vomiting to lose weight. Did she start out throwing up after eating too much, and it became a habit?

Trucks line the road in front of José's house. The crooked bleachers are filled with men of all ages. Two men inside the chain link cage are boxing, but they don't have gloves. One of the men's faces is covered in blood. I squeeze my eyes closed as Ryan's death stare fills my head.

Mom sends Drew to Leah's to feed the dogs, and she orders me to my room. She barks, "Stay!" and pulls until my door scrapes closed.

I lean against it and eavesdrop on her Skype conversation with Brenda, her old teaching partner in Northside. She tells Brenda everything that's happened, and she's sobbing by the time she's finished. Mom wails, "I'm not equipped to deal with this—*this shit*—by myself! I knew that Colby had food issues when we were living in Northside, but it's gotten worse! Just when I start to think she's going to come out of this okay—I mean, she tried to stop Ryan from killing himself, so she's not *totally* stuck inside herself—but then she goes off and does something like this, and I don't know how to get her to stop!"

Brenda's voice is soothing. "Aw, honey, you're doing the best you can. Maybe if you call the high school, the counselor will be able to recommend someone who can help her. Have *you* thought about getting counseling, Sonya? You all might need it after what you've been through since Reese...you know..."

Mom's not calming down. If anything, she's ramping up the hysterics. "I don't know how I'll *pay* for a therapist! Reese won't even help me with the medical bills I already have. He claims he's broke, and—"

Brenda interrupts, "But don't you remember how our school counselor would refer people to the mental health center? They didn't have to pay, or if they did, it was very little. There is help available, Sonya. Colby's eating like she is for a reason. I'm taking a psychology class for my master's degree, and—"

Mom blasts, "Well, I wish she'd stop eating so much! People can't even tell that she's mine, and to tell you the truth, sometimes I prefer it that way. I look at her, and all I see is Reese. They used to do these baking sessions together, laughing and eating the whole time, and it always disgusted me. Food, food, food. No wonder they're both so fat."

Oh, my God. Why didn't that truck run me over? Oh my God I want to die.

My eyes fill with tears and I feel as if I just slammed into the side of the road again. My mom has said awful things before, but this is a whole new kind of *awful*. It's *awful* times a thousand. *Why did I have to listen in? I'd give anything to unhear that.*

Brenda is silent for a long time.

Mom asks, "Are you still there? Did our Skype session freeze up?"

Brenda's voice is high when she finally speaks: "Can Colby hear you, Sonya? I'd hate for her to hear you talk about her that way. And, you know, maybe she misses her dad, and she's using food like a Band-Aid. Have you thought about that?"

Mom sounds defensive. "Brenda, you *know* I don't have a mean bone in my body. Anyway, Colby's in her room. She *shouldn't* be eavesdropping; I've made clear to her that listening to other people's conversations is unacceptable. Let me check..."

Mom's footsteps thud toward my room. I rock back and forth, trying to get to my knees, but I can't. I reach up, pull my iPod off my dresser, and slip in my ear buds. I pull *The Scarlet Letter* off my bed and open it to the middle, then shift so that I'm leaning against my bed. I lay the book on my lap and try to turn on my iPod, but my hands are shaking too hard. I pick up the book and pretend to read it as my mom forces my door open. I act like I don't see her come in.

"Colby?"

That's it; nod your head to the beat of the nonexistent music.

"Colby?" She steps in, nudges my foot with her toe.

I snap my head up and one of my ear buds falls out. "Huh?"

She gives me a close-mouthed smile that doesn't match the look in her eyes. "Nothing. Just checking on you. Wanted to make sure you're okay."

My eyes fill with tears, and I hope she doesn't notice. My voice sounds like Kermit the Frog's when I answer. "Yeah. I'm just fine."

She starts to pull my door closed but stops. "Did I give you back your iPod?"

I nod.

"Hmm. I guess I don't remember doing it."

I slide in the ear bud and pretend to start reading again. Mom pulls my door closed, and I stare at the words in the open book. My teardrops fall on the pages and I rub them in, darkening a conversation between Roger Chillingworth—who is Hester Prynne's husband, and Arthur Dimmesdale, Hester's minister and Pearl's father. They're talking about secret sin. Chillingworth says that he can't understand why some men would rather hide their sins than confess them, and Dimmesdale says that if certain people were revealed to the world as sinful, they could no longer do God's work. Turns out,

Arthur Dimmesdale is getting sicker and sicker, trying to keep his secret about being Pearl's dad.

I close the book and think about telling Mom the truth about Ryan. I trace the title on the cover and the red icing stains on my fingers are enough to convince me that my mom can't handle finding out any more about me right now.

Chapter Eighteen

Mom drives us to school the next morning. She kisses Drew on the forehead and sends her on to the elementary wing, then barely says "Bye" to me before she heads toward the counselor's office. I play dumb, like I don't know she's on a shrink-seeking mission. "Where are you going, Mom?"

She snaps, "Don't worry about it." Then she smiles, but her lips curl like they did when she spied that empty icing cup on the floor in the bathroom.

My body is in my desk during class, but all I can think about is what Mom said to Brenda. She's *relieved* when people don't realize she's my mother?

At lunch, I slide my tray onto the *Nobodies* table and sit across from Anna. She looks surprised, but she doesn't yell at me or flip me off, so I get the idea that it's okay for me to stay.

Sean says what Anna's probably thinking: "Oh, so you decided that we're good enough? Yesterday you sat with *Abercrombie and Bitch*, and we figured you'd gone over to the *Dark Side*."

I snort. "I'd burst into flames if I went there. I was just trying to find out who made the Facebook page in my honor."

Anna asks quietly, "So, did you?"

I shake my head. "Not for sure, although I'm pretty sure that Kara did it since she had Ryan's cell phone." I drag a French fry through ketchup and think about what happened in the bathroom at Sugar's yesterday. I remember sneaking the icing and Mom banging on the door, but everything in-between is fuzzy.

Maybe I'm crazy. Seems like eating four cups of cake icing in ten minutes would be a memorable thing. To tell the truth, though, I often don't remember everything I eat when I pig out. It's a blur, and I can't feel myself.

Which makes me think...maybe that's the point?

In English class, Mr. Van Horn moderates a debate on the nature of Pearl, Hester Prynne's daughter. He assigns half the class the point of view that Pearl is a little demon seed, so she's bad for Hester's soul, and the other half is to argue that Hester is bad for Pearl. In other words, we're supposed to explain Pearl's problems—like, she runs at other kids, screaming and shouting at them—by deciding if she's possessed by Satan or if her mom's a crazy bitch.

I tune out the discussion of *The Scarlet Letter* and imagine the class debating my nature.

> *Colby's a fat ugly liar!*
>
> *Look at her dad. Did you expect her to turn out differently?*
>
> *Her mom's right, you know. If she'd just lose weight...*
>
> *She's genetically doomed. You know what she needs to do.*
>
> *If she's dead, then her poor mother won't have to be*

ashamed of her anymore.

So, we agree, then?

Yes: Colby has to die.

I knew you'd see it my way.

I pull *The Scarlet Letter* out of my backpack, plop myself onto the bleachers, and settle in for P.E. class. My classmates head for the bay door and the sunlight, but I don't exactly mind that the cast on my arm is keeping me from participating.

From the doorway, Coach Sharp blasts her whistle. I look up. "Come on, Denton! Your excuse note is only for strenuous workouts. You can walk the track and get some fresh air. Starting tomorrow, I'll expect you to dress out."

Shit. I shove the novel into my backpack and crab-crawl off the bleachers. Coach Sharp waits, as if I'd go sit back down or something.

I blink in the sunshine and frown: Becca is waiting just outside the doors for me. I do a double-take because she's wearing her pearl-snap western shirt over her gym shirt and shorts.

"Get moving, ladies. Walk one, jog one; walk one, jog one. If you can jog more than one, go for it. I'm looking for cross country candidates."

I snort; Coach Sharp snaps, "Something funny, Denton?"

My voice drips with sarcasm. "Um…I'm not exactly in shape. I doubt you'd want me on your team."

Coach Sharp shrugs. "No time like the present to find out what you can do, is there?"

We aren't five steps into our lap when Becca says, "So? Have you thought about it? Are you going to do the right thing and tell the truth about Ryan?"

I ignore her question and take off in as much of a burst as I'm capable of, but she must be a charter member of Drew's *Ask a Million Questions* Club, because Becca's every bit as annoying as my little sister. She catches me easily, and she won't shut up.

By the time we reach the U in the track, I'm wheezing. "Leave *[gasp]* me *[wheeze]* alone *[gasp-wheeze]* about it!" I bend at the waist with my right hand on my thigh. I concentrate on long, deep breathing, but mostly I just cough and watch Becca's feet, hoping they'll walk away.

Instead, they step closer. She puts her hand on my back. "Are you okay? Do you have asthma?"

I straighten, shake my head, and cough some more. "No; I'm *fat*, in case you haven't noticed." The sun is beating down on my hair, and it feels like my skull is melting. I wave my hand in front of my face. "Damn, it's hot!"

A shrill whistle blasts and Coach Sharp yells from her place in the grassy center of the track, "Move it, you two! No stopping and standing!"

"We'd better keep going," Becca says worriedly. "She'll have us running sprints if we piss her off."

I wave her off. "You go on. I'll catch up."

"No, I'm sticking with you. Think of me as a reminder of how much time you have left to tell the truth." She glances at her watch. "Two and a half hours."

I roll my eyes. "Lucky me: my very own time keeper."

Becca gives me a close-mouthed smile and tilts her head at me. "Tick-tock."

"The only help I need from you is keeping your mouth shut. It's *not* like telling on me is going to bring Ryan back from the dead!" I turn on my heel and resume my lap.

From behind me, Becca calls, "5:00 P.M., Colby!"

I flip her the bird, walk on, and try to breathe instead of wheeze.

Mom's waiting in the Sugar's parking lot when Drew and I get off the bus. She's got her purse on her shoulder and her car keys in her hand. "Hey, girls. Drew, go on inside. Colby's got a doctor appointment, so you're riding home with Leah today."

"Is Colby getting her cast off? I want to go."

Mom gives Drew a little nudge toward Sugar's. "No, it's not that kind of doctor. Just be a good girl and go inside so that we make the appointment on time."

My sister digs in her heels. "What kind of doctor is it?"

"Enough!" Mom's sharp voice seems to propel Drew toward the front door. My mother locks eyes with me and nods toward the car. I move to it and wait for her to unlock my door.

I slide in at the same time she does. "Where *are* we going?"

Mom sighs. "After what I saw in that bathroom yesterday, I know that you need help. I don't know what to do, and I'm hoping that someone much smarter than me will be able to tell me."

I blurt, "So why am I going? *You're* the one who needs help." *Go ahead, Mom. Tell me how you really feel, like you told Brenda last night.*

Mom's right hand flies off the steering wheel, and she stops just short of backhanding me. "Colby!" She breathes in deeply, exhales shakily, and wraps her fingers around the steering wheel so tightly that her knuckles are white. She repeats her breathing thing a couple more times, then starts the car and backs out of the parking space.

We pass the memorial that marks where Ryan died. The flowers, teddy bears, and notes are beginning to fade in the late summer heat. A few of the items have blown into the road and been run over, but the white cross bearing his name and yearbook photo stands tall above everything else. *I'll bet if I had succeeded, the only thing marking my spot would be the Coors bottle that was on the ground by my head.*

The liquid rage flares up so suddenly that it takes me by surprise. "Doesn't it strike you as weird that all these people are making such a fuss about Ryan, when he *chose* to put himself in the road like that? If he'd lived, can you imagine how many jobs Grandpa would tell him to get to pay off the medical bills?"

Mom scowls. "That's terrible, Colby! How can you come up with such hateful ideas?"

I cross my arms tightly over my chest, glare out the window, and seethe. "Gee, Mom, I have no idea. I guess I got that from Dad, too."

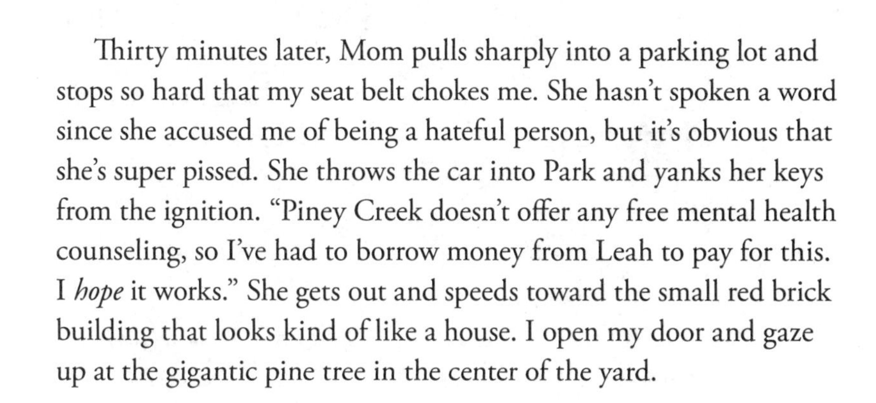

Thirty minutes later, Mom pulls sharply into a parking lot and stops so hard that my seat belt chokes me. She hasn't spoken a word since she accused me of being a hateful person, but it's obvious that she's super pissed. She throws the car into Park and yanks her keys from the ignition. "Piney Creek doesn't offer any free mental health counseling, so I've had to borrow money from Leah to pay for this. I *hope* it works." She gets out and speeds toward the small red brick building that looks kind of like a house. I open my door and gaze up at the gigantic pine tree in the center of the yard.

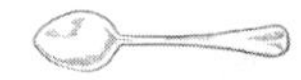

It smells like sugar cookies when I push open the front door. I glance around, but I don't see any cookies for the taking. Mom's standing with her back to me, talking to some man behind a long counter. She tosses her hair and gives a little laugh. *Bitch Mom* may have driven us here, but *Beauty Queen Mom* has taken over now, charming as ever.

The place looks like somebody's living room. There's a fireplace, matching red and white checked sofa and love seat, and a little kid's table and stools painted black and white to look like a dairy cow. I wander over to a bulletin board and study some faded cartoon strips. There's a notice for a parenting class called "The Teenage Brain," and a list of signs that a kid is depressed. I scan but don't really read it.

Somebody laughs, and I turn to see a lady with a girl about my age on the love seat. They're passing a smartphone back and forth and smiling. The phone makes a sad trombone sound and the lady exclaims, "You beat me again, Ashley! Think we have time to play again before your dad gets here to pick us up?"

The girl nods. "Let's try, Bev."

I watch them. *Why can't my mom and I do stuff like that? Oh, wait: that girl's normal-size. I'll bet if the girl was a big fat disaster, Bev wouldn't want a thing to do with her.* The girl catches me staring and gives me a quizzical look.

Mom calls, "Colby, have a seat." I join her on the sofa. She's got a clipboard with several pages to fill out. I plop down next to her and try to spy what she's writing, but she turns away to keep me from seeing. Finally, she turns the clipboard face-down. "Just…um, there's some magazines over there; go pick one and read it. The doctor said he'll be with us in a little while."

"Thought you wanted me to sit next to you," I snap.

"No, I just wanted you to sit *somewhere.*" Mom gives me a warning look. "You'd better fix that attitude, young lady. I'm doing this to try to help you."

I return her laser-like stare. "You mean like I helped Ryan? That worked out well, didn't it?"

"Colby Diane Denton, you are out of contr—"

"Mrs. Denton? Would you and Colby like to come back now?"

The same guy Mom was talking to before stands in the doorway beside the long counter. He's about my dad's height but not as stocky, and he's wearing a navy blue T-shirt, black jeans, and cowboy boots. He looks more like he should be on a tractor mowing a field than shrinking people's minds.

"I'm not quite finished with the paperwork," Mom says in her honey-sweet voice.

"That's okay; you'll have time to complete it while I talk to Colby." He smiles and holds the door open for us, waiting.

"If you say so." Mom picks up her purse, and I follow her to the doorway. My heart is pounding in my ears; I dread having to listen to Mom tell a perfect stranger what a complete clusterfuck I am.

My head's down, and I nearly miss it when he holds out his hand to me.

"Hi, Colby. I'm Dr. Matthews. But you can call me Dr. Matt if you want."

We follow him down a short hallway and into a small office. It's lined with bookcases, and there are kids' toys on the floor in front of a wall of windows with closed blinds. His desk is against the same wall as the door, and there's a chair next to his desk, a rocker in the middle of the room, and a small love seat opposite his desk. Mom takes the rocker. I take the love seat. He settles into his desk chair and pivots it so that he's facing both of us.

"What brings you in today?" He leans back in his chair and crosses his legs. I grab a throw pillow and hold it over my stomach. It doesn't even begin to cover all of me, but at least I don't have to look down and see that part of myself.

"First of all, thank you for getting us in so quickly. It's our good luck that you had a cancellation." Mom smiles and tilts her head at him. I swear it looks like she's posing for a picture.

"How can I help?" Dr. Matthews asks. He glances at me, then back at Mom.

"Well, it's like I told you on the phone; I caught Colby covered head-to-toe in cake icing yesterday. She'd locked herself in the bathroom of my sister-in-law's bakery. About a week ago, I caught her with a bag of sugar cookies that she stole from the bakery. She'd eaten them all. A. Gallon. Sized. Bag." Mom pauses for effect, then continues. "But yesterday, eating the cake icing in the *bathroom*? That's just gross, don't you think?"

Dr. Matthews's only response is a stony gaze.

Mom rushes to fill the silence. "I mean, *look at her*: You can tell that she's not missing any meals." She punctuates her sentence with a nervous laugh.

Still nothing.

Mom sits up straight, smoothes her blouse over her tummy, flicks her hair back over her shoulder, and seems to be waiting for him to agree that I'm a big fat pig, but instead he slowly turns back to his desk for a bottle of water, untwists the lid, takes a drink, twists the lid, and just as slowly places it back on his desk. It reminds me of how everything seemed to be in slow motion after I blabbed about Dad's kissing photo, but this time it's for real.

I study my fingernails. I scrubbed and scrubbed my skin and nails last night, trying to make the redness go away, but I can still see the icing stains. I close my eyes and visualize the shiny steel grill of that semi-truck heading straight for me. *Boy, do I wish Ryan had stayed out of it.*

Mom's shrill voice interrupts my nail-gazing. "So, Colby? What do you have to say for yourself?"

I readjust the pillow on my lap and stare at a loose thread.

"How'd you break your arm?" Dr. Matt's voice is soft. I glance at him to make sure he's talking to me—well, *of course* he is; I'm the only one in the room with a cast—and he raises his eyebrows and gives a little nod.

I start to answer, "I—was—" but Mom cuts me off.

She babbles, "Her cousin Ryan was trying to kill himself by standing at the top of a hill where there's a blind spot for drivers, and Colby ran into the road and attempted to knock him to safety, but she slipped on some gravel and broke her arm, and Ryan was hit by the truck and died. But she *tried* to save him. I wish she'd push away from the table the way she tried to push him!" More nervous laughter.

Dr. Matthews doesn't even acknowledge that he heard her. Instead, he prompts, "Colby, you were saying that you were…?"

"I just told you." Mom is obviously irritated.

He leans forward a little in his chair. "I'd like to hear it from Colby, without interruption, please." He sits back and gives me a gentle smile. "You were saying?"

"Oh, um, it's—it was just like Mom said."

He nods and seems to choose his words carefully. "Why…did Ryan want to kill himself?"

"Are you asking me this time, or her?" Mom asks.

"Either one is fine."

Mom glances at me. "Do you want to tell about the video he made?"

I shake my head slowly and reach for the other pillow. I lay it flat atop my chest. I wish I had a couple more pillows; I'd line them up to the top of my head.

"Ryan made a video of Colby getting dressed. He stood outside her window and filmed her. She was stomping around her room trying to squeeze into these pants that were at least two sizes too small. I tell you, Dr. Matthews, Colby has *really* piled on the pounds in the last six months! So, Ryan claimed that his phone—the one he made the video on—was stolen, and that someone *else* created a Facebook page and uploaded the video, but I guess we'll never know now. Anyway, he said he felt like killing himself because of the video being uploaded and having, oh, gosh, I think it had over two hundred shares by the time the page was taken down." Mom turns to me. "Colby, what was it? Two hundred shares of that video? At least?"

Just thinking about it makes me feel like throwing up. I move the chest pillow up and cover my face.

Dr. Matthews's voice is soft. "Colby, can you look at me?"

I lower the pillow just enough to reveal my eyes.

He asks, "How did you deal with that? Having your privacy invaded and the video seen by others...That seems like that would be devastating."

"Mom said it was all my fault," I whisper into the pillow.

He tilts his head. "I...couldn't quite hear you, honey. Could you say it again, please?"

I cut my eyes to Mom. She's watching me with that look in her eyes, the one that says, *"Careful what you say, Colby...Don't embarrass me...We're not dogs, Colby. We don't reward ourselves with food... People can't even tell that she's mine, and to tell you the truth, sometimes I prefer it that way."*

I lower the pillow back to my chest. My voice is flat. "According to my mom, Ryan never would have made that video if I wasn't so fat." I raise my chin and look Mom in the eye. "*You said* that. Right before I went outside and tried to—"

Mom bolts out of the rocker like it's on fire. "You always do that! You take the slightest thing that I say and twist it! I don't have a mean bone in my body, Colby Diane! I am a good mother! Just look at Rachel and Drew!"

"Time out," Dr. Matthews calmly says. He rises from his chair and moves to the door. "Mrs. Denton, I'd like to speak to Colby alone now."

"You—you think I'm a bad mother, don't you? Just because I said *that*, you think that I'm a horrible person." She shakes her head. "I knew this was a bad idea to bring Colby. All I want is for you to tell me what to do to fix her." She backs down into the rocker. "Can you do that? I just want her to stop eating like she does so that she can be happy. I grew up in a girls' home, and the thing that got me out of that place was beauty pageants. I want all of my daughters to have a way to be successful, and, well, even if we don't have any money, we can always get sponsors, and—"

Dr. Matthews smiles kindly and sounds like he's talking to a little kid. "I'm sure you're doing the best you can, Mrs. Denton. I don't think that you're a bad person. You brought Colby here so that she can get help, right?"

Mom nods, and she *looks* just like a little kid to me, too.

He continues, "We're finished with the first part of the interview, when I speak to parent and child together. Now, I'd like to speak to Colby alone. At the end of the session, I'll call for you, and we'll make a plan for the next several days, okay?"

Mom looks confused. "You mean—this is going to take longer than just today, to fix her?"

Dr. Matthews looks taken aback, and he nods slowly. "Yeah, I think so. Sounds like we have quite a bit of work to do. Now…you wait outside, all right?" He opens the door a little wider and gives her a reassuring nod.

Mom picks up her purse. "I-I'll finish the paperwork for you while I'm waiting."

"That's fine, Mrs. Denton." He watches her go to the waiting room. "See you soon."

Chapter Nineteen

Dr. Matthews pushes the door closed, walks slowly to his desk, and stares at a framed photo of his family. He raises his eyes to the ceiling, like he's thinking about something, and then settles back into his chair. "I'm...curious about something you said, Colby. When you were telling what your mom said about the video being your fault, you said, 'Right before I went outside and tried to—' but your mom cut you off before you could finish that sentence. What were you going to say?" He tilts his head, watches me.

"I—don't remember," I lie.

Dr. Matthews narrows his eyes, shakes his head, and says gently, "I don't know you well, or really at all, yet, but I have to say, I don't think you're telling the truth. Let's make sure I understand the situation here, though, because I could be wrong." He holds up one finger. "First of all, it looks to me like your mom gives you a lot of static about your weight and the way you eat. Am I right?"

I nod.

Two fingers. "Second of all, your cousin filmed you at a very private moment, and whether he meant for it to be shared or not, the video was posted to Facebook and seen by at least a couple hundred people—and probably more, since the friends of the friends of the friends..." He makes a pained face at me. "Man, that sucks. I can't even imagine how awful that would feel. I think I would feel betrayed, violated, enraged...Would you say you felt any of those emotions?"

I bury my face in the pillow again and nod.

He takes a big breath in and blows it out. I look up. He holds up three fingers. "And *then*, your mom, who, you know, it would be nice if she had your back on this one, but your mom actually blames *you* for the video being made...right?"

I nod and feel my face crumbling. "Yes." I start crying, and I don't know how long it takes me to stop. The doctor finally picks up a box of tissues off his desk and walks it over to me, then sits in the rocker, and we're pretty much knee-to-knee.

"I know," he says softly. "I know that must have hurt. Bless your heart."

I pull out some tissues, wipe my eyes, and draw some shuddery breaths. Just hearing Dr. Matt give words to the pain makes me feel like I'm going to break into little pieces and ooze all over the floor in a puddle. It's like the relief a balloon must feel when it's so full of air that it bursts. If a balloon *could* feel, I mean.

"So then when you went outside, Colby, what were you going to do?"

I breathe the word, "Try," but it comes out mostly as a sob.

"Were you *trying* to go for a walk? Or *trying* to get some fresh air?"

I shake my head slowly and close my eyes. "No," I whisper. "I tried to...die." I raise my eyes to his, then immediately look away. "When I went outside, I tried to get hit by a big truck. But instead, Ryan did."

"So...Ryan wasn't suicidal?"

I shake my head. "No. *I* was." I inhale shakily and breathe out, "He just got in the way of my plans. That's all."

"Why did you want to die, sweetheart?"

I restack the pillows on my lap and look down at them. "I—I'm a terrible person. I'm a disaster and...so, so...fat. I don't fit anywhere. I destroyed my family. I—"

Dr. Matthews holds up a hand. "First of all, you're not a terrible person, and you're not a disaster. And, what do you mean, you destroyed your family?"

I roll my eyes to the ceiling and envision the photo taped behind our family picture, then bring my gaze back down to the doctor's. I tell him everything that's happened in the past few months, and I don't stop until his talking alarm clock announces that we're out of time. Dr. Matt gets out of his chair to call my mother in.

"Wait!"

He turns to me.

"You can't tell her that I didn't try to save Ryan. Please! It's the first time in my life she's ever been proud of me for anything. Please, *please*, Dr. Matt. Please don't tell her how it really was."

"Colby, you are definitely a danger to yourself, and I am ethically obligated to tell your mother that I believe you are at risk for suicide."

"Can you…Can you tell her that without telling her that Ryan died saving me? Can you just give me some time to figure out how to tell her?"

"Will you agree to a contract with me, where you promise to call me if you are about to harm yourself? Can you do that, Colby? Can you promise that you won't do anything to yourself and that you'll come for another session next week?"

"Yes, yes, I promise; just don't tell my mom that I'm a lying sack of shit, please."

He frowns. "You're *not* a lying sack of shit."

I swallow hard. "I promise. I won't hurt myself and if I feel like I'm going to do anything stupid, I'll call you."

Mom starts spewing words the second she steps back into Dr. Matthews's office. "See? What did I tell you? Now can you see what I've been putting up with?"

Dr. Matthews sits back down and orders her, "Have a seat."

Mom looks a little surprised but does as he asks. She babbles, "I just don't understand why Colby is so different from her sisters; I've mothered her the exact same as Rachel and Drew. It's like she eats the way she does to get back at me." She looks to Dr. Matt for some kind of response, but all she gets is that same stony gaze.

He leans forward with his elbows on his knees. "Listen to me, Mrs. Denton. You may not like what you're going to hear, but I'm going to be straight with you because you need to act like a parent, not a self-centered child."

Mom's jaw drops, and her eyes get as big as CDs.

"Colby is severely depressed and at great risk for suicide. I know that you are most concerned about the eating and her weight, but the first thing we need to do is stabilize her so that she is *alive* to work on the other issues."

Mom furrows her eyebrows and shakes her head at me. "Colby, you're *not* suicidal. You'd tell me if you were depressed!" She glares at the doctor. "My girls can talk to me about anything. There's no way that—"

Dr. Matt cuts her off. "I can assure you that she *is* depressed, and she *is* suicidal. And, she *is* telling you, in other ways. People with eating disorders are at greater risk for suicide. The binge eating disorder is Colby's way of unplugging from intense emotions. By eating massive amounts of food in a short period of time, she creates the problem of feeling guilty or ashamed of eating so much, rather than the guilt or shame she feels about something else: disappointing you, for example. I will work up a plan of treatment goals, but the short-term goal for this week is to keep Colby safe: That's paramount! Do you understand what I'm saying to you?"

Mom gives me her skeptical face, and I look at my hands. *Damn these icing stains.*

"Mrs. Denton?"

Mom drags her eyes back to Dr. Matt, and he continues. "Colby's agreed that she will contact me if she feels like hurting herself. In the meantime, you can help by seeing that she's not left alone.

Spend time together doing activities that don't involve food."

Mom waves her hand dismissively. "Well, that's going to be impossible because of where we work."

He turns to me. "Where do you work?"

"At my aunt's bakery."

He shakes his head. "That's just like an alcoholic working in a bar. I'd like to see that situation changed."

Mom blurts, "But we *owe* Leah for taking us in when we had nowhere else to go. Colby's father left us, and the F.B.I. seized our—"

"She told me about it." Dr. Matt reaches around for his appointment calendar and pulls it into his lap. "Same time next week?"

Mom murmurs, "Well, I certainly didn't expect to be spoken to like this when I brought my child here for help. I—I'm not sure that this is a good idea."

Dr. Matt's voice is rough. "The key words in what you just said are 'my' and 'child,' Mrs. Denton. Regardless of how you feel about your husband and his actions, Colby is *not* responsible for what he did. She may look like your husband, but she is *not* her father. She is a unique, smart, capable, tough young woman, and she deserves to be loved and appreciated for who she is, regardless of her size. I suggest that you get counseling, too, and learn what is missing inside of you that your focus is so exclusively on your daughter's weight that you don't, for example, understand what an act of evil that boy making that video was."

Mom opens her mouth, closes it, and leans forward with her head in her hands. Finally, she speaks. "But...Colby's so...big! Are you saying I'm wrong to be concerned about her health?" She lifts her head, locks her gaze on Dr. Matt, and they have a bit of a staring contest.

Finally, Dr. Matt says matter-of-factly, "If you're bringing your daughter to me expecting me to force her to lose weight, you're going to be disappointed. It's *not* about the weight, Mrs. Denton. It's about health and positive self-care. Weight loss may occur as a result of altering the other behaviors, but it's not the ultimate goal. At this point, Colby sees herself the way you do: as just *The Fat Girl.* And she's so, so much more than that."

Mom's voice is thick. "Well…will you work with me?"

He shakes his head. "No. I am Colby's therapist, and it is my responsibility to be her advocate. I need you to hear that loud and clear. However, I am happy to recommend someone to work with you." He pulls a business card from a drawer and hands it to Mom. "Leslie Trevino is my associate. Just call the number and leave a message, and she'll call you back. Now, Mrs. Denton, can you promise me that you will do your best to keep Colby safe this week, or do I need to set up intake at a mental health facility?"

Mom squeaks, "You want to have Colby *committed*?"

"If you're going to continue berating her and carelessly throwing out comments as if they don't inflict more damage on your already very vulnerable child, then, yes, I will be forced to have Colby committed until I feel that she's stable enough to put up with you on her own. She's promised me that she won't hurt herself, but if you don't modify your behavior, I don't think her promise to me will hold up in the face of it."

Mom throws herself back in the chair, gives a little snort, and shakes her head. "You're testing me. This *must* be some kind of joke. I'm a good mother; I—"

"Mrs. Denton, I have over twenty years of experience in working with traumatized people. You're right to be concerned about the binge eating disorder. It will eventually kill your daughter if we can't get it under control. But suicide is the immediate threat to Colby's well-being. Between your husband's bone-headed actions and your callousness—the likes of which I've rarely seen—Colby has to find better ways of coping, or she's going to be dead. You may not like the way Colby looks, but I hope that somewhere inside of yourself, you love *her*."

"Well, of course I do! That's the most ridiculous thing I've ever heard!"

"Then prove it to me, Mrs. Denton. And more than that, prove it to Colby."

"You...think that I don't love my child!" Mom laughs, but it's not a happy laugh. Her face practically melts off her skull, and she bolts from the chair. She jerks open the office door so hard that it bounces back off the wall. Seconds later, the outer office door slams against the wall, too.

I set the pillows aside and wriggle forward on the love seat. Dr. Matt offers a hand and pulls me up to stand.

He looks down at me. "You got this, Colby? You'll call me, right? You promised." He hands me a business card with his phone number circled on it. "If you need to talk, leave a message and I'll call you right back. Okay?"

I nod, and we shake on it. "Yeah."

"If I don't hear from you before, then we'll talk next week. Agreed?"

"Yeah."

Mom's terse voice from the waiting room: "Colby!"

I can do it. I can hold on for a week. I won't try again for at least a week.

The second we get into the car, Mom blares, "What *on earth* did you tell that man, Colby Diane? He definitely got the wrong impression of you, and he's totally wrong about me!" She digs in her purse for her keys, but her hands are shaking too much.

I drag her purse into my lap and pull the keys out for her. My face burns and I murmur, "I'm sorry, Mom, I—"

She snatches the keys from me, throws herself back against her seat, and covers her face with her hands. Her voice cracking, she cries, "I can't take any more, Colby!"

I lean against the window and watch as my mom has a meltdown in the therapist's parking lot. A man pulls in next to us. His eyes grow huge at the sight of my mother wailing and pounding the steering wheel.

Mom catches him watching her and immediately stops throwing a fit, tucks her head. After a moment, she asks, "Is he gone?"

I watch him move to the sidewalk. He glances back at us one more time, and I shoot him a dirty look. "Y-yeah, Mom, he's gone. Why do you care what a total stranger thinks, anyway?"

Mom ignores the question. She tilts the rearview mirror, takes a look, and grabs her purse from my lap. She pulls out her makeup bag and starts repairing the damage.

I watch her a moment. "Why does it matter so much that your makeup's all runny? We're just going home, right?"

She pauses in reapplying foundation and snaps, "Appearances *matter*, Colby. You're born alone and you die alone, but you can use what you've got in between. It's like I told that doctor, but he was too busy yelling at me to listen: Beauty pageants are what got *me* out of that girls' home."

I point at my face. "You think that I'm beauty pageant material, Mom? I don't even wear makeup!"

She softens her voice and puts her hand on mine. "You have an interesting face, but nobody notices it because the rest of you is so... overwhelming. At this point, wearing makeup would just be a waste of time for you."

"Didn't you hear a word Dr. Matt said, Mom?" I choke out. "You say these awful things to me like I don't have feelings, but I do!... You're going to call that lady, right? His associate?"

Mom's eyes flash. "The only problem *I* have is a daughter who gets back at me by eating everything in sight and having a bad attitude. I would think that you'd try harder to make me happy. After everything I've been through with your dad leaving, do you really think I should have to put up with this...this...*shit*, too?"

"God, Mom! You're so mean! I don't even know you anymore!"

"You're just saying that to hurt *my* feelings. And—*you* act like a person you just met an hour ago knows you better than I do. All you need to do is go on a diet. Push away from the table. Have some self-control. I borrowed three hundred dollars from Leah to get help for you, and as of this moment, we have two hundred left. Figure out how to stop pigging out by the end of the third session. *Just do it*." She uncaps her mascara and reapplies it. "Why don't you get to know that girl we bought the clothes from? Find out how she lost weight."

I stare out my window. "I *know* how she did it, Mom! She throws up what she eats!"

Mom doesn't say anything, and I turn back to her. "Did you hear me? She throws up. You don't want me to throw up, do you?"

She shrugs and drops her mouth open as she applies mascara to her lower lashes. "I knew lots of girls who did that. Seemed to work for them."

I stare at my mother in disbelief. She caps the mascara and tosses it into her makeup bag. The guy who saw Mom having a meltdown must have said something to Dr. Matt, because he steps out onto the porch and gives us a worried stare.

Mom sees him watching and reaches over, pats me on the shoulder. "Look at him coming out here to check on us. He doesn't know when to quit. You know, we could just take a hundred dollars and go clothes shopping, and I could send the other hundred to Rachel."

I talk fast. "Look, I *promised* Dr. Matt that I'll come back next week, Mom! I *promised* him that I won't—" I stop short when I realize that I almost told her the truth about why Ryan is dead.

She cuts me off. "What? You won't pig out?" She laughs ruefully. "Oh, you're *not* going to pig out. I guarantee that you won't do that anymore."

White. Hot. Rage. "You can't stop me! I'll eat what I want when I want, and you can't do a thing about it! If you were mean to Dad like you are to me, I'm not surprised he cheated on you!"

Mom looks like I slapped her. "How can you talk to me like that? I am your mother!"

"Yeah, but you don't want other people to know that you are. I *heard* you! You're ashamed of me!"

"Heard me...Were you eavesdropping again?"

I answer her with a cold stare, and Mom looks like she's going to cry. She starts the car and backs out of our parking space so fast that she nearly clips the truck behind us.

I kick the underside of the dashboard and scream so loud that my throat feels like it's ripping open. "Why don't you love me like you love Rachel and Drew? *Why*?"

Mom ignores my question and instead cruises along the highway while sermonizing about children honoring their parents, but I tune her out and listen to my "Fuck You" playlist in my head.

I'm starting my mental playlist for the second time when we pull in to Leah's driveway. Just then, Leah and Drew step off her porch, each carrying dried-out flowers from Ryan's memorial service. They add them to the other wilted arrangements spread along the pavestone retaining wall that edges Leah's yard.

Mom and I get out of the car and join them there. Drew plucks a still-vibrant daisy from the pile of shriveled flowers. She pokes a finger into the soil and inserts the daisy's stem.

My throat raw from screaming, I croak, "Why are you *doing* that?" Drew pats the dirt around the base of the cut daisy and cuts me a sideways look. "So it can come back to life again, silly."

Leah's voice is hollow. "That's not how it works, honey. Dead is dead. And...there's no resurrection. That's just a story that people tell themselves to feel better." She turns from us and moves away. Charley and Zeeke run ahead of her to the house. She slowly ascends the steps and sits in the rocker on the porch, staring blankly toward the road. Her eyebrows furrow, and I follow her gaze to the police cruiser winding down the driveway toward us.

Chief Taylor pulls in behind our cars. It almost looks like he's blocking us in so that no one can leave.

Drew paws through the funeral flowers for more candidates to "bring back to life." Mom bends down and touches her shoulder. "Come on, Drew Ann."

"In a second." She straightens the bent bloom again and again, but it stubbornly refuses to face the sun.

Mom glances back at Chief Taylor exiting his car. She says sharply, "No. *Now.*" She pulls Drew to a standing position, then hooks her other hand through my arm. "Let's go, girls." She drags us along the dirt path toward the trailer. "We'll leave them alone to talk." Her voice is louder than it needs to be for just us to hear; it's kind of obvious that she's talking to Leah and the police chief.

"Actually, Mrs. Denton, I'm here to speak to all of you. I have some new information pertaining to the circumstances of Ryan's death."

Chapter Twenty

Chief Taylor's face is grim. He nods toward Leah's house and waits while Mom, her arms still looped through ours, ascends the porch steps with us.

His voice is soft but firm. "I think it's best if we go inside."

Leah leaps to her feet and for a second I think she might punch Chief Taylor in the face. "Why should I care what *you* think? Your son beat Ryan to a pulp, and you got rid of the evidence. I have no respect for you *or* your opinion. What? You think you're going to *prove* to me that Ryan killed himself? I'll never believe that, no matter what you say, so get off my property right now."

Chief Taylor removes his hat and holds it in his hands. "Ms. Ellis—Leah—we can talk about what happened last May another time. I may have made some bad decisions regarding my son, and I can understand why you feel that way about me. But"—he shakes his head, glances at me—"I *truly* think it would be best if we all go inside and have a talk." He leans forward and opens Leah's front door, then steps back and waits for us to enter ahead of him.

"All right, but I'm telling you now, if you're going to try to sell me that line of bull—" Leah chokes up. She doesn't finish her sentence; just shakes her head and leads the way into her house.

Chief Taylor waits until we're settled, pulls his notepad from his back pocket, and sets his sights on me. "This afternoon, one of your classmates, a"—he consults his notes—"Becca Schuler—and her mother, Kate, informed me that they were witnesses to the accident that took Ryan's life. They said—"

Leah cuts him off. "*Accident*? Did you say, '*Accident*'? So you admit that it wasn't suicide?"

He holds up a hand. "Now, I'm getting to that, just—"

"I *knew* it! I knew my baby wouldn't leave me on purpose!" Leah's voice cracks. She covers her mouth with her hand and her shoulders shake with sobs.

He watches her a moment, sighs heavily, and frowns at me.

Mom says defensively, "Wh-why are you looking at Colby like that?"

"Young lady," Chief Taylor says to me, "would you like one last chance to be the one to tell the truth about what happened on the road that day?"

"She *told* the truth!" Mom gives me a little shove. "Didn't you? You saw Ryan in the street and you saw the semi coming and you—*you*—tried to save him."

I fix my eyes on the framed print on the wall above Leah's head. It reads *Hope Will Find You*. I can feel Leah's eyes locked on me like lasers, and I don't dare lower my gaze to meet hers.

Mom shrieks, "Colby! *Tell them* that you weren't the one trying to die that day!"

Chief Taylor's voice is every bit as flat as Mom's is hysterical. "Mrs. Denton, we need to hear Colby's version of the events." He pulls a ladder-back chair from Leah's dining room table and turns it toward me. He sits heavily, and his leather gun belt squeaks a little. He leans forward with his elbows on his knees and says softly, "Listen to me, sweetheart. Becca told me that you're bound and determined to keep the circumstances of Ryan's death a secret, and that she gave you twenty-four hours to come clean…which you have apparently opted not to do." He shrugs. "Would have been nice if they'd spoken up sooner; I'm just glad that they came forward now."

I lock my arms at my sides and slowly draw them across my chest. I cradle my cast and curve my shoulders in.

Chief Taylor says gruffly, "Look at your aunt, Colby. Don't you think you owe her the truth?"

I won't do it and he leans forward, cups my chin in his hand, and forces my face toward Leah. I close my eyes, and he gives my face a little shake.

His voice is rough. "I said, look at her!"

Mom's voice is sharp. "Colby!"

I open my eyes, and in Leah's cold stare, I see Ryan's bloody face. I grit my teeth and try to swallow, but the lump in my throat makes it nearly impossible. I shake my head.

Chief Taylor releases my chin, straightens, and pulls a piece of paper out of his shirt pocket. He unfolds it. "This is Mrs. Schuler's witness statement, signed and dated today."

He clears his throat, then reads matter-of-factly. "My daughter and I were cleaning our family's rental property on the day Ryan Ellis died. We were finishing up and about to leave, when we witnessed Colby Denton step in front of a car, as if she was trying to get hit. The driver swerved to miss her, but circled back around and appeared to be yelling at her. We watched as Colby went back up the street toward Sugar's bakery.

"About thirty minutes later, we saw her walk determinedly—" He pauses. "That's the word they used, Colby: *determinedly*."

He bumps up his eyebrows like he's waiting for me to talk. When I don't, he continues reading. "We saw her walk determinedly into the street and hold her arms out as if she was trying to keep her balance. She stood just at the cusp of the hill, and within moments, an eighteen-wheeler appeared. As if out of nowhere, Ryan Ellis came running from the side of the house. He barreled into Colby, knocking her clear of the semi. It happened in the blink of an eye. Next thing we knew, Ryan was lying in the road. We saw his mother when she discovered his body. There was a little blonde girl standing in the road, screaming. I took her by the hand and we found Colby just off the shoulder of the road, near a bar ditch. I placed my purse under Colby's head and stayed with her until help arrived."

Chief Taylor refolds the paper and slides it into his pocket, then leans forward again with his elbows on his knees. He clasps his hands as if in prayer and asks, "Is that about the way it happened, Colby?"

I bite my lip, close my eyes, and lower my head. A tear runs down my nose and lingers a moment before falling onto my forearm.

Mom shrieks, "Why did you make up that story? *Why*?"

I whisper, "I didn't."

She slaps the side of my head. "What did you say? Stop mumbling! Why did you make up that story?"

I sigh. "*I* didn't. *You* did. All I did was keep it going."

Chief Taylor asks loudly, "Mrs. Denton? Is that true? Did you *purposely* derail my investigation?"

Mom snorts. "I did *not* make up any story. Colby Diane Denton, tell him that I did not make up that story."

My head snaps up. "Yes, you did. You said it in the ambulance, when you told the paramedic that I didn't remember trying to save my cousin! I never told you I did. *You* decided that I did!"

Mom's face has that melting-off-her-skull look. She latches onto my wrist, digs her fingernails in, and shakes her head. "But the police officer said…*I* never…"

"Yes, you did, Mama. I heard you."

All eyes turn to Drew. Her voice is tiny. "I remember, Mama. You told Colby not to look at Ryan when we were getting in the ambulance. I asked you if Colby was in trouble and you said, 'No, she can't help it if Ryan tried to kill himself.' Then Colby tried to talk, and you told the man in the blue shirt to help her calm down because she didn't remember trying to save Ryan."

Mom's eyes are huge. She's still got a death grip on my wrist and she looks down at her hand as if it belongs to someone else. She releases her claws and crosses her arms tightly over her chest.

Leah sobs, "How *could* you, Colby? How could you let me think that Ryan committed suicide? Why didn't you say anything?"

My heart is pounding in my ears. No one is speaking; it's like they're waiting for me to make some kind of profound statement that will explain why I'm a terrible person. "It…was…I mean… Mom was…" I stop, realizing that no matter what I say, no one will understand how badly I needed my mom to be proud of me for *something.*

"I'm sorry," I whisper. "I wish it had been me. Every day, I wish I had been the one who died." I shake my head. "That day…the Facebook page…the video of me getting dressed…and…Mom said it was all my fault because I'm so…" I sob, "I just wanted to die. I *needed* to not be here anymore."

I reach for my mother's hand and try to pull it into my own, but she keeps her arm locked firmly against her chest. "Please, Mom, please don't hate me. I…I *need* you not to hate me anymore."

Mom won't look at me. Leah rocks herself back and forth in her chair, and Drew stares at our mother like she's an exhibit in a museum.

Chief Taylor scribbles on his notepad for what seems like forever. At last, he stands and says quietly, "I'll forward my findings to the medical examiner. Leah, I think it's safe to assume that Ryan's death will be classified as an accident."

She nods and gets up, moves to the front door, and holds it open. "Thank you for letting me know the truth," she says softly. "I knew it. I *knew* he wouldn't leave me on purpose." She closes the door behind him, then turns to us. "I'd like to be alone now." She goes to her bedroom, and when she turns the door lock, the sound makes me jump.

Mom gets up without a word and walks out the front door. Drew follows her immediately, but I remain frozen in the same spot. I think about the promise I made Dr. Matt, and I hear his voice in my head: *"You're not a terrible person."*

Even after I told him the truth about what happened, he didn't seem to change his opinion of me. I shake my head. Maybe he wasn't listening closely. If he *had* been, there's no way he would have been so nice to me…

That sound—the waterfall of loss that I heard when the truck's brakes stopped squealing—is coming from Leah's bedroom. It sends me slamming into the pavement all over again and the horrifying moment I knew that Ryan was dead and I was alive.

I've *got* to get away from it. I work my way off the sofa and start for the front door, but stop in the hallway. I stare at Ryan's closed bedroom door, trying to work up the courage to open it. I swallow hard, then twist the doorknob and step inside his room. I turn on the light and sit on the edge of his bed, breathe in his scent, take in my surroundings.

He never invited me into this place when he was alive.

There's a framed photo on his desk of him and Leah. She has her arm draped around his neck and they're both making silly faces. Another shows Ryan staring full on at the camera while Leah gazes at him with love in her eyes. My stomach clenches with pangs of jealousy. I *wish* my mom would look at me like that, but I know she never will. Especially now that she knows the truth about Ryan's death.

I rise and close Ryan's door quietly behind me. I step out the front door and start down the steps. Charley briefly raises her head from her place on Dad's recliner, but lowers her head to the armrest and goes back to sleep. There's no sign of Zeeke. He probably followed Drew home to the trailer.

I start toward it, too, but I know what awaits me: Mom's disappointed face and more affirmation that I've achieved a new level of being a big fat disaster. Can't face it.

Just can't.

There's still enough sunlight to see that the barn door is ajar. I open it wider and step inside, startling some birds nesting in the rafters. I duck when they fly out over my head. I straighten, and my eyes light on the solid-looking wood beam about five feet over my head. There's a crossbeam above it...and an idea begins forming in my mind. A way I won't have to see that look on my mom's face anymore.

I look around for a rope. I'm not sure how to make a noose—especially with one arm in a cast—but I'll bet if I tie it just right, it'll break my neck as perfectly as that semi broke Ryan's. The same crackling electricity that drives me to pig out—or to march into the center of Main Street on the prowl for a semi-truck—is in charge of me now. I'm not even thinking; my heart is racing like I'm jet fuel–powered with the idea of hanging myself.

The barn is so full of our crap that I can't get back into the depths of it. I open the doors wide since nobody's paying any attention to me anyway. I drag the bits and pieces of our lives that didn't fit anywhere else out into the yard. Zeeke reappears; he and Charley sit off to the side like they're watching a furniture parade.

I clear enough of a path to get to a workbench in the back of the barn. Next to it, dangling from a hook, is a rope. The perfect rope. It looks like the kind a cowboy uses for a lasso. I lean against the workbench and futz with it, trying to figure out how to form a noose. I'm able to wiggle the fingers on my left hand perfectly; it just takes a little while to figure out the best way to work the rope with a left arm that's in an L-shaped cast. After a while, I give up on making a noose and loop the rope across my shoulders, pull it into position, and try to get the stiff material to loosen enough to knot.

I sigh loudly; it's getting darker and I'm having a hard time seeing what I'm doing. I move to the doorway, dragging that long-ass rope behind me like a tail on the ground.

I glance toward the trailer and remember what it was like to look in the window at Sugar's and wait for my mom to come talk to me...that feeling when she smiled and went to help Drew decorate her fucking day-old cookies, when I was dying inside because everyone and their brother was watching Ryan's video of me dressing.

Fuck her. Wait'll she finds me hanging in this barn. Bet she won't be laughing then.

I finagle the rope into a knot, then a double knot, and check to make sure there's not too much room between it and my skin. It reminds me of pulling my bed sheet up just under my jaw so that I can't feel my double chin sticking to my neck. I pull the end of the rope even tighter, grunting as I do so.

I drag our end table back into the barn and place it under the beam. I step onto the wobbly table, and—

"What are you doing?"

—I nearly jump out of my skin at the sound of Leah's voice.

She steps into the barn and flips the light switch just inside the door. Harsh fluorescent light floods the small space.

Leah shrieks, "What *the fuck* are you doing, Colby?" She stomps over to me and pulls me off the table by my good arm, then stands between me and my plans. "Huh? Tell me."

I say nothing; just look at my feet. She tries to pull the makeshift noose over my head, but it catches on my chin.

"Jesus H. Christ, Colby!" She uses both hands to loosen the knot a little and work the rope over my head, then tosses it to the ground. She wraps her beefy arms around me and sobs, "What are you thinking?"

I don't know how long Leah and I stand in barn. She weeps and babbles and to be honest I can't understand most of what she says, but I do catch this: "Not you, too. Please. No."

Leah drags me back to her house. I'm rubbing my neck, wondering if the itchy feeling means there are telltale signs of rope burn, kind of like the icing streaks. Seems like every time I let the crazies take over, I end up with an outward sign that I've been up to something. Sometimes it's red food coloring stains; sometimes it's more whale blubber.

Leah takes my hand away from my neck and leads me to the sofa. She sits, pulling me down with her. She holds her hands over her face, and I think she's going to burst out crying again, but she doesn't.

I whisper, "Leah, I'm—I'm so, so sorry. I should have told you the truth, but I couldn't, because..."

I can't say it.

She lowers her hands and tilts her head, whispers, "Why?"

I force the words to come out: "I killed Ryan, I—"

Leah holds up her hand, shakes her head rapidly. "*No.* Uh-uh. *No.*" She closes her eyes, lowers her head, whispers, "No, Colby. What happened was a horrible accident. Ryan saw you there and"—she stops, takes a deep breath, and blows it out—"he did what I'd have expected him to do."

She looks toward his room and says softly, "My son *wasn't* perfect. I know that. I have no idea what possessed him to film you through your window, and for that"—she looks back at me—"I am so, so sorry." She rounds her shoulders and crosses her arms. I force myself to look at her face but can't for long, because it's like seeing Ryan all over again.

Leah takes my hand and turns to me. "It seemed to me that you and Ryan were good friends when you were little and we'd visit your parents, before his dad and I got divorced and, you know...my relationship with my family completely went to shit. I hope you have at least *some* good memories of him from when you were young, when he wasn't so angry. That's the only explanation I can think of for what he did, filming you while you dressed. Anger can make people do things they never would otherwise. It's what drove you to stand in the middle of the street and try to die, isn't it?"

I shrug, and the ache of my mom blaming me for Ryan making the video feels just as strong now as it did then.

She chews her lip, like she's trying to choose the right words. She takes a big breath in and blows it out. "The way his dad abused us really messed up Ryan's sense of trust. He witnessed it when Mark decided that I was going to come back to him, and when I refused, he grabbed a pot of boiling water off my stove and threw it at me. That's the reason I have tattoos covering my body like I do. I was lucky enough to find an artist who was able to make beauty out of this evidence of Mark's rage." Leah straightens her arm, and I notice for the first time the unevenness of her skin, and how the winding flowers and vines conceal splattered scars.

She continues, "And when Ryan reported that girl's rape and nearly all his friends turned on him—even beat him so severely that he ended up in the hospital…it left him with an anger so big that it just about broke him. Top it off with that disaster of a Fourth of July picnic, and…" She shakes her head. A tear runs down her cheek beside her nose. I watch it until it slides down her jaw and drops off her chin. Another one immediately follows, and I am watching her tears, because looking into her eyes is more than I can do.

"I'm sorry I didn't speak up for him at the picnic," I murmur. "I *didn't* agree with what was said…I've never been good at speaking up for anyone. Including myself."

Leah's eyes are soft. "Oh, honey, it'd be nice if my family would actually *hear it* when others disagree with them, but they don't. That's part of the reason I had to get away from them. No matter what I said, I wasn't heard. Problem is, *my* idea of getting away from them when I was just out of high school was to marry a slick talker who didn't listen to me any more than they did. Mark had a weakness for beer and a fondness for knocking me and Ryan around." She shrugs and snorts. "No wonder my parents love him so much!"

I laugh uneasily.

Aunt Leah brushes my hair out of my eyes and runs her hand

down the back of my head. "The scars that Mark gave me aren't the only ones I have." She turns up her forearms and shows me the long scars, disguised by ink as flower stems, extending from her wrists to her elbows.

I gasp. "*You* tried to kill yourself, Leah? When? *Why*?"

Leah stares at the *Hope Will Find You* print on the wall. "It was a long time ago. I was about your age. I was beat down with my family's bullshit, and I thought that checking out was the answer." Her eyes take on a far-away look and she says softly, "I've been thinking lately that it might still be. My life has a hole in it now. What do I have left? I just want to be with my boy…"

I gasp. "Leah, you can't!"

She turns to me, takes my face in her hands, and I *have* to look her in the eye. She chokes out, "My life will never be the same. *Ever.* Yours won't be, either, Colby."

"Please, Leah, don't kill yourself. *Please*!"

She sobs, "You're telling me that *I* can't kill myself, but what were *you* trying to do in the barn when I found you?"

I try to pull out of her grasp, but she holds tight. "Please. Let me go." She leans in and kisses me on the forehead, then releases me.

We sit in silence for a few minutes. Shame fills me from head to toe: *I took* Ryan from her, and because of what I did, Leah wants to die, too. That thought in my head—*I'm done. I can't* be *here anymore*—is tidal-wave strong, like the urge that propels me face-first into a four-cup measure of cake icing. I squeeze my eyes tightly and bite down hard on the inside of my lower lip.

Leah touches my knee just as I'm tasting blood. I open my eyes. Her head is bowed, and her voice is barely above a whisper. "I think…you and I need to have an agreement."

What does she want from me? I'm surprised I can't see my heart pounding through my shirt. "…What kind of agreement?" *Are we going to kill ourselves together?*

Leah faces me, and I see Ryan in her eyes. Not the bloody Ryan.

Her eyes are soft and a little scared, like his were when he apologized to me and said that he doesn't mean to be such an asshole.

"Ryan gave up his life trying to save you from taking your own. You wanted to die, and I'm spending most of my waking hours asking myself just what I've got to live for—"

I sob, "I'm sorry, I'm sorry. I...I wish I had died...I do, I wish it had been me."

Leah moves closer and pulls me tightly against her. She holds me while I cry, running her hand over and over my head and shoulders.

When all I've got left is shuddery breathing, she speaks in a low, soothing voice. "Let's agree that we're going to live. It's a choice, you know. *You* promise not to throw the gift of a second chance away, and *I promise* to stick around to be here for you in a way that your own mama isn't."

Mom's face flashes through my mind: that tight-lipped look of hers that says, *"Don't embarrass me."* I pull out of Leah's embrace and try to sound convincing. "My...mom...it's not so bad—"

Leah waves me off. "*Psssht.* Save it, girl. You don't have to maintain appearances with me. I *see* the way she looks at you. I *hear* the little digs she makes, and a person would have to be deaf, dumb, and blind not to notice how she favors Rachel and Drew over you. Sometimes parents beat their kids—like Mark used to knock Ryan around—but words hurt, too, and they can totally skew a person's view of themselves. You're going to have to learn to separate what you know about yourself to be true from what your mom *thinks* is your truth."

Her mention of the word "truth" is like a knife through my heart. I choke out, "What I've done...H-how do I—what do I—everyone's going to hate me now..." I cover my face as shame threatens to drown me.

Her voice is soft. "Didn't your mom take you to some kind of counselor today, sweetie? He ought to be able to help you deal so that you don't...you know...try again. I mean, you and I have an agreement, right? You've got a second chance at life, and I can decide to hang in and make sure you don't fuck it up."

She pulls my hands from my face, takes them into her own. I swallow hard and nod. "Y-yes. I promise not to waste the gift I've been given. At least...I'll *try* not to fuck it up, Leah. I'll *try* to be someone who will make you...proud. Somehow."

"You don't have to be anybody but who you are, Colby. We *need* to be each other's reason to keep going when it feels like there's not one." She gives me a tiny smile. "That's why you need to work hard in therapy, so that wanting to live is not such hard work."

"Are *you* going to get some help, Leah?"

She closes her eyes, nods. "Yeah, I think I'm due for a tune-up. I was in therapy for a long time after my suicide attempt, but I think I'm going to need support to get through...this."

"How many sessions do you think it'll take you to get better?"

Leah gives me a strange look. "Why do you ask?"

I pull Dr. Matt's wrinkled business card from my pocket and stare at it. "Well, my mom told me that I have to get better in three sessions, because that's all she's got money for. I only have two left."

My aunt snorts and rolls her eyes. "Your mother is an absolute trip, Colby."

I lean forward. "Soooo...more than three?"

"Colby, darling, I will see that you have as many therapy sessions as you need to get well." She sighs loudly. "I need to have a talk with your mother."

I yawn, and Leah does, too. She pulls me up and envelops me in a hug. "You *are* loved, Colby Denton. Just the way you are. And don't you forget it."

Something breaks loose inside of me, and it hits me: Leah doesn't care how much I weigh or if I eat ten boxes of Ding Dongs. It's like...amazing. I haven't felt that kind of love since my dad and I used to play "Ask Me Anything" while we looked at the stars on my ceiling.

"Thank you, Leah. Thank you."

Leah whispers, "No matter how rough it gets, remember our agreement. I'm here for you."

My words are smothered against her shoulder, but I know she hears me: "I won't let you down."

Leah walks me back to the trailer around eleven that night. I push open the front door as quietly as possible, and I'm relieved to find that Mom and Drew have already gone to sleep.

I shower and put on my pajamas, then crawl into bed and close my eyes, dreading what I fear will come as soon as I fall asleep. But tonight, for the first time since Ryan died, I don't dream of his bloody face, and…I may have imagined it as I went to sleep, but I could swear that the star on my ceiling is glowing.

Chapter Twenty-One

Mom doesn't talk to me the next morning. She tells Drew to eat breakfast at school, then goes back into her bedroom and closes the door.

Drew's eyes get big and she whines, "But I don't like eating breakfast at school."

I pull a box of cereal off the shelf and hand it to her, then turn to the cabinet for a bowl. "You don't have to, Drew. We have time before the bus comes."

Drew asks, "Do you *want* to go live with Daddy?"

I nearly drop the bowl. "What?"

Drew takes the bowl from me and dumps cereal into it. "Mama called Daddy last night and told him to come get you...Do you *want* to live with Daddy?"

My head is spinning. I don't answer; just uncap the milk and pour it on Drew's cereal, sloshing it over the sides and not caring.

Drew takes a bite of cereal and speaks through her food. "Daddy said you can't come live with him because he's got enough problems already. Mama yelled at him and made me go to my room, but I still listened anyway...What's a spineless asshole? I know what an asshole is, but what's a spineless one?"

Michael Taylor boards the bus and asks no one in particular, "Have y'all seen my Facebook status this morning?"

A flurry of people whip out their phones and silently read.

Within moments: "Are you kidding me?"..."Wow. That's some cold shit."..."That sucks."

I try to make eye contact with Tina, hoping that she'll tell me what's on Michael's Facebook page, but she's staring at her phone.

Chief Taylor's exiting the school as I'm going in. Mr. McDaniel turns without a word and enters the office when I glance at him. I get a sinking feeling in the pit of my stomach.

At the end of morning announcements, Mr. McDaniel asks all the teachers to check their e-mail immediately. Mrs. Clay glances at the speaker in the ceiling and mutters, "I long for the days when my lectures weren't interrupted by technology."

She shuffles around her desk to her computer, sits in her chair, taps a few keys, and leans in close to the screen. She sighs heavily, then rises, comes over to me, and gives my shoulder three rose-scented pats. She stays by me, sighs again. I force myself to look up at her. She shakes her head sadly, gives me a rueful smile and a couple more pats, then moves back to stand within reach of her fresh roses.

Whispers break out in the back of the room. Mrs. Clay clears her throat. "Continuing our discussion of homeostasis..."

Anna turns to me, hisses, "What's going on? Why did Mrs. Clay look at you so funny?"

I shrug.

I enter Fun Math to find a red rose on Ryan's desk. I try not to look at it. One by one, girls place handwritten notes alongside the rose. I pick up one to read it.

"That note's not for you," Kayley blurts from her place next to me. "It's for Ryan, because he died trying to save *you*. Now we *all* know the truth."

"How did you—?"

She tosses her hair over her shoulder. "It was on Michael's Facebook page. His dad's the chief of police so I *know* it's the truth. You know: the opposite of *lying*…?"

"Is she for real, Colby?"

I turn to see Anna.

"Wh-when Sean and I came to see you after Ryan's memorial service, you said that *you* tried to save *him*. Why would you lie about that?"

My voice doesn't even sound like it's coming from me. "I'm sorry, Anna. I didn't mean to; I…just…"

Coach Allison cuts us off. "Okay, folks, we're not having this discussion here. Mr. McDaniel has instructed us staff members to direct you to Mrs. Healey if you feel the need to talk about it." He turns and reads directly from his computer screen. "This is a tragedy, no matter who died and who was the real hero. Students may feel betrayed, but we must emphasize the need for compassion."

He frowns first at me, then at the impromptu memorial growing on Ryan's desk. "Y'all get out your workbooks."

In the hallway, some people stare and try to conceal their whispers, while others don't even attempt to keep me from hearing. Girls write Ryan's name in big bubbly letters and tape signs to their lockers. Some of the same guys who used to call Ryan a traitor are squaring their shoulders and talking about him like he was their brother.

I open my locker door to find a note shoved through the vent: *LIAR. Go back where you came from!*

I shake my head and snort. *Like I don't wish every day that I could hit Rewind on my life.* I crumple the paper and throw it to the floor.

I slide into my seat in life skills and hear Angela and Kyle talking about dedicating the yearbook to Ryan. When they notice me, they stop talking and glare at me. I pick up my things and walk out the door.

"Colby, wait! Where are you going?"

I freeze in place and hang my head. Mrs. Lowe approaches and puts her arm around me. "Honey, where are you going? Class is about to start."

I whisper, "I can't do this. Everyone hates me because of what I did to Ryan."

Her brow furrows; she shakes her head. "You didn't *do* anything to him, sweetheart. It was a terrible accident."

I snort, "I guess you haven't heard. He was trying to save *me*. *I* was trying to kill *myself*." I look away, unable to meet her eyes.

"No, I've heard." She leans down, looks up into my face, and says softly, "You *still* didn't do that *to* him. No matter what you call it, Colby, Ryan's death was an accident. He didn't intend to die, and you didn't intend for him to die, either. That's an accident in my book."

"But...I lied about it. I let everyone think that I was a hero. How am I supposed to live with myself?"

The tardy bell sounds, and Mrs. Lowe waits until it stops to speak again. "Everyone messes up sometimes. There's not one of us who find it easy to own up when we're ashamed of what we've done." She tilts her head, and her blue eyes are soft. "I just wonder how much pain you must have been in to get to the point of standing in that road, and how much you must be in, now. Are you getting professional help for the feelings you're having?"

I nod. My promises to Dr. Matt and Leah are heavy on my mind. I've gotten so used to thinking about dying as a way of escaping pain that I have no idea how I'll be strong enough to let go of the idea and deal with my *life*. I can't even imagine getting through the next eight hours.

"Well, I'm really glad that you're still here with us, Colby. I'm sorry that Ryan's not, but I don't hold you responsible. Think you can just try to come back to class? Please?"

I allow Mrs. Lowe to take me by the hand and lead me back into her classroom.

Becca slides a note across the table to me. It's just a couple of lines:

> *I know you probably hate me, but I don't regret telling the truth.*
>
> *Truth is the only thing that saved Kimmie's life. Find your voice.*

I slide the note into my binder cover and stare at it until class ends.

There's no way I can face Anna and Sean at lunch. I head for the bathroom and enter a stall, close the door, and hang my backpack on the hook. I unzip the front pocket and pull out *The Scarlet Letter*, sit on the toilet fully clothed, and pick up where I left off. Reverend Dimmesdale is punishing himself for his sin by whipping himself and fasting, and Hester Prynne is setting herself apart from other women by thinking for herself, seeing as how they won't have a thing to do with her anyway. If she can survive being hated by everyone, maybe I can, too.

I lift my feet when I hear someone come in, and I nearly fall off the commode when Tina's face appears under the door. "I thought I'd find you in here." She goes into the stall next to me. I keep watch, expecting her knees to hit the floor.

"I wish you wouldn't make yourself throw up. It's not good for you."

She sits on the toilet, taps one foot. "You're not exactly in a position to give advice to anyone about what's good for them, Miss *I Tried to Commit Suicide*...Anyway, barfing's not something that I like to have an audience for. If I'd known you were in here before, I wouldn't have done it. What are you doing in there? Are you sick?"

"No, I'm reading."

Tina snorts. "Seriously?"

"It's better than facing all these people who hate me for what happened to Ryan." My throat's getting tight, and I'm on the verge of crying.

"Yeah, what were you *thinking*? Why didn't you just tell the truth?"

"You wouldn't understand...Look, Tina, if you want to yell at me for being a liar, you'd better get in line. *No one* can hate me as much as I hate myself. Why would I want everyone to know that I meant to die? Kara told me she wishes I'd died with Ryan."

Tina sounds shocked. "God, she's such a bitch sometimes!"

I'm blunt: "But you hang out with her!"

"I know." She sounds like a sad trombone.

"Anyway, me telling everybody the truth is as likely as *you* letting on that the reason you're skinny is that you barf all the time. I Googled that, by the way, and *you* have no room to judge *me*. You're trying to die, too, you know. Bulimia can kill you. You could have a heart attack. And your teeth are going to rot out. It's a sucky way to go."

Her voice is flat. "So I've been told. My mom caught me a few months ago, and if the shrink I'm seeing can't fix me by Christmas, she's putting me into a treatment center." Tina lifts her feet off the floor, too.

"But you barfed just the other day!"

She snaps, "Don't judge me! It's progress, not perfection. Anyway, I was freaked out because you were bugging me about the Facebook page."

"I'm sorry—"

Tina slams the stall wall and says caustically, "No, it's not *your* fault. My therapist would be *proud* to hear me tell you that *I alone* am responsible for *my* recovery. If I binge and purge, it's my choice, because I always have another response that I can choose instead. *I* slipped, but *I* chose to get back up. What about *you*, Colby? You prefer death by semi-truck?"

I gasp, "No."

She asks in a singsong voice, "Why'd you try to kill yourself?"

"Did you see the video that my cousin, *Saint Ryan*, recorded of me?"

"Yeah. So?"

"My mom said it was my fault that he made that video. Because I'm so fat."

"So?"

It's my turn to hit the stall wall. "What do you mean, 'So'?"

She answers by kicking the wall. "So, just because your mom said that doesn't make it true. It just means that your mom's a hot mess."

I feel pissed and more than a little stupid. "If *you're* so smart, why did you start throwing up in the first place?"

"I told you, I'm trying to stop. I'm in therapy, and it's fucking hard work."

"Well, how hard can it be? Just don't do it anymore."

"Are you telling me that you have no idea what it's like to be out of control when it comes to food? I mean, no offense, Colby, but you didn't get to be the size you are without pigging out."

I stand, unlock my stall door, and move to Tina's. "Open your door."

She slides the lock, and the door swings open.

"How do I stop? Eating like I do is the only thing that makes me feel better. I've always done it once in a while, but my whole life has gone to shit in the last few months and it's like I have no control *at all*. You might have been fat like me, but you have *no idea* what it's like to have my mom as a parent. She's a former Miss Texas, for God's sake."

Tina stands and wags a finger at me. "*You* have *no idea* the kind of pressure my mom put on me to lose weight. I'm only fifteen and she was already worried that she'd never have grandchildren if I didn't lose weight. *My* mom is certifiably crazy."

"Oh, yeah? Has your mom ever given you diet books for your birthday?"

Tina makes a face. "No! That would be the absolute suckiest birthday gift ever!"

"*Mine* has."

"No way!"

I nod. "It's true."

We spend the rest of our lunch period sitting under the windows in the girls' restroom and comparing bizarre Mom stories.

"You *can't* beat this one," I brag. "My mother wanted to sneak a tapeworm egg into my food so that a parasite would make me lose weight, like, by eating me alive. She wasn't going to tell me about it, but my dad caught her trying to order one online, and I heard them fighting about it."

Tina makes a face. "That's off the charts wacko! Hello, CPS? Come arrest Miss Texas!...This one isn't *that* crazy, but my mom tried to get the pediatrician to prescribe weight loss drugs to me when I was eight years old."

I'm shocked. "That's terrible!"

She waves her hands. "No, no, that's not *even* the worst of it! When *my* doctor refused, she asked *her* doctor, but she told him they were for me! So *he* said, 'No,' and she said, 'Aw, hell, just prescribe them to me, then, and I'll cut them in half for Tina.'"

"Did you take them?"

"Not for long. The pills were basically speed, and my teacher kept complaining that I wouldn't shut up and that I was vibrating in my chair."

"Wow. Okay, it's a draw. Our moms are both nuts."

We laugh so hard that I snort. I can't remember the last time I did that.

It feels good, and sort of normal.

We walk to English together. I'm still getting the stares and whispers, but I'm not alone.

Mr. Van Horn starts class by displaying Jonathan Edwards's fifteen *Resolutions* again and asking for volunteers to share their progress. I silently reread the one I chose: *Resolved, to think much on all occasions of my own dying, and of the common circumstances which attend death.*

I can practically feel the scratchy rope around my neck and the way the table wobbled when I stepped up onto it. Would I really have stepped off?

Leah's question: What the fuck are you doing, Colby?

Yeah: what the fuck?

Mr. Van Horn's voice: "Colby? You look like you're deep in thought. Care to share your *Resolution* with us?"

Kara hisses, "I don't see lying about killing somebody on the list!"

Mr. Van Horn snaps, "What's that, Kara?"

"Nothing."

He moves over to stand by her, arms crossed over his chest. "Since you're so eager to speak up, share your *Resolution* with the class."

Kara stammers, "I...um...the one about...not talking bad about other people." She reads aloud, "*Resolved, never to speak evil of any person, except some particular good call for it.*" She sits up straight and squares her shoulders. "That one."

The class breaks out in laughter. Even Mr. Van Horn seems to be having a hard time not busting out.

Anna blurts, "You're supposed to be *already* keeping the *Resolution*, Kara. You couldn't make it through ten minutes without talking shi—I mean, talking bad about other people!"

Kara's neck is breaking out in red splotches, but she sits up as tall as she can in her seat. "Um, you'll notice the part that says, '*except some particular good call for it*'?" She scrunches her face up, which just makes her look like a scrunchy-faced rat, and jabs a finger in my direction. "If *anybody* deserves to be trash-talked, it's Colby Denton. She *lied* to *everyone* about what happened to Ryan, and he was one of us!" She sits back in her seat, like that settles everything.

My eyes fill with tears; I stare at Becca's note inside my binder cover, and the words jump off the page at me: *Find your voice.*

Mr. Van Horn strides over to my desk and stands between me and the rest of the class. He puts his hand on my shoulder, and minutes seem to tick by before he speaks. "Guys, it's like I told Fredrick the other day, when he was talking about Hester Prynne being a dirty skank. When you know the whole story, your perspective can change. I know that a lot of you go to church, so perhaps you remember this Scripture: *Do not judge, or you, too, will be judged.*"

He looks down at me. "I, for one, am here to support you, Colby. I know that what you're going through can't be easy, and that none of us would want to be in your place right now. What happened was tragic." He pauses, looks around at everyone, and emphasizes the word: "*Tragic.* And, given the right circumstances, it could have happened to *any* of you. Before you sentence Colby to stand on the scaffold, I suggest that you consider how you would want to be treated if you were in her shoes. Open your books. We're on to Chapter 13."

Becca clop-clops quickly past me on the way to the gym. She has her chin tucked into her binder like always, and her eyes are on the ground. She nearly smacks into a pole, and to be honest, I'm disappointed when she doesn't. She may have felt that she had no choice but to tell what she saw, but she's right: I do hate her.

Chapter Twenty-Two

The next morning, I have to get through a crowd of people to reach my locker. Then I see why they're standing around: "*Killer*" is written on my locker door in blood-red nail polish, and my reaction is the payoff they've been waiting for.

Mr. McDaniel's voice can be heard from far off. He claps his hands and says gruffly, "Break it up, people. Get to class." He finally makes it through the throng to see the artwork on my locker. He scowls, turns to my classmates, and bellows, "Any one still standing here in ten seconds will have three weeks of detention!" People take off, and hc pivots back to me.

"I-I didn't do it—"

Mr. McDaniel crosses his arms, frown firmly in place. "I know you didn't." He steps back and takes in the other lockers, but no one else's has been painted. "I'll get the custodian to start working on this immediately." He turns abruptly and starts toward the office.

The voice in my head whispers, *"I want to die."* I press my forehead against my locker door and answer, "Shut up."

Fredrick's in the middle of presenting his *Resolution* to our English class when the P.A. speaker beeps.

"Yes?" Mr. Van Horn addresses the ceiling.

The secretary says, "I need Colby Denton to come to the office. She's leaving."

Kara hisses, "Good riddance."

Mr. Van Horn shoots her a look.

I gather my things and find my mom standing outside the office door. She's not wearing makeup, and her hair is pulled back from her face in a ponytail. She looks pissed, and she's doing the thing where it looks like if she uncrosses her arms, her guts will fall out all over the floor. My stomach clenches: Either Mom found out about the rope in the barn last night, or she found my second snack stash.

I really don't want to know.

We pull away from the curb, and my mother comes unhinged. "Leah told me that she stopped you from hanging yourself in her barn last night!"

I give the smallest of nods. I reach down, unzip my backpack, and pull my iPod and headphones from it, but Mom grabs them and throws them in the back seat. I turn my body as much as I can toward the car door and pretend that I'm looking out the window, but I can't see anything because my eyes are full of tears.

"She also tells me that you two had a long talk, and that she'll pay for your therapy as long as you need it. Hmph! She doesn't know you as well as I do; or maybe *she does*, since you're just like her. A couple of fat peas in an XXL pod!"

I turn on her. "She sees you for what you are, Mom. She knows that you don't love me the same way you love Rachel and Drew!"

Mom puts the accelerator to the floor. "*They* don't put me through half the shit you do, Colby! Is it attention you want? Is that why you pretend to want to kill yourself? Well, she convinced this—this—*therapist* that it's for real. You left his business card at her house last night, and when I told her that I didn't believe for a minute that you're depressed, she called him and told him about what she saw you doing with that rope."

My voice is shaky. "Leah's not lying, Mom. I've nearly killed myself twice now. Maybe you should pull over."

Instead, she speeds up and passes some cars against oncoming traffic. We squeak back into our lane at the last minute.

I yell, "Mom! Please! Pull over!"

"I can't take anymore, Colby! Do you understand me? Now, you're going to straighten up and stop making my life harder than it is!" She speeds up even more.

The countryside is whizzing by. I'm terrified, holding my breath. I gasp, "Mom! Please! Please, stop this!" I try to think of something to say to get through to her.

"What—what would all those people who knew you as Miss Texas think if they saw you right now? Would they even recognize you? What would *Dad* say about what you're doing?"

Mom doesn't answer, but she does slow down. I don't know if she wanted to or if she eases off because the highway patrol is ahead, shooting radar. Her chin trembles, and she starts to cry. She sounds like a little girl when she speaks. "Why should I care what your father thinks? He doesn't love me anymore."

"Where are we going?"

Mom doesn't answer me until we pull up to a stoplight. "Dr. Matthews told Leah that if I know that you're a danger to yourself but won't seek help for you, he would call Child Protective Services and report me for neglect. He acted like he really didn't want to, but he said he would." She reaches over, pinches the fat on the back of my upper arm, and twists it. "If anyone calls CPS on me, I'll put you in a group home like the one I grew up in. Then maybe you'll learn to appreciate what you have with me as your mother."

She doesn't say another word until we bump into the curb in front of Dr. Matt's parking lot. She pulls a hundred dollar bill from her purse and points it at my door: "*Out*."

I take the money and step out of the car. I barely get out of the way before she throws the car into Reverse and squeals out of the parking lot.

My heart is thudding hard, and I think my legs may give out on me. Our car is out of sight, and I look back toward the building.

Dr. Matthews is standing in the doorway. He gives a small wave, then disappears inside, leaving the door open.

I practically fall onto the sofa in Dr. Matt's small office and immediately assemble my throw pillow "wall."

He sits and pivots his chair to me. "What's up?"

I feel like I've been hollowed out on the inside, and my hands start shaking. "I—I...I'm not sure. I was at school and my mom picked me up and...here I am."

Dr. Matt nods, says, "Hmm. So there's no reason that your mom might have wanted me to see you today, given that we only met yesterday?"

There's a big framed picture of Dr. Matt standing next to a giant petrified tree, and I lock my eyes on it. "W-we left here yesterday and the police chief and—everyone knows that—that it was me. That I'm the one who kil—I mean—that Ryan was trying to save m-me, and I—I..." My throat is dry and I choke on my spit. I take my eyes off the photo for a microsecond, glance at him, and go back to the big tree. I'm shaking all over.

His voice is gentle. "Are you frightened?"

I give a tremulous shrug. "M-maybe a l-little."

"Why are you afraid? Do you think you can try to look at me?"

I shake my head, and whisper, "You wouldn't *believe* the ride I just got off of. And...I don't want to tell you about last night."

He waits a few beats, says nothing. Finally, he says, "You can tell me. This is a safe place."

I look down at the pillow that's just inches from my chin. Teardrops darken the material. "I know I promised that I'd call you if I…felt like doing something stupid…to myself, but…at that time… I couldn't think."

"So…what did you do?"

"You already know. Mom said that Leah called you."

"I'd like to hear it from you, though, so that we can start working on disrupting the impulsive behavior pattern. What happened just before you went to the barn and found a rope?"

"My mom found out the truth. Everyone did. A girl who saw 'The Accident' tried to get me to tell the truth about it, and when I wouldn't, she and her mom reported it."

Dr. Matt tilts his head. "You call what happened in the road that day 'The Accident.' Why do you call it that?"

I'm taken aback. "What do you mean? Do you think I *meant* for Ryan to die?"

"*Did you?*"

"*No!*"

"Does my asking that question make you angry?"

I feel myself blush. "No…it's just…everybody's been telling me that it's not my fault that he died."

He nods. "To make you feel better about it, right?"

I look down. "Well…yeah. *Am I* supposed to hate myself for what happened?"

"Don't you? Think about it. Isn't that why you felt that you needed to try again? To pay for his dying instead of you?"

I'm confused. *What does this guy want to hear? What's the right answer?*

Dr. Matt leans forward in his chair. "What are you thinking right now, Colby?"

I chew my lip. "I'm…I…" *It wasn't about Ryan. Last night wasn't about Ryan! Should it have been? Would I be a better person if it was?* "Can you repeat the question?"

"Sure. I asked if you were going to hang yourself last night as some sort of penance for Ryan dying when you tried to kill yourself by being hit by a truck. Does that help?"

"I wasn't thinking about him," I say softly.

Dr. Matt rolls his chair a little closer. "So, you were thinking about…"

"*Me*. And my mom, and how when she found me hanging, she'd be sorry for not coming outside to talk to me when everybody in Piney Creek was watching the video that Ryan made."

I sit up taller, shove the pillows onto the floor, and yell, "I wanted Mom to be sorry for decorating fucking day-old cookies with my little sister after she said that it was my fault for the video being made in the first place! *I* wanted *her* to hurt as much as I do!"

Dr. Matt's voice is quiet. "So, what you're saying is, both times you've tried to kill yourself, you were really, really pissed off. You're pissed that when you hurt, your mom doesn't give a shit."

"*Yesssssssssss*!" The same rage that coursed through my veins the day Ryan died is erupting from me now.

Dr. Matt grins. "That feels good, doesn't it? Getting that anger out?"

The tide of emotion is receding, and I breathe in deeply and nod my head. Tears roll down my face.

He hands me the box of tissues. "I'm going to tell you something about suicide. Are you ready for this?"

I swipe at my tears and my voice is tight. "Y-yeah."

"Suicide is not about pain. It's about anger. *Rage*. It's the ultimate rage directed back at oneself. To stop directing that anger back at yourself, you've got to learn some coping skills for dealing with it appropriately. The first thing we need to do is deal in the truth here, okay?"

I nod and sniffle. My tears won't stop flowing.

"One thing you need to do is stop calling what happened "The Accident." You didn't mean for Ryan to die. Please hear me clearly:

That part was an accident. But *you chose* to put yourself out there on the road that day, and last night *you chose* to try to make a noose to hang yourself with. We need to process what got you into that state of mind in the first place so that you don't find yourself there again. But make no mistake: You have a choice. *Always have, always do, always will.*"

I protest, "But the video was removed from Facebook, and now everybody knows that I didn't try to save him. And…it's not like Ryan can take back filming me while I dressed!"

Dr. Matt shakes his head sadly. "Sweetheart, this is about a lot more than one video that your cousin made. You were pissed about *a lot more* than what your mom said about it being your fault, or decorating cookies with your sister when you were devastated. We need to work on what's got you so angry, so that you can have the life you want. Wouldn't it be nice to look forward to your life instead of just hang on?"

I frown. "I've never even thought about having a life, really. I just pretty much go from one day to the next trying not to pig out and doing it anyway when I can't take it anymore. I mean, I go to sleep hating myself, and I wake up the same way. And…I've got this voice in my head telling me that I ought to just die and get it over with."

Dr. Matt's talking alarm clock chimes in, signaling the end of our session. "It's four o'clock."

"Until we see each other again, I want you to remember that you have a choice about how to respond to your feelings. Sometimes the best thing to do is *Just Wait*. While you're waiting for overwhelming feelings to pass, write down how you're feeling. Get the rage out in a healthy, safe way. And: same agreement applies as before—call me if you feel overwhelmed and out of control, and we'll work together to find a way out of it. Can you agree to that?"

"Yes. And I will keep the promise this time, no matter what happens."

He stands, retrieves a business card from his desk, and hands it to me. "This is going to take some time, Colby, because we're working on ingrained behaviors. Be patient with yourself, and remember: You have a choice. *Always did, always have, always will.*"

Mom is waiting in the parking lot when I go outside. She's on her cell phone, and from the sound of it, she's not much calmer than when she brought me to see Dr. Matt.

She shrieks, "There's no way to appeal this? Are you sure? Rachel, how could you? *How could you do this*? I know you were desperate for money, but…*what will people think* when they find out you've been kicked out of Lewis & Clark College for selling essays?"

They talk a while longer; basically it's just Mom trying to come up with ways for Rachel to blame someone else for selling essays for fifty bucks a pop. When they finally disconnect and Mom tosses her cell phone in her purse, she sits motionless, hands on the steering wheel, staring into space.

I reach into the back seat and retrieve my iPod, slide in my ear buds, and push Play.

I don't let Mom see it on my face, but inside, I am smiling from ear to ear.

Chapter Twenty-Three

So, today I arrive at school to find the words "*Lying Bitch*" in neon orange marker on my locker door. I *also* find Tina there. She's gotten to school early for the express purpose of using her phone to take pics of anyone who stands near my locker and gawks at it. For *some* reason, there's no crowd present. Just Tina.

A kid stops near us and she snaps his photo.

He holds up his hands like she's got a gun. "Hey, I'm just going to my locker!"

Tina arches her eyebrow. "Make sure that's *all* you do, Alex."

"Okay, okay. Jeez." He retrieves his backpack and hightails it down the hall.

I smile. "Thanks, Tina."

She throws her arm around me. "I'm sticking by your side in every class we have together, *and* in the hall. If they're going to mess with you, they're going to have to take me on, too."

It's pretty cool to have a friend.

We have a substitute teacher in biology. She can't get the DVD player to work, so we have to miss out on the video that Mrs. Clay left for us, *The Mysteries of Homeostasis*. Everyone is *extremely* disappointed.

Most people pull out their phones and start texting. My dad took my phone with him when he left. I'd lost it anyway for throwing a bowl of ice cream at Drew and shattering her best friend, the mirror...I guess that's one instance when I could have *written* my feelings about my little sister being a brat instead of trying to peg her with a bowl.

Truthfully, the mirror wasn't that big a loss. Not to me, anyway.

I start working on my *Resolution* for English class. I signed up to do my presentation on Friday, but, for someone who has thought a lot about killing herself, describing how I've applied this *Resolution* to my life is surprisingly difficult. I center it on the page:

"*Resolved, to think much on all occasions of my own dying, and of the common circumstances which attend death.*"

Common...circumstances...which...attend...death. Hmmm. What are those, anyway?

Tina and I sit together at lunch. She's finishing her *Resolution*, too. She chose the one about temperance in eating, and she's going to come out to everyone about her bulimia.

"My therapist thinks it would be a good idea to stop hiding my eating disorder. She thinks that keeping it a secret is part of what"—Tina forms air quotes with her fingers and speaks in a nasally voice—"enables me to continue to perpetuate the cycle of destructiveness." She rolls her eyes and shrugs. "Also, she thinks that if I know people are watching for it, I'm less likely to bolt for the john after I eat lunch."

"I really hope you get better so that you don't have to go into inpatient treatment," I say. "I mean...I'd miss you."

I'm opening a ketchup packet just as Kara bumps into our table. Ketchup squirts onto my shirt. She dramatically exclaims, "Oh, I'm *so sorry*, Hallister! Wow, I hope you don't get any of that on your hands, you lying bitch. Might mix with the *blood* already on them."

"Speak clearly, please, Kara." Tina holds up her phone.

Kara looks confused. "Wh-what?"

Tina calmly repeats, "Speak clearly, please. I'm recording everything you say, and I'm playing it for Mr. McDaniel when he comes through here in about five minutes."

"You're a *bitch, too,* Tina. I thought we were friends."

Tina grins and pushes Stop on the recording. "And…that'll do it. Thank you, Kara. *Thank you very much.*"

That afternoon in English class, I approach Mr. Van Horn. "Is it okay with you if I go last to give my *Resolution* presentation? Writing it isn't going so well."

He pulls me away from the other students and says quietly, "Given your recent circumstances, if you'd prefer to just turn in an essay, that'd be fine."

I think about Tina and her bravery in revealing her bulimia. "No. I think I'd like to say it."

He looks surprised. "Fine with me. Tomorrow it is."

Coach Sharp reminds me that I have to dress out today. I follow the other girls to the locker room and strip down to change in a shower stall. I've pulled the curtain but there's still this gap, and I can hear snarky little comments about someone letting a cow into the locker room.

I face the back wall, finish dressing, and when I turn around to pull aside the shower curtain, I see a skinny figure standing in the gap so that no one can see me anymore. She's wearing a plaid western shirt with her gym shorts. It can't be anyone else: Becca.

I pull the curtain aside and step out. "Thanks. Um, I appreciate that."

Becca looks away and mumbles, "I was just doing the right thing."

I put my hand on her shoulder. "I know. Thank you. Want to walk one, jog one, together?"

She looks surprised. "Sure."

Drew and I get off the bus at Sugar's in the afternoon, but after I told Leah what Dr. Matt said about me working in the bakery being like an alcoholic tending bar, she said that I can't work there anymore.

I was *so relieved.*

When Dr. Matt believes that I'm completely out of the woods, suicide-wise, I may even get to go straight home to do my homework instead of sitting in Sugar's dining room, breathing in those icing fumes and being tempted to get into that box of broken cookies. But for right now, I can't be alone.

I do my best to ignore the cake ball lollipops calling to me from the display case, and I try to write my *Resolution*. A group of cheerleaders stop in. I overhear them talking about ordering cupcakes for Homecoming, and I take my work outside and sit on the bench next to the big window. I stare at Ryan's memorial and think about what I want to say to my classmates, but I'm stumped for words. I read again what I've got on my page:

"*Resolved, to think much on all occasions of my own dying, and of the common circumstances which attend death.*"

I turn my paper over and sketch the cross with Ryan's name on it.

A car lurches to a stop right in front of me. Anna gets out. The car pulls away.

She seats herself next to me on the bench and glances at my paper. I cover the cross with my hand. She looks away and says, "Hey. Nice cross."

I sigh. "Hey." I uncover the cross and darken the R in Ryan's name. "The bakery's doing a special rate for students on Homecoming orders, if that's why you're here."

"Oh, *please*. Like *I'm* going to order a possum cake or something?" She kicks a big piece of gravel and it skitters across the parking lot. "Nah; my mom's got to go to the drug store, and I saw you sitting outside. I asked her to drop me off so that I can talk to you."

I trace the cross over and over again. "Oh."

Anna leans forward with her elbows on her knees. "Ryan was one of my best friends. We knew each other since we both moved here in second grade. He was one of the only people who would talk to the weird girl."

I nod.

She sits up, kicks another chunky rock. "I mean me. *I'm* the weird girl."

"I know."

Anna's voice cracks. "And I—I really miss him. A lot. And…I hate it that he's dead, and I hate it that you lied about how it happened."

"I'm sorry." I tuck my *Resolution* into the back of my notebook. "You don't know how much I wish that it hadn't happened at all. I wish I could take it back; I—"

"I know." Anna stares across the street at Ryan's memorial, silent. Then, "I'm the one who put the cross there."

"Really? So you're *not* a devil worshipper?"

She sits back against the bench, crosses her arms. "I never said I was a devil worshipper. People just assumed that because I never said I wasn't." She shrugs. "Why would I bother telling *Abercrombie and Bitch* anything? They're going to make up their minds about me whether they know me or not. Know what I mean?" She swats at a mosquito, then re-crosses her arms.

"Yeah. I get what you're saying." I watch her a moment. "…You know…I *wish* we could still be friends, Anna. But I understand if you can't forgive me for what I did." The invisible giant hands are around my throat again. A tear escapes my eye and hangs on the tip of my nose. I close my eyes and whisper, "You reached out to me when I really needed a friend."

Anna puts her arm around me, and I can tell that she's crying, too. "The weird girl needed a friend, too, and Ryan was there for her." She puts her head on my shoulder. "You can be my weird girl. I'll be your Ryan."

Chapter Twenty-Four

The next day in English, Mr. Van Horn announces, "Our last presenter is Colby Denton." He imitates the guy on *The Price Is Right*: "Come on down, Colby!"

I hear my heartbeat thumping in my ears when I walk to the front of the room. It feels like my fat is multiplying times a thousand, and for a fleeting second I think about just placing my paper on Mr. Van Horn's desk and bolting for the door.

But I don't.

Mr. Van Horn prompts me just as he has the other presenters: "And, pray tell, which of Jonathan Edwards's *Resolutions* did you adopt?"

I gesture to the list displayed on the screen and read aloud, "*Resolved, to think much on all occasions of my own dying, and of the common circumstances which attend death.*"

The only sound in the room is the air conditioner clicking on.

I close my eyes and envision the plastic star on my ceiling. After Anna left Sugar's, I finally figured out what to say. Then I stayed up late, reading this paper to that star until I fell asleep. I open my eyes and remind myself that I've got at least three pairs of friendly eyes in the room: Tina, Anna, and Mr. Van Horn. I swallow hard, shakily raise my paper, and lean against Mr. Van Horn's desk so that I don't fall over.

I lower my paper and stare at a spot of ground-in chewing gum on the carpet. "I'm not sure I'm doing this right. I chose the *Resolution* about dying, but I had a really hard time writing about it, I guess because..."—I search for the right words—"...I've been thinking about dying for so long, that I just..."—I shrug—"...don't want it to be all I think about anymore."

I force myself to look at Mr. Van Horn. "I hope that's okay, that you won't count off points or anything. But if you do...I guess I could rewrite it later when I'm...better."

He says gently, "I'm sure it'll be fine, Colby. No worries."

I nod and swallow hard. "Okay. Here goes." I glance at my audience, but immediately look back down at my paper and lock my eyes on my words:

"I was trying to figure out what Jonathan Edwards was talking about when he wrote this *Resolution*. I mean...was he talking about what happens to people's bodies when they die? Or...like, the way that people die when they're really old and they just don't wake up? Or...tragic deaths, like an accident or...suicide?"

This isn't sounding as put together as it did when I read it to the star on my ceiling last night. Crap. I scan the page, flip it over, and read the back...

Mr. Van Horn prompts, "Colby, do you need a second to collect yourself?"

"Huh? Oh, no, no. It's okay, I was just...This isn't coming off like I mean it to...I'm sorry."

"You're doing fine. Keep going. If you *want to*, that is." He moves from his podium to his desk and sits on the edge, leans over, and pats me on the back. Then his classroom phone rings and he turns to get it.

I glance up at my audience. Kara's smirking, and her back row buds are giving me the evil eye. Tina clears her throat and gives me a thumbs-up. Anna clears her throat, too, but *she's* making sure that Kara sees her flipping the bird.

Mr. Van Horn wraps up his phone call. "Yes, Mr. McDaniel, please wait until later this class period to do that. I understand that it's important, but this is, too. Thanks." He returns to his spot on the edge of his desk. "Sorry about that, Colby. Please continue."

I take a deep breath and blow it out. "Okay. Here's what I think Jonathan Edwards was talking about: What do people who *know* they are going to die think about? What do they *say* to other people, if they have the chance before they go? What do people *hope* they'll be remembered for?

"You all know how my cousin Ryan…died. His death was an accident. He died saving my life, and"—I choke up—"…he didn't know he was going to die that day…The same day that y'all saw a video of me on Facebook."

A few of Kara's friends on the back row giggle at the mention of the video. Mr. Van Horn points at them. "You, you, and you: *out*! *Now.*" He waits until they leave, shoots a warning glare at Kara and the remaining students, then nods at me. "Continue, Colby. You're doing fine."

"I didn't know Ryan like a lot of you did. We were friends when we were little, but then family stuff got in the way, and by the time I moved to Piney Creek, he was a different person, and so was I."

I swallow hard, will my hands to stop shaking. But I can't steady my voice when I continue. "I think that…if Ryan had known he was going to die, he would have wanted to be known as someone who did something honorable…something brave…even though none of his friends supported him in doing it." I look across the classroom at the football players, but all of them are looking at their desktops.

My throat feels like it's closing up because I know what's coming in the next part and I don't want to read it out loud, but I do.

"I don't think that Ryan would want to be remembered as the guy who videoed his *Fat Ass* cousin trying to put on jeans that were too small, then his video somehow ended up on Facebook, you know? Because that's such an awful thing for somebody to do to another person. And…if I *had* died that day, I know that I would not want to be remembered only as *The Fat Girl* in the video.

"I'd rather think about what I want to try to leave behind when

I'm gone, instead of *how* and *why* I go. I'd want to be remembered as a *person* who was kind, and funny, and loyal, and that when I was alive, people saw me for who I am as a person, not what I look like, or what my dad did, or mistakes I made like lying when I couldn't face the truth about myself."

Kara—or somebody on the back row—coughs, "*Fat Ass*!" Mr. Van Horn moves from his desk to stand by the wall next to their row. His arms are crossed and he looks pissed.

My face feels like it's on fire, and my Kermit the Frog voice is back when I start speaking again. "I—I hope that someday, you will be able to remember Ryan as the guy who did the right thing when a girl was raped, and that because of him, she's still alive. And—and I hope that someday, people will look at me and see Colby. Not *The Fat Girl*." I shrug. "So...that's my *Resolution*."

I place my paper in Mr. Van Horn's inbox and even though my legs feel like they're going to give out any second, I force myself off the edge of the desk, straighten up to my full height, and head back to my seat.

Tina and Anna stand, Mr. Van Horn joins them in clapping for me, and eventually, a few other people join them in a standing ovation. I don't even realize that the classroom door is standing open, and that Mr. McDaniel and the School Resource Officer are just inside the room. Both of them look very serious.

Mr. McDaniel says, "Mr. Van Horn, we need to speak with one of your students about items found in her locker." He holds up a bottle of blood-red nail polish and a neon orange marker. The officer walks over to Kara, grips her arm, and walks her out of the classroom.

Tina gives me double-thumbs-up and smiles so big that I think her face will crack.

Dr. Matt closes the door behind us and takes his seat. "How was your week? I didn't hear from you, so I hoped that you were hanging in there."

"It was okay. I brought my journal so we can talk about some stuff I wrote. My sister *really* pissed me off."

He smiles and leans back in his chair. "She's only seven, right?"

"That's my little sister, Drew. My older sister, Rachel, is eighteen. *She's* living with us again because she got kicked out of college for selling essays."

Dr. Matt grimaces. "Ouch! How's Mom taking that?"

I shake my head. "My mom is *a wreck*. She's not used to being disappointed in anyone but me. The good thing is, since Rachel moved back, she needed a room in our trailer and I volunteered to move in with my Aunt Leah."

"You find your aunt to be a supportive person, then?"

I nod. "Definitely. We get along really well, and she loves me the way I am. *She* doesn't think I'm a big fat disaster. Sometimes, I even forget that I'm *The Fat Girl*."

Dr. Matt makes a face. "You're *much more* than your body. You know that, don't you?"

"I'm getting there. Every day, I get closer to who I want to be."

He leans forward in his chair. "And who's that?"

I look down, notice that I don't have a pillow in my lap, and smile. "I just want to be *me*: Colby. A person who wants to live."

Note to the Reader

Big Fat Disaster is a very personal book for me. I struggle with binge eating disorder and have done so since my mid-teens. I have also struggled with suicidal thoughts. I wanted to write a book that would let others dealing with these same challenges know that they are not alone in their pain and shame—and that there is hope for recovery.

Suicide is never the answer. There is **always** another choice, and I promise, **there are people who care about you**!

There is help available: The National Suicide Hotline is 1-800-273-TALK (8255). You can also check them out online:

www.suicidepreventionlifeline.org/GetHelp

If you are suffering with an eating disorder, *there is help available.* You do not have to continue the vicious cycle! The National Eating Disorders Association website is a great resource for people who suspect they have an eating disorder and those who love them:

www.nationaleatingdisorders.org/learn

Acknowledgments

Thank you to Gina Panettieri, my tigress of an agent and blessing of a friend. Thanks for encouraging me to see where else this story could go and for always having my back. Love you, G.!

Thank you to Kim Storey and Dawn Lowe for reading *Big Fat Disaster* throughout its stages of development and giving me feedback on it. I am blessed to call you my friends! Love you both!

Thank you to my school family for your love, support, and lending your names to my stories.

Thank you to Christine Kohler for her ninja copyeditor skills and willingness to give *Big Fat Disaster* a once-over before I returned the final draft for publication.

Thank you to Merit Press and Jacquelyn Mitchard for believing in *Big Fat Disaster*. Thank you, Jackie, for pushing me to explore the characters more deeply.

Thank you to my brother, Sergeant Brett Beene, for advising me on the legal aspects of Reese Denton's crimes. I love you, Brett!

Thank you to Matt Jaremko for advising me on how a therapist would help a kid like Colby begin to attain a sense of power, and for the myriad other ways that Matt has been an incredible blessing in my life and that of my family. I owe the life I have today to you. I love you, Matt!

Most of all, thank you Daniel, Mandy, Alissa, and Kristen, who are, for me, the reasons the sun comes up in the morning. I am here because of you. I love you.

Zeekie-man, I love you and will miss you always. Good boy.